Moving in

• • •

Moving In

• • •

Elisabeth Leigh

ARROW

Published in the United Kingdom in 1998 by
Arrow Books

3 5 7 9 10 8 6 4 2

William Heinemann
Random House UK Limited
20 Vauxhall Bridge Road, London SW1V 2SA

Random House Australia (Pty) Limited
20 Alfred Street, Milsons Point, Sydney,
New South Wales 2061, Australia

Random House New Zealand Limited
18 Poland Road, Glenfield
Auckland 10, New Zealand

Random House South Africa (Pty) Limited
Endulini, 5a Jubilee Road, Parktown 2193, South Africa

Random House UK Limited Reg. No. 954009

A CIP catalogue record for this book
is available from the British Library

Papers used by Random House UK Limited are natural,
recyclable products made from wood grown in sustainable forests.
The manufacturing processes conform to the environmental
regulations of the country of origin

Typeset in Melior
by Palimpsest Book Production Limited,
Polmont, Stirlingshire

Printed and bound in the United Kingdom by
Cox & Wyman Ltd, Reading, Berks

ISBN 0 7493 2364 7

For Vivian, and Clancy, who have given me appreciation, wisdom and love

One
• • •

Dripping onto the terrazzo floor, Alice pulled off her one-piece underwired classic black costume where the jagged edge of a ripped-off label destroyed the evidence. Size sixteen. Last year, after a murderous two weeks of pre-party abstinence, she had squeezed into size twelve, now squeezing was out of the question

'Watch out,' said Beatrice as she vacated the shower cubicle. 'The water's scorching hot.' Then she added, 'You've lost weight. Your hips look much slimmer.' Alice knew that both statements were untrue. The water would be just hotter than warm and the reason her hips appeared slimmer was due to the mirror placed at a flattering angle by the customer-conscious management of the Lansdale Club.

Alice had to tell her now, which was why she stood, loitering, with a towel swathed round her full hurting breasts. Being pre-menstrual wouldn't make it any easier. Would Beatrice kiss her or fly off the handle and storm out hurling invective? 'Bea?' Alice tried to distract Beatrice from rearranging her long auburn hair into ear-loops, but she was deep in the creation of a new self. Although Alice had known her for many years, she never quite knew which was the real Beatrice, or whether there was one.

'What do you think? Is it me?'

1

'Maybe.' The slight tilt of Alice's head registered disapproval.

Beatrice was expert at picking up body language. 'Too severe?'

'Yes, too severe.'

'You look sweet when you're severe. I have to be so careful. Perhaps a change of colour. A darker chestnut, do you think?'

Alice summoned up every inch of determination and stood next to Beatrice, watching her in the mirror as she began the delicate process of embellishing a face which needed none. 'Bea, I want to tell you first. Robert and I have fixed a date to get married.'

'Brilliant, darling. I'm so pleased.'

Beatrice's reaction appeared so instant and spontaneous that Alice's mouth dropped open. 'Really pleased? Honestly?'

'It's the best thing I've heard in ages. And you're going to be amazingly happy.' Having paused half-way through defining her Rita Hayworth mouth with a slim gold-wanded lipstick, Beatrice turned her back on the mirror, but not before giving a fleeting over-the-shoulder glance at her image. 'How did you manage it? Robert's always been hopeless at dates.'

'You're not upset?'

'Upset? I'm thrilled.' Beatrice took Alice's hand and laid it on hers. 'What kind of a ring? Strictly speaking, for your sign, it should be an opal.'

'No ring.'

'Ah.'

Alice waited in suspense while Beatrice raised her chin, wondering whether to revise her opinion.

'Rather retro, I suppose. Rather Paula Yatesy to have a ring. You're quite right, as usual.' Beatrice conjured up her lipstick once more and carried on talking while Alice had a quick shower, shutting her eyes to avoid the sight of a bulging tummy and a barely perceptible waist.

'Whatever you do, don't order the cake from Maison Blanc. Did you know I was going into cakes? Only for special friends, though.'

'You don't mind? Really?'

'You two are perfect, utterly perfect. Imagine Robert marrying someone I didn't know. I couldn't bear it.'

When she emerged from the shower, cocooned in a towel, Beatrice flung her arms round Alice's neck and kissed her dramatically on both cheeks. 'And you must get married somewhere gorgeous like the Philippines and we can all fly out there and throw garlands at you. I've always wanted to do that.'

'A register office. Somewhere quiet, I expect.'

'Not Kensal Green, I hope?' said Beatrice, as she sank onto a bench and deftly pulled up her sheer black tights. 'At the very least, do it in a church. I'm sure God forgives mistakes.'

They laughed. Alice was relieved that Beatrice was taking it so lightly.

'It doesn't seem right to get married in church. Robert wouldn't want to provoke Him, even though he doesn't believe.'

'He used to.'

'Did he? How can you be sure? Robert hates anything to do with religion.'

'Alice, darling. All men are religious; they just don't want to admit it. I hope you haven't chosen September. Your signs aren't in harmony in September.'

'The end of September.'

'That's just about bearable but not marvellous. Not what I would have chosen for you.'

Alice couldn't see why you had to consult the entire planetary system before writing a date in your diary, but she always underestimated the power of Beatrice's belief in orbits, coffee grounds and having beds and tables facing the right way, which had a fancy phrase which escaped her. For Alice, having grown up on a farm, a full moon meant good harvests and a skyful of stars warned of late frosts.

'You must be firm with Robert. He can be very stubborn, you know.'

'I think I can handle it.'

Alice smiled happily, turning her back on Beatrice as she dried herself and pulled on leggings and a full top, her usual uniform.

'I'll order some champagne from the bar. If you insist on dieting, why don't you try the champagne diet? Much better than horrid beansprouts and carrots. I don't know why you torture yourself. You've a lovely figure, I'd give anything to have breasts like yours.'

It was totally untrue, but she had said it so often she must have believed it by now. Beatrice, being small-boned and slender as a baby carrot, couldn't appreciate the agonies of being not quite grotesquely fat but none the less far from thin.

Alice wanted to be thin almost as much as she wanted to marry Robert. Was there a single successful member of the fashion fraternity who was fat? It was unthinkable. Her yearning for thinness arose not from vanity, but from a practical sense of her career. (Well, that was one reason. She didn't wish to go too deeply into the others even though Beatrice had given her Susie Orbach for Christmas.) Just as you doubted the capability of a thin chef, it was the same with a fat designer. It made absolutely no difference that Alice designed for the head only and not for the whole body. Those who imbued the female body with fabulous chic – the hairdressers, the make-up artists, the shoemakers, the tailors, the dress designers, the milliners, the makers of lingerie and gloves – were at the very least expected to embody some of the style and elegance they gave to others. Alice was convinced that you shouldn't call yourself a milliner – what an Edwardian ring it had, evocative of hourglass mistresses

4

and music-hall chanteuses – without being a little exotic and mysterious, or witty and wacky. Being none of these things, or so she thought, the least she could do was to lose some weight.

Once, in a thoughtless moment, Beatrice had flung out a remark, which stayed with Alice like a deeply embedded splinter that refused to rise to the surface: 'Robert's never gone for fat girls, he just doesn't fancy them.'

If Alice ever stopped secretly monitoring herself every day and counting her calorie intake she felt sure she would be hurled over the border between plump and fat. And Robert would find somebody else. 'I like beansprouts and I've lost nearly two kilos this week,' she said defiantly.

'Didn't I say you looked slimmer?'

'Is nine months enough to lose fifteen kilos?'

'Alice. How many times do I have to say it? You're absolutely gorgeous as you are. Repeat after me, I . . . am . . . not . . . fat.'

'Plump, then,' Alice insisted.

As they made their way along the pink corridors towards the club bar, Beatrice came to a sudden halt. 'What about Simon? Have you told him yet?'

'I expect Robert has. They were going to have a sauna together.'

'Simon will be upset. Brooding over it for months.'

'He never broods.'

'Even though it doesn't show, believe me, Simon is a secret brooder. Strange, considering he's a Leo. Remind me, when's his birthday?'

'The twenty-third of July.'

'That explains it,' Beatrice concluded. 'He's on the cusp of Cancer.'

Simon had been the first boyfriend to cause Alice to think about the future. Would she share it with him? At the time she had few doubts. When they were together everything was so easy, so affectionate, so natural and enjoyable that she assumed that the mind-spinning, obsessive, crazy love they all talked about incessantly, sprawled across the tightly-clipped lawns of Corsham Towers, was a schoolgirl fantasy. Then she met Robert.

Simon said why didn't she just have a passionate affair and he'd wait for her to get over it? Better that it had happened before they were married than after. But it hadn't worked out that way. In the end, without any demonstration of the pain and anguish he must have felt, Simon had managed to keep Alice as a friend, while never referring to the days when they were lovers.

'Things needn't be any different. We'll see each other as we always do.'

'Simon is a one-woman man,' said Beatrice.

'If you're about to say I should have married him, forget it,' replied Alice crossly.

'Virgo with Leo is a harmony combination. Not that one should take these things too seriously.' Beatrice contradicting herself again. None of Alice's friends apart from Beatrice showed such a passionate concern with heavenly influences.

Leaning against the bar, Simon was already onto his second pint, since he needed extra liquid to help him digest the news. He was of a stocky build, a good height but not tall, with well-cut glossy black hair, expressive dark-brown eyes and a slightly ruddy face. He liked to wear what *GQ* and suchlike magazines told him was in this season, regardless of whether it suited him, in order to distinguish himself from the rest of his colleagues, who tended to sport ill-fitting suits or voluminous sweaters. 'Congratulations, Robert. Alice is nuts about you, always has been. I hope you popped the question in the proper style.'

6

'It was all rather casual. Alice was chatting while she cooked supper. Then I found myself saying, "Could you bear the idea of being Mrs Norham?" Suddenly, we'd fixed a date. September. It didn't feel like a momentous decision. Not like the last time, thank God.'

'Same again? I'll get some champagne when the girls arrive.'

Robert shook his head, having made a rapid calculation that twenty minutes on the exercise bicycle didn't warrant two pints of beer.

Today, Robert looked relaxed and healthy, which meant things must be quiet on the work front. However, Simon wouldn't bring that up and certainly not at the club. He surreptitiously examined Robert. The club management, recognising the need for constant comparison with one's peers, had covered most of the available wall with mirrors. He wondered how it was that Robert – who had a long, lean, sinewy body – never seemed to attract the slightest deposit of fat, unlike him. His waving light-brown hair, Simon thought, could be shorter, but he supposed Alice liked it long. He could see what she saw in him, physically that is, and sometimes felt envious of the fact that Robert was tall but well proportioned, had a firm jaw-line and slightly mysterious (so the girls said) bluey-grey eyes. However, his own muscles were better developed even though he exercised less than Robert. This was puzzling; Simon would find the answer at some point. He liked finding answers.

'It doesn't mean things will be any different,' said Robert. 'Alice will keep on her place at Kensal Green for a while – and I'll get cracking on the basement. It'll make a splendid workroom for her, lots of space.'

'Excellent.'

'I never thought I'd be sharing my house with someone again. But I'm getting used to the idea.'

Simon allowed himself a consoling thought. When

he had proposed to Alice it had been a truly momentous, unforgettable evening. It was during his opera phase, a box at Covent Garden (*Aida*) followed by a gastronomic experience, roses with a handwritten note tucked in the glossy leaves, vintage champagne, smiling waiters . . . and she had said yes without hesitation. So he immediately contacted every estate agent possible (http:/www.houseseekers.co.uk) and found a run-down place in Shepherd's Bush, a few minutes' drive from Lidgate's the master butcher's, the impelling reason for his choice of location. Who better than Robert, old friend and sought-after architect, to transform a Victorian red-brick monster into a high-tech dream?

Simon swiftly closed down his memory file and reduced it to a sleeping icon (regrets, no point) and opened another one. He was beyond his high-tech phase and now he was mulling over plans to resurrect the original Victorian features he had once despised, with the help of a computer-generated 3-D image of each room. Or he might go for rustic Afghani. Or both. What was wrong with mixing styles? As yet he hadn't dared tell Robert of his plans. Robert believed in renewal rather than restoration and thought that the National Trust was stifling Britain's architectural talent. And he wouldn't tell Alice until the builders were in.

'I've got out of the way of being a husband,' reflected Robert. 'I wonder if it needs practice. I'm sure you'd have been much better at it than me.'

'It's going to work out very well, you and she. If she'd married me, I expect she'd have thrown me out by now. You can't have two people who like eating living together. They end up the size of houses. At least it's only me the size of a house, well, a bungalow let's say.'

Robert grinned, put his elbows on the bar and leaned towards Simon. 'You're welcome to come round any time. Any time at all. Don't feel that anything's different just because . . .'

'You're tying the knot,' said Simon quickly, finishing his sentence.

Even when Robert wasn't feeling awkward, which he was now – any friend would be in his situation – he had a tendency to speak slowly. It seemed irritatingly slow to Simon, who had trained himself to increase the speed of his reactions by two hundred per cent, which included a more rapid speech delivery. The new Simon had taken a few years to emerge, following his decision to abandon commercial art and start up a customised computer company. Since clients needed to feel he had a natural affinity with these rapidly developing machines, Simon worked out that the more he resembled the human version of a computer, the more machines he could sell. This turned out to be the case. To his surprise, Simon was becoming quite rich. 'Alice has made the right decision, as always,' he continued. 'After all, in comparison with me you're taller, more good-looking, miles more talented and creative – and relatively tidy. Much better husband material. Anyway, I'll still be taking Alice out for the occasional meal.'

'Of course you will.'

'And I won't have to be dutiful to her parents, that's quite a plus. Mummy will probably want you to design an extension once you're in the family. Don't say I didn't warn you!'

'You don't feel too . . . Alice was worried, in case . . .'

'She needn't be. Besides, I like being a bachelor. I like taking my shoes off without bothering about smelly socks, cooking up sausages and baked beans at two in the morning if the mood takes me, leaving the dirty dishes, zapping e-mails across the world and generally ignoring time. Women are stuck with time, I don't have to be.'

'Only if they have kids.'

'Ah yes. Kids.'

Simon hoped Robert had changed his mind about fatherhood since, according to Beatrice, his resistance to procreation had hastened the decline of his marriage. He didn't want that to happen to Alice. Avoiding Robert's gaze, he gave a quick glance at the ceiling and turned his head slightly, as though contemplating something from the bar. 'I've always thought Alice would be good at motherhood. Better than Bea, that's for sure.'

Robert gave that slow, easygoing smile which Simon envied so much, since every woman who'd met him commented on it. 'Alice is in no hurry, she says. One day.'

'And you?'

'I can't think about them at the moment. I'll need to adjust to the idea. After Bea walked out, I found a box full of baby clothes and toys at the back of a cupboard. It was a real shock. Still, she's got what she wanted now. Shame they've both got her temperament. Poor David.'

'Poor nanny, more like,' said Simon.

Robert is too easygoing, Simon thought. Beatrice had some cheek, bringing round the children of marriage number two to husband number one, while she went on a shopping spree. This, he knew, happened quite often. He didn't want Alice to have to put up with that. 'I hope Beatrice realises her child-dumping days are numbered. I don't imagine Alice would appreciate it,' he remarked.

He could only think of Alice, when he ought to be thinking of Robert and Alice. Switch gear, he told himself. A couple. Robert and Alice. RbtAl. Married. In-laws and all that. At home together. Get used to idea. Gtusdea. His mind was accelerating and short-circuited past the steps required for tact. 'You do love Alice?'

'Love Alice? I must do. I want her to live with me.

10

She makes me feel I can start again. Yes, yes, I love Alice.'

'I just wanted to hear you say it. You know, like girls do.'

Edging her way round the cane armchairs grouped round the window on the far side of the bar, Beatrice strolled over in the direction of Robert and Simon. She had mastered the right swing of the hips and the stretched ankle during a short modelling course and adopted it instead of her former girlish lope. Alice followed behind her, admiring the heavy belt which sat low on Beatrice's narrow hips. Ralph Lauren skirt, she noted, last season's shimmer look. The long jacket had to be Armani, Armani sludge colour. Alice's designer eye was constantly on the look-out for cut, seaming, colour, even at moments of high emotional tension. She looked over to Robert and Simon. Did Simon know? What had been said? They appeared to be at ease. Simon was tipping back on his bar stool, talking away. Robert was standing – he rarely sat down – bending down slightly towards Simon with an amused smile on his lips. In a few months' time she would be saying, 'This is my husband. Meet my husband.' Husband only for formal occasions. Robert. This is Robert. Yes, we're married, if asked. Mrs for tradesmen. Was it true what they said, that signing a piece of paper had a subliminal effect and everything changed? She wanted only slight changes, like living at Robert's house all the time instead of just at weekends.

By now, Beatrice had reached the bar and was brandishing two empty beer glasses. 'How long have you two been here? It's disgraceful. I bet you've skimped your exercise programme.'

'Skimping? Me?' Simon adopted an incredulous grin.

'Look at those glasses. How much have you drunk?'

'We're celebrating. That's allowed,' said Robert.

Alice kissed first Robert, then Simon. They all knew. Soon it would be over and they could carry on bickering and laughing and teasing as usual.

'What about the champagne?' demanded Beatrice. 'Where's the champagne?'

'Ordered,' replied Simon.

'Decent, I hope.' Beatrice threw Simon a warning glance, which he ignored.

'We've been waiting for you,' added Robert. 'But we're used to it.'

'Aren't I allowed to wash my hair? Or have a shower?'

'No, not today,' said Simon. 'It's a significant occasion. Although you probably don't see it that way.'

'That's outrageous. I'm absolutely thrilled, aren't I, Alice?'

'Bea wants us to get married in the Philippines. I think she's got some gorgeous man hidden over there and she needs an excuse to go,' said Alice, smiling at Robert.

'Nonsense. I'm completely faithful to David.' She caught Simon's raised eyebrows. One drunken evening at the club she had boasted of her conquest, the landscape gardener who'd made her a pergola. She smiled as she remembered him again, irresistible nut-brown limbs and a thick tangle of hair. 'Well, almost faithful. I'm the only one who's realistic around here. That's the way to be when you're married.'

'For you, Bea.'

'I was faithful to Robert for three years, three whole years, but he never believed me. Did you Robert?' Since he refused to comment, Beatrice turned to Alice. 'Robert's incredibly jealous. Still, I suppose all men are.'

'I haven't noticed,' said Simon.

'You wouldn't. You only notice things on little screens,' replied Beatrice, mustering a contemptuous sniff.

'I've never been jealous,' remarked Alice. 'No, that's not right. I was jealous of Mary Bartlett. Heavens, I haven't thought of her for years. Mary Bartlett.'

'Should I know her?' enquired Beatrice.

'She was in my year at Corsham Towers.'

'Was she your friend?'

'Oh, no. She kept herself apart. I remember her being rather quiet, always in the library.'

'And naturally she got top marks in exams.'

'She was good at exams. I was hopeless.'

'No wonder you were jealous.'

'That wasn't really the reason. Mary Bartlett was five foot ten and size eight, her parents had a flat in London, another in Paris and a huge country house somewhere near Barcelona. Or so she said. No one was ever invited, not even for a weekend.'

'So she was thin and had rich, mean parents,' said Simon.

'Like several thousand others,' added Robert.

'I'm trying to think why I was jealous,' said Alice. 'Oh, I know. Her mother bought her clothes from Sonia Rykiel and she flew in aeroplanes on her own. And Mary was clever, too. Four A levels, or was it three? Anyway, the headmistress adored her and invited her for tea on her own.'

'There's nothing worse than a girl at school who gets special treatment. I'd have been fiendishly jealous, too. Did she marry a magnate's son? Bet she did, the bitch.'

'Probably,' replied Alice with a smile. 'But I'm sure she's desperately miserable.'

A bottle of champagne in a bucket was handed over the bar by a resting actor who was a favourite at the Lansdale Club.

'When's the wedding going to be?' asked Simon. 'Not at the beginning of September because I'll be in the States. Conference time. Unless you'd rather I wasn't there . . .'

'I'd cancel if you couldn't make it,' said Robert. 'No, it's the end of September.'

'I'll have to pencil in the cake now. I'm unbelievably booked up.' Beatrice fished out her omnipresent electronic organiser from her bag. 'Traditional or wacky? I can do it with pillars or without pillars. Something architectural would be fitting. How about that?'

'We don't need a cake, Bea,' said Alice firmly. 'We'll just all go out to dinner afterwards, somewhere special. I'd rather you made a cake for my birthday.'

'No wedding bash?' shrieked Beatrice, horrified.

'Maybe later,' said Robert.

'I should have known. You hate parties. But you always enjoyed them once you got there.'

'That is simply untrue. We didn't go very often, anyhow.'

'Yes, we did. We went to masses. You pretended you hated parties and then got all dressed up and excited. You've forgotten. We used to go to at least one party a week.'

They were all accustomed to Beatrice's conviction that because she had lived with Robert for four years she knew every byway of his personality. It was easier to let her assume that this was the case.

'Well, then, I must have forgotten,' muttered Robert.

Robert's house was within walking distance of the club. Alice walked her bicycle beside him; his arm was on her shoulder. 'Happy?' he asked.

'Very. Blissfully.'

'Should we ask Bea to make a cake? I know she'd love doing it.'

'If you like. But do you really think it's a good idea, the first wife making a cake for the second wife?'

'Why not?' said Robert. 'She adores doing things for friends.'

Without realising it, Alice had paused at the window

of Maison Blanc, making a mental picture of the chocolate croissants, strawberry tarts and flans as smooth as a skating rink. The days of swift, guilt-ridden trips to the patisserie would soon be over. Once she was married, she told herself, a new leaf would be turned.

'Wait there,' said Robert.

To Alice's dismay, he bounded through the glass doors and she saw him pointing at the creamiest confection in the window. A few moments later he emerged with a gold box, smiling. 'As I'm working tonight, here's a treat.' Robert placed the box carefully in the capacious basket of her upright bicycle, formerly owned by her mother.

'You're a darling,' Alice said, wondering if she could muster enough self-control to make it last two days instead of demolishing it all as soon as she arrived back home. Then the guiltless solution came to her. 'Why don't you take half? I'll never eat all that.'

'It's for you. You know by now I never eat cakes.'

Alice could feel the juices in her mouth rising in anticipation. 'I really mustn't make a habit of this. Otherwise I'll have to live at the club and spend all my time doing work-outs.'

'There's no need for that.' Robert smiled as he slipped his hand over her bottom.

Alice was about to blurt out, 'I've been putting on weight again' but quickly decided that it was better not to draw attention to it. She didn't want Robert to think she spent all her time worrying about her thighs, her bottom and the fold of flesh above her waist, which expanded, in her imagination, to the size of a watermelon. If he had viewed her body with the revulsion she felt herself, how could he have asked her to marry him? Or maybe he didn't notice. Maybe he was just delighted to find himself in a calm oasis after hurricane Beatrice. If he only liked thin girls once, he could have changed his mind. Alice hoped he wasn't

15

being tactful, refraining from comment. Otherwise, she feared it would come out suddenly, once they were married. *Do you think it would be an idea if you went on a diet? Only you have put on a tiny bit of weight, darling.*

'Before you go off,' said Robert. 'I thought we could work out the details of what to do with my basement. I want it all ready for you by September.'

'Are you sure you won't mind me working down-stairs? I'll understand if you decide against it. You might need extra room some day.'

'Then I'll build an extension.'

'You hate extensions.'

He laughed, crinkling up his eyes in a way that Alice found irresistible. 'You know me too well. No, that basement will be an ideal space for you.'

They veered off Holland Park Avenue and walked northwards, stopping outside a glass-fronted house which was sandwiched between two dreary Victorian dowagers. 'When it's finished, this will be my wedding present,' said Robert as they went down the basement steps. He unlocked the door and gestured across a wide area of concrete floor, with a stretch of glass-sheeted window on the far side. The view outside was of a low brick wall marking the edge of the garden above, from which trailing plants hung down in patches of green. Pushing back a pile of cardboard boxes to clear a path, Robert took a notebook from his pocket and showed Alice a rough sketch. 'Shelves here. Work tables here. And a display area here.'

'And my desk?' added Alice.

'I thought I could knock out a door here. Then I could pull down the coal storage area, just big enough for a tiny office. How about a pale wooden floor?'

'Wonderful. Just perfect.'

Alice made her way round the piles of debris and stood in the middle of the room. Once he had cleared out all the clutter, it was quite a considerable space, larger than she remembered. 'I must have a fish tank.'

'Are piranhas fashionable this year?'

Alice giggled. 'Goldfish, silly. And waterweeds and snails, like I used to have at home. When everything's quiet, I'll look at the fish.'

'I'll make you a proper entrance, too, so I won't be distracted by hordes of visiting ladies.'

'You think there'll be hordes, then?' Alice said with a smile. As yet, she had only a handful of good customers, friends of friends from fashion college days.

'Once you have a show, they're going to come crowding in, you'll see.'

Alice laughed. 'I can't possibly afford to put on a show. Anyway, I haven't made nearly enough hats.'

'You're going to do well, darling. Trust me.' Robert took her hand and they paused by the window.

'You've forgotten one thing, though. A cloakroom.'

'Ah yes. Perhaps I'll be able to fit one in leading from the office.'

'Can I have a small sign up, at the entrance to the basement?'

'You can have anything you like. This is your part of the house. All yours.' Robert came behind her, circled his arms round Alice's waist and kissed her neck. 'Now I must get back to my drawings.'

They kissed again, then Robert climbed the circular metal stairs to the rooms above. Alice let herself out of the basement and collected her bicycle leaning against the front gate. She could see Robert standing by the window at the front, blowing a kiss. Then he turned his back to take his place at the large drawing-board, his face illuminated by a single anglepoise lamp.

Her mother had decided to come up to town. Alice made an effort to arrive a quarter of an hour early to avoid being chided for lateness. There she was, striding through the tables of a little old-fashioned cafeteria in Soho as though it were the Ritz, conspicuous in a navy felt hat and a bright-red suit with box pleats (size twelve, but she could have got into a size ten). And her lipstick matched perfectly. 'Sorry I'm late, darling. I had to see the new vet. Awfully nice man.'

She planted a light kiss on Alice's cheek and arranged the fruits of her shopping trip around her, as though laying out sandbags before a flood. After studying the menu, she gave a brief, pained glance towards the 'home-made' scones and teacakes arranged on a nearby table. 'No one can make scones nowadays,' she said, as she lowered herself carefully onto a chair, so as not to crease her skirt. 'But we'll try the cream tea. I feel like a cream tea.'

'A cup of tea will be fine, Mummy,' said Alice. Then she lied, 'I had a huge lunch.'

'Cream tea for two,' said her mother firmly, as the waitress wielded her notebook beside her. 'How often do we meet for tea? This is a special occasion, Alice, darling. Still worrying about your figure? I was twice your size when I was your age.'

'Everyone's thinner now. People change their shape.'

'They don't in the country, thank goodness for that. And Arabs won't marry a girl unless she's absolutely whopping.'

'I'm not marrying an Arab,' Alice replied tartly. 'I have to lose fifteen kilos before September.'

'Then your face will be too thin. It doesn't suit you, having a thin face. Do be sensible.'

Once the plate of scones, turgid pot of cream and virulent jam were placed in the centre of the table, Veronica ignored the offering and settled down to serious business. 'Daddy and I thought you should have a reception at the farm. We can clear out one of the barns. Remember your twenty-first? Wasn't it super? I can't believe you're thirty now. It only seems like yesterday.'

Alice swallowed hard and took a minute bite from a leaden scone, which suddenly seemed horribly desirable. 'We want to get married quietly. Thanks all the same, I know it would have been lovely.'

'You mean it's not fashionable. I don't care what people in London are doing. You must have a proper wedding.'

'It will be proper, Mummy.'

Alice could see that her mother was making an effort. It was difficult for her to realise that she was thirty, even more so to try and understand that she had changed since the days when she drove the tractor around the farm and rode her pony out into the fields in the rain. 'A white wedding?'

Alice shook her head.

'You know I'm disappointed. But never mind. You must have wanted one.'

'Robert had a church wedding the first time, he doesn't want it to be at all the same.'

'Of course he doesn't. But what about you? Doesn't he consider you? I do hope he's not going to get his own way all the time. He won't respect you if he does.'

Alice smiled and layered some cream onto a second scone. 'We get on very well. And I love him to bits, you know that.'

Having dabbed her lips on the edge of the napkin, Veronica kissed her daughter on the cheek. 'Then I shan't interfere. Did I used to interfere? I tried not to. Your father was always telling me to put my foot down. As though I was about to squash a beetle. We must get to know Robert better. I hope we'll see him more often now. Is he shy? I imagine he is, he never says much. I expect you're very good for him.'

'He's making me a workroom in his basement. Just you wait till you see it. I'm so excited.'

By the time the scones had disappeared and the teapot was replenished, Veronica was able to mask her regret that Alice was missing out on a proper wedding. Her only daughter – after Alice she had produced three sons – was marrying an architect. At least she wouldn't have to endure the stench of cow-dung, the fears of disease and the invincible hold of those awful people in Brussels. 'We're both terribly pleased, darling. And we'll love having the grandchildren to stay.'

'One day. We're in no hurry.'

Again, Veronica forced a smile. 'Everyone has children so much later. I do have to keep reminding myself. I wonder how it will be when you're my age?'

'You'll probably be able to go into a baby store and get your sperm from a fridge. And there'll be a picture on the bottle, showing you what the child will look like.'

'I'll be buried under the turnips by then, I hope.'

Veronica paid the bill, gathered up her bags and suddenly remembered something she had to give to Alice. 'Here, something for you addressed to the farm,' she said, passing over a large white envelope. 'Your old school. I had a look inside to see if it was urgent. There's a Corsham Towers reunion. Why don't you go?'

'I might, if I've the time,' said Alice doubtfully. 'It's a long way to go to talk about what happened in the dorms years and years ago, and who's married a farmer and who's married a stockbroker and who isn't married at all.'

'Who knows?' said Veronica brightly. 'Some of them might want a little hat for a garden party or a wedding. And I'm sure they'll all be pleased to see you.'

'I could go, couldn't I?' said Alice. She hadn't given much thought recently to life before Robert.

'Don't do what I've done,' Veronica said, as though reading her thoughts. 'I sometimes think I should have considered myself a little more, kept up with my old friends, even gone away on holiday a few times without Sam.' She checked some of the objects in her bag – purse, car keys, letters to post – and clicked it shut.

'But your father's always been such a demanding man. I'm sure Robert's quite different.'

'No. I'm not marrying my father,' said Alice, grinning.

'Mind you, I'm not complaining. I hope you have as good a life as we've had, darling.'

Alice left her mother heading for Bond Street, her quest being a nice little scarf from Fenwick's for a neighbour's birthday, something with horses on.

Two

• • •

Hattie found the best seat, half-way down the gloomy Victorian hall and near to the aisle in case they decided to leave early. Today, the treacly brown wood panelling was enlivened by sprays of catkins and bunches of blue-bells forcing their way out of irregular ceramic vases, the product of Miss Lisle's pottery classes. Miss Trelawney was pressing down on the organ keys as though about to produce a prime vintage, grimly addressing the keyboard with pursed lips. The military thump of the Corsham Jubilation anthem boomed against the shields and cups, and off the walls whose peeling paint was masked by strategically placed blackened gilt frames of former headmistresses, all depicted with a serene expression and eternally gazing above the heads of the audience. Two percussive chords summoning the entry of the voices immediately followed a raised hand, belonging to Miss Armitage. The Corsham Senior Choir was uniformed in dark-burgundy skirts and red-checked Viyella shirts half covered by grey blazers. Alice remembered the words, but her throat was dry. She could never sing on command.

She heard a familiar cough near her. Mrs Rowlandson, whose husband had run off with the gym mistress, suffered from asthma but managed to overcome it for the special option of Public Speaking. *With eyes upraised as one inspired, Pale Melancholy sat retired.*

Alice, I want to hear your vowels, dear. Vow-els. Your voice is an instrument of power and beauty. You either speak or keep silent. You do not mutter.

Alice was restless, changing her position on the hard wooden chair, closing her nostrils to the smell of lavender polish mingling with the chemical stench of recently treated worm-eaten oak.

'I fancy a bun,' whispered Hattie. 'I had to get up at six. No breakfast.'

'Shall we go out for tea, then?'

'Super idea.' A smile lit up Hattie's freckled face. Alice felt closest to Hattie, who had a reassuring presence, with broad shoulders and plump arms like a matron. Her hips were still slim, though the pleated skirt she was wearing was far too long. Hattie had always hated her legs, Alice recalled, and no one could persuade her otherwise.

During the speeches and presentations they both glanced furtively to either side, then turned round to assess the rows behind them. All the old girls were sitting as they did then, quelled by the atmosphere of propriety and seemliness, knees close together, backs straight, mostly in suits. It was strange how mature they looked, as though they had all entered their mothers' bodies. Do I look like that? Alice wondered. They seemed nearer forty than thirty, but most were in their late twenties or early thirties. A couple had brought babies along, who occasionally gurgled and grunted under the girlish chorus. Alice smiled at a familiar face. It was Pen, who'd cut her long black hair short as a boy's, razored up the back.

Hattie had noticed her, too. 'Pen's new husband is rather weird, apparently,' she said in a low voice.

Others continued chattering, as the determined headmistress (there had been two since their day) issued a stream of negative statements about the evils of lying league tables, followed by gushing positive ones about the achievements of the school and those who had made major contributions, in particular the parents who had raised enough for a small tractor, most appreciated by Bill the groundsman.

Hattie raised her voice to its normal pitch. 'He's something in therapy.'

'You mean he's a therapist.'

'I don't think so. He does shifts in a hospital therapy department, apparently. She's expecting the baby in August.'

'His?'

'Oh, yes. His all right,' answered Hattie.

Alice sighed. Pen had got herself pregnant, working-class boy, parents heart-broken, all that education, money and sacrifice down the drain. 'I hope she's happy with him,' she said. 'Pen was always such fun. Wouldn't it be dreadful if he made her put his supper on the table every night?'

'They don't do that any more, do they?' asked Hattie in wonderment.

'Some still do,' Alice remarked, reverting to her customary role of understanding the world.

'I wouldn't stand for it.'

'You would if you loved someone.'

As the stream of nervous girls walked up to accept their prizes, Alice thought of all the resolutions she'd broken with Robert. Waiting by the phone, would he call? Collecting his dry cleaning. Typing out letters. Emptying the Hoover bag. Declining a supper party because he was working all night without considering she might go on her own. But she suppressed her own wishes for a good reason. She had known right from the beginning, when Robert began to talk about his disastrous marriage, that she would have to lay the ghost of Beatrice. If only his former wife were living somewhere like Outer Mongolia, but there she was in Holland Park, two minutes' walk from Robert. Alice came to with a jolt as the final march ushered out the staff, followed by the rumble of wooden chairs pushed back as Assembly rose to its feet.

For old times' sake they would visit the netball and tennis courts, the lily pond, the Animal Park (still devoted to rabbits, guinea-pigs and a mangy donkey). They were about to set off to the Vegetable Garden when a figure in a track suit and baseball cap came careering down the path. 'Hi, guys!' cried a jubilant voice. The run was a give-away, arms flailing, heels kicked up like a young pony let out of the stable. 'I saw you in Hall. I was at the back. I persuaded Duane to come to England; there's an agricultural fair, that was my excuse. He's got the kids, doing London. Duane loves doing things. My, you two look neat.'

It suited Jilly, being married to an American. Even at school she had affected what she imagined was an American accent, now she had mastered it. She was always chafing against restrictions, forever saying England was far too small for her. Alice noticed that, two children later, she had graduated from size twelve to size fourteen. She wondered if it was a fact of life that she had missed out in biology: having babies made you fat. It would be a tough decision, risking being fat for life in the cause of motherhood. Losing Robert.

'Great seeing you all. I never expected Alice would come!' said Jilly, as they caught up with Pen. The gang was now complete.

'I'm longing for tea,' replied Alice. By now, she had thought of a solution. She would adopt an orphan baby from a war-zone. Or maybe two. Robert would approve of that.

'Anyone for the Corsham Grange? Refectory tea will be ghastly,' Pen began.

'Right. Let's go.' Alice smiled.

Pen was just waiting for the gatekeeper to release

the electronically controlled gates – there had been a mention in the *Corsham Trumpet*, the school magazine, that particular emphasis was now being placed on security – when Alice caught sight of a familiar shape walking down the drive, clearly in sensible shoes judging by the speed with which she was negotiating the gravel. 'My God!' Alice exclaimed. 'Isn't that Mary Bartlett?'

'It's her all right,' groaned Hattie. 'I don't understand why she's come, of all people.'

'She looks just like one of the teachers. Perhaps she's been sucking up to the new Head, trying to get a job.'

Pen was working out if the gates would open and close before the new arrival came up to them. 'It's not as though she'd be looking up old friends,' she said. 'She didn't have any.'

'One, I think,' said Alice. 'Didn't she sometimes go around with Millie Price-Jones?'

'Only because she had a fifteen-hand bay, stabled at home.'

'Shucks, we're all grown up now.'

'Jilly's right. Let's wait and invite her for tea.'

'Do we have to?' asked Pen, undoing the tight collar of her blouse now that they were almost out of bounds.

'It would be nice,' Alice remarked. They all knew perfectly well that it would not be nice at all, but Alice was right.

The only change to the Corsham Grange Hotel was that the mats showing hunting scenes had been removed from the mahogany tables in the tea-room and replaced by bright-yellow checked cloths.

'We do hot snacks now,' explained the waitress with a touch of haughtiness she considered appropriate. She recognised the group, since she had formerly worked at

Corsham Towers in the kitchen and was climbing the ladder towards being Head of Customer Relations, the new name for Manageress.

'Like hamburgers and fries?' asked Jilly.

'We do serve meatballs, chips and peas.'

Hattie winced at the long duration of her smile. 'Set tea,' she declared defiantly. 'And lots of cream. I shouldn't, but I'm going to. It's all right for you, Pen, you don't have to worry. You can have anything you like.'

Even with a pregnant bulge, Pen managed to look waif-like, with those wonderful, long, bony arms and slender neck, which Hattie knew she would never attain, even if she starved for a week. Pen drummed her fingers lightly on her stomach. 'Jolly old meatballs for me and him inside. And lots of gravy. It is a he, I checked. He'll be called Albert.'

'Like Prince Albert.' Hattie smiled approvingly. 'It's time they brought back the name Albert.'

'Actually he's named after our local pub. The Albert.'

Mary Bartlett drew up a chair at the table for four and Alice shifted slightly to let her in, but without looking at her. 'Meatballs? For tea? How could you?'

'You're allowed to eat freaky things when you're pregnant.'

Mary was showing unsisterly revulsion. Hadn't she learned that friends never make disparaging remarks? Perhaps, Alice thought, she was unaware that it was disparaging. Looking back, hadn't she always managed to come up with remarks which were inappropriate? Only faintly so, but enough to threaten the good feeling between the group. One did not criticise unless criticism was sought and even then there were accepted ways of doing it.

'You must all come visit me and Duane in Wyoming,' said Jilly, ladling out thick dollops of cream. 'We'd have a great time. And I make a terrific pecan pie.'

27

Alice, Hattie and Pen tried to hide their consternation. Didn't Jilly realise that Mary would consider herself included in the invitation? And she was the kind who might stay for weeks.

'When I was in New York, nearly all the Americans I met lived on salads.'

'Jilly doesn't live in New York,' said Hattie in an acid tone. She instantly regretted being unkind but sometimes it just came over her. She turned to Jilly, searching for a safe topic of conversation. 'Do you miss England? I suppose you must.'

'Only my friends. I don't have a clue what's happening over here; there's hardly ever anything on the TV about Britain.'

'Not even the Royal Family?'

Hattie was the archive source for anything relating to Royal lineage, having worked out that she was seventy-third in succession to the throne. She had excelled in history but was unavoidably absent to take her A levels. Only the gang knew that she had had the bad luck to get pregnant at a house party in the summer holidays.

'Nothing's changed here,' remarked Pen. 'Except Daddy lost a lot at Lloyds and I've got married.'

Hattie glanced at Alice, indicating by a few rapid blinks that she was Not Meant to Know. 'Who to? Who to?' they chorused.

'I call him Archie.'

'What does everyone else call him?' asked Mary.

'His real name is Buddy, but you can't call your husband that. At least I can't.'

'I bet he's gorgeous,' said Alice.

'He's got a wonderful voice and plays the guitar like a dream. His father is thrilled, he's a look-alike Buddy Holly, you see. He had the voice but couldn't manage the chords. Which is why he called his son Buddy. We're very happy. Poor, of course.'

'Does he play professionally?' enquired Mary.

'If you call doing a gig in the local pub being professional,' said Pen.

'We're dying to meet him,' said Alice. 'You could stay at my place, you're always welcome.'

'A holiday, how super.'

Pen knew she would pull out all the stops and she and Archie wouldn't be expected to take Alice anywhere smart. No one was expected to be rich any more.

'I've just realised I know some people who live near you,' interjected Mary. 'Aren't you in Oxfordshire somewhere?'

'My parents are,' Alice replied with a smile.

'Do you know the Alleyn-Shipworths?'

'Only vaguely.'

'They're very good friends of mine. Always asking me to stay. I could pop round and see you next time I'm down there.'

'I'm only there for the occasional weekend,' said Alice. 'I live in London.'

'Do you? I happen to be working in London at the moment, engaged on research for Professor Norrington. He's a special adviser to National Heritage and a very highly respected man. Somewhat academic, of course. But I do persuade him to deviate from the straight and narrow sometimes.'

'I've always wanted to fall in love with someone clever,' said Pen. 'But I only seem to attract the ones who aren't very bright.'

'I'm not in love with him, please don't think that. In any case he's married and over fifty.'

That wouldn't be an obstacle for Mary Bartlett, thought Hattie. It was as though Alice had picked up her train of thought and they both giggled. Jilly and Pen and Hattie now looked impatiently at Alice, while Mary emptied more hot water into the teapot.

'Are you still with Robert?' enquired Pen. 'We're dying to know.'

'Or has someone else come along?' suggested Jilly. Being married, she imagined that all her friends who weren't had a string of different boyfriends every year.

'You remember all that business with Beatrice and how I thought Robert would never get over her?' Alice began. 'Well, things are so much better now you wouldn't believe. And Bea and I get on quite well, we're good friends, actually.' She paused to accept the beaming smiles.

'And has he asked you to . . . ?' asked Jilly.

'Robert and I are getting married in the autumn.'

Hattie, Jilly and Pen clapped their approval. During interminable phone calls they had followed the agonies and torments of Alice, who despaired that Robert would ever dare to take the plunge. Now, at last, he was behaving as he should. Now they could like him, instead of hating anyone rotten enough to give Alice a hard time.

'I always knew Robert would come round to it in the end,' said Hattie. 'You just have to be patient, don't you?'

They all knew to what she was alluding, except for Mary, but it wasn't the moment to refer to Hattie's fiancé who repented of his decision during his stag night and never arrived at the church. Jilly, Pen and Alice always tried to protect Hattie, but secretly admired her capacity for constantly falling into disasters and extracting herself from them with aplomb. Following the marriage disaster, she had flung herself into the married-man disaster, waiting for him to come round to it in the end. Compared with her, Alice thought her life had been safe and a little predictable, but the others appeared not to see it that way.

'Alice went through the most terrible time,' said Pen to Jilly. 'She didn't make anything for a whole year and we were all terrified that . . .'

'That I'd end up in the loony bin?' said Alice, smiling.

'Goodness no,' retorted Pen.

'What do you make, Alice?' asked Mary.

'We didn't say anything at the time,' continued Pen. 'But we both thought you could be in for a nervous breakdown or enormous doses of Prozac.'

'Even though we knew that Robert really wanted you. It's not as though he was playing around.' Suddenly Pen dived into her shopping bag. 'Here. I found some old photographs. Take a look, you won't believe this.' One by one, Pen passed round a series of gaudy photographs, mostly out of focus. 'A load of tarts taking a break. Remember when we did that Channel trip together?'

'And Jilly's boyfriend forgot his passport and driving licence.'

'And Pen lost her purse.'

'And we all got fantastically drunk in that little place in Le Havre.'

'And ate all those oysters '

'And nearly missed the boat back.'

'And Hattie picked up that rugby player in the bar and invited him home for tea.'

'Look, you can just see his back.'

'What happened to him?'

'He sent me two tickets for a match, but I never went.'

'And did he come for tea?' asked Mary.

'Of course he didn't. Hattie couldn't remember picking him up till we told her afterwards. What a laugh!'

'We must do it again.'

'On our own. Girls outing.'

'When shall we go?'

'They have special off-season deals on the ferry. Unfortunately, I'm hopeless on boats. I throw up even when it's calm,' said Mary.

'I'll find out about the crossing. We'll do it when Jilly's next over.'

'Great, Alice. It's a date.'

Pen was already working out how many hours of extra cleaning she'd have to do to finance the trip. Something to look forward to. Later on, she might mention that she was bringing Archie along. By then she'd be a mum, you needed two to look after a baby. 'Let me show you a picture of Archie,' she said, pulling a crumpled photograph from her wallet. She would have to get them all used to the idea. 'I've only got this snap. Here he is, after a gig, all sweaty.'

'Oh, wonderful,' they chorused.

'Such a gentle, sweet face,' said Hattie, relieved that he was obviously not building-site material, like some of Pen's former beaux. Shame about the beard, though. Jilly took her cue from Pen and pulled out a leather-bound baby book, American-style, with gold lettering announcing every significant occasion in the development of Hank and Melanie, culminating in a portrait of check-shirted Duane holding them both up to camera in a shopping mall. They listened attentively to the running commentary, unaware of the waitress who removed the plates and cutlery with an aggressive clatter.

'He looks tall there, but he's shorter than me.'

'Isn't he adorable? What a fabulous face.'

'And how about you, Hattie?' asked Alice.

'Same as ever,' she replied with a winsome smile.

'You mean he hasn't done it?'

'No, he's still with his ghastly wife.'

'He doesn't deserve you. Honestly, Hattie.'

'I never want anyone else, however hard I try. I do try.'

'I do know what it's like,' Mary announced, determined to contribute to the conversation. 'You're locked into a beautiful room and you can never escape, not unless someone breaks the door down. And you don't want to escape, because outside is grey, always grey. You'd rather stay imprisoned in the beautiful room.'

'There's no point dwelling on it,' said Hattie, without having a clue as to what Mary was trying to say. 'Anyhow, we're going to hear about Robert and Alice. Alice, I do hope you've brought some piccies, too.'

'Not of Robert. He hates having his photograph taken. When they wanted his picture for the *Architectural Review* he kicked up such a fuss. In the end I took a snap and they had to use that.'

'Robert who?' queried Mary.

'Robert Norham,' said Hattie. 'And I've met him. You'd all be wildly jealous. Everyone adores him; he's the ideal man for Alice. Sweet, modest and unbelievably brilliant. At college they said he was the best pupil they'd ever had.'

'One of the best,' corrected Alice. 'But I'm not marrying him because he's brilliant. I really don't understand much about architecture.'

'I've heard of him. He's very well thought-of. They say one day he'll put Sir Richard Rogers in the shade.'

Mary's remark was greeted with puzzled silence. Then Hattie came to the rescue. 'I'm sure you're right, Mary. I expect he will.'

'Professor Norrington says he's one of the few architects to break new ground in the last ten years. Of course, he is controversial.'

'Like Prince Charles,' added Hattie. 'All the most interesting people are controversial, I think.'

'Prince Charles is a frightful bore. And I bet he wears bedsocks and thermal underwear.'

'Pen, we're not getting into an argument about the Royal Family,' said Alice, firmly. If there was one topic which created ill will and resentment it was this. Alice swiftly changed the subject by pulling a brown envelope from her bag. 'I have brought a few transparencies along to show you what I'm doing. Just in case you're interested.'

'Oh, let's see.'

33

Hattie, Jilly and Pen passed them round, holding them up high to catch the light of the plastic candelabrum above their heads. Alice didn't consider the occasion an appropriate one, but Simon – who was trying to teach her business basics – had insisted. Every occasion was appropriate for Marketing. Without Marketing, what would she be? A little drop in the big ocean of commerce and Alice was too good for that. Poo-pooing her indifference to the processes of promotion, he had brought along his Hasselblad, rustled up a couple of resting actresses and lo, publicity stills of a selection of Alice's hats.

'Could I have a look?' enquired Mary, as the transparencies were handed back to Alice.

'Of course you can. I didn't think you'd be interested.'

Mary smiled for the first time as she reverently took them from Alice. 'These are beautiful, such wonderful shapes. I might be needing a hat. I do like them, as a matter of fact. But after you've been forced to wear one at school it takes a while to regard hats as fun. Do you make to order?'

'Oh yes,' replied Alice.

'Have you a card on you by any chance?'

Simon pontificating again. Rule number one, Alice darling, when you start, you do anything. And I mean anything. Even for Mary Bartlett? Alice scrawled down her phone number on the back of the Order of Events for the Corsham Towers Jubilation Ceremony and hoped Mary would lose it.

By the time Alice arrived home, she had the kind of headache that had used to bear down before exams when she hadn't prepared properly. She couldn't quite work out why her head felt as though it would burst like an overfilled dumpling and was attempting to recover in a steaming bath, when Hattie rang.

'We should meet more often. It's so wonderful that everything's going so well for you. And you've lost so much weight. How on earth did you do it?' was how Hattie began, in her cheerful, well-elocuted telephone voice. They all spoke in the same way on the phone and anyone bugging their conversations would have had difficulty distinguishing them. The Corsham Towers voice was unmistakable.

'I haven't really. I've got to lose at least fifteen kilos before the wedding.'

'How ridiculous. Fancy imagining you've got a weight problem. And I'm so excited that you're marrying Robert. I really am.'

Hattie continued chattering until Alice's bath had run cold and caused yet another reminder that her padded-out skin was several sizes too big for her frame.

'Of course we'll keep in touch,' Alice said, attempting to conclude the conversation.

But Hattie declined to take the hint. 'Mind you, next time I hope that Mary Bartlett will be doing something exciting in America or Timbuktu. Whatever it is that she does. What is it about her? I mean she isn't nasty or anything like that. She never says anything important, nothing I want to hear anyway. Was she always like that at school?'

'I think so. I never knew her, really,' replied Alice, stretching out for a towel and attempting to clutch her phone at the same time. Downstairs, she could hear the other phone ringing. And ringing. 'The other phone, I'll have to answer it.'

'How marvellous to be so busy. Never mind, I'll go and feed the cats. Michael never rings me in the evening. He doesn't go to pubs and he can hardly phone me from his home, can he? And it's so hard being intimate, driving along with a mobile pressed to your ear.'

'Goodbye, Hattie. Talk soon.'

'Do you think he'll ever leave his wife?'

'It takes time. One day, he'll turn up on your doorstep and say "I've had enough. I want to be with you."'

'Do you honestly think so?'

'Yes, I do,' said Alice, trying to sound confident. 'Must go.'

It shouldn't have happened to Hattie, Alice thought. Some girls were cut out to be mistresses and some stayed at home dreaming of church weddings and making lovely meals for two. They all thought that Hattie would be married and Pen would end up as the mistress, having secret assignations with rich and powerful men. Alice, who was convinced she would marry a farmer, might well have escaped marriage if Robert's divorce hadn't been coming through when she met him. It was only an accident of time, of timing. But married or not, she had the overwhelming sensation that she was going to stay with Robert for years and years and would never ever, ever want anyone else in her whole life.

Alice tried to imagine herself old, older, in ten years' time. The future was as remote as a tiny cloud high up in a clear sky, which could either drift away or imperceptibly meet up with others to mask the sun and dampen down the day. What had made her different from Hattie? They had gone to the same classes, played the same games, pinned up the same photographs over their lockers, gained comfortably average Cs. They would make no waves, wed no lord or foreign baron; they would be unlikely to have their names printed in anything of greater import than the local parish magazine. They had never sought fame. Fortune might, if they were lucky, come to them from Making the Right Marriage, someone in the City perhaps, but they were all aware that Huge Fortune was beyond their reach. You married for love and one day you would inherit a beautiful old house filled with beautiful old furniture and some relative would make sure that the children went to the Right School.

As soon as she went downstairs, the phone stopped ringing. Alice hoped it had not been a call from Robert, expecting to find her at home. Then she noticed a message on her answerphone. 'Ring me as soon as you're back. I'll drop round.' She knew what that meant. He would come when he could, but not at the time he said he'd come. Robert was never on time. By now, she had learned not to wait expectantly for him, but to continue her evening's work as though he might, or might not, show up.

'I haven't seen that before. What are you making?' asked Robert, as she ushered him into her workroom a couple of hours later.

Alice hastily covered up the length of material she had coveted and bought when on holiday with Simon. 'Just trying something out. Some stuff I've had for ages. Nothing special.'

When she had bought the fabric she'd intended to make it up into a going-away dress for Hattie after her wedding – a go-anywhere dress, vibrant colours, strong abstract design, a positive fabric. Since Robert had now agreed the date, she would make it for herself but two sizes smaller as an incentive to lose weight.

'Shall we go to bed?' Robert said, stroking her fingers and kissing the palms of her hands.

Alice felt a warm rush suffusing her body. A small gesture, a few words and she would abandon everything.

'I don't want to stop you working,' Robert said, enfolding her in his arms.

'I want to be stopped.'

Alice smiled, then returned his kisses. Her headache had melted away; nothing mattered except the moments with him.

'I'll have to go back home later tonight, darling.'

'Never mind, I thought you might,' she said.

'Don't get to know me too well. I want us to have some surprises, even when we're living together all the time.'

'When you've done my workroom I could always put a bed in there. We don't have to sleep together every single night of our lives, do we?' said Alice.

'But you won't be allowed to go there if we've had a row.'

'Why should we have a row? I don't throw saucepans and I promise never to throw your car keys into the Regent's Canal.'

'Beatrice could be such a bitch sometimes. And sometimes . . .'

'My bedroom's a mess. I left early to go to Corsham Towers,' said Alice.

'Sorry, I forgot to ask. Was it good, seeing your friends?'

'Most of them. Tell you later,' Alice replied, starting to climb the stairs.

Three
• • •

Alice carried a satchel into which she had crammed her make-up, her toilet-bag, two pairs of knickers, a spare T-shirt and an uncrushable dress in case they went out somewhere. Since Robert had never once suggested that she might leave a few things in his wardrobe for when she came to stay, even though it would have been more convenient, she refused to deposit personal items in his house. It was a feminine tactic with which he had become all too familiar and one that Beatrice had used with abandon. He ought to have known better, Robert had told her, when Beatrice left a black lace night-dress 'by mistake' in one of his drawers shortly after they had begun to sleep together. The first stage of conquest was to leave a trace of identity, like a dog marking a favourite spot, and Beatrice could always find something to leave behind – her address book, a pair of ear-rings, a bottle of perfume – all of which warranted an unscheduled visit the following day. It was a good sign that Robert was now able to talk about his past without seizing up or erupting with bitter recrimination.

Alice was careful to allow Robert to feel that she was still a guest. Once she became his wife, all that would change, but even then she would always maintain a space between herself and Robert. Her parents had never spent a night apart, but they were the old generation. Their kind of marriage, Alice thought, suited them and they were happy. They would never understand the need to maintain a separate identity, but she knew it was essential for the kind of marriage she wanted. The subject had been exhaustively discussed over thirteen years ago, as they sat on the Corsham lawn and the ragbag of suggestions had been ordered into the Ultimate Plan for Successful Marriage. Pen had been the instigator, Hattie the reluctant follower, Jilly the wild enthusiast, Alice the firm believer, when they had aired their views on the best way to avoid divorce, with the help of articles from *Cosmopolitan* and an illustrated sex-manual bought at a railway station by Pen. Only Alice's parents were still on their first marriage, the others were about to repeat the same mistakes, or had already done so. No one, they swore to one another over Cup-a-Soups brewed late at night in the sixth-form kitchen, should repeat mistakes.

Alice propped her bicycle against the railings surrounding Robert's house and locked a wheel to one of the uprights. The railings were dull and chipped, but he hadn't got round to completing the painting of the exterior. Like a supermodel who paraded high fashion on the international catwalks and spent her private time in jeans or track suits, his own house would lack the refinements, which he sweated to provide for his demanding clients.

Having phoned to say when she would be arriving, Alice let herself in. Robert had given her a spare set of keys. The door of his studio was closed. 'Hi. It's me,' she called.

When she came into the room, Robert hopped down from his high stool, abandoned his drawing-board and gave her a welcoming kiss.

'Are you finishing something?' Alice asked.

'I've done enough. It can wait.'

'Are you sure?'

'Absolutely. Simon's asked us for dinner tonight, he's got some friends coming round. Business friends.'

'Oh.' Alice sighed. 'I haven't seen you all week.'

'You don't want to go?'

'Not really, not tonight.'

'I was hoping you'd say that. Why don't you call him and say we'd promised to see someone.'

'And that I'd forgotten to tell you?'

'Something like that.'

'I hate lying to Simon. I'll just tell him the truth, that we want to be alone. I'm sure he'll understand.'

'Coming from you, he will,' said Robert.

They settled in the one room that Robert had completed, a living-room extending from front to back, newly floored in pale maple, with white walls and black lacquered Venetian blinds. There was nothing comfortable to sprawl on, only striking chairs made by his favourite designers and a metal-framed, stiffly upholstered couch, which was modern and classic, and apparently significant in the history of furniture design. When Alice had once suggested he might get a squashy sofa on which she could lie down full length Robert was amazed. If you want to lie down, he said, what's wrong with my beautiful bed? Over the time she had known him, Alice had come to appreciate his purist approach, his concern for line, surface and texture, rather than what he called the 'three-piece-suite' idea of human needs. The Japanese were appalled at the European penchant for heavy sofas and lumpen armchairs. And he had persuaded her they were right.

Alice had become accustomed to sitting cross-legged on a sea-grass mat, while Robert leaned against the mantel of the black marble fireplace. He seemed unsuited to sitting in a chair, as though he couldn't wait to leap up and move to another place. Alice liked watching him. In this room he appeared taller, his skin more golden, his greyish eyes more blue, as though the spring light were caressing him.

'What shall we do? Simon was raving about some

new restaurant in a converted laundry. The food's marvellous, the design's yet again by Julian – wouldn't you guess? – but it's in Lewisham. Of course, he started explaining some amazing back route he'd discovered, said we'd get there in no time,' said Alice, after she had finished her call. 'Or we could see a film.'

'Take-away something, then watch tele in bed? How about that? I'm slightly shattered as I had to be on site at eight this morning, that place in East Cheam.'

'The one you loathe. It's not fair, having to go all the way out there.' Alice repressed her impulse to wing off into the evening somewhere where they could dance until they dropped, and rose to her feet. 'I'll find a nice bottle of something.'

'You don't have to, darling.'

Alice grabbed her coat, slung it over her shoulders and said with a grin, 'I like choosing pretty labels.'

On the way to the off-licence, she lingered by the closed patisserie shop. The girls were cleaning up, white-coated, swabbing down the floor as though it were an operating theatre in the aftermath of a Saturday accident night.

One of them recognised her and gestured for her to wait. 'Not gift-wrapped I'm afraid,' she said, pressing a paper bag into Alice's hand. Inside was a bulging, buttery cream slice, oozing raspberry jam and demanding to be devoured immediately.

'I'll make you a hat!' Alice called out through a mouthful of cream. She so much preferred exchanging favours, rather than money. Thinking about the kind of hat which would suit the comely, freckle-faced girl delayed her realisation that she shouldn't have. Three hundred calories at a guess, maybe more. A fifth of the daily ration. Although she had been hopeless at mental calculations in the classroom, Alice had discovered a surprising facility for remembering the calorific values of various foods and making quick additions without the aid of a calculator. She had underestimated, she decided. Double cream four-hundred and sixty-one calories per 100 grams. Must be 100 grams in that cream slice. Jam two hundred and forty-eight calories per 100 grams. Alice reflected. There couldn't have been 100 grams of jam, could there? That was the equivalent of one light meal, which she would now have to subtract from her daily intake. Eat less tomorrow, she promised herself.

By the time she returned, Robert had spread out a Chinese feast for four in appropriate bowls and plates.

'Why did you order all that?' Alice cried in horror. 'Those are Simon portions.'

'If you can't manage all of it I'll finish it off tomorrow.'

Alice felt her urge to eat melting away in a swamp of regret. Next time, she swore she would look the other way as she passed the window. Taking up the chopsticks, she picked at a few grains of rice as Robert stuffed down a giant battered prawn. Alice could see him observing her out of the corner of his eye.

'My appetite's a bit feeble, even though it looks delicious,' Alice explained. The regret was rapidly passing and she told herself to count ten after every mouthful.

Suddenly Robert leaned towards her across the stainless-steel table. 'Darling, you're not going on some stupid diet, are you?'

'Certainly not. I'm just not very hungry.' She allowed him to pass some spare-ribs into her bowl. Nibbling slowly at the bones would give the illusion of eating. A hundred calories, maybe less.

'How was your school get-together? You still haven't told me. Did you see Hattie and Pen?'

'And Jilly. The one who got married and went to America. You've never met her.' Alice sketched a brief portrait of the missing member of the group.

By now, Robert was familiar with the lives of her closest friends, as well as her family. Unlike Alice, he appeared not to feel the need for the kind of friendships she enjoyed. It was a strange idea to him to entrust every detail of your life to people you rarely saw. Hattie, her closest friend, would call several times a week with news she had garnered through letters and telephone calls. Alice knew who was meant to call and hadn't, what rows had broken out, which cat had had kittens, why the car had broken down, which hyped-up movies had been disappointing, every minor accident, passing fancy and pleasure of life. Alice's soap opera, Robert called it.

'And someone we never expected turned up, a girl called Mary Bartlett,' concluded Alice. 'Still, she says she wants me to make her a hat.'

'Another commission? Aren't you pleased?'

'Not all that much. I hardly knew Mary at school. No one liked her. I only enjoy making hats for people I like, you know that.'

Robert laughed. 'If I only did things for clients I like, I'd be twiddling my thumbs all day.'

'It's different for you. You're patient with difficult people.'

'Am I? I hadn't noticed.'

'It's not so important for me. I'm only making hats, after all. Not creating buildings or transforming old ones. People wear a hat for a day and shove it in a box to the back of a cupboard. It's not the same.'

'You're creating something . . .'

'Only a little something for the top of someone's head. A dot on the i.'

Not long after the Corsham Towers reunion Mary Bartlett happened to find herself in the vicinity of Kensal Green. She came unannounced, far too early for Alice who was washing her hair at the time, nor did she offer any apology. It was as though she had arrived for a pre-arranged appointment.

'Such an interesting house,' Mary said, stepping back to encompass every detail of Alice's red-brick terrace house which had neither ruched net curtains, nor a stamped-out Home-Base Georgian door. It was quite unlike the long line of clumsy, bow-windowed Edwardian villas on either side. Only Alice could have combined seemingly discordant hues so that they appeared to have grown up together. Mary appeared undeterred by Alice's grumpy expression as she held open the front door, swathed in a towel, having expected a demand for overdue payment from the milkman.

'You've given it a new character it never had. It's so bold and original.'

'Glad you like it.' Alice tried to sound pleased.

'I really do. Did you use National Trust paints? They have such unusual shades. That green, for example, and the red. Have you been to India by any chance?'

Alice took a step inside, since it was starting to splutter with rain. 'Come in. You'll get wet.'

'I love rain.' Mary appeared to be staring at a squat chimney pot. 'My great-grandmother was Vietnamese.'

'I don't see the connection,' said Alice, disappearing inside.

Mary followed behind her into the workroom. 'I have the rainy season in my blood, dripping leaves, muggy tropics, then the rush of downpour sounding like a distant waterfall.'

'I've never been anywhere really hot.'

'Oh, but you should. It's surprising, really, that you haven't. All those lovely warm colours. I wonder what drew you to them?'

'Escaping from my parents' taste I expect. They like everything pale green and pale pink and pale yellow. Won't be a minute. Must dry my hair. Have a look around, if you'd like to.'

When Alice came back, she found Mary roaming round the room, staring in fascination at the old wooden hat-blocks, collected over the years, different forms of ovals and rounds, featureless faces straight out of some surrealist canvas. She lingered by a hat press whose function she didn't recognise. Completed hats waiting for collection were balanced on wooden hooks, sculpted straw, layers of felt, one or two which looked out of place swathed in tulle. Mary then stopped in front of a large cork board covered by images, scraps of coloured paper, swatches of fabrics, quickly drawn sketches, dried flowers and yellowing, jagged cuttings from magazines, which featured Alice's hats. 'I've always seemed to end up wearing dark brown or dark grey. But now I've decided to give more thought to my appearance, to strike out in a Technicolor direction.'

'Bright colours, then.'

'Bright *interesting* colours. They needn't be crude.'

'No, naturally.' Alice sighed impatiently. Mary sounded as though she was correcting a phrase in an essay. 'Is there anything here which is the kind of thing you'd like?'

'Not quite, I have to say.'

Was Mary going to be one of those customers who could never make up their minds? Large brim, small brim? Big crown, small crown? Toning with the outfit? Contrasting with the outfit? Making a statement on its own? Not making a statement at all? Alice wandered over to a sofa she had been meaning to re-upholster, covered in a thick rug. As long as you weren't too thin, you couldn't feel the protruding springs. Mary was too thin.

'That's quite comfortable,' Alice said, pointing to the one respectable armchair in the room.

'Do you mind if I sit on the floor? It's better for my back.'

It was difficult to visualise a hat from this angle. If

her favourite position were to be cross-legged on a floor the hat would have to be interesting from above. Still, it wasn't often you sat on the floor at weddings. 'Is your hat for an occasion, Mary? It helps if I know. For example, if it's a wedding, will it be a town wedding, a country wedding . . .'

'Oh, no. Nothing like that. It's for a very important cocktail party my professor's giving. The Chancellor of Oxford University will be there. Very grand indeed.'

'Formal, then.'

'I don't know why, but I seem to see a little frivolous cocktail hat from a Noël Coward play. It might have a gardenia over one ear. I like gardenias. You could sketch out different styles. I'm very open-minded. Do you think I could carry it off?'

'Lovely idea. I haven't made a cocktail hat for ages, not since college.' Alice beamed, little having expected a licence to experiment.

'When the guests come into the room I want them to look at me immediately and think, "What an interesting-looking woman. So unlike the others." People tend to forget what my face looks like. Take a proper look, I don't mind. I want the hat to create a mood around me, like ivy draped over an ancient pillar.'

It was a challenge, to make the connection between ancient pillars and Noël Coward, but Alice was used to it. Customers created confused images while believing they knew clearly what they wanted. Alice's task was to persuade them that the hat she created was what they had had in mind right from the beginning. 'Mary would you mind standing up, so I can get a good look at the shape of your face?' As Mary sprang quickly to her feet, Alice positioned herself at the side of her long mirror. 'Come over here. I find it helps to see a reflection.'

Alice asked her to turn round slowly. Now she could examine her as though she were hanging in the National Portrait Gallery. She'd never thought of it before, but she did have the kind of face which could look completely different from one day to the other. Today she looked almost pretty, but Alice remembered her as undistinctive and plain. Her skin hung softly over the bones of her face in an indeterminate way, but when the light caught it from certain sides it appeared strong and well defined.

Mary obligingly tilted her head through several different angles, as though waiting for a painter to select a pose. 'Having you design my hat is the beginning of my personal revolution. Hats make you remembered.'

'Yes. They heighten personality, so people say. But you don't need that!' Alice had said this before, a phrase which caught the imagination of older clients, but Mary showed no response. There was an awkward silence.

'Are you going to the cocktail party with someone?' asked Alice in a tone of friendly enquiry.

Mary looked straight at her as though she'd been hit between the eyes. 'No. That's the point.' Then, to Alice's consternation, a couple of tears erupted without warning and coursed down her cheeks. 'Don't take any notice, please.' Pulling a lacy handkerchief from her pocket, Mary swept it across her face with a brusque movement.

'I'll get you some coffee,' said Alice.

It was a shock, seeing Mary Bartlett in tears. No one had ever seen her cry, not unless she wept under the bedclothes at night. Some girls did.

'Could you possibly make it tea? Earl Grey if possible, no milk.'

'I've got some herbal, it's part of my diet regime.'

'That would be wonderful.'

She could have said something like 'What you? On a diet? Whatever for?' as everyone else did. But she made no comment and seemed completely to have regained her composure.

*   *   *

Mary sipped her tea delicately, as though the rough pottery mug were bone china and liable to crack between her hands, which Alice noticed were elongated and veined, like the Leonardo hands. Robert had a print of them in his studio.

'Sorry about that. I'm not usually weepy.'

'Please don't apologise. I get like that sometimes, too.'

They smiled at one another, on the edge of formality, then Mary's voice brightened. 'I'll be wearing an emerald-green dress – I've never worn green before – and I brought it along to help you. I realise you can't design a hat without knowing what lies below it. Is there somewhere I can change?'

'If I pull down the blind, no one will see, don't worry.'

She turned her back, and Alice surreptitiously watched her slip down her long, full skirt and throw off the heavy sweater she was wearing, far too warm for a muggy day in April. Her tiny breasts were held aloft by an extravagant black lace confection and below it she wore fine black stockings held up by an embroidered silk suspender belt. Suddenly, Mary turned round to face her. 'I bought this ridiculous underwear for him,' she said. 'It wasn't my idea.'

'It's fantastic. You should wear a see-through dress over it.'

'I'm not the sexy type, although I did try. Too bony in my view,' Mary said, as she pulled down a fussy, panelled, emerald-green silk dress over her head (Laura Ashley trying, thought Alice, but it could have been Belleville Sassoon) and secured a series of tiny gilt buttons up to her neck. 'What do you think?'

'It's a bit . . .' Alice faltered. Obviously Mary had spent a fortune.

'Do tell me. I want your frank opinion.'

'Well, quite honestly it reminds me of something you might wear at a hunt ball.'

Mary seemed surprised for a moment, then gave a slight laugh. 'You think it's too outrageous. Never mind.' The smile remained on her face, as though she wished to demonstrate her good humour. 'I've probably gone over the top.'

'A little.' Alice smiled back.

Mary removed the dress, folding it up and replacing it in a plain plastic bag, and quickly pulled on the full skirt and baggy sweater in which she had first appeared. 'You're probably right. I knew it was wrong at the time. Do you do that sometimes? Buy something, and as you're signing your credit slip you know it's going to be a disaster, but you daren't say anything, it's too late?'

'All the time,' Alice lied. 'Always reassure the client' was one of the refrains she had to learn on a seminar for small businesses which she had attended at Simon's insistence. She hoped the day would come soon when she could afford a business manager and was featured in *Vogue* and *Harper's* and *Women's Wear Daily*, and Joan Collins was front-page *Hello!* wearing one of her hats. One day she would be a Great Dictator like Coco Chanel and Giorgio Armani, but only in the hat department.

'Who was the man who liked black underwear? He sounds exciting,' said Alice, unable to stifle her curiosity. And after all, it was Mary who had brought up the subject.

'His name was Roland. I was married to him.' Mary pronounced it in the French way. 'He came from Montpelier, dark, menacing and totally irresistible. Brilliantly intelligent, artistic, elegant, passionate, sensitive, oh everything. We were following the same course at the Sorbonne, though I never completed it.'

'Because you fell in love?'

'That's putting it too mildly. It was a *coup de foudre*, a grand passion. I never do anything by halves. And something always goes wrong. Always. Do you smoke, by any chance?'

Groping in a drawer, Alice extracted the client pack, a few stale Benson and Hedges left by a careless visitor.

'Thank you so much. I'm so relieved you're not puritanical about smoking.'

'What went wrong? Did he run off with someone? I hope you don't mind me asking.'

'Worse.' She inhaled deeply and stared into space. 'He killed himself.'

Alice gulped. No one she knew had ever taken the final step. Or even talked about it. 'How dreadful. How absolutely dreadful.'

Mary had covered her face with her hands, but she slowly removed them, making an effort to regain her composure. 'Whenever we had a serious argument he threatened to commit suicide, because he thought he loved me more than I loved him. Which wasn't true, by the way. Then one day he threw himself under a train. In the Metro. Barbès Rochechouart. I'm certain he did it to spite me, to show that he could do it. People I love always die.'

Alice searched in vain for an appropriate response. How could she react when she hardly knew her? Mary wouldn't accept the usual remarks of polite sympathy and concern, but she had to say something. 'I'm sure it only seems like that,' was the only remark she could muster.

'Could I have some more tea?' said Mary, smoothing back her hair. 'And then perhaps you could make a suggestion about a dress. I am rather hopeless at choosing things for myself.'

While the kettle was boiling up, Alice went upstairs to her bedroom and surveyed her wardrobe from thinner days, kept as a reminder. She pulled out a smoky blue chiffon dress with a faint stain on one side, which

Simon had bought her once. It hardly showed. Mary needed a dress with happy memories.

When Alice came back into the workroom with two cups of tea and the dress over her arm, Mary carried on talking as though there had been no interruption. 'You see why I was rather awkward with all the girls at the reunion. I could hardly say I'd married this fabulous man who went and threw himself under a train, could I?'

'When did it happen?'

'Six months ago. You're the first person in England I've told. I wanted to tell you, I hope you don't mind. But I won't go on about it. I'm here for a hat, aren't I?' Her tone had changed abruptly, as though the relief of confession had gone to her head. Now she looked alive again, her eyes bright, a smile on her lips. 'I wanted to hear about Robert. I didn't intend to . . . to spill over like that.'

Alice smiled. 'I'm glad you told me.' Then she went over and picked up the chiffon dress, which she had thrown onto her table. 'I thought this might be good on you. I'm far too big to wear it any more and it would look marvellous with your colouring. Try it, go on.'

Mary excitedly threw off her clothes and took hold of the chiffon dress. It was on the loose side but she pulled in the belt. (Size eight, still size eight. What bliss to be size eight!)

'It looks far better on you than it ever did on me.'

'I'm not sure.' Mary walked over to a long mirror. 'To be absolutely honest, I don't think I want to wear blue, although it is a gorgeous dress. I hope you don't think I'm being difficult only Roland said it was my best colour. I doubt if I'll ever wear blue again. Do you understand?'

'Of course I do. It was only a suggestion. You'll find something absolutely right, I know you will.'

'As I told you, I've a bad back. I can never undo

things; it makes me feel like a cripple. Would you mind undoing the zip?'

Her skin was cool, her back fine-boned, her waist indented to the right degree. Alice knew she could never attain that smoothness, that elongated willow-like shape. Even so, she could fine herself down, she could be an 'After' while now she was a 'Before'. And she would work, slave and force herself to concentrate on the slim image, which lay hidden beneath the gross covering of flesh.

Moving to her work-table, Alice pulled out a drawer stuffed with feathers of various hues, pieces of silk, fabric flowers, small shells and buttons, and collections of multi-hued chocolate wrappers and ribbons, which had taken her fancy. Then she placed a small black base on Mary's head, and experimented with various shapes and colours.

'Alice, you must wear that wonderful blue dress again.'

'I'm miles too fat now even to think of getting into it.'

'Yes, you do need to be a little slimmer. Only a little. Do you mind me saying so?'

'No, no, of course not,' Alice stammered.

'Between friends one can say these things. I know you've always been worried about your weight. Do you remember, at school you were forever cutting out diet articles and hiding them in your desk?'

'How did you know?'

'During prep, I saw you a few times studying them. You used to stick them in the back of your geography book.'

'I hated geography.'

'Didn't we all?'

'You were good at it.'

Mary smiled dismissively. 'I could draw maps, that's all.' She sank down into the client armchair and sat bolt upright with clasped hands, while Alice continued experimenting. 'If you like, I can help you. I'm quite an expert on weight problems. My mother, when she was alive, became gross in a week if she didn't mind her diet. I take after my father, luckily.'

'And is he still . . .' Impelled to discover whether all Mary's family had died in strange circumstances, Alice was apprehensive about overstepping the bounds.

'Yes?'

'Alive?'

'Married for the third time. She's younger than me,' said Mary contemptuously. 'An American post-graduate student. My father is a professor of classics. Brilliant but unstable, unusual in the field of classics. I wish I had his mind but, as he's always reminding me, I don't.'

Alice nodded politely, wondering who else shared the field of classics and what they spent their time doing. She preferred not to enquire too closely. 'It's boring for everyone else, when you're on a diet,' she said. 'Robert thinks I've got a tiny appetite because I don't want him to know. So I hardly eat anything when I'm with him. Naturally, he thinks I'm not interested in food.'

'By the way, what size are you?' asked Mary. 'Fourteen?'

'Not quite. Nearer sixteen.'

'And your height?'

'Five foot six. I should be about fifty-five kilos.'

'That's on the low side. But you do need to get rid of . . .'

'Fifteen kilos,' Alice quickly replied. 'And I've got to lose it by September, when we get married. Got to, got to. Robert hasn't said anything, of course he wouldn't, but I can see him looking at me sometimes, doubtfully, as though he can't bring himself to make a comment. And I couldn't bear him to tell me after I was married.'

54

Mary frowned, as though she was searching for the right words. 'Some women get fat little by little and their husbands don't notice. When the fire has gone, as it were. And they become resigned and find themselves glancing furtively at slim thighs and small waists. Usually their secretaries!' Her voice had changed, she giggled slightly and there was a hint of warmth that she usually disguised in a clipped delivery.

'Beatrice thinks I'm crazy,' said Alice.

'Beatrice?'

'Robert's ex-wife, he was married to her for four years. She is unbelievably slim and tall, and perfectly proportioned. At first I thought we'd never get on, but now I've got to know her she's become one of my friends. Strange, really.'

'Why? Interesting people usually take a little time to know.'

Alice shrugged 'I suppose so. I sometimes wonder why Robert was attracted to me, I couldn't be more different from Beatrice, in every way.'

'I imagine that you both represent different parts of Robert. But you're the one he wants to live with.'

'Do you know, I honestly believe Beatrice wants me to marry Robert. That's what she told me, anyway.'

'Why shouldn't she want him to be happy?'

'She does admit that her marriage was a failure, but no one expects her to give a big welcome to wife number two. That's what most people think. You can't blame them.'

'Some people are idiots. If you can't make a success of a relationship, why shouldn't someone else? Why be bitter about it? I don't understand that mentality.'

'That's a really generous thing to say, Mary.'

'Not particularly.'

Alice stood by the window and watched while Mary wandered round her room yet again, like a blind person sensing the position of each object, recording texture and smell, seeking out individuality in the dark. She stopped by a plastic case enclosing a neatly folded pile of fabric. 'What's this? Can I look?'

'Take it out. I found this fabric a few years ago, when I was in Rome. Italian silk, there's nothing like it.'

Mary held up the filmy material, splotched with deep vermilion reds and resonant cornfield yellows. 'Oh, I do love this,' she said, placing the length against her. 'My favourite colours. You have such a wonderful eye. I would have picked this out immediately, too. You can feel the influence of that Mediterranean sun, rich and powerful.' Then she came towards her, full of emotion. 'Alice, could you make me a dress out of this? It would be absolutely perfect. I'd only wear it once and then when you'd finished your diet, you'd be the same size as me and you could wear it. I'd give it back to you, it would be yours anyway.'

Taking the fabric from her, Alice folded it carefully along the creases, back into its former shape. 'I'm sorry, Mary, really sorry. I'd love to give it to you, but I can't. This is going to be made up into the dress for my wedding day. It'll be in a register office, so I thought I had to wear some good strong colours. I could try and find you something else like it.'

'No, no. It was just an idea. A stupid idea. Forget about it. How was I to know?'

'Of course you weren't.'

A sudden smile lit up Mary's face. 'I was married in cream lace. Roland wanted me to wear purple, he was unconventional like that, but I put my foot down.'

Alice thought for a moment and suddenly felt she had been ungenerous. 'I think you should have that material. I'm sure to find something else.'

'Absolutely not,' said Mary sternly. 'I wouldn't dream of it. It will look stunning on you and I'm sure Robert will love it.' She glanced at her watch and frowned. 'Is that the time? I really ought to go, but I would love another cup of tea. Would you mind?'

'Not at all.'

When Alice returned, Mary was sitting on the floor again, leaning against the wall. She came and sat beside her. 'I'm dying to hear more about Robert. How did you meet? It always fascinates me knowing how people come across one another,' Mary said.

'He was a friend of Simon's. I was going to marry Simon.'

'But once you'd met Robert, even if you'd been married to Simon for only a few days, you'd have run off with him.'

'How did you know?'

'Great passion arises from the unexpected. You don't come across a great love in a mixed doubles on the tennis court or sipping sherry at a cocktail party. And it usually happens when it seems impossible that it will ever reach fruition. Luckily, in your case, it did.'

'I'm not sure about great passion,' said Alice with a smile. 'I just want to be with him.'

'But you've never thought, why him? Why Robert?'

'There was never anyone else, not in that way.' Alice was unable to explain further, but she felt that Mary was demanding a more original explanation. 'He's everything I've ever imagined,' she added.

'You don't have to say any more. I'm always asking questions, you can ignore them, I don't mind. I'm sure you've masses of work to do, I've taken up enough of your time. It was lovely talking to you.' Taking up her bag, Mary made it clear that she was leaving with reluctance.

Having agreed a time for the first fitting, Alice showed her to the door.

Afterwards, she suddenly regretted talking as she had – talking about her weight, admitting her fears – and wished she had maintained the business-like exchanges and polite enquiries which normally accompanied the genesis of a hat. She hoped Mary would forget their conversation. Rushing to the fridge in her tiny kitchen, Alice took out a ready-prepared tiramisu and poured the contents into her mouth with a dessert spoon. Chocolate, cream, nuts and liqueur, which floated unctuously down her throat. Five hundred and sixty-five calories of ecstasy.

It was club night and Alice had arrived late. Beatrice, who resembled a sleek baby otter, shining in gunmetal Lycra, stood over Alice as she was marathon cycling, going nowhere, sweat pouring down her neck.

'Don't stop me,' shouted Alice breathlessly. 'Another five minutes.'

'I don't know why you do it.'

'Because I need to.'

'I'm going to shower and then I'll have a calzone in the bar. Shall I order one for you?'

'No!' Alice screamed, pedalling ever more furiously.

The bar was crowded, but Simon had arrived long before the others, commandeered a table and spread pages of the *Financial Times* over three chairs to indicate occupancy. A nearly demolished wadge of dough lay on his plate and he would shortly repeat his order. Being hungry, he had suspended his critical faculties. Robert, in a track suit with a towel round his neck, looked at Simon quizzically since he resembled an extra from *Goodfellas*, costumed in a brown pin-striped suit with a buttoned waistcoat, straining to close.

'What do you think?' said Simon, putting his thumbs in the waistcoat. 'It's my power-dressing city look.'

'Which city? Chicago?' Robert grinned as he pulled out a chair.

'New York via Milan. I bought it there after I'd got the contract.'

'What's this one?'

'Stopping computers doing their nut when the year 2000 comes along, helping them face up to the new millennium. They're like kids, you have to help them adapt to unfamiliar environments. Do you realise, when we eventually get them to communicate, we'll have to reduce all the problems of the world into a format a dim five-year-old might be able to grasp? That will be the next giant leap for mankind.' Simon pointed to his plate. 'Do you want one of these things?'

Robert shook his head. 'I thought I'd give the gym a miss today. It's bad to exercise on a full stomach and I had serious lunch.'

Sweeping into the bar like a powerboat heading full throttle for the open sea, Beatrice threw her bag onto a chair. 'Something has happened to Alice. She is cycling away like a maniac and refuses to have supper with us.'

'I'll go and get her,' Simon said, rising from his chair.

Pushing him back into his seat, Robert said, 'No, I'll go.'

'Tell her we won't have a thing till she comes,' said Beatrice. 'She's taking it all far too seriously. Perhaps she's fallen for her gym instructor. I must say he's rather dishy.'

As Robert hurried away, Simon frowned at Beatrice. 'Was that necessary, Bea?'

'Do him good to be kept on his toes.'

'You're in a bad mood.'

'No, I'm not. Yes, all right I am,' exclaimed Beatrice defiantly. 'And so would you be if you'd had to make three hundred miniature quiches with two children getting under your feet.'

'And the au pair?' he asked sweetly.

'Don't talk to me about Hilda. Why does her mother have to fall sick in Oslo? How am I meant to manage? She just doesn't understand what it is to be a working mother.'

59

'You could always ask David to help out. Don't husbands do that nowadays?'

'David's very good in the house, but he's extremely busy. It's so marvellous when someone loves his work. And he adores the children.'

Beatrice was in no mood to discuss her domestic arrangements with a bachelor who only had to think of himself. Fortunately, Simon and David no longer shared the same business premises. David had performed so brilliantly as Simon's accountant that he had been able to leave his company and set up as an independent financial consultant shortly after they were married. This improved the funds available for housekeeping and luxury holidays, and enabled Beatrice to have numerous pricey business lunches with her friends, disguised as client tasting sessions. She rarely talked about David, because there was nothing much to say. She hadn't married him for his brilliant conversation or his dazzling charm; neither was he the kind of man who would kindle uncontrollable flames. He was decent, reliable and above all, David wanted children, the more the better. But no one could spend all day with little ones (two girls, one three, one five) who screamed 'I want' from morning till night, without seeking refuge in a demanding job.

'No one's forcing you to make quiches, Bea. It's not as though you're on the breadline.'

'Cooking is my career, Simon. Everyone has to have a career. Imagine if I did nothing all day? What would happen to my mind?'

Simon was about to reply that cooking did damn all to broaden the mind, but veered onto a safer topic. 'I haven't seen David in ages,' he said, trying to sound as though he had just thought of him.

'Why should you want to?' replied Beatrice. 'He hasn't changed since you saw him last.'

Simon retrieved the pages of the *Financial Times*

heaped on the two vacant chairs and held one up to his face.

'What are you reading?' asked Beatrice.

'The gardening column. I think I'm going to get into gardening. Everyone else is. I shall grow vegetables on my patio, I've decided.'

'Vegetables don't thrive in London. The soil's not right.'

Simon let Beatrice have the last word and waited until Robert came back with Alice. They were both laughing, which was a welcome change from Beatrice's stormy countenance.

'Who's for a late-night movie?' asked Alice.

'I'm up for it,' said Simon.

'Me, too.' Suddenly Beatrice looked radiant. 'But I choose, okay? The quiches can go to hell.'

As they all sat giggling at Woody Allen, Alice took handfuls of the communal popcorn, consoling herself with the fact that she had missed supper. She knew they would all emerge from the cinema good-humoured, having laughed loudly at the same jokes and exchanged knowing glances down the row. Robert had asked if she could stay the night. Mary was going to find the solution to her weight problem. She felt Robert's fingers tightening round hers in the dark. Turning to him in the flickering light, she mouthed, 'I-adore-you.'

Four
• • •

Alice was at home in the middle of stitching hanks of straw when Beatrice came up the path, shepherding Sasha and Drusilla in front of her. 'Darling, could I just leave the girls with you for half an hour?' said Beatrice breathlessly. 'Only I've got to make a delivery and it won't look wonderful if I charge into Coutts's boardroom with them in tow. Hilda isn't coming back. She's left.'

Making hats is a process in which you lose yourself, a long, slow meditation while the three-dimensional form grows beneath your hands. Unlike others in the business of fashion, milliners are the dreamers who have adapted to the slow, patient rhythm of intricate creation. When the outside world intrudes the spell is broken. Alice had barely learned to master her irritation but Beatrice was too frantic to notice.

'Just half an hour, then. And they'll have to amuse themselves. I'm busy.'

Beatrice thrust a shoe-bag of toys into Alice's hand. 'Of course you're busy; but they won't disturb you. You're a darling. Here are the toys. You can put them in one of the bedrooms upstairs, they'll be quite happy. It's quite ridiculous! Why do nursery schools finish so early? Must rush, cold buffet in boot.'

Drusilla and Sasha quickly showed their dissatisfaction at Alice's inadequate bedroom – they told her it was tiny, not like Mummy's – and the moment Alice thought she could leave them with a box of dressing-up clothes Drusilla told Sasha that dressing up was what babies did. She found a new game, which involved hurling their toys in relays down the stairs. Surprised to find that an arm had become detached from her favourite doll, not yet able to understand that physical force caused breakages, Sasha started to scream. It was no use Drusilla standing primly at the bottom of the stairs telling Alice she was always screaming. Or that she shouldn't take any notice, Mummy didn't.

'You can help me make a hat,' suggested Alice, tossing a box of tatters in their direction.

'Daddy looks silly in a hat,' confided Drusilla with a smirk. 'He's got a straw one. And he wears it in the garden so his skin doesn't go burnty.'

'You're burnty,' lisped Sasha.

'I am not.'

'You are.'

Another scream as Drusilla lashed out at Sasha, who then attempted to retaliate by pulling her hair.

'Just stop it,' cried Alice. Then, in desperation, 'Or I'll tell Mummy.'

'Don't care.'

Beatrice came back in a couple of hours, which seemed closer to a week, and gasped 'coffee' as Alice opened the door. Bumps and bangs reverberated round the hall. 'Darlings, I told you to stay upstairs,' said Beatrice, hauling her charges from Alice's workroom. 'And no scissors,' she added, wrenching a pair of pinking shears from Drusilla's grasp. She won a few minutes' silence by presenting them with a couple of sticky lollies, which they first complained about, then decided to suck, before discarding them on the carpet. 'It's so sweet of you to have the children. I don't know what I'd do without you.' She gave such a genuine smile of relief that Alice didn't have the heart to ask if they were always so difficult. 'Ghastly traffic,' groaned Beatrice, pulling up a kitchen chair. She threw off her trenchcoat to reveal a clinging T-shirt with Considerate Catering blocked out on the front and stretched out her legs, tightly encased in a zebra print.

'New leggings? Lovely,' remarked Alice, revelling in the apparent calm Beatrice had effected, judging by the lack of thumps from upstairs.

'Cost a fortune. I had them rung up in Harrods's Food Department. David doesn't mind if it's gourmet on the bill. Christ, why can't I find someone to do deliveries? They all want to be bloody chauffeurs in uniform.'

'You could try the Job Centre.'

'Is there one in Holland Park?'

Beatrice had persuaded David to relocate from South Kensington to Holland Park after a couple of years coping with minimal space. That the house she chose — or rather the only one available which suited her needs — happened to be two hundred metres from Robert's was pure coincidence, she insisted, once the sale was completed. And besides, in London you could live next door to someone and see them only a few times a year.

Alice began to assemble a jar of instant coffee, a couple of mugs and a carton of milk.

'And sugar, please, Alice.'

'I don't have any sugar in the house.'

'Honey'll do fine,' retaliated Beatrice.

Alice withdrew from the cupboard a large jar with a smear of honey still remaining. It had disappeared with alacrity ever since she had read that mountain dwellers scraping an existence somewhere in remotest Russia, or whatever they called it nowadays, ate nothing but yoghurt and honey. Thirty per cent of them reached the staggering age of one hundred and five and obesity was unknown. If the calorie content was high, it would be outweighed by the health advantages, Alice persuaded herself.

Beatrice held up the jar. 'Honey's so much better for you than sugar. Did you read about those Russians . . . ?'

'Yes, I did.'

'They lived a long time, it said in this article, but their sperm count was unbelievably low.'

'Really? I don't remember reading that.'

'You never read anything properly, you're a skimmer just like David,' said Beatrice, running her finger inside the honey pot. 'Children been okay?'

'I let them have a go at making a paper hat.'

'Wonderful, they love making things. They're so fond of you, Alice, always asking when they can see you.'

'I'm not sure why. I'm much better with little boys. I suppose it's because I had to cope with three brothers, but I always wanted a sister.'

Looking at her intently, Beatrice leaned forward. 'You know, you're so good with children. Has Robert talked to you about it?'

'About what?' asked Alice.

'Having babies. No, of course he hasn't. You'll have to bring up the subject, he won't. You are going to have them, aren't you, Alice?'

'I'd like to. Eventually. I don't really think about it much, not at the moment.'

'You will, once you're married.'

Alice grinned. Beatrice would never understand that their views on marriage were totally different. Being an Irish Catholic, Beatrice would have seen it as the gateway to motherhood. Alice wanted a few years of freedom with Robert, but Beatrice wouldn't understand that either. Her women friends were far more important than her husband, Alice sometimes thought.

'If I were you, I'd have it out with him,' Beatrice continued. 'Not that it did me any good, but he might have changed. I hope he has.'

'Not all men want children, Bea.'

'Maybe not, but they do once they're old. Men love to

65

be doting grandpas, haven't you noticed? Anyway, I've no intention of doting. I'm going to be an amazingly glamorous granny. I'm quite looking forward to it when all this slog is over.'

'You have people around to help,' said Alice, thinking of the endless procession of child-minders, au pairs, cleaners, baby-sitters, nursery schoolteachers and a steady pool of relatives available to lift the burden of motherhood.

'Oh, dear, that's not the point.' Beatrice sighed. 'You can't imagine, of course you can't. They're constantly in my thoughts – am I doing the right thing, suppose they turn out dyslexic, suppose they're insecure, suppose they're not getting enough affection, suppose they have bad teeth, suppose they get Mad Cow disease. There's always something which could blight them for life. I may not show it, but I worry all the time. Being a mother is so draining.'

'I know. Anyway, as I said, I'm not thinking about it yet.'

Alice knew by Beatrice's knitted brow that she was about to impart some advice, or report another doom-laden message from the stars. 'Listen, I've heard about a marvellous therapist who does Tai Chi as well, lives somewhere up your way, Chinese but trained in Freud. Or maybe she's an analyst, I never know the difference.'

'Bea, I don't need a therapist.'

'Everyone does, at some time in their lives. Or perhaps you'd be better off with a more alternative solution. Meditation is very good.'

'For what?'

'Reaching the inner self.'

'I've got to finish three hats by the end of the week.'

Beatrice looked mildly disapproving, pursing her lips. 'Alice, darling. You must give yourself some space.'

'I told you, I'm having a workroom in Robert's house.'

'Not that kind of space, silly. Space for personal development. At least half an hour a day, that's what I do. I shut myself in the conservatory and watch the plants growing.'

'Really?' Alice suppressed her amusement. 'Do they grow faster if you watch them?'

Beatrice was instantly thrown into confusion. 'Oh! Is that true? Actually, I can believe it. I really can.'

Before she left, Beatrice insisted on visiting the workroom. She regarded Alice's creations as part of her responsibility and took her hats from the stands with the veneration with which she would have lit candles in church. 'Beautiful. They should hang in the Louvre. Oh, you're so creative, so full of imagination,' she cried. Although unable to believe such praise, her genuine pleasure touched Alice. But she tried to stop her when she laid her hands on The Dress, even though it was hidden in a carrier bag. 'What's in here? Oh! Look! I must see how you're getting on with it.'

'I haven't done much since you saw it last.'

Beatrice ignored the havoc in Alice's workroom, stepping over upturned boxes and torn sheets of paper covered with scribbles. She held up the tacked-together sheath. 'Stunning,' she remarked. 'You're so clever. You won't let him see it till the day, will you?' Then she held it against herself and laughed. 'It would fit me. Isn't it a fraction small, though?'

'Wait and see. I'm getting a new diet.'

'You're not still worrying about your figure? I thought we'd had all that out ages ago. You definitely need therapy, Alice. I see now that we have to take this seriously. You have a problem.'

'No, I don't. But I do have to get back to my hats.'

'All we creative people have problems,' Beatrice declared as she went up the stairs to collect the children. 'That's why we're different.' Then Alice could hear her yelling, 'Come on, you two, Mummy's in a hurry, time to go, time to go. Why don't you come when I ask you to?'

Closing the door of the workroom, Alice began to pick up the debris. There was the thumping of feet descending the stairs.

Beatrice poked her head round the door and blew a kiss. 'Thanks so much for looking after the children. You've been marvellous. See you at the club.' The front door banged shut and the house suddenly seemed horribly silent.

Towards evening, Mary would be arriving to view the hat, an event she told Alice she had been looking forward to all week. She had phoned to ensure that the time was in Alice's diary, just to confirm. It was a habit she had, of constantly confirming times and dates. Times and dates were so crucial in research, although she understood that, being artistic, Alice tended to ignore them. Not that carrying out research was lacking in artistry, but no one came to view the fruits of your labour with gushing praise.

Alice stifled her panic and said the hat would be ready. She stitched the last of the white satin petals together with the crystal raindrops and stretched the cap over the canvas base. Then, searching through her drawer, she pulled out a selection of feathers and trimmings and began to place them against the hat. Several hours later, she set the hat in the centre of the room and prayed that, after five solid days of work, Mary would respond with delight. This was always the moment she dreaded, when she would either be greeted with a pout of disappointment or a burst of enthusiasm. There was no telling what the reaction might be.

Holding a hand-mirror in one hand, Mary turned slowly to appreciate every angle, staring at herself in the long mirror in Alice's workroom, giving nothing away by her expression. If Mary wanted changes, that could be another two days' work. Or she might decide against the black satin. Or she might have changed her mind completely and opted for a quite different shape. 'Alice,' she said at last. 'This is going to be a work of art.'

'I'm quite pleased with it,' Alice replied. She wanted to laugh with relief, but smiled instead.

'Pleased? It's perfection. And I can see you love what you create. That makes all the difference.' Mary stroked her hand down the crystal beads. 'Look how they catch the light. I want to wear it all the time. Much more exciting than feathers, how brilliant!' Removing the hat, she balanced it delicately between her hands and put her cheek against the black satin. 'It feels like a Burmese cat we used to have, called Artemis. A beautiful cat. It was run over by an articulated lorry. I've an affinity with cats. I imagine you're a dog person.'

'I like both,' Alice said diplomatically. 'But Robert is definitely a cat person.'

'I knew he would be. Men usually are. They represent the independence of the female they dream of but hate when they find it.' She stretched out her arm and held the hat at a distance. 'I was wondering, would it perhaps be better in deep chestnut brown, instead of black? Wouldn't it go better with my hair?'

'Well,' began Alice, rapidly thinking her way out of yet more hours of labour. She contemplated the mousy brown framing Mary's face. 'It might be an idea if you dyed your hair. Just for the evening.'

'Really? What an amazing thought!'

Alice waited as impassively as she could while the idea sank in.

'I might try. But only if you choose me a colour. I'd really appreciate it. If you're wearing a hat, everything has to be right, don't you agree?'

'I'll think about it. A coppery colour, maybe.'

'Wonderful.' Mary clasped her hands together decisively, drawing attention to a succession of bunched-up silver rings encumbering each finger. 'Now let's celebrate.' She dived into her large leather bag and took out a wrapped bottle. 'Do you drink sherry? It's my weakness. Roland used to find it so funny.'

Alice nodded and smiled.

After Mary had opened the bottle and poured generous measures into two tumblers, the only containers available, Alice brought out a battered black exercise book with the Corsham Towers crest on the front. 'I was looking for something and I found this, my diet diary,' she explained. 'I've been keeping it ever since school. Would you like to see it?'

'Of course, I'd love to.'

Mary opened the lined pages of the exercise book one by one, as though she were holding a rare book in a library. Then she let out a gasp. 'This is incredible.' Raising a pair of half-glasses to her eyes, she peered at a tiny drawing, a grotesque caricature of Alice under which was written 'Big fat blob'. 'Who on earth did that? I bet it was Pen, she was always doing things like that.'

'No, Mary, it wouldn't have been Pen.'

'She was malicious at times, you know. Very malicious.'

'If she was, I'm sure she didn't mean to be. Pen has a wicked sense of humour, that's all. She'd never hurt anyone.'

'You know her better than I do,' Mary replied calmly, scrutinising the pages. 'You seem to have tried every diet under the sun. Now I know why you hardly ate anything in the Refectory. I thought you had some terrible disease.'

'Matron used to bring me up a special tray, so I could follow my diet,' Alice said.

'I still don't understand how you were allowed to go

70

along with it. I mean, look at this. No fats, no carbo-hydrates, only high protein. Who at Corsham Towers knew the difference between high or low protein?'

'No one. I used to give them diet sheets and say they'd been given to me by my doctor.'

'And they believed you?'

'I stole some notepaper from the doctor's surgery at home, photocopied it and forged his signature.'

'How very brave of you.' Mary turned another page. 'This one's ridiculous. As much fatty food as you want but no fruit or vegetables? Where on earth did you get that from?'

'A cousin in America used to cut out diets for me, from health magazines. They have lots over there. That's why I did the Scarsdale diet, the Beverly Hills diet, the bran diet, the egg diet . . .'

'Alice, it's shocking.'

'Then I did amphetamines for a while. Look at this page. "Hooray hooray tried on Pen's jeans and fitted into them. Now I am size ten." Next day, I've written down: fish and chips, two portions, five Mars Bars, three bags of crisps. And a week later . . .' Alice went forward a couple of pages. 'Put on five pounds. Shit.'

Mary pushed aside the diary. 'This is so sad. If only I'd known, if only you'd talked about it.'

'Everyone else had secrets. This was mine.' Alice laughed. 'I told Matron I was dieting because I had dangerously high blood pressure. It did no one any harm, and it got me off games. All I ever dreamed of was losing weight permanently. I'd have done anything, I even thought of having part of my gut removed. That was the height of my ambition, how daft can you get?'

'I didn't realise it was so serious! You must have been so miserable,' said Mary, horrified.

'Silly not serious. I don't throw up or anything like that.'

'Have you told Robert? Does he know about this?'

'Goodness, no. And Simon never knew because we spent all our time eating gorgeous meals. He never notices even now if I put on the odd stone. Of course, Beatrice does, though she always denies it. She doesn't miss a thing.'

'I hope she keeps it to herself.'

'She teases me at the club when I do extra work-outs and keep my eyes glued on the calorie counter they have on the bicycles.'

'Oh? Which club is that?' Mary enquired.

'It's a health club where we all meet each Thursday, me and Robert, Simon and Beatrice. A kind of a weekly ritual, though only Robert and me take it seriously. Most of the time we sit in the bar, gossiping.'

'What a coincidence! Only the other day I'd been wondering whether to join a fitness club. My doctor said it might strengthen my back. Sitting all day in libraries is so bad for one. Does your club have a pool? Apparently swimming's one of the best things you can do.'

'Yes, a beautiful one.'

'I would have gone before, but I haven't enough courage to swim on my own. In some ways I'm rather wimpish I'm afraid.'

'Heavens, I wouldn't go on my own, either!' said Alice.

Clearly in no hurry to leave, Mary stood contemplating the view from Alice's back window, a tangle of bushes interspersed with a few straggly plants. 'When I was with Roland I never gave much thought to being fit. Perhaps it's time I did.'

'Why don't you come along one evening?' Alice suggested.

'Are you sure I wouldn't be intruding?'

'Of course not. We sometimes bring friends along as guests.'

'This Thursday's out. But I could come Thursday of next week,' said Mary, consulting her diary. 'And I'm going to apply myself to your weight problem. I have got someone in mind – that's all I'll say for the moment. One can't rush these things.'

'Do you really think there's a solution? After everything I've tried?' said Alice, her voice rising in excitement.

'There could be, Alice. Leave it with me,' replied Mary.

After her meeting with Mary, Alice felt that something had changed. For the first time, she had an intuition that despite all her efforts and experiments she had somehow overlooked the perfect and permanent cure for her secret obsession. And although she had promised nothing, offered no instant answer, she was convinced that Mary would find it. She would discover a miraculous diet which no one else knew about, or some extraordinary doctor who would send her to sleep so she would fall asleep fat and wake up thin. Or a pill you could take with no side effects, which she could hide in her bag. Or some rare extract which made you shed the kilos. Or a simple operation which would dissolve away the fatty tissue. She knew that Mary was about to change her life.

Clutching her visitor's card from the Lansdale Club, Mary followed Alice down the corridor into the gym. Gazing apprehensively around her, she was transfixed by the banks of machines pedalled, pulled and manipulated by shiny, sweating creatures who stared rigidly ahead, eyes blank, as though they had been metamorphosed from humans into programmed aliens. Swinging onto the saddle of a clamped-down bicycle, Alice motioned to Mary to occupy the one next to her, just being vacated by a body-builder.

She waited while Mary applied herself to the task of

mastering the complex set of indicators in front of her, peering at them with her half-glasses.

'Do you want any help?' Alice asked.

'No. It takes me a while to get to grips with machinery, but I'll work it out. I'll be fine.'

They pedalled together in silence until a ping on Alice's machine reminded her that she had finished her task. Then, having taken Mary to admire the pool from behind a sheet of viewing glass, she suggested a swim.

Mary declined, saying that next time she must remember her swimsuit. 'There are far more efficient ways of losing weight than putting yourself through all this,' she remarked, as she stared through the glass at the swimmers below.

'It's meant to keep you healthy.'

'Mm. But that's not the reason you come, is it?'

Alice smiled; there was no longer any need to spell it out. 'Look, there's Beatrice. She's the girl clutching onto the steps, kicking her legs in the air,' she remarked, having picked out the only person who wasn't swimming. 'And there's Robert. Oh, he's about to dive.'

Robert jumped a few times on the diving board and plunged vigorously into the water, creating a volcanic splash.

'A very attractive man,' Mary commented. 'Though not my type, I have to say. But I can see why you're mad about him.'

'What is your type, Mary?'

'Always dark. I always go for dark men.'

'You'll like Simon, then,' said Alice with a laugh. 'Let's go and meet him.'

When they reached the bar, Alice took Mary to settle at the group table, where they were joined, shortly afterwards by Robert, Simon and Beatrice.

'This is quite a decent bar, very distinctive. Not what I'd expect in a health club,' Mary commented, once the introductions had been made.

'Designed by Robert,' said Alice proudly.

'Really?'

'Some time ago. I'd change it now. It's very eighties.'

'I don't agree, I think it works extremely well today.' Mary thought that Robert would acknowledge her compliment with a smile, but he remained impassive. 'I never thought of architects designing bars,' she added.

'Architects design interiors, you know. Not all, but some. We don't spend our entire time putting up office blocks.'

'That's where the money is, Robert,' said Simon. 'Why don't you knock one up from time to time?'

'Yes, I could do one next week. I've got a few days with nothing much on. Where do you want it, Simon?'

'Is my back garden big enough?'

'Might have foundation problems.'

'Can't have it falling over. But you could design it that way. Has anyone ever planned a building which looks as though it's falling over? That's what I call a bright idea.'

'Like the Tower of Pisa?' suggested Mary. 'One of my favourite buildings. But of course it wasn't designed to lean.'

'Really? Are you sure?' said Simon, with a knowing glance at Robert.

Beatrice disrupted the flow of conversation by rising languidly and announcing that she'd been overcome by a desire for bangers and mash. The club menu was going more traditional since the latest chef had taken her advice, unlike the last one who said he'd trained with the Roux brothers, clearly a lie. Beatrice was unperturbed when the waiter told her he'd only sold five portions of sage and saffron forcemeat rings with purée de pommes Lincoln. 'Our members are so backward.' She sighed. 'They keep insisting on grilled goat's cheese and radicchio. We must educate them.'

'Bangers, then,' said Simon. 'Bangers all round?'

75

'You don't have to say that to please me.'

'I could never please you, Beatrice. I don't have the imagination.'

Beatrice stared at Simon a moment, wondering if this was a compliment or an insult. You never knew with Simon. 'I think I will have saucisses à l'anglaise.'

'What would Mary like?' said Robert. She was sitting far back in her chair, as though she didn't wish to be noticed. 'You just have anything you fancy. Here.' He pushed the menu towards her, but she merely smiled.

'I'm going to be horribly traditional and have goat's cheese.'

'Then I'll have it, too.'

'Surely not, Alice? You never have that.'

Alice gave Simon a gentle prod under the table. He knew perfectly well that she was longing for those burned, crusty sausages.

'You can have one of my sausages, Alice. I only want one,' said Beatrice. 'And I must have your opinion.'

After Beatrice had sounded out everyone on the sausages – too much seasoning, too little seasoning, too fatty, not fatty enough, better without saffron, without sage – she brought up the subject of the wedding cake, to which she had given much thought, even though the occasion was several months away.

'We're not having a cake, Bea,' Alice reiterated.

'Alice is right not to,' Mary said. 'No one ever actually eats wedding cakes, only if the fridge is empty and there's nothing else. Much more fun to have sugared almonds like the Greeks do. Or the Italians. How about amaretti?'

'Wait till you see my ideas, then you'll change your mind. I've abandoned the pillars, by the way,' continued Beatrice.

'What a relief,' said Simon. 'Something cantilevered instead? Now that would be a technical challenge . . . but you'd need special icing sugar.'

'Where do I get it?'

There was a gale of laughter from Robert and Simon, and Beatrice quickly realised that she had made a fool of herself. Why did architects use all those technical words? She would have to look up 'cantilever' in David's dictionary – she wouldn't dream of asking Simon. 'Incidentally, Simon, I read in *Good Food* magazine that they're bringing out icing sugar which sets in two seconds.'

'Ideal for an extension, then.' Simon grinned at Robert, then at Beatrice. He could see that Mary was bewildered. 'Don't worry, we're always like this,' he said by way of explanation. 'It means nothing.'

'Everything means something,' muttered Beatrice.

'That's rather philosophical for you, Bea.'

'Well, Simon, I must have read it somewhere, mustn't I?' she said, with a giggle.

'Are you working on anything at the moment?' Mary asked, still picking at her goat's cheese when everyone else had finished.

'Nothing desperately interesting. Only a few small things,' said Robert.

'Robert is all for keeping things small,' confided Simon, leaning towards Mary. 'He thinks we take up too much space, but I like having room to move around. One day, I might convert a church. But there aren't any going in Shepherd's Bush at the moment. A friend of mine has just bought one in Kensal Green, near you, Alice. It could mean a job for Robert.'

'It's bad luck to live in a church.'

Simon ignored Beatrice's sally. 'I like the idea of having supper in a chapel, don't you? Faint echoes of the Last one, maybe I should do that. I wonder what Jesus had for dinner?'

'Jesus was a vegetarian. Anyone spiritual has to be vegetarian.'

'Not necessarily, Beatrice,' said Mary. 'It has never

been part of the Christian religion. Only the poor ate vegetables.'

'How do you know that?'

'Mary's a scholar, she researches all kinds of subjects.'

'It must be so satisfying,' said Robert. 'Really going into something in depth. I'd love to, but I have so little time.'

Mary looked at him with a shy smile. 'If there's anything you need to know I'd be delighted to help out. It would be no trouble, I'm always in some library or other.'

'She's working at the moment for a very famous professor,' Alice added.

But Beatrice was unimpressed. 'Why doesn't he do his own research? If he's that clever? Why does he need a girl to do it for him?'

Simon immediately leapt to Mary's defence. 'Bea can observe sexual politics in the choice of a sausage. Don't take it personally.'

'I'm not a feminist, if that's what you're implying,' Beatrice said calmly.

By now, a series of empty plates were ready to be removed, but none of the staff was paying attention to the cluttered table.

Mary whipped round to face the bar. 'Shall I go and ask someone to clear this away?'

'Good idea,' said Alice.

While Mary absented herself from the table, Simon began buttoning up his waistcoat, which he had loosened to accommodate the sausages. 'I've got to get back,' he muttered. 'The e-mails will have been piling up.'

'And I can't be late, either. I promised David I'd stay in for the children tonight; he's been so sweet during the week. It's the least I can do.'

'I need to get back, too,' said Robert.

By the time Mary came back to the table, both Beatrice

and Simon had disappeared. Robert kissed the top of Alice's head. 'Come round tomorrow, won't you? We might be able to go away for the weekend. In fact, we will. Definitely. How about it?'

Alice turned round and kissed him on the lips. 'Wonderful idea, darling.'

Mary kept her eyes fixed on Robert, as he hurried out towards the bar exit. Then she drew her chair closer to Alice's. 'I like your friends. They're all so different, so interesting.'

'And Robert? What did you think of Robert?'

'He's very fond of you, Alice. He doesn't make it obvious, but I can see he's always aware of you. I think he probably feels more than he can express.'

'He's quite private.'

'I guessed that. He reminds me so much of Roland, not physically of course. The same kind of hidden sensitivity.'

They smiled at one another complicitly, as though they were the only two people who could appreciate his qualities.

A member of the bar staff came over and placed the bill under Alice's plate.

'What do you think of the club? Do you like it here, Mary? Would you like me to propose you as a member?'

'I'm abroad so often, it would hardly be worthwhile. But I did enjoy it. Maybe I could come again.'

'Why not?' said Alice, picking up the bill.

'I'll look after that, Alice.'

'I couldn't possibly let you.'

With a gracious smile, Mary allowed her to pay. 'Next time it's on me.'

Outside the club, Mary hailed a taxi, but not before enquiring whether Alice needed a lift. This time, Alice explained, she had brought along her ageing Fiat Panda instead of her usual bicycle. She had done enough exercise for one day and Mary agreed. Just before they parted, Mary said, 'I've managed to contact one of the only people in the world who really knows about eating problems. I didn't want to say anything until I'd found out if they were free. These people are so incredibly booked up.'

'Is he in England? I hope I don't have to go somewhere like America,' said Alice apprehensively.

'Oh no. In fact, it's a woman. She's a doctor who does sessions in England. I'm going to see if she could take you on.'

Mary refused to say more. On the way home, Alice made one of her frequent diversions to the patisserie shop. A particularly enticing lemon curd tart, glowing a desirous eggy yellow and brushed with icing sugar, attracted her attention. Quickly parking the car nearby on forbidden territory, she rushed inside. She would buy it, eat half and leave the other half in the boot hidden under a raincoat. And when she met the eminent doctor she would confess all.

Five
• • •

Away from London, Alice viewed the unfamiliar landscape through Robert's eyes; it became identified with
him, part of him. With no one else did she feel that
the world had been freshly created, each colour more
intense, each shape eating into her memory. 'Are you
happy with me?' she asked, to confirm her own joy in
his presence.

'You know I am.'

He swung her over a puddle and she pulled him
towards an empty barn. 'Isn't that beautiful?' she said,
looking up at the blackened timbers stretching to support one another.

'We excel at vernacular architecture. Yes, it's splendid.'

Alice smiled. 'Imagine living in somewhere like that.'

'We could, I suppose. Create a warm, wonderful
space, bare wood, great windows. But the farmer needs
it. It was built for him, not for people like us. Gener-
ations of men have laboured to fill it with straw for their
cattle in winter.'

'I bet he's built a brand new one that he prefers, like
Daddy did. Whoever owns this barn hasn't used it for
years. Look, it's falling to pieces. It would cost a fortune
to restore it properly.'

Alice knew Robert disapproved of the way her father
cut down the hedgerows, invested in hunks of machinery

which reduced his work force to a minimum and sprayed his fields to prosper. When he had announced that he was going to convert his old barns in order to sell them off at a decent price to the young aspirers from the City and liberate some capital, he offered Robert the commission. Robert resolutely turned it down, merely saying that he had too much work. Although he said nothing at the time, afterwards he told Alice that he had to stand by his principles without needing to give his reasons.

But Alice disagreed. Shouldn't everyone shout it from the rooftops, when they believed in something? 'You should say something to Daddy,' she had said. 'He never takes it seriously when I tell him that he's spoiling his land. All he says is, "And how do you think you got to Corsham Towers? And bought your little house? And didn't end up on the dole like some of your other friends?"'

'Supposing he's right, Alice?'

'Don't be ridiculous. He needs to be shaken up. All he ever meets are people who agree with him.'

'I can't change him, I wouldn't try. I'd rather seek out people who understand what I'm on about. You can't convert people, just like that.'

'You can try, can't you?'

Robert was so unlike her, so contained and confident in his beliefs. She was sure that one day his worth would be recognised, that he would be truly successful – and she would help him to be so. If he needed a gentle push here, a subtle prod there, she would encourage him. Not like Beatrice, not screaming at him, not telling him he should go off and teach somewhere (those who couldn't, taught), not insisting that he didn't understand what people wanted, not mistaking his convictions for arrogance. She sometimes wondered how he had put up with Beatrice for so long.

Later that night, as they lay back naked on the

crumpled sheets of a modest-sized bed in a modest hotel, Alice caught sight of her body, dimly lit by the pink-shaded bedside light, reflected in the mirrored wardrobe. 'He pretended not to notice,' she thought. 'I really am getting grotesquely huge.'

They had made love in the gloom, the moon shining feebly into the barely furnished room. Afterwards, she realised, his hands had avoided her hips, her waist and her thighs. He had only briefly stroked her breasts, putting his arms round her neck. She had lain on top of him and he had said, did she mind? she was getting heavy. He had eaten too much for dinner. Heavy, he said. Heavy.

She rolled onto the other side of the bed and felt the bloated mass of her body. Naturally it would be bloated — after how many? at least three hundred, then at least six hundred, then, my God, another six hundred calories of pudding, not forgetting a liqueur — she really could have refused that — another three hundred; it didn't bear thinking about. No wonder she was weighing down like a ton of bricks onto the thin mattress. She imagined every cell expanding, swelling like a boa constrictor, which had swallowed a goat. Horrible. Horrible. Her stomach was rumbling with the effort of digestion, so she drew up her legs to stifle the sound. Had Robert heard the repulsive gurgle? If only she could be sick, spew out the vile evidence, call a halt to the inevitable absorption of all that fat, all that sugar, all those evil, useless calories engorging, seeping into her muscles, her tissues, soon to transform themselves into visible lumps, visible folds, to deform her body like some grim photograph in a medical text.

Was he asleep or pretending to be asleep? She tossed on her pillow, crunching it beneath her head, pumping it full again, then burying her face to hide her shame. While she was lying there, eyes wide open, Robert shifted in his sleep away from her, right onto the far side of the bed, his arm hanging over the edge. His deep breaths meant he probably was asleep. The unconscious doesn't lie, they say.

At breakfast, she vowed to wave aside the bacon, eggs, sausages, fried bread and tomatoes tantalisingly displayed on a cardboard menu on the dressing-table and order a lightly boiled egg.

Alice said so little on the return journey that Robert was concerned at her silence. 'Have I said anything to upset you?' he asked.

'No, no. Everything was wonderful. It's just . . .' She could only think of the lamest of excuses. 'I don't know why, I've got this ghastly headache. I've had it since this morning.'

'You should have told me. I'm sure we could have found some aspirin.'

'It'll be gone by tomorrow.'

His concern seemed a charade. Alice supposed that Robert was thinking the same thing. Hadn't they shared the same thoughts so often that they used to laugh and say, 'I know what you're thinking'? She knew what he would be thinking now – *how can I break it to Alice that if she gets much fatter I'm afraid I'll stop wanting her, afraid I'll start desiring someone else, afraid I won't be able to go through with the marriage*? Because she was thinking: *he's pretending to be concerned, but actually he can't bear to spend another night with me. Not even Robert could hide it. He found me heavy. No wonder he turned to the other side of the bed. I don't blame him.*

Alice knew she needed help. The one person she was longing to see had been out of touch for what seemed an eternity – although it was only days. How could she expect Mary to recognise that hers was a crisis case? You couldn't collapse into a full-blown nervous break-down just because you were too fat. It was unheard of.

84

Mary I'm desperate. Absolutely desperate. Please can I see that doctor you mentioned? I need to see her very soon. No, she couldn't say that, Mary would think she had gone out of her mind. Alice decided on another approach. She wanted Mary to identify more strongly with her problem, with her. Then she would have to take her seriously. If she took Mary to meet her family, it would give her an opportunity to show her where it all began. It would make her realise the urgency of her situation.

Next morning, Alice rang and left a message, trying not to sound as knotted as she felt.

Mary rang back a couple of hours later. She sounded tense. 'I'm sorry I didn't call. But I've had some money problems – nothing serious, just the bank being unpleasant. I need to sort a few things out.' The mobile phone waxed and waned, then she began to sound more choorful. 'I'd love to meet your family.'

Encouraged by her reply, Alice decided to take the plunge. 'Mary, I was wondering if you'd had time to get in touch with . . . you know who I mean . . . I'm sure you've had more important things to do,' she said haltingly.

'It's top of my list. I haven't forgotten. I'll see you on Saturday.' Alice sighed with relief. Mary did have an uncanny instinct for realising what preoccupied people. Almost a gift.

Early on Saturday morning Alice was outside her house, throwing into the open car an ancient waxed coat, rubber boots and a thick sweater of Robert's. She kept running inside, then back again in a flurry, for although she had made a mental note of what to take she knew that she would forget something. Somehow, when she visited her parents, she lost her usual ability to order things. Was it because she could hear her mother's disappointed voice? *Alice, darling, never mind, bring it next time.* Then her father's — *still the same, aren't you Alice? I'm surprised you know which day it is.* As though she had never changed, never been in charge of her own little business, wasn't about to be married, but had stuck at somewhere around twelve. The fact that they expected her to forget things made her forget things. Like the specially ordered hat, the principal reason for her visit. William, one of her three younger brothers, had just got engaged to Judy, a sturdy physiotherapist who had won Daddy's approval by strapping up the leg of a lame horse better than the vet had managed. A plain hat, she insisted, a little boater with a ribbon, nothing too over the top. How could she have omitted to put Judy's hat in the car? As she rushed inside to retrieve the box, Alice could hear her mother's painfully cheerful voice repeating, *Oh never mind, darling, bring it next time.*

There was a light tap on the car window. Alice was crawling around in the back, trying to find her car keys. 'Hello, Alice.'

Alice extracted herself bottom first from the back of the Fiat to find Mary standing to attention in a loose, unbuttoned tweed coat almost down to her ankles and a matching tweed pleated skirt. Jaeger, Alice thought. Sizes always too big.

'Will this do?' Mary said, turning round, looking down at her feet shod in over-shiny leather lace-ups. 'I wasn't sure what to wear. So I brought some jeans with me in case.'

'That's absolutely fine. Won't be a moment.' Alice continued rummaging on the floor.

'Have you lost something?'

'Car keys. They're in here somewhere.'

Another light tap on the window. 'These?' Mary was holding up a small bunch of keys. 'They were in the gutter, just by your car.' As she handed them to Alice, she said, 'I'm good at spotting things.'

'Great. Let's go.'

Alice treated her car like a lazy horse, slapping her foot down on the accelerator and getting a surprising burst of speed from the sedate engine. As she veered round the corner, she noticed Mary clutching the door-strap. 'Are you all right?'

'Don't take any notice,' Mary said. 'I always get nervous in cars.'

'Robert can't bear my driving, but I always get to places before him. And I've never had anything more than a few bumps. But we won't speak about my parking.'

Alice bombed down Holland Park Avenue, pulling in and out, switching lanes with alacrity, then swung round the roundabout and headed off towards the M41. She giggled. 'Funny how I never get better at parking the car. That's how I met Simon. It was just like in a Woody Allen movie. Stupid and commonplace, like it often is when people come into your life.'

'Could you go a little slower, just for a while? I know it's ridiculous.'

'There's no hurry, anyway,' said Alice, slightly reducing her speed. 'It's just habit.' Then the thought struck her that Mary must have suffered in some ghastly car accident. It was obvious, why had it taken her so long to work that one out? Because it hadn't happened to her, or to any of her friends? Suppose she had some dreadful scar, some shameful mutilation, which she kept hidden from sight?

To her relief, Mary had leaned back in her seat and seemed more at ease. 'You were telling me how you met Simon? Do finish the story.'

'I was desperate to find a parking space in Earls Court somewhere and I found one I knew I could get into if I tried. You always know when the space is right, even if you can't manage it. Anyway, I was very naughty and kept bumping the car in front and the car behind, trying to wiggle in. Then this man came up and I thought "Christ! He's going to tell me off." But he didn't. He just bent down and said through my window, "Would you allow a male chauvinist pig to park your car for you?" I roared with laughter. That was Simon.'

'And he made a date?'

'No, I did. I said I fancied a coffee and a bun after all that. And so did he. That was ages ago. I was going to marry him once.'

'And you still see him?' Mary sounded puzzled.

'After that, he introduced me to the architect who was doing out his house. Which is how I met Robert.'

'And you fell wildly in love.'

'I suppose I must have done.'

'You can't be properly in love without falling wildly, can you?'

Automatically, Alice put her foot down again once the motorway stretched ahead.

'I hate being a bore, but you are doing eighty-five. I can just about stand up to eighty, but over that, I get queasy. I'm sorry. It's worse when I'm worried. It's so ghastly having to worry about money. I never had to with Roland.'

'Would you like some music?' said Alice. She knew how Mary must have felt, wondering whether the phone would be cut off, counting every penny.

'I wish I could lend you some money but at the moment . . .'

'I wouldn't dream of it,' Mary replied quickly. Then she stretched out to search through a pile of discs in the glove compartment. 'I'll find something, shall I?'

For the rest of the journey, Mary was calmer. 'I do like Chopin,' she remarked, having chosen a 'Romance in Classical Mood' album which had come free with a box of Black Magic chocolates. 'Although Roland dismissed him as a hothouse flower. I could never predict his tastes. He liked Liszt, though. Do you like Liszt?'

'Sometimes,' replied Alice, for want of anything better to say, hoping Mary wouldn't seek out her opinion when she didn't have one.

'Same here,' Mary said with a contented smile.

They had almost arrived at the farm. Alice turned down a lane which still had a few hawthorn bushes lining the edge and stopped in front of a solid, red-brick Victorian building.

'The Victorians knew how to build,' Mary remarked as she got out of the car. 'Wonderfully functional and sturdy. It must be worth quite a lot, in this part of the country.'

'Mummy thinks it's ugly but she's got used to it,' said Alice, as she heaved herself out of the car. Then she sighed. 'I hope they don't notice, but I've put on weight since I was last here. And it was only a few weeks ago. Does it show?'

Mary gave her a brief glance. 'Country clothes always make one look fat. By the way, I did try to contact the diet doctor, but she's in Los Angeles at the moment. Seeing her clients in Hollywood,' she said, as she picked her way over the muddy yard.

'I hope she comes over here soon. I do need to see her quite urgently, Mary. Actually, I was afraid you might have forgotten,' said Alice.

'You remember things for friends. Important things, anyway.'

As they came up to the front door, with its ugly storm porch, they were assaulted by a cacophony of barking dogs, which made Mary stand still in her tracks.

'Don't worry,' said Alice. 'The dogs are all chained up and anyway the only savage one is a tiny Jack Russell.' She pulled an iron bell by the door, which echoed round the yard. 'There'll be a huge lunch, I warn you. Steak and kidney pudding, most likely, with mounds of mashed potatoes and gravy and greens. And pudding. And cheese. And Mummy's chocolate and walnut fudge with coffee.'

'Will these do? I didn't know what to bring,' said Mary, pulling out from her deep wicker basket a large bunch of gift-wrapped roses.

'You needn't have been so extravagant. That's very sweet of you. Beautiful colour.'

'They only had red. I prefer white, myself. Roland always used to buy me white roses.'

They were all waiting in the hall.

'Mr Miller, call me Sam.'

'Mrs Miller, I'm Veronica. And here are two of Alice's brothers.'

'Tim.'

'William. And he's one of the dogs, Chirpy.'

Mary looked bewildered, then rallied with a firm handshake, before presenting Alice's mother with the flowers, which she insisted on arranging in a vase. Veronica took her through to the kitchen, after apologising for the frightful mess. Sam would insist on preparing lunch and he was rather careless about clearing away.

'You're doing a frightfully professional job there, Mary, I must say,' said Veronica, admiring the way she had trimmed the stems to different lengths and fanned out the leaves to create a pleasing symmetrical shape.

'I've never learned how to do it properly. I don't know anything about flower design.'

'Neither do I, though I'd love to. But you seem to have an instinct for it.'

'Take that apron off, Ronnie,' commanded Sam, putting his head round the door. 'It'll look as though you've been in the kitchen all day.' He winked at Mary. 'She hasn't, you know. It's me that cooked the lunch.'

'I'm sure Mary won't mind.'

'Follow me. We'll be eating in five minutes. The only

time Alice eats a decent meal is when she comes here.'

William laid the table, Tim opened a bottle of wine and Sam sat in the only chair with arms.

'No, not those plates, William. The other ones.'

Alice winced at her mother's insistence on propriety. 'The other ones' meant the best china, not the dishwasher-proof set for every day. Any minute now the linen napkins in rings would make an appearance from the large stained-oak cupboard in the dining-room.

The predicted meal made its appearance and it took great determination for Alice to decline a second helping. How could she possibly stuff herself, with Mary at her side, lifting mouse-sized portions onto the heavy silver-plated fork?

'Alice has caught the London disease. No appetite, *nouvelle cuisine* nonsense,' Sam remarked, as he dolloped out extra portions for his boys.

'You've said that before, Daddy.'

'And he'll say it again,' Tim stated, scooping up a pile of potatoes.

Alice didn't stand a chance; she came from her father's line. Why couldn't she have taken after her mother, still slim in early middle age, with the narrow hips and legs of the properly bred Englishwoman, so birdlike that they barely needed to taper into the ankle? Alice looked at her brother's filled-out faces, stocky limbs and healthy muscles – both took after Sam – and wondered if she could ever fight her inherited genes and whether she had embarked on a fruitless quest.

'Shall we have coffee in the drawing-room?' This was not really a question, more a statement of intent. Mrs Miller, having also attended Corsham Towers, had long ago mastered the art of polite suggestion.

Sam pushed his cheese plate aside and finished off the remaining biscuit. 'All right then, Ronnie. We'll move to the lounge.'

The class tussle had been going on for years and was still the subject of minor skirmishes between Veronica and Sam. Yet Sam was proud that his children talked properly, that his wife could sit down with anyone in the county, just as long as he could stay as he was. He didn't mind that she went to National Trust lectures and played bridge with her posh friends, but he wouldn't tolerate being shouted at, or asked how many beers he'd had. For her part, Veronica had had to resign herself to being called Ronnie by her husband, a nickname she loathed. At least she had stopped him using it on public occasions.

It was time for Alice to produce the hat.

William tore off the surrounding tissue paper. 'Judy'll look good in that. Try it on, Mum, let's have a look.'

'Gently, Will. My head's far too big. Why doesn't Mary put it on?' Veronica balanced the hat between her hands and placed it carefully on Mary's head.

'Looks good on her, doesn't it? She looks quite different in a hat,' said Sam.

'What's that meant to mean?' said Alice.

'Some people look just the same. Others don't. Don't ask me why.'

There now followed a discussion of what to order for the small garden party to be given by the Millers to celebrate William's engagement to Judy. It would be held on the lawn at Ling Farm. To call it a lawn was excessive, but Sam was made to see that you couldn't say back garden on an invitation, even though it was.

'I hope you'll be having a proper wedding party, Alice. Since you refused to get engaged like any normal person.'

'We haven't decided yet, William.'

'She's keeping him guessing. Or maybe she'll decide the day before. I know Alice.'

'Few people nowadays make a fuss of getting married,

I find,' Mary began. 'It's what happens afterwards that matters.'

'That's what I say,' confirmed Sam. 'All that fuss and money to strut around in fancy clothes.'

'How can you say that?' Veronica remonstrated. 'When we had such a marvellous wedding. Would you like to see some photographs, Mary?'

'I'd love to.'

This was an appropriate moment for William and Tim to make for the door, mumbling an excuse, which no one could catch, as they left.

'Mummy, I'm sure Mary has seen wedding pictures before,' groaned Alice, dreading yet another appearance of the leather-tooled album.

'No, I really do like looking at old pictures. It's what I do a lot of the time, anyway, carrying out academic research.'

'How fascinating, what a wonderful job to have.' Veronica went over to a glass-fronted bookcase and extracted her treasures. 'It's something I've always wanted to do, to spend all day in a library. But of course I couldn't, not with three sons and a daughter to bring up.'

'You could do it now we're all grown up,' said Alice.

'If only.' Her mother sighed. 'But there's always so much to do, so many people who need help.'

'Charity, Ronnie does a lot of that. Very good at it, chatting to old ladies.'

'That's only part of it, Sam. There's so much adminis-tration nowadays, committee meetings, lobbying, fund-raising.'

'If you do all that work, you should get paid,' said Alice.

'You know that's not why I do it. It gives me such satisfaction, the same as when you're making hats. Why do something you hate?'

'I wouldn't make hats for free. What's the point?'

'Our generation is different. We always wanted to give back something, especially when life has been good.'

'You mean, I've made it good, my bloody hard work has made it good.' Sam swung round abruptly to face Mary. 'You married, are you?'

'I was.'

'You have to get used to it today, everyone being divorced. Stuart, that's our eldest, his marriage didn't work out and such a nice girl, too. Married at twenty-two, didn't have a bloody clue. And now he's looking for another, silly bugger. I told him he's not cut out for it, but he doesn't listen.'

'I'm not divorced. My husband died,' Mary said. Veronica glanced disapprovingly at Sam.

'I'm sorry, my dear. Very sorry. The best die young, so they say. More coffee? Give us a hand, Alice.'

Alice followed her father back into the kitchen and started washing the coffee-cups. It was another ritual, having clean cups for the second pot.

Sam knew better than to say it was a waste of time. 'Funny girl, your friend Mary.'

Alice laughed. 'Whatever makes you say that?'

'Don't ask me. She's too thin.'

'You're being ridiculous, Daddy.'

'If she wants to find another husband she should be more friendly. And put on a bit of weight.'

'She was desperately in love, she married a Frenchman called Roland.'

'That explains it. No wonder he died young. No stamina, the French, have you noticed? Kick up a fuss about everything. I'd have a Hereford over a Charolais any day.' Sam stuck his chin out assertively and pondered. 'I would, you know.'

By now, Alice had replaced the cups and spoons; the coffee was brewed and would have to rest. Mummy could tell if it hadn't rested. 'It must be so hard for Mary, not even a child to remember him by.'

'Too thin for children, that one. Still, your mother managed it. Your turn next, then? Decent hips, that's what you need for kids.'

'William will beat me to it. You'll be a grand-dad soon.'

'It's not the same. Not the same with different blood.' Sam peered at the glass pot and judged it ready for serving. 'I'll have some more fudge, Alice. In that tin,' he said as he carried the silver tray triumphantly towards the lounge.

When the coffee was poured, Sam took a cigar out of his pocket, went over to the fireplace, took a flaming twig to one end and sucked vigorously at the other. The smoke curled lazily round the room and plumed hesitantly towards the open fire. Then he applied himself to the farming pages of the local paper.

Mary and Alice took their places on either side of Veronica, who was seated on the capacious chintz sofa, with the albums balanced on her lap, reverently turning the cellophane-wrapped pages.

'Heavens, don't I look enormous there?' exclaimed Alice. 'Was I really that big, Mummy? Even bigger than now.'

'Puppy fat, that's all. You were only fourteen at cousin Charles's wedding. Everyone's fat at fourteen,' Veronica said comfortingly, slowly turning the pages. 'And you're not really big now, anyhow. What a foolish thing to say.' Under each photograph she had carefully written the date and persons present from left to right, which Mary insisted on reading. Uncles, aunts, grandparents, cousins, second cousins – all those tedious faces smirking at the camera. Not at all interesting to someone like Mary. What could she see in them?

Alice couldn't wait to leave. At long last, the albums were replaced in the glass cabinet. Alice glanced at

Mary and tilted her head to suggest it was time to go.

But Mary ignored her cue. 'Miller is a fascinating name. I wonder if you're related to the Berkshire Millers. There was a General Miller who was part of Cromwell's army, I seem to remember. Do you know Sir Gerald and Lady Miller of . . . ?'

'Ronnie might,' said Sam, from behind his paper.

'I can't say I do. But Miller is a common name, after all.'

'No names are common, each one has a history,' said Mary. 'It just means that the Millers managed to survive better than others. They must have been a strong breed.'

Sam turned a page and looked over to where Mary was sitting. 'Is that so? That explains it.'

'Would you like me to find out more for you? I do this kind of thing on occasion, for friends. I find it fascinating.'

Now the paper was pushed aside and Sam leaned forward, his hands clasped somewhere over his stomach. 'Could you do that?' he asked.

'Certainly.'

'I'd pay good money, wouldn't expect you to do it for nothing.'

'I'd have to visit a few churches, look at local archives, check on parish registers.'

'Sounds all right to me.' Sam beamed. 'I could be heir to a title, then? I can just see their faces in the Fox and Eagle. Lord Miller. Another pint for Lord Miller.' He paused, then threw the remains of his cigar in the fire. 'Lord and Lady Miller, of course.'

'And then you'd have a coat of arms,' Mary added. 'Although, naturally, one has to pay for these things.'

'It'd be worth a few grand, that would,' commented Sam, smiling broadly at Mary.

Following Sam's invitation that they should both stay

for supper, Mary just had time to say 'How very . . .' before Alice interrupted her. She knew that she was only able to humour her family for so long, before the simmer of past conflicts boiled to the surface.

'I really do have to get back to London,' Alice insisted, just as Sam was reaching into a cupboard to offer his favourite brandy.

Mary, fortunately, had taken the hint. 'Yes, we really must go. You've been wonderful hosts. And I won't forget about the history of the Miller family.'

Mr and Mrs Miller shook her warmly by the hand.

On the way home, Alice took a detour to the Cromwell Road. This was where Mary had settled, for the time being she explained, since she never stayed anywhere for long. As Alice climbed the thinly carpeted stairs, flight after flight, she began to fight for breath. Following behind Mary, who tripped lightly in front of her, she wished she had refrained from the fudge, at least.

'It's small, but it suits me for the moment. Once I've collected all my material I'll need somewhere larger with a separate room to work in,' Mary remarked, pushing open the door. 'Let me know if you hear of anything. A three-roomed flat, preferably.'

The lofty room was painted white, every wall covered with books, and it was crammed with incongruously heavy French furniture, a curlicued and gilded mirror, an elaborate inlaid table and an escritoire cluttered with silver-framed photographs nestling among a host of leafy pot-plants. The walls were covered with oil paintings in great gilded frames, which Alice couldn't resist examining. 'Is that really a Matisse?' she asked, unsure whether she had read the signature correctly.

'Yes. I rather like it, though it's not from his best period. It was a present from an aunt. She never liked me much, but she liked the idea of avoiding death duties,' said Mary with a smile.

Alice suddenly realised how wealthy her family must

be, for you never knew at school whether girls would inherit thousands, millions or billions. For someone who must have had everything, Mary was remarkably modest. 'A lovely place,' she remarked, admiring the large, airy room if not the style.

'I just took some of my favourite things from Paris after Roland died. The things we enjoyed most, which meant something to us. Look over here. That's Roland,' she said, walking over to the desk and pointing to one of the photographs. 'Isn't he beautiful?'

Alice peered at the gaunt face, with black hair half blown across his eyes, the face of a student, unremarkable except that he looked as though he was making an effort to smile. (He must have been much younger than she was.) Still, she thought, everyone else's boyfriends and husbands seemed ordinary, compared with the one you adored. 'He's quite something,' she said.

'He was devastating. Roland looks happy there, don't you think?'

Alice gave a sympathetic smile. 'Very.'

'I have to remind myself that we *were* happy together.'

After apologising for having consumed the last bottle of decent wine, Mary produced a bottle of sherry and poured it into a couple of tiny glasses. 'The glasses are purposely small. Otherwise I don't notice how much I'm drinking. Do feel free to help yourself to as much as you want.' Mary settled herself in a heavy armchair, clutching the tiny stem of the glass tightly as she balanced it on the arm. 'It was a struggle at your parents' house, wasn't it? Suddenly I started to see everything more clearly. I had clues about what was going on. Although I might be wrong, naturally. One can only take in tiny indications, but if you remember them afterwards, that must mean they're important, don't you think?'

'You mean the wedding photographs?'

'No, no, that was just a ritual to display the family. That wasn't about you.'

'Not the picture of me looking unbelievably gross? Mummy refused to take it out of the album, I can't understand why.'

Moistening her lips with sherry, Mary leaned back thoughtfully. 'Do you mind if we discuss it? It helps if I have some background, so I can talk to the doctor I have in mind for you. She's always besieged by people trying to make appointments, so naturally she has to make careful choices about who has the greatest need.'

'I don't know how I'd qualify,' said Alice. 'It's not as though I'm a hopeless heap, is it? Even though I feel I am.'

'Ah, but that is the precise nature of the problem. Because it isn't expressed, it doesn't mean it doesn't exist. Often the most powerful conflicts are masked by a calm, controlled exterior. It doesn't mean the sufferer is unable to get on with life, unlike having an acute mental illness. What matters is the *way* they get on with life. It could well be destroying them little by little, or wrecking their capacity to make rational judgements.'

'And then Robert wouldn't want to marry me,' Alice blurted out.

'What we're talking about has nothing to do with Robert. It lies in your childhood. I'm no therapist, but I do know that.'

'Oh, God, don't tell me I've got to spend hours every week talking about what happened when I was five. All I want to do is to lose some weight. I have to, Mary. I know it's silly, but it's getting really urgent.'

'You will,' replied Mary confidently. 'There's no point in losing weight if it isn't permanent, is there?' Getting up to shut out the dusk and illuminate the darkening room, she appeared serene, like a nun going about her daily rituals. Almost beautiful, Alice thought. 'Why were you always trying to diet at school? You could have done it in the holidays, wouldn't it have been easier?' Mary said, as she pulled the cord of the heavy curtains. Then she switched on a heavy bronze lamp held in position by a couple of open-mouthed cherubs.

'My dream was to get off all the weight during term and come home absolutely different, completely slimmed down. Then I could wear anything I wanted. The only garments which aren't affected by what you eat are shoes and hats. I wonder if that's why I became a milliner?'

Mary drew a chair up close to Alice. 'This is going to take some time. It isn't just a question of finding a sensible diet and seeing that you keep to it. Food is not the issue. Your problem is far more complex.'

Alice suddenly had a vision of all the complexities she had refused to recognise. Until now, she had allowed herself no time for problems, which were rarely deep, usually the product of lack of time or not getting enough sleep, or losing an address book, or having a client cancel an order – or simply not seeing enough of Robert. 'No one can understand what it's like being fat. They just don't see it as a problem. But it is, it really is.' Alice was aware that her voice was betraying desperation.

Mary quietly handed her a glass of sherry. 'Have you heard of Dr Dorothea Grossman?'

'I don't think so.'

'In Hollywood they swear by her. It can make all the difference to an actress's career, being a beautiful shape, having the perfect figure. But it's not just actresses. The Americans take the subject of weight gain far more seriously than we do, quite rightly. Everyone has enormous respect for Dr Grossman, who's generally recognised as the leading expert in reduction. She spends a lot of time lecturing round the world.'

'She sounds rather frightening,' said Alice.

'Not when you know her. She's a very kind, concerned woman. Otherwise she couldn't do what she does, or get such incredible results.'

'What kind of results? It sounds rather awe-inspiring for me. Do I have to be stuffed full of drugs?'

'No. You don't take any drugs whatsoever, nor any chemical replacements for sugar and fat. Nothing like that. In fact, you can eat anything you like.'

Alice studied her fingernails, one of which was growing out of control. Then she felt a wave of panic. 'And you're sure to lose weight?'

'Yes, that's the marvellous part.'

'Even if you have a mammoth binge?'

'You won't want to.'

'I hope I don't have to have my mouth chained up,' Alice said with a nervous laugh, little imagining that Mary would take it seriously.

'No, certainly not. Dr Grossman doesn't agree with that kind of treatment. Everything is carried out on a solid scientific basis.'

'Where can I see her? In London?' asked Alice, trying to conceal her concern. If this famous doctor was unable to see her, what then?

'You go for consultation only in her Harley Street clinic,' said Mary. 'For treatment, she has a country clinic in Derbyshire which is particularly orientated to women's eating problems. She has trained all the staff herself. I went there once, it's enormously impressive. And, very sensibly, men are excluded, unlike so many of these places which rely on landscaped parks, pretty nurses and luxury gyms to provide adulterous opportunities away from home.'

'Not my scene at all.'

Mary smiled, then looked intently at Alice. 'Of course, you have to give total commitment. Dr Grossman will only take you for a minimum of two weeks, but recommends four.'

'Four weeks?!' gasped Alice. 'I can't take off four weeks. Not possibly.'

'It depends how serious you are. Any less won't effect a permanent change. Isn't that what you want? Permanent change?'

'Yes,' said Alice lamely.

'Look, Alice. Do you want to spend the rest of your life obsessed with the supermarket and the fridge, hiding your obsession from Robert, from your friends, from your family? Surely it's far better to come to terms with it now. I'm not pushing you into anything. I'm sure I could find you yet another diet . . .'

'No,' said Alice, regaining her resolve. 'I know really that there's no such thing as the magic diet, whatever they say. But it's like praying to a saint when you don't believe, on the off-chance someone is listening.'

'If you plan it properly I'm sure it can be done.'

Running through her commissions, Alice quickly realised that a four-week break could be possible if she simplified some of her more elaborate ideas. 'I could cancel a couple of things . . . Is it possible to meet Dr Grossman first, before I commit myself?'

'It's not for me to say, but you might need to examine your attitude to commitment. At a certain point you have to trust.'

'Usually I do tend to trust people too easily,' said Alice. 'But if you're recommending this doctor . . .'

'I had a friend who went to Dr Grossman's clinic not so long ago, she came over from Paris specially. She said it was the most remarkable experience she'd ever had. I've heard lots of people saying the same.'

'And did she lose weight?' asked Alice.

'Oh yes, I believe so, but she said the weight loss wasn't important. She felt she had achieved the rebirth of her personality. Afterwards, her work developed in an extraordinary way. She's a painter, you must meet her when she's next over. Dr Grossman is particularly good with creative people.'

Fired by Mary's description, Alice conjured up a secluded country house, a secret hideaway surrounded by leafy trees, smiling nurses and grave white-coated doctors, all devoted to transforming the fat duckling into a slender swan. 'I wouldn't want anyone to know. How would I manage that?'

'Just say you're going to a health farm, that's quite acceptable. When I had an abortion once, I told everyone I was researching in the Tuamoto Archipelago and would be away for some time. As no one had ever heard of it, but didn't want to display their ignorance, they merely said "how exciting".'

'Does it exist?'

'Of course. In the South Pacific. I'm always careful about the facts.'

'You didn't tell me about the abortion.'

'I thought I had. Some other time.'

How would it be possible to hide her secret from Robert, from Simon and above all Beatrice, who was capable of winkling out the answer to the Sphinx's riddle? How would she explain that she had gone away fat and returned thin? What story could she invent which would inevitably take her away for a month? There seemed no way out, a lesser time than a month would not effect a permanent change.

'There's no need for anyone to know the reason that you're going to the clinic, or rather health farm,' said Mary.

Alice brightened. 'Of course! Beatrice went to one once, said it was much better than a holiday.'

'You're exhausted, running out of ideas . . .'

'And I need a complete rest.'

'To get away . . .'

'To recharge. And Robert will be working all the time, so I wouldn't be seeing much of him anyway.'

'I envy you,' said Mary. 'Once in a lifetime, you have the opportunity to change your life. I know that the time has come for you now.'

When she left Mary's flat, Alice ran down the stairs, feeling light as a newly risen soufflé.

After she had made her evening call to Robert she decided to work through some of the night. The energy, which seemed to have been sucked from her at the farm, came rushing back. She opened the fridge, fingered the luscious goodies ready for such an occasion, opened and shut the door several times and eventually allowed herself one sausage roll. Two hundred and thirty-five calories. Having worked out that she would be burning up ninety calories an hour if she continued until four in the morning (she knew the calorific value of every activity she carried out), that would be three hundred and sixty calories on the credit side. The sausage roll was easily allowable.

Back in her workroom, she carefully glazed a large-brimmed hat made of split hanks of straw, each a different shade of brown, from deepest caramel to palest cream. Then, when she had almost finished, she placed it on a block and gazed at it. Each hat was as individual as a piece of sculpture. The straw she was working seemed to have formed itself into a shape as though it had a will of its own, like a vase rising from a potter's wheel.

After a couple of hours in which she thought of nothing but the evolving shape in front of her, Alice got up from her stool and went over to the mirror. Size ten. The world was about to change. Size ten. She began to chant it like a mantra, walking round her workroom glancing sideways at her reflection. Then she took hold of the tacked-up shape of her wedding-day dress, started up her sewing machine and defined the seams for ever. Alice Miller, size ten.

Six
• • •

Why was it that unexpected and unwelcome news always came on a Friday, as though on purpose to blight the weekend? Alice started to panic. How would they manage? She wasn't earning enough to keep Robert during his lean periods. Once married, he would feel the pressure even more. Now she began to regret having paid the deposit for Dr Grossman's clinic. The fee for the course had taken her aback, but you couldn't expect a world expert on weight loss, who could only see so few patients, to give her services at pensioners' rates, like some local hairdresser. It would take several hats and many months to complete the payment, but Alice had convinced herself that she must at all costs go ahead. It would be an investment, she told herself, although not of the kind Simon would have recognised. But now everything had changed.

They had just returned from garnering the treasures of a supermarket, proud that they squirrelled away enough provisions to last through a riot. Robert turned everyday shopping into a design experience, lingering by displays, analysing the colours of packets and tins, and examining the graphics on labels as though visiting an art gallery. He seemed oblivious to the sort of practical concerns that dominated when Alice went on her own. As she was unpacking the bags in the kitchen, delighting in the special treats they had allowed themselves for the weekend, she heard an anguished shout from Robert's studio.

'It's off. I haven't got it.'

Alice wished that Simon had never suggested adding a fax facility to Robert's computer. Then the message would have come in a letter delivered by the wisecracking postman who had been well trained in customer relations and showed special sympathy with brown envelopes. Robert removed the message from the computer before Alice could read it properly. 'Are you sure it hasn't just been delayed?' she said, wishing desperately that he had misread the scanty text she had glimpsed over his shoulder.

'They loved the design. Hated the costings. After all I'd done to make it a viable project. They're idiots. They'll go for some half-baked version of what they really wanted and hire some architects who specialise in cheap rip-offs of other people's ideas. I bet they've gone for Wendover Millington Glover.' Robert left his desk and slumped into a chair. 'There's nothing for it but to open our special bottle.'

'That's for tonight, for when Simon and Genevieve come round.'

'I can't stand Genevieve. Why can't he find someone we can talk to?'

'She's all right.'

'She isn't. She's thick and tedious.'

'That's unkind. She's a beautiful girl with a wonderful figure.'

'Anyone whose idea of a day out is going to the Brent Cross shopping centre shouldn't be allowed into the house.'

'Snob!' said Alice with a laugh. 'Anyway, Simon goes to Brent Cross sometimes.'

'But he doesn't talk about it. That's the difference. Will you call Simon and say I can't make it, darling?'

Alice picked up the phone. '*We* can't make it.'

While she was leaving a brief message with Simon's secretary, Alice kept her eyes on Robert. He had his hands clamped behind his neck, which Alice recognised as a gesture of either disbelief or anger. This time it was anger. 'I know it was bloody good. All wasted. Weeks of ideas and planning, and knowing it would have worked. Another sheaf of plans bites the dust. Why do I do it? Why can't I find a bloody client who understands the difference between a dishcloth and a roll of silk? Someone who isn't concerned with saving a few hundred quid on using proper wood instead of fucking MDF? And then spends several grand on crappy drapes.'

'You're an artist. You can't expect most people to understand that,' Alice said, in a desperate effort to restore his equilibrium. 'One day you'll meet someone who appreciates you. You will. You know you're more talented than any of them.'

Robert stopped in his tracks; his expression suddenly changed from fury to a tender vulnerability. 'You believe that, Alice? You're not just covering up my disappointment?'

'You know me better than that.'

He kissed her as though he were drawing out all the comfort she could give.

'It would have been ghastly, even if you had got the commission. You would have been miserable for weeks and weeks. What's the point of working if you loathe every minute of it? If you hate what they're asking you to do? If you despise your clients? If it destroys our pleasure and makes you dread the following day?'

'I don't mind it happening once. But it's happened too often. Perhaps I should do something else.'

'No, no,' Alice said vehemently. 'You can't stop doing what you love. You can't bury your talent, just because no one sees it.' She understood the risks he took. Weeks and weeks of spinning ideas around, then alighting on the one, the only one that was right. First there was the elation. Then the leaden rejection. The joy of achievement was ripped away from him. How unjust it all was!

Suddenly, Robert leaped to his feet. 'Why should the bastards get me down? Let's go dancing. We haven't had a good whirlaround for months and months. How about the Adelaide Club? Barty said he was going with a gang of mates. Yes?'

Alice's eyes opened wide with delight at the thought. If she jigged about all night she could lose at least five hundred calories.

'And fish and chips afterwards.'

'Anything you want, darling. I'll have to find something to wear.'

'The silver dress. You haven't worn that for ages.'

'No one wears things like that any more. I wore it when we were first going out.'

'I love it.'

Alice knew she would never fit into it. Why had he thought of that? It must have been at least a year ago that she had squeezed herself into that glittering sliver of a dress. 'It doesn't suit me any more. I need a tan to wear that, anyhow.'

'Nonsense. You looked fantastic in it. Remember Simon's barbecue when it burst into huge flames and his bushes caught fire and he had to get the fire brigade? You wore it then. The reflection of the flames made you seem like a fiery madonna.'

'Is this an order?'

'Don't do it to please me.'

Alice grinned. 'You want me to go back home and get it, don't you?'

'Yes. I'll even drive you.'

'No. I'll go on the bike. It'll be quicker.'

As well as being quicker, cycling would produce a minus of several hundred calories, an investment for the fish and chips later. She would pedal fast on the way to Kensal Green, go for the burn-up and make herself breathless, pouring with sweat. Then she would loiter on the way back, cool off, have a bath at Robert's . . . she would dig out something else, say she couldn't find it, seek out a loose top, tights to give the illusion of slimness. He must have realised, surely, that the seams would burst if she pulled herself into the silver dress? She could imagine the noisy rending of stitch after stitch; gaping chasms spreading from the waist; the revelation of fleshy folds caught in the lurid light pulsing and flashing to betray her.

As she pushed down on the pedals, Alice thought how Robert managed his life so much better than she did. How well he coped with disappointment. He delivered a quick outburst when she would have moped for days, been bad-tempered, discarded things she was working on and had a row with Beatrice. Above all, she would have believed her critics were right. *No, Alice, sorry it's not for us*, the expression which said you really aren't much good, we expected better of you, never mind, we'll bear you in mind for the future. A famous store had turned down her favourite hats with the familiar, polite rejection: *not quite for our customers, why don't you try somewhere else*? The following season she saw copies in the window, being pointed out by a group of ogling Knightsbridge ladies. Robert had said stuff them, find someone else. Simon, of course, urged her to go back again and again until they took something, but then he had the kind of determination she would never understand. You either like pushing in business, she thought, or you want nothing to do with it.

Now, what to wear? Alice piled up a load of clothes on her bed and pulled out the silver dress. Had she really worn that? Even then, it must have seemed a size too small. What a fright she must have looked.

Burrowing in her wardrobe, she found a peacock-blue dress, which hung by straps from the shoulders and flared out in a nebulous triangle. She would wear a large Perspex necklace in bright pink to distract from the lower layer. And earrings hanging down like giant spiders. And clumpy shoes and riotous tights. On second thoughts, she would take a lukewarm bath at home, for she never felt at ease in Robert's bathroom. Then, she would cycle slowly back towards Holland Park. Cycling slowly didn't burn up so many calories but you always had to wind down after exertion. Besides, the last thing she wanted was to arrive sweaty and breathless.

When Alice let herself in again she heard voices. Beatrice's, Robert's and for God's sake, had she really brought the children? Didn't the little horrors have a bedtime?

'Alice, darling. I've got a crisis on my hands.' As Alice came into the living-room, Beatrice moved forward to embrace her. She was dressed in a dark moiré suit with a plunging silk shirt underneath and Alice hoped she was dropping by before going somewhere else. 'I know it's absolutely the wrong moment, but David's abroad and some clients of mine are giving the most amazing dinner party, very good for business, and the baby-sitter's gone and let me down. They're expecting me in an hour, it would be absolutely appalling if I didn't turn up.'

'I'm really sorry,' said Alice, resisting the gale force of Beatrice's demands, 'but Robert and I are going out. Otherwise, of course we'd have helped.'

'I know, I know. And you look wonderful, you really do. But . . .'

'Bea, we can't do it tonight. Not tonight,' said Robert.

'Please, please. I'll go on my knees, I'll ladder my tights, anything. Tell you what, the children can sleep over, they love sleeping in other people's houses. They'll be no trouble at all. And then I'll collect them early in the morning.'

'No. No. And no,' repeated Robert.

'We don't want to. We want to go with you, Mummy.'

Beatrice took Drusilla and Sasha firmly by the hand. 'It's only for one night.' Then she turned to Robert. 'Is it so much to ask?' Judging by her despairing tone, it was possible that she would let forth a stream of tears. And then the children would start. But on this occasion Beatrice appeared to be making a gargantuan attempt to control herself. 'I am your ex-wife, after all. It's not as though I were some vague friend taking advantage of you.' There was a concentrated silence while Robert and Alice waited for her to come to the right conclusion.

'We're going out, Bea. Come on, Alice. I'm going to order a cab.' Robert started to walk towards the phone.

'Please wait, Robert!' cried Beatrice, to no avail.

Sensing that drama was in the air, Drusilla and Sasha sat on the floor expectantly, gazing at Robert.

'Will you play with us?' asked Drusilla. 'We've brought our Lego and Mummy says you're good at Lego.'

'Another time,' said Robert, starting to dial.

'I can do that. Mummy showed me.'

'Another time,' repeated Robert. After his third attempt to get through to a local minicab firm he gave way and allowed Drusilla to do the dialling.

Alice beckoned to Beatrice who followed her out of the room into the kitchen. 'We're not just being difficult. Robert's had a shock, something's fallen through. He's got a crisis, too. We can't bear to stay in, not tonight. I'm sorry.'

'No, of course you can't. I'm so thoughtless sometimes, Alice. You know how it is, when your emotions take charge and you just can't stop . . . Never mind, I'll think of something.'

Alice knew she would. One of Beatrice's redeeming

111

qualities was her quickness to adapt to refusal and to change her plans. Why couldn't Robert understand that? Why was she so different with him, so reasonable with her?

'It's always been the same.' Beatrice sighed. 'Every time something doesn't work out, Robert has to rush out and forget about it. He can't accept rejection, he really can't.'

'He doesn't want to dwell on it, I understand that.'

'And then, afterwards, he's in a bad mood for days. It used to drive me crazy.'

Only occasionally and it never lasts long, thought Alice.

'Oh, Alice.' Beatrice sighed again. 'I do so want things to be different for you. Don't make the same mistakes as me. I couldn't bear it.'

'I won't, I promise. After all, I'm not you, am I? We're so different.'

'I know, I know. But it doesn't stop me worrying. Robert has always been such a handful. Still, you don't need me to say that.'

'We're fine,' Alice said with a smile.

Robert put his head round the door. 'The cab will be twenty minutes, darling.'

Beatrice leaned against the fridge and frowned at Robert. When she spoke, it was in the argumentative tone which, Alice noticed, she only used with him. 'It's very early to go to a club, Robert. Why are you going so early?'

'Because we want to, Bea,' said Alice gently.

'Because *you* want to, Robert.'

'No. That's not true.'

'You never asked me what I wanted to do, ever. Everything ran according to your timetable. It didn't matter what I was doing. At least David fixes everything up in a diary.'

'Good. He's more organised than me.'

112

'No. Just more thoughtful.'

Alice attempted to restore harmony. 'Bea, this isn't the time. Robert has been working for weeks and now his project will never happen. Do try and understand.'

'Oh, I do. I know this script off by heart. I lived with it for months and months. He'd dream up these impossible schemes and expect everyone to fork out for some lunatic idea which would never work.'

'So you're the expert now?' said Robert sarcastically. 'You never even learned how to read a plan. For God's sake, don't start telling me how to be an architect.'

'Someone has to. Just because I didn't fart around for seven years at that bloody school of architecture you think I'm not entitled to have an opinion? If you had listened to me, you wouldn't be where you are now. But you never listened, did you? You always had to be right, about everything. And I was supposed to tag along saying "darling how marvellous" to every scribble you made.'

'Well, you don't have to any more,' said Robert.

'I was usually right, as it happens. Remember the Archer Street project? They ended up doing just what I'd said in the first place.'

'Bea,' said Alice. 'It's hurtful for all of us, bringing up the past. And it doesn't help anyone.'

Bea opened the fridge, found a piece of cheese and started to demolish it. 'You can't imagine what it's like, trying to run a house, bring up children and make a business work.'

'They're not my bloody children, it's not my house and it's not my business.'

'It could have been, Robert, if you hadn't screwed everything up. Didn't we spend all those years together? Didn't it mean anything? Did you think I'd just walk away and forget what we had?'

Flushed with anger, Robert stormed out of the kitchen.

The awaited tears began to trickle down Beatrice's face. She threw her arms round Alice's neck. 'I'm so sorry, darling. I didn't mean all that. Only it's so hard. Robert refuses to talk about it. You can't throw away a marriage and put it in a bin bag. I've tried, I've tried really hard. If only he'd just come to terms with . . . Forgive me. Please.'

'Go home, Bea. Please. We can't help you tonight,' said Alice as she walked to the hall to collect her coat.

Beatrice followed her. 'You don't hate me?'

'You know I don't hate you.'

'Robert does. Do you think he always did?'

'There's no point in torturing yourself about the past. It's over, Bea. You must take Drusilla and Sasha home and get them to bed. It's getting very late.'

'You're right. Everyone else's children go to bed far earlier, but somehow I don't seem to manage it. Do you think I'm an awful mother?'

'What nonsense. As long as they're not falling asleep, why shouldn't they stay up? But it *is* getting rather late, it's well past nine.'

Beatrice brightened. 'Is it really? I was supposed to be in Barnes for pre-dinner drinks at eight. Oh well, I've missed that, haven't I? It would have been a very boring dinner party, no one I could talk to. I should have made an appearance. But it doesn't matter, not really.'

They kissed at the front door and Alice followed her out. Robert waited until he heard the click of the gate and Beatrice calling to the children, who were racing ahead, 'Shall we go and get a video? What shall we see? Something scary?'

Alice leaned her head against Robert's shoulder. 'It'll be easier once we're married.'

'She wasn't always like that.'

'Robert! Of course she was. Only you didn't notice it so much when you were in love with her.'

'I shouldn't have lost my temper. It's only because . . .'

114

'I know. Let's forget about it for the moment.'

The cab was waiting outside. Just before he opened the door for Alice, Robert suddenly remarked, 'Maybe I should stop being an architect and try something completely different.'

'Like what?'

'Having a flower shop, selling weeds at vast prices to Chelsea restaurants and hostesses who want to make a splash.'

Alice laughed. 'But it would turn into a business.'

'That's the trouble.'

'You wait; everything will be different tomorrow.'

The club had been hot and Robert's hands, clutching her back when the music slowed pace, left trickling rivulets, which insinuated their way to Alice's waist. At least five hundred calories, surely. And Robert rejected the idea of fish and chips, thus saving Alice the burden of putting back the weight she would have lost, according to her calculations. They returned home exhausted and satisfied, rid of the irksome reminders of a hostile world.

The following day Alice gave Mary's cocktail hat the final touches, then wrapped it carefully in swathes of tissue so that once Mary arrived she could pull it from the box like a surprise present. Always give the customer a sense of occasion. *The act of buying is the key to success.*

Exactly as she had planned, Mary made a beeline for the box. 'This must be for me. Is that right?'

Alice nodded and watched her slowly untwist the tissue paper and remove the hat. Taking it to the mirror, she positioned it on her head. 'It's just what I had envisioned. How often does that happen?'

The crown nestled snugly, lending Mary a distinction, which surprised Alice. When you made a hat for someone you were often surprised at the transformation of the face, the shape of the features. She is beautiful, Alice thought, and I had never recognised it.

'You've made me so tremendously happy.' Mary walked round the studio, glancing in the mirror from all sides, accustoming herself to the halo augmenting her face. 'And it feels as though it has grown organically over a period of time. You're a genius, Alice. It's far better than I could ever have imagined.'

'I'm rather pleased myself,' said Alice with a smile, modestly allowing herself a tiny surge of pride.

'Has Robert seen it yet?' asked Mary.

'No, he hasn't.' Then Alice's face fell. 'Things aren't very brilliant for him at the moment.'

'Whatever's happened?'

'Work,' Alice replied quickly. 'A big job has fallen through. It always takes Robert a while to adjust to disappointment, but he says he'd rather be on his own than make me depressed as well. So here we are, both pretending not to be depressed. Saying "Are you all right?" all the time. Isn't it ridiculous?'

Since Mary wanted to know the background, Alice recounted the history of the never-to-be building. She kept asking questions, some of which Alice couldn't answer, like the names of the clients, the exact site, the other competitors. 'So it really is a huge project,' concluded Mary, having extracted as much as Alice was able to give. 'Let me think.' She wrapped the hat lovingly back into its tissue paper, then took up her usual position, leaning against the wall, her legs crossed loosely in front of her. 'We must try and find Robert something big which does happen. I wonder what he's doing wrong. Is he rather unworldly when it comes to business? I mean, does he take people out to nice lunches, send them champagne at Christmas, that kind of thing?'

Alice shrugged, she wasn't aware of the way in which

Robert conducted his business. 'I don't know. I've never asked.'

'You should know everything about him,' said Mary with a laugh. 'After all, you are about to get married. Anyway, I was just wondering whether he didn't pay enough attention to his potential clients.'

'Flatter them? Robert doesn't go in for that. What are you getting at, Mary?'

'I'm only trying to decide if there might be scope for improving Robert's chances, nothing more than that. I might be able to help, put in a word. Gerald, a friend of mine, has just bought a dilapidated warehouse down by the river. He was talking of creating a series of studios, lofts whatever he calls them – the latest craze, apparently. He's been interviewing architects but it's all the usual high-profile ones. He might well take to Robert, he sometimes likes wild ideas.'

'People want wild ideas in theory, then, when it comes down to it, they want the same old thing. That's Robert's experience, anyhow.'

'Leave it to me, Alice. I'll have a try, but whatever happens don't say anything to Robert. I don't want to raise his hopes. And he'd hate it if anything happened which wasn't due to his own efforts.'

'I promise,' said Alice, marvelling once again at Mary's sensitivity, her ability to understand how people felt.

'And I mustn't forget this!' exclaimed Mary, suddenly rising to her feet. She opened her bag and produced an envelope, which she placed on Alice's table.

'Your cheque.'

'Thanks a lot. I appreciate that,' said Alice, thinking of the customers who never paid on time.

'Open it. I hope it's the right amount,' Mary said.

Alice opened the envelope and quickly scanned the cheque. She was puzzled by the name printed below. 'Duchesse de Guerlidan'. 'You never told me that

Roland was an aristocrat. How romantic!' exclaimed Alice.

'I never use my title,' said Mary with an apologetic smile. 'But it's useful at passport control. Besides, in France titles are two a penny.'

'I'm sure my bank will be impressed,' Alice said, placing the cheque in an old button box. 'The Duchess of Kensal Green. It's not the same, is it? It sounds so much better in French.'

Now that the transaction was completed, Alice was relieved. The work was done, the money was paid over and it would make it easier to enjoy the closeness of their friendship.

'You know I hate talking about money,' Mary began. 'But I was wondering if you'd pay the deposit for the clinic. Otherwise your place can't be guaranteed and there is a huge waiting list.'

'Of course I'll pay it,' said Alice hastily. 'And your cheque will be a big help.'

'I know Dottie Grossmann is rather expensive, but then she has to be. Her time is so valuable.'

'Dottie? Is that what you call her?'

'Dottie to close friends.' Mary gave a knowing smile.

Alice took a breath and told herself she had to say what was on her mind. 'It's rather difficult,' she explained. 'I didn't expect the deposit to be so much. If I pay what she wants, it would go way beyond my overdraft, even with your cheque. Do you think I could possibly ask her for reduced fees? I mean, does she make adjustments for people with hopeless bank accounts? Obviously, I can't ask Robert.'

'You don't need to do that, Alice. I'll help you out.'

A look of shock crossed Alice's face.

'I suggested Dottie in the first place. It's the least I can do. And I did put in a word, so that she would give you priority. I'll give you anything you need. Pay me back when you're able. At the moment, I don't have money worries, I really don't. There's no reason to make a big deal of it.' Mary pulled out her cheque-book. 'How much would you like?'

'I can't, Mary.'

'How much? Tell me? A thousand, two thousand, more?'

Alice gulped. 'Two thousand would help a lot.'

Mary began to write out the cheque. 'If it's not enough I'll write another one. I don't want you worrying about money. The important thing is to sort out your problem, because this means as much to me as it does to you.'

Alice kissed her on the cheek and placed the cheque carefully on top of the first one in the button box.

When the call came from a property developer who was known to Robert only by name and reputation, he decided to say nothing to Alice. Gerald Dinely had asked him if he could come up with some ideas for a warehouse conversion. He was unlikely to be in the running for such a large commission, especially as he hadn't proved himself as yet with a major work, which would have established his name. He would give himself time to prepare for disappointment. This time, he would make life simpler by refusing to undertake any unpaid work, which he knew from past experience Dinely would expect him to produce. Without great hopes of any result he agreed to have a half-hour meeting.

Once Robert had entered the Dinely Corporation's Mayfair offices, which took up the second floor of a grand residential house, he was kept waiting for over half an hour. Containing his anger, he was on the point of leaving. Then Gerald Dinely burst into the room and apologised, holding a mobile phone to one ear. He was olive-skinned, small and wiry, with black curly hair and was wearing black leather trousers with a bright turquoise shirt open at the neck. He paced round the reception area as though his brain would stop functioning if he remained still. Robert wondered how he managed to continue talking to him and his client at the same time, changing voices like a ventriloquist acting two parts at once. In a brief pause, Robert had time to notice that the furniture bore the hallmark of the French designer Philippe Starck and that the huge glaring abstract on the wall was by an American painter who was no doubt approved and selected by Christie's in New York.

'Sorry, sorry, sorry about this Robert. Won't be a sec,' Gerald kept repeating. He was so unlike the property developers Robert had met that he found himself warming to his manic behaviour. Eventually he replaced the mobile phone in his pocket and gestured Robert to follow him. They ended up in a nearby Italian café to run through a few ideas, as Gerald put it. Instinctively, Robert warmed to his open approach, his infectious enthusiasm. He was just draining his *cappuccino*, when there was the old-fashioned toot of a horn.

'Come on, we're off to see my baby,' said Gerald. Shouting 'On my tab, Mario!' to the café owner, he rushed outside. His chauffeur, whose uniform consisted of a studded jeans jacket and a baseball cap, was waiting in a vintage Rolls to drive them to the riverside warehouse site.

By the time they arrived, Robert had begun to abandon the caution and reserve with which he defended himself. They both looked up at the jagged, derelict profile of a vast warehouse. The size of the place amazed him and he tried not to think that a commission like this could keep him going for at least a couple of years.

'You like it?' asked Gerald, as though Robert were about to buy a suit.

'Very exciting. You could do wonders with this.'

'You brought some of your stuff along? I'd like to have a look.'

'I've nothing with me, I'm afraid.' Robert began to regret treating the meeting so casually and wondered whether Gerald might think he was not terribly keen.

'Come tomorrow then. Nine a.m.? That do you?'

'I'll be there,' said Robert with a smile.

Next day, Robert brought over a portfolio of drawings and sketches, which Gerald quickly scanned. They appeared to meet with his approval, for he immediately cancelled all his plans for that day and insisted on seeing a couple of small developments which Robert had designed in north London.

In between and during phone calls, they talked of buildings, clients, other architects, new materials and millennium projects. For a developer, Gerald was one of a rare breed, someone who cared about the life of the city, had passionate ideas about planned regeneration and was prepared to condemn what was admired by the majority. Robert could see that he liked to take people over and had the determination to push through big projects in the direction he wanted, like a tug pulling a ship into harbour. They might argue, but Robert thought they would make a good team. Still, the chances were small that he would get the job. All the major partnerships would be queuing up, laden with awards and confidence. Robert decided not to give it too much thought.

Only hours later, Robert was completely taken aback when Gerald phoned him and let slip that a friend of his, whose judgement he very much respected, had highly recommended him. He would pay for some initial plans and take it from there. Another meeting was fixed for a week's time.

They were all assembled at their usual table in the bar of the Lansdale Club – Simon, Beatrice and Alice –

waiting for Robert. He had phoned Alice to say he would be delayed, he was waiting for a fax to come through. When he arrived, he promptly ordered a bottle of champagne.

'I knew it would be good news before you came,' said Beatrice. 'Did you know? Your stars are absolutely amazing at the moment.'

'He's called Gerald Dinely and he's just asked me to draw up plans for a conversion of seventy loft studios in a London warehouse.'

'Official? Contract?' said Simon.

'Official and contract,' echoed Robert.

'Proper money?' pursued Simon.

'Proper money.'

Alice threw her arms round Robert's neck and kissed him. The faces of all his friends lit up, as though they had been personally responsible for his triumph. Beatrice said she knew all along that Robert was going to make it. (Alice smiled to herself. How many times had she accused him of being a failure?) Simon gave a speech about the right time comes for everyone, Robert's time had come. Alice wanted to cry with happiness and did, sitting there with quivering lips, tears trickling foolishly down her face.

It was only when her euphoria died down that she recalled the reason for Robert's success. How tactful of Mary to keep it secret, not to give the smallest hint that she was responsible. But Alice knew she was, that Robert's contract was entirely due to Mary's efforts. How generous she had been. How could she thank her enough? How could she express in words what Mary had achieved for Robert – and for her? How could she return the kindness? Without Mary's help, they would both be in despair. He would be depressed and broke – and she would be endlessly repeating the vain attempts to reduce her weight. How rare it was to find someone who had suffered so much herself, yet still wanted to help others, expecting nothing in return. Instead of feeling weighed down with a sense of obligation – as she was when her father lent her the money to buy her house – Alice was joyful. Mary had taught her the real meaning of friendship. One day, she would find the right occasion to help Mary as she had helped them.

When the congratulations had died down Alice downed her champagne in a gulp. 'I've something to tell you, too.' She would try and make it sound like a ridiculous impulse. 'I know you'll think I'm crazy, but before Robert and I get married I'm going to spend a month on a health farm. Which means I won't be coming here for a while.' She was dreading the hoots of derision, but none came.

'Marvellous idea,' said Simon. 'It'll stop you working like a maniac and Robert can work enough for two maniacs. Knowing him, we won't see him for weeks.'

'A month is a long time. Wouldn't a week be enough?' Robert appeared so crestfallen that Alice almost changed her mind on the spot.

Luckily Beatrice charged in. 'Alice deserves it. Anyway, the holistic cleansing process takes at least a month. You can't just book in and stay for a few days like going to a hotel. Your body has to adjust to total renewal. A friend of mine goes once a year. If only I had the time . . .' Then, turning to Alice. 'Maybe I could join you for a couple of days? Which one are you going to?'

'I haven't decided yet,' Alice replied quickly.

'Everyone needs time alone to have a creative recharge,' Simon declared; although they all knew he had difficulty in being solitary for half an hour. 'I'm thinking of going to a monastery myself. I can't decide on whether it should be in Scotland or Tibet. Actually, I've been looking into it. There's a lot to be said for the Tibetan approach.'

'My God,' said Robert. 'Don't turn hippie on us.'

'Don't discourage him,' countered Beatrice. 'Anything spiritual would do Simon good, he's a material-world man. He can't go on like that all his life.'

'Why not?' said Alice. 'Simon is happy where he is. He doesn't long for the transcendental experience.'

'Maybe that's true,' continued Simon. 'But I would like to know what I'm missing.'

'There's hope yet,' said Beatrice with a laugh.

The rest of the club caught their mood. Dan, the latest barman, offered round a plate of spanakopitta and the hilarity grew as more and more bottles were produced from the chiller cabinet.

'You will come back tonight?' Robert said, clasping Alice's hand, his face unusually wreathed in smiles.

It wasn't one of Alice's nights so his offer caught her by surprise. 'Are you sure? Won't you be flat out from now on?'

'I want to feel you close to me before you fly off to the frigid zones of the health farm. Where will you be?'

'Derbyshire, I think.'

'Do they allow you to use the phone? Or is that against the rules?'

'Don't be silly,' Alice said, giving him a light kiss on the lips. 'I'm not going to prison.'

Soon afterwards, Alice packed a suitcase including some aromatherapy oils donated by Beatrice and there was also a gift from Mary – an electronic calorie counter that beeped riotously when the day's limit was exceeded. Lingering in her workroom, she picked up the sewn-up dress she would wear on her wedding day. How narrow, how impossibly tiny it looked. And when she returned, she would slip it over her head and it would slide voluptuously down her hips, without meeting impossible resistance.

As she travelled up to Derbyshire in the train she

124

could almost feel the extra pounds loosening, ready to be shed. At the station she had bought a pile of fashion magazines, no longer fearing to linger over the images. Soon she would be a few steps closer to the gossamer, wind-swept girls with their racehorse legs and childlike hips.

Seven

• • •

It was not what Alice had expected. There were no Venetian-blinded gleaming rooms with bright modern furniture, no corridors hung with water-colour landscapes, no trim nurses gliding through with a smile, no serious white-coated doctors, no immaculately landscaped gardens. Cloudesley Hall was formerly a hotel, which still betrayed its inferior status in dingy brown paint and woodchip wallpaper painted over in cream. The dense smell of gravy browning and lingering fat from the ancient frying pans of the defunct one-star Cloudesley Hall Hotel had given way to the Cloudesley Clinic's equally pungent aroma, redolent of brown rice and fast-fried vegetables heavily laced with soya. However, the former hotel bar was still in use and stocked with drinks of every description. When Alice peered more closely at the enticing blue, green, orange and purple bottles she just managed to read the minute lettering on a series of handwritten labels: Cloudesley Organics – Grape juice, Carrot juice, Beetroot cordial and Nettle nectar. She had a strong desire for a long, cool glass of wine. Still, considering the number of calories in just one glass (about one hundred and fifty), a soft-drink bar did make sense.

'Hi! Isn't this a great place? Such a fabulous atmosphere. I haven't seen you around. Did you just arrive? My name's Candice.'

These were the first words that greeted Alice as she entered the Meeting Hall, where a small crowd of women had gathered and were sitting on faded cushions. The words were uttered by a woman of gargantuan proportions who was chewing on a celery stick. She was quickly joined by other female figures ranging from size sixteen to size twenty at least, some in flowing garments, some in clinging ones as though to advertise their difference from the norm. Whereas usual introductions consisted of enquiries like 'What do you do?' or 'Where do you live?' the questions directed towards Alice concentrated on pounds, kilos and sizes. They quickly confirmed her as a member of the group, having established that she clearly had a weight problem, even though it was not apparent. Why else would she be at the Cloudesley Clinic? But they had to ask. Why was she so slim? Was she bulimic? Dr Grossman was brilliant with bulimics. In vain did Alice deny her condition. That was so typical of the illness, that the sufferer refused to recognise it.

Onola, approximately one hundred kilos, entered whole-heartedly into the discussion – which, she explained to Alice, was usually referred to as a communing session. Although, Alice admitted to herself, Onola's comments showed a degree of understanding, she found herself resisting the hectoring tones. And she also had to stop herself from comparing herself with the other women. It was not their fault that their complexions were grey, their faces unanimated, their hugeness almost a parody of the human figure. She was unused to being surrounded by women like this. Why are you all so ugly? Why do you look so sick? she thought. Then she wondered what they all thought of her. How was she to know that they didn't see her in the same way?

While waiting for supper to arrive in the Women's Diner, Alice made her first mistake by asking for sausages. One of the women sitting next to Alice – four of them were crammed round one of the small tables – made an involuntary grimace. Quickly realising that she should not have indicated disgust, she smiled instead.

'There's nothing wrong with sausages, Alice,' said Onola, putting a friendly arm round her shoulder. 'What kind were you thinking of?'

'Great big spicy beef-and-pork bangers.'

'Wonderful, Alice. We'd like to share your meal.'

A rosy-cheeked girl in a beige tunic and draw-string trousers came over and placed a terracotta soup bowl in front of each of the guests.

Alice took a spoonful of the greyish liquid and winced. 'Do we get a menu? What's this, exactly?'

'What would you like it to be?' The voice was warm and friendly and the fleshy face crinkled up in approval of Alice's answer, should it come.

'Tomato soup' was all she could muster. 'And could I have some bread?' she added.

'Of course,' came a chorus. 'What kind would you like?'

'Any kind would do,' said Alice. 'Actually, what I'd really like is a huge hunk of Italian bread with loads of olives inside.'

Smiles wreathed all their faces as a plate of carefully fanned-out Ryvita was placed on each table by the smiling waitress. 'I forgot to put this on the table. Do forgive me,' she said in a soft Californian voice. 'Enjoy.'

The main course turned out to be a mixture of stir-fried carrots, courgettes and chickpeas, accompanied by a bowl of watery yoghurt. Alice leaned forward to speak to the thin creature opposite her. 'Surely you don't have to eat all this low-calorie food, do you?' she asked.

The haunted face was briefly lightened by a thin

smile. 'Why should I be different from the others? That wouldn't be fair.'

The end of the meal was marked by small glasses of dried-mint tea, followed by the group standing round the table and joining hands.

'Thank you She on High for providing us with sustenance,' said Iris. Then she added, 'We believe in higher powers. But we don't make a thing about it.'

'I'm glad,' replied Alice.

The Women's Diner closed once the meal had been consumed, but the conversation continued round the bar, where Onola offered to treat everyone to a juice of her choice. Alice was about to ask why they should have to eat such a dismal meal and whether there was an alternative menu for the guests who were trying to gain weight, when the exchanges suddenly came to an abrupt halt, following the chime of a distant clock. All the women closed their eyes and gripped one another's hands. Alice wondered when she could let go of the two pairs of clammy fingers clasped round hers, but they continued to maintain their grip.

'There's a visiting group of Chinese gong players. They'll be starting in the Meeting Hall at nine. We're all going. We'd love you to come,' Onola whispered.

'I'm feeling completely exhausted,' Alice replied.

'Everyone's like that for the first few days. Before the collective karma raises your energy level. You mustn't resist it. Fatigue is nature's way of restoring balance. Don't feel bad about it.'

'I won't,' Alice promised.

Having left the group, she prepared to follow the grimly illuminated signs to her far-off corridor where she might find her bed and extract her sponge-bag. Her bedroom, labelled 'Cowslip' on the door, was more like a narrow dormitory with four iron-framed beds facing in different directions. Further down the corridor there was a room marked 'Wash Room' in which she found a large, chipped enamel bath cheered up with a vase of orange dried flowers in the place where the soap might have rested. What a relief to find hot water! The steam belched upwards, creating a thick fog so that Alice could barely see her folds of flesh. From far away she could hear the rhythmic bong of an instrument she didn't recognise. She would call Robert in the morning.

Outside in the corridor a phone rang just when Alice was accustoming herself to the spongy, polystyrene mattress, which reflected back her body heat at an alarmingly increased temperature. She was hungry, but not feverish, she told herself. And she wasn't quite desperate enough to take out the box of Tampax in which she'd hidden a multi-pack of Mars Bars. At first, she resisted the piercing tone echoing outside in the corridor, then decided to get up and answer it.

'Hi, Mary. Yes, it's fine. Well, to be honest, a little strange at the moment.'

'It'll take time to settle in. Dottie doesn't like to rush things. Have you had a session with her?'

'Not yet. I think I'm booked for two days' time.'

'What are the other women like?'

'Interesting,' Alice said evasively. 'It's not quite what I expected. The place, I mean. I thought it might be a little more luxurious. Considering what I've paid.'

'That's deliberate, Alice. Dr Grossman doesn't want to attract women who don't have empathy with what she's doing. The surroundings aren't important. What happens is.'

'Nothing's really happened yet,' said Alice, her feet turning purple in the unheated corridor.

'Wait till you meet Dottie. It's like judging a foreign country by the airport. You've only just arrived.'

'I thought I might have a room to myself. There are three other girls in here. And the bed is soft and mushy,' said Alice, growing more and more irritable. Then she apologised to Mary for being so tetchy, but it was only because she was tired and hungry.

'Everyone feels like that on the first night. But it will pass.'

'I hope you don't mind, Mary, but it's freezing cold out here. I'll have to ring off,' said Alice.

'Do give Dottie my regards. I'll call you after your first session. Sleep well.'

Padding back to her room, Alice folded back the nylon quilt and inserted herself between the thin, slippery sheets. She felt as though she was in some kind of alternative prison for female offenders. Was this punishment therapy? Why had Mary said nothing about it? After a brief sleep, she was roused to semi-consciousness by prying torches and whispering female voices. An overhead light bulb shrouded in a grubby Chinese lantern was briefly switched on. Half expecting to see a prison warder, she was relieved to recognise some of the faces she had seen at lunch. She read through the items on her typewritten card, headed 'Alice's Per Diem Schedule', then buried her head under the nylon quilt.

Day One – Morning
Relaxation Workshop

Determined to arrive promptly for her first session, Alice searched for the room number indicated on her programme. When she had located it, at the end of a dimly lit basement corridor, she stopped in her tracks. What was she meant to do? There was a notice on the door, which read: 'Please Wait. Transformation in Progress.' Checking the number again, she found it corresponded to her programme details. She gingerly let herself into the room and was immediately greeted with a hug by Kirsty, the statuesque blonde group leader.

131

Alice was provided with a set of royal-blue leotards and leggings with a generous stretch capability. Once she had changed in a corner of the room, Onola and Iris waved at her to join the group, who were spread out over the floor, lying on their backs. Kirsty was urging everyone to imagine a warm Mediterranean sea lapping around them as they breathed in long slow gulps and gasps, in and out, in and out. The relaxation work continued for a long time.

'Alice. Alice! Are you sleeping?'

Alice opened her eyes and realised that she had drifted off. She grinned at her mentor, responding to the fully displayed set of even, dazzling teeth.

'When you relax, Alice, that's quite different from sleep. Sleep is the body's way of shutting out. We are making ourselves open.'

'Sorry,' Alice said, as an apology seemed in order even though there wasn't an ounce of rebuke in Kirsty's soft-edged mid-American drawl.

Kirsty picked her way round the supine bodies lying in various positions on rubber mats like porpoises about to perform on cue for *Sea World*. 'Well done, everyone. Now you've nearly reached seven out of ten on the relaxation scale. Doesn't that feel just wonderful?' she said encouragingly, though Alice was unable to determine the principles by which she was judging. It was curious that the women who were grossly overweight appeared to have spent time at the clinic on previous occasions. Alice vaguely remembered Mary mentioning that the clinic effected permanent change, but she was sure there would be some explanation. It was only the first day, after all.

Day One – Afternoon Role-play
and Communing Evening Fun-Jog

The afternoon began with a pretty speech from Kirsty

about the mind-releasing powers of role-play which would be focused on a realistic shopping scenario. She suggested Harvey Nichols or Harrods as a venue, but when Rhoda objected that she wouldn't dream of entering places of blatant capitalist exploitation Kirsty said they could choose any shop they wished. The first exercise involved selecting a cocktail dress in their own size, which was a challenge in itself, since mass-production had failed to satisfy the demands over the over fourteens – let alone size twenty.

Alice was relieved that the allotted time was not sufficient for her contribution, but Kirsty appeared not to have noticed her silence. She was already conjuring up the most marvellous cocktail party she had attended at the American embassy and she invited everyone to imagine that they were there too, wearing the dreamy dress they had previously selected. Alice stood at the back, pretending to hold a glass and smiling awkwardly, while the others circulated vigorously around her. After Kirsty had effusively congratulated the group on their performance – how many actors could improvise so well? – she resuméd the session. How did they feel? Who did they talk to? Did they stand against the wall? Did they dare to talk to a handsome man they fancied? Were they already fingering the sausages and vol-au-vents piled high on a plate? Had they fought back hateful thoughts about the slim girls in black? Had they wanted to go home? Yes, yes, yes, came the replies, the grateful glances of recognition.

'Now!' Kirsty continued, flashing a luminous smile. 'Suddenly you have become the shape and size you wish to be. I want you to arrive at that party, take off your coat and give it all you've got.'

The Transformants crossed the floor, flung out their arms in wild gestures and came to a triumphant stand-still. After being congratulated once again, they were invited to observe themselves in the mirrors lining the walls, to determine their skin type. Alice realised that her skin fell far short of glowing radiance and she was just able to distinguish a few submerged spots, which she hadn't noticed before. She screwed up her face in revulsion.

'That's right, Alice,' said Kirsty, pointing a perfectly manicured finger in her direction. 'Isn't that always our first reaction? To pull a face? I do it myself. We all do that, don't we? [Nods of agreement.] Let's all take a long, hard look at ourselves. We're going to gaze in the mirror and guess what I want you all to do? I want you to give a great big smile. As big as you can manage. Don't be afraid to show your teeth.' She worked her lips into a formidable cheerleader grin, which seemed to divide her face in half. 'Like this, everyone. Smile in the mirror, now smile at your neighbour.'

Since many mouths were incapable of stretching to the required capacity, Kirsty showed them how to enlarge their apertures in a series of exercises, which involved sticking their fingers in their mouths and kneading their cheeks. After half an hour of oral gymnastics Alice decided this session was not for her. While the others were pulling their mouths apart like dentists about to insert an overlarge set of false teeth, she made her way unobtrusively towards the door.

But this time Kirsty noticed Alice's defection. 'Is something wrong? Are you feeling ill?'

Although tempted to give this excuse, Alice decided to come clean. 'I'm sorry, Kirsty. I honestly can't see the point of all this. I mean, I don't think it's what I need. At the moment, anyway.'

The rest of the group took their hands away from their mouths and stared at Alice. Kirsty came up to her, put a hand on her shoulder and looked straight into her eyes. Her complexion, which Alice could see in giant close-up, was completely flawless and smooth. 'Now tell me, Alice. What is it you think you need? We can then decide whether it's a good need or a bad need.'

'All I want is to find a diet so I can ...'

'Yes?'

'Fit into a size ten dress.'

'Is that all? Really all?'

Alice was disconcerted by Kirsty's staring delphinium eyes. 'Yes,' she said defiantly.

'You want to fit into your dress, Alice, and there's nothing wrong in that. But I have a feeling there's something you're unwilling to say. Don't be afraid. Here you can be honest. That's why we've come together.'

'I am being honest,' Alice replied, trying to contain her impatience. 'But I wasn't expecting this.'

'What were you expecting?'

Alice glared at Kirsty and she rarely glared. For some reason the sickly Benolin voice had started to get to her. 'Maybe I expected to learn about the reasons some people can binge and stay thin and others only have to eat two wafers of Kit Kat and they put on weight. And I wanted someone to help me stop eating all the time. Why are we doing all this? What's smiling got to do with losing weight?'

'That is a very big question, Alice. We're not ready to answer that one yet. This is only day one, remember.' To signal her seriousness, Kirsty sank to the ground and sat cross-legged in a yoga position. 'Alice, I believe you're angry. Later on, we're going to explore hostility but we won't go deep-diving in that area just yet. However, we could talk about negativity. Does anyone else feel overcome with negativity?'

'Yeah. I do. Alice is three sizes smaller than me.'

'That's very honest, Rhoda. We all appreciate your honesty, don't we?'

Alice looked round at Rhoda, who was slumped onto a chair, her arms folded tightly against her belly. 'We're all overweight, we've all got the same problem.' She

135

instantly regretted her remark, which seemed inappropriate considering that Rhoda's vast proportions made Alice seem like a waif.

Kirsty glanced at Alice and quickly corrected her pained expression to a half-smile. 'There's no such thing as overweight, Alice. What we're looking at is a false ideal of body image dreamed up by a consumer society and promoted by advertising to keep us in a permanent state of dissatisfaction and anxiety.'

'But I'm part of the fashion industry, it's what I do. I make hats, I make hats for thin models sometimes.'

Kirsty leaped to her feet and faced the group. 'Am I saying thin is bad? Am I saying fat is bad?'

'No!' came a chorus.

After the evening fun-jog, which covered several miles, Alice was congratulated on overcoming her hostility and having a positive bonding experience. She had sustained her tolerance and good humour by using Mary's counter to calculate her calorie loss. The meagre meals and two-hour jog must have consumed enough to lose a kilo at least.

Day Two – Afternoon
The Exploring Game
Cutting the Grass
Seminar with Dr Grossman: The Negative becomes Positive,
a new interpretation of domestic tasks.

Alice decided to pass over the exploring game in favour of treating herself to some of the beauty therapies on offer. However, she was astonished to learn that they were not included in the overall fee – which amounted to over three thousand pounds plus VAT – and were based on Knightsbridge prices. When she questioned the expense she was told that the Cloudesley Clinic Beauty Trainers were world famous and featured in *Vogue*, *Marie-Claire* and *Options*. In the meantime she was strongly advised to attend the afternoon session with Melody, an alternative gardening expert who taught organics and a new approach to group bonding in a unique combination. This activity centred on cutting the grass borders surrounding the flower-beds in front of the clinic with blunt shears, while reciting mantras. Melody was also a world expert in Flower Essences, and her seminar on this subject was an optional (and therefore pricey) extra, which Alice declined.

Candice, who had attended the clinic on several occasions, informed Alice that the real high point of Day Two would be Dr Grossman's lecture. That evening, Alice sat at the back of the hall, fascinated by the elegantly suited woman with short, carefully styled grey hair and grey eyes enlarged by an imposing pair of scarlet designer spectacles. She had a crisp New York accent and was expounding her theories that would soon be followed by a series of practical and liberating experiences encapsulated in positive-action plans.

After the herbal tea-break work began in earnest. The action plans involved Hoovering the corridors, cleaning the bedrooms, swabbing down the kitchen surfaces and floors, doing the left-over lunch-time dishwashing and drying up, sorting the rubbish into appropriate bags, then taking it to a tip near the compost heap in the Copse. Alice could see the value of having a dedicated unpaid labour force, but she knew there was a missing link which evaded her. How did all this relate to losing weight? She hoped Dr Grossman would soon enlighten her.

Day Three – Morning
Private Consultation with Dr Grossman
Afternoon: Free Period for Reflection And Meditation

Alice made her way to the Annexe, an exquisite Georgian house built to the rear of the hotel. In her flower-strewn office, with walls covered with reproductions of luscious Renoir nudes and plump Renaissance cherubs, Dr Grossman received Alice in a flowing gown, very different from the formal suit she had worn for her lecture. This gave her the appearance of being large, although Alice quickly realised she would have been a size twelve at most. The slim arms and neck gave her away. All Alice wanted was to be weighed. Was that too much to ask? Wasn't she meant to be losing weight?

'That will come later,' said Dr Grossman, her lecture-hall voice now softened to a throaty contralto. The dress, Alice thought, could have been Yamamoto, all those drapes. Definitely not a quick bargain from Evans. 'But I have good news, Alice. You are going to be pleasantly surprised. The process of going through the sessions with our lead trainer, Kirsty, and all the other wonderful experts we have here will enable you to reorientate your perception. Incredible though it may seem, fat will no longer accumulate in the body tissues. This has been scientifically proven, although no one yet understands the relationship between obesity and mental perception. My former professor is undertaking a vast study on this subject.'

Having accepted a couple of phone calls, Dr Grossman finished instructing her callers and sat bolt upright in a chintzy armchair, which would have seated two size fourteens with ease. 'Are you finding our sessions valuable?' she asked, staring fixedly at Alice.

It was hard not to feel intimidated by Dr Grossman's intense gaze, but Alice thought she would appreciate an honest response. 'Well, actually, I'm not sure that I am.'

Dr Grossman cleared her throat and opened a folder placed on a table at her side. 'I see here', she said, consulting a sheet from the folder, 'that Kirsty suggests possible participation resistance. In ordinary language, let me put it this way. Do you have difficulty in relating to women?'

'I . . . I've never thought about it. I mean, no one's ever said anything,' Alice stuttered.

'It's an underlying problem that concerns us here. What is fear of body shape about, after all? Is it not a false comparison with others of our sex? Is it not an imposed condition devised by men to make women competitive and distrustful of one another? If we distrust, do we not also fear and loathe?'

'Mm,' said Alice, stunned into incoherence. How could she have known? She hadn't mentioned Beatrice, or her fear that she would always be inferior to the size eights and the size tens. It was as though Dr Grossman had dived down and dredged up the secret she had kept all this time. She felt naked and exposed. Then she experienced a surge of resentment. It might have been an inspired guess. Hadn't Dr Grossman spent years studying the female psyche? She could merely have picked on one theory at random, which happened to fit. Enough of this, Alice told herself, I've come to lose weight permanently and that's what I'm going to do.

'We all have the same fears,' said Dr Grossman. 'But you must resist your desire to run away, however painful. That way you will conquer them.'

'Yes,' said Alice firmly. 'But I would still like to lose weight. That's the reason I came here. I would like you to give me a diet, which I can follow at home, and this time I'm really going to make the effort to keep to it. I would like to be weighed now, if you don't mind.'

A broad smile crossed Dr Grossman's face. 'But of course you can be weighed. Come this way.'

Alice followed Dr Grossman into a side room, where a pair of electronic scales and various pieces of apparatus she didn't recognise were ordered in a line. Alice removed her clothing, was given a towelling robe and stood on a crystal pad, which registered her weight. Minus slightly less than one kilo after only three days.

'That is excellent. What we would have expected,'

139

said Dr Grossman, pulling a printout from one side of the machine. 'As you progress, you will find a more rapid weight loss. The momentum curve will be quite dramatic.'

'I don't think I'll be able to stay more than another week because I really have to get back to work,' Alice explained.

'If that's what you think is best,' replied Dr Grossman, still smiling.

'But I'd like to see you in London. Perhaps I could just pay for the time I've been here,' Alice added.

Dr Grossman clasped Alice's hand. 'I'm afraid that won't be possible. Of course you can leave at any time, but clinic policy does not allow for refunds.' The buzzer sounded on her desk and she escorted Alice to the door.

That evening, Alice called Mary and told her of her extraordinary meeting with Dr Grossman, but she didn't seem surprised.

'I told you she was special,' said Mary. 'Trust me, Alice. Would I have sent you to someone who was useless?'

'No, of course you wouldn't. But why do I have to go to all these ridiculous classes and sessions? Couldn't I have seen her in London? Here I am, paying all this money to sit around with a load of . . .'

'A load of what?'

Alice checked herself. 'Women I have nothing in common with.'

'You must see it through, Alice. You can't possibly leave now. It's important. You'll realise later.'

'Do you think so?'

Alice could hear something sizzling in the background, or it could have been running water. 'Is this a good moment? Are you taking a shower?'

'Oh, no,' Mary said with a nervous laugh. 'I never take showers. I'm just cooking something. I've a friend coming round.'

'Sorry. Shall I ring later?'

'Could we talk tomorrow? Only it's so long since I've cooked properly; I haven't done it since Roland died. You think you can't do it any more, like riding a bicycle.'

'Don't worry, I'm sure it'll be wonderful,' said Alice encouragingly.

'I'll call you tomorrow. Do forgive me.'

The phone went dead before Alice could ask what she was cooking. She wondered whether to call Robert and was reaching out to dial his number when she remembered suggesting that apart from her weekly phone call they would only contact one another in an emergency. This was a period for both of them to be alone with themselves, a time of reflection and recuperation for them both. Alice stopped dialling.

Eight

• • •

In Alice's absence, Robert surveyed his house. The kitchen was neat once more, without the usual parade of mugs waiting to be washed, or piles of cutlery stuffed into a jar to dry. He roamed round the basement which would be hers, imagining her hats hanging like resting butterflies on the walls. When he had a moment he would start on the shelving, strip down the windows, find her some blinds. For now, though, he couldn't imagine when he could find the time. Gerald was a demanding client, asking to be informed of the tiniest step. He assumed he had the right to take over Robert's life. Robert found himself longing for the contented routine of marriage to begin, so that he could have some respite from the warehouse. He was barely allowing himself enough time to eat and sleep seemed an indulgence. Just when he had settled the following week's scheme of work in his mind he received an unexpected call.

'I'm know it's rather late, but I've been out of London and wanted to talk.'

Robert was unable to identify the voice. 'Sorry?'

'Mary, Mary Bartlett. Don't you recognise me?'

'Of course. I expect you want to talk to Alice, but she's left for the country. She's gone away for a break.'

'Actually, Robert, I need to talk to you.'

'What about?' he said suspiciously. 'Not bad news, I hope. I'm getting used to good news at the moment.'

'I know, I've been following your progress. I thought it was about time I told you. Gerald Dinely's a very old friend of mine.'

'Is he really? Alice never told me.' Suddenly Robert felt startled and confused. Did that mean that it was Mary who had pulled the strings? And would she expect payment, a percentage of the commission, like others he'd heard of?

'I knew you two would get on. I've an instinct for these things. Isn't it wonderful? Alice must be so pleased.'

'I . . . I didn't realise . . .' Robert stuttered. 'That I owed it to you, Mary. There was no reason for you to . . .'

'Oh, yes, there was. I care about Alice's happiness, she's a very dear friend. And that includes you, naturally. Anyway, you owe me nothing. Gerald has a mind of his own, but he really likes your work. And he likes you, too. I'll be in Holland Park tomorrow, someone I have to see. Shall I drop by?'

'Certainly. You won't mind if it's rather brief? Only as you can imagine, I'm up to my ears.'

'I'll come for coffee at eleven.'

At two minutes to eleven the following day there was a tap on the window. Mary was standing on the doorstep, smiling. 'I wasn't sure which bell to press. Since there are three of them. You never know if an angry lodger might come storming down the stairs.'

'There's no lodger,' said Robert, as Mary entered the hall. 'The bottom one's for Alice, the middle one's for me at work, the top one rings in the living-room. So you know who's coming for what reason.'

Robert hung back as Mary entered the living-room. She immediately walked round it, gazing in wonder at the space, looking up at the tall ceiling, admiring the mouldings. 'Do you mind if I sit down? I've been walking to and from libraries all morning.'

'Please do.' Robert smiled at her, he appreciated the formalities of behaviour.

Mary perched on the edge of a metal chair and praised details of the room, the rug, the wood, the shape of the windows, the way he had placed the table in a manner that did not impede the space. 'I hope you don't mind, but I'm fascinated by houses. This one is beautiful.'

'It will be, when it's finished. You seem to have an architect's eye. Did you train as one by any chance?'

Mary gave a slight laugh. 'Heavens, no.' Then she added in a faintly flirtatious tone, 'Though I'm very flattered that you thought I did.'

The slight intimacy caught Robert off guard. 'Would you like some coffee?'

'If you're making it, that would be wonderful.'

She followed Robert into the kitchen, striding behind him so that he was aware of her positive movements. 'Would you tell Alice that her hat was a spectacular success? Everyone was coming up to me and demanding to know who made it. So I gave her phone number to a few people. Do you think she'll mind?'

'That's kind of you, Mary. I'm sure she'll be very pleased.' Robert stirred the instant coffee in the mugs and presented one to Mary.

She seemed more at ease, having abandoned her earlier formality, and was leaning against the kitchen cabinet. 'I've known Gerald for years. He can be quite tough to work for sometimes. And his taste needs . . . well, let's say a bit of guidance. But he does have an open mind, which is rare. I heard your first meetings went wonderfully well.'

'We seemed to be on the same wavelength.'

'Let's hope it stays that way. But if you have any problems, do get in touch with me. I know how his mind works and I'd make sure he wasn't making outrageous demands on you. He does sometimes, but he listens to me, ridiculous though it sounds.'

'Why ridiculous?'

'Because I'm only a researcher, I just know a little about architecture, things I've picked up over the years.' Suddenly she lifted her head and looked directly at Robert, for until now she had merely glanced at him briefly, either studying objects in the kitchen or contemplating her mug of coffee. 'Could I possibly see some of your work?'

'Of course.' Robert escorted her into his studio, showed her some models of previous projects, then drew out a series of sheafs from a plan chest and spread them over his table. As she pored over them, her bobbed hair swinging round her face and hiding her eyes, Robert became aware of a complex floral perfume, which seemed at odds with what she was wearing, a grey, full skirt and black polo-neck sweater that looked like the uniform of a teacher or a council official.

She made few remarks, but appeared to be absorbed in the details of what was before her. 'I'm keeping you, Robert. I do apologise,' she said at one point.

'Please, Mary . . . take your time.'

'I'm very impressed. You're good, very good indeed. Still, I knew you would be. Alice isn't the kind of girl who'd marry a talentless nobody, is she?'

Robert gave an embarrassed smile. 'No, I suppose she wouldn't.'

'You must be missing her. Still, I expect she phones regularly. She called me last night, as a matter of fact.'

'Oh?'

'She's only just beginning to settle in, of course. But I know she'll get a lot out of it. As it happens, I know a couple of people who went to the clinic and it totally changed their lives.'

'Clinic? She told me it was a health farm.'

'They call them clinics now, it sounds better.'

'Do you think Alice's life needs changing?' said Robert, looking hard at Mary.

'No, not changing. But she needs to open herself up to new possibilities. When you're stuck in work, it's often difficult to keep hold of a vision. Alice told me she was getting stale, she felt she was repeating herself. At times like that you need a completely new invigorating environment.'

'Alice complains sometimes, when she's tired. Do you think she means it? I do know that she demands a lot from herself. Like me, I suppose.'

'And says little about it. That's her nature.'

'You seem to know her well.'

'Only a little. As you're probably aware, we were at school together at Corsham Towers. We shared all the things schoolgirls do, nothing very profound. You get to know one another's habits, taste in music and clothes and books, but it doesn't go beyond that. After I got married we lost touch, even though I never meant to. Then, recently, we discovered we had a lot in common. It came as quite a surprise; you don't expect people to change, do you?'

'Some of my friends have changed. Most of them I haven't kept up with. One loses touch.'

Mary smiled sympathetically, as though she had shared the same experience. 'Of course. But it's so rare to find someone with whom you have an understanding. Alice may not be intellectual, but she grasps things intuitively. A precious quality. I appreciate her a lot.'

'I'm pleased,' Robert said with a warm smile, which masked his reaction. He suddenly felt uncomfortable. He didn't want Mary to have known Alice before him. He didn't want Alice to have had a past in which he did not figure, to be excluded from what had made her into Alice. How could Mary pretend to know her as he did? Then he was ashamed of his arrogance, his possessiveness. Perhaps that meant he really was in love.

Mary failed to detect his discomfort and continued,

'This clinic – health farm – she's gone to is a gorgeous place, friendly staff, acres of woodland nearby. I rather envy her, staying there. Still, she deserves it.'

'Yes, she described it to me. I can't imagine anything more tedious, but Alice seems to like it.'

'And she really needed a break.'

'It's been a tough year, we haven't had time to go away much. Still, we'll have a honeymoon, I'm determined to make space for that whatever happens.'

Mary rose to go, then suddenly made a request. 'Could I possibly see the rest of the house? I'd love to see what you've done. Alice told me you're making her a marvellous workroom in the basement.'

'There's still a lot to do, but the basic stuff's done. Come down and have a look.'

While Mary was contemplating the space she remarked to Robert that, strange to say, she considered it was the best part of the house. But then she did have a weakness for low ceilings, she always went for rooms without full light, so much more conducive to study and creative work. 'I mustn't keep you, Robert. But I'm so glad I've seen what you've done. By the way, I thought I could arrange lunch with you, Gerald and me. Just so that things continue smoothly. I'd hate you to get messed about.'

'Thanks. That's very kind.'

'Gerald always keeps Friday free for last-minute meetings. Could you manage Friday if I can arrange it? Café Royal, one o'clock? He always has a table there.'

'Fine.'

'I'll ring to confirm, but I'm sure it will be all right.'

Shortly after Mary had left, Robert was interrupted by a visit from Beatrice, who knew he would be working at home. He was relieved they had not coincided as he had no wish to discuss Mary's involvement. Beatrice would be bound to jump to the wrong conclusion and criticise him for obtaining work through someone else's influence. She had never been able to understand the politics of behaviour which, he supposed, was one of her charms.

'I won't stay, I promise.' Beatrice was standing on the doorstep with a large basket covered in a linen cloth. 'I've brought you something. Here take this.'

'Bea, I'm working.'

'I know, I know. But since Alice is away I had to bring this marvellous pâté I made, which didn't get eaten yesterday. It was a directors' lunch but they had bad news, being taken over or something, so they didn't feel like eating. Cost them a fortune! Feel that cheese, it's superb. I thought you might like it.'

Taking the basket, Robert headed for the kitchen, followed by Beatrice. Here she unpacked the pâtés and cheeses, and stacked them in the fridge. 'Nothing to eat in the fridge, as usual. I can tell Alice is away. Robert, could I just make myself a cup of coffee? Only I was up at a lunatic hour.'

'If you must.'

Beatrice clattered round the kitchen, inspected the cupboards, made some coffee and sat down comfortably at the kitchen table. 'So the warehouse project is really happening. I'm so glad, Robert. You've no idea, I've always been longing for you to get something enormous, something that's . . .'

'It's work, that's all. I don't make a distinction between large and small.' Robert spoke curtly when he didn't want to discuss things, she recognised the tone. Don't talk to me, I'm busy.

Well, she felt like talking. 'How are you getting on with Gerald Dinely? David's heard of him, you know. He's so pleased you've got something prestigious going. But you really need to find out his background. David said the City was wary of him and he knows about these things.'

'Why is that necessary? He's a client, not a merchant bank.'

'For God's sake, he's incredibly successful. You ought to check it out if someone's that rich. Who knows where the money came from? He might be an arms dealer.'

'It makes no difference. As long as he pays me.'

'You never used to think like that, Robert. Anyway, I hope you stick it out.'

'What do you mean by that?'

'Remember the Shaftesbury flats? You backed out just because they wanted aluminium windows.'

'That wasn't the reason. Anyway, we won't go on about that.'

'I just mentioned it, no need to get all upset about it.'

'I wasn't.'

'Yes, you were. I could never talk about anything without you getting hurt about something. I got hurt, too. Did you ever think of that?'

'Bea, this isn't the time.'

'It's never the time.'

'The past is over.'

'Never mind, I didn't come here to argue. You will try that cheese? It's delicious.'

'Yes. And I thank you.'

Beatrice waltzed round the kitchen, then changed her mind about going and sat down again. 'I've been worried, Robert.'

'What about this time?'

'Alice's stars aren't very good at the moment. She's suffering negative influences, which she may not know about. How much longer is she staying at that place?'

'Three weeks or so, I think. I haven't a clue about time at the moment.'

'Ten days is quite enough. Can't you think of an excuse to make her come back early? She'd come like a shot if you asked her.'

'Bea, why don't you keep your superstitious nonsense to yourself? I could never understand why someone so, so . . .'

'So what?'

'Sensitive to what's going on could go along with that outdated rubbish.'

'Rubbish? Oh, yes? So why did Ronald Reagan consult an astrologer? Or Princess Diana? Or Gorbachev? Answer me that?'

'Moments of weakness.'

'Don't be silly, Robert. Ronald Reagan was never weak. He did it because he knew there was something in it. A lot in it. And most American presidents have had astrologers, believe it or not.'

'All right. If it makes you happy, Bea, I'll believe it. For today, I'll believe it. Now will you let me get on?'

'I feel uneasy about Alice. You must take this seriously, Robert. Please.' Her green eyes opened wide and she looked beseechingly at her former husband.

'So what should I do? Ask her to come home? She's having a wonderful time.'

'Then I'll ask her.'

'Bea, can't you just leave Alice alone? What are you trying to do? Can't you stop interfering for once? We're getting married, we're going to make our own life together. We can still be friends, I want to be friends. But you must let us be for a while.'

'What do you mean?'

Although he had promised himself to say briefly what he had to say, Robert was unable to stop, as though he had lost his balance and was rolling faster and faster down a steep hill. 'Stop bringing the children round for a start. And I'd appreciate it if you didn't ring up so often.'

'I only rang you twice this week.'

'Several times.'

'Were you counting, then? For Christ's sake, Robert,

if you say you're busy I'll hang up. What's the problem? Give me one good reason why we can't still say things to one another? I talked to my Chinese acupuncturist about it. He said you couldn't reconcile your ying and your yang. You're not in balance and it's so important to be in balance. Especially now.'

'Utter nonsense. What does David think about all this?'

'He knows we like to talk, of course he does. Why should he mind?'

'The acupuncture, I meant.'

'I don't discuss it with him, Robert. He wouldn't understand.'

'Accountants understand about balance, surely?'

'He's not an accountant any more. He's a financial consultant, I'd have you know.'

'I forgot,' he replied with a grin, enjoying Beatrice's expression of umbrage, the way she tilted up her nose and looked through her lashes, as though delivering a rebuke at a cocktail party. 'Why don't you suggest he takes up numerology? He might take to it.'

'What do you know about numerology?'

'As much as you know about architecture, Bea.'

'How dare you!' Beatrice leaped off the chair and put her face close to Robert's. 'I'm not having it. I will not allow you to insult me. I'm not your wife any more. I'm not having it.'

Reeling at the taunt, Robert took her hands in a firm grasp. 'That's enough, for God's sake calm down,' he shouted. 'Do you behave like this with David?'

'Fuck David.' Her eyes filled with tears. 'Oh, Robert. He's so . . . he's so . . .' Her voice disintegrated into sobs.

'Come out with it and stop snivelling. I can't bear it.' Robert walked to the window and looked out. He wanted her to go, but he couldn't let her go, not in that state.

Straightening herself, Beatrice managed to find a tissue and blew her nose delicately. 'David never says anything which lights up my mind. I know it's unkind of me, but I do find him slightly . . .'

'Slightly what? You might as well say, I won't repeat it.'

'Boring.'

'What's so terrible about that, Bea?'

'You aren't.'

Having decided that there was little chance of returning to his studio for a while, Robert came over and sat opposite Beatrice. 'It's what you need. You're the kind of woman who needs a boring man. What do you want anyway? Dr Jonathan Miller to discuss the neuropathology of the female response?'

'About which you for one know nothing. Why do you like insulting me so much, Robert? Do you know how patronising you sound?'

'I didn't mean to be unkind, honestly. But David is obviously a decent, caring husband who works hard to give you a good life.'

'I work hard to give me a good life.'

'All right, all right.'

Suddenly Beatrice leaned across the table and slipped her hands round Robert's neck. 'Do you still love me?'

'No, Beatrice. I don't.'

'We can go to bed, then. If you don't love me.'

'I've loads of work to do.'

'Is that a no or a yes?'

She kissed him and he breathed in the light fragrance of her powder, her hair, always slightly scented as though she had just washed it. Everything seemed comfortably familiar. The time in between appeared to have been erased. His mind went blank, he was overtaken by a demanding lust. He took her against the broom cupboard, lifting up her skirt, running his hands over something lacy, she was never without sexy underwear. What did they used to say? *In case you got run over by a bus*? He pushed aside the crotch of her pants and penetrated quickly. Why? Perhaps out of revenge, maybe because he had never resolved whether he hated or loved her.

'I think about us when I'm in bed with David. Is that terrible? I'm sure it is,' said Beatrice, already hearing the chiding tones of Father Thomas in the Confessional.

'It wouldn't have happened if Alice had been around. Bea, we mustn't do this again.'

'Oh, I know we mustn't. Really I do,' said Beatrice, straightening her clothes. 'But it will never be the same with anyone else.'

'For you, perhaps.'

'But you can't face up to it. All those fantasies locked up in filing cabinets, poor Robert. Your mother has a lot to answer for.'

'Like yours. Like anybody's. You believe all that Freudian nonsense, don't you? It's a substitute for thinking. But I don't expect you to understand, I don't blame you for it.'

'You don't talk to Alice like that.'

'I don't need to.'

'Because Alice is intelligent and I'm dumb. Well, let me tell you something. At school, she didn't get better exam grades than I did. Does that surprise you?'

'Alice is an artist, you don't have to get good marks in A levels for that.'

'And I'm not.'

'What?'

'An artist. I'm uncreative, aren't I? I'm just a mother. Go on, say it. Bringing up children makes women uninteresting. They stop seeing the outside world, I'll never forget you saying that.'

'I didn't say anything of the kind, Bea.'

'We'd been round to have dinner at Phyllis and

James's, and afterwards you said how she hadn't come out with one thing which didn't relate to the children all evening. And that she never used to be like that.'

'Someone else must have said it.'

Beatrice shook her head with a smile. 'Oh, no, I've a good memory. Do you know what some of my friends have told me?'

'No?'

'That out of us two, I am by far the most talented.'

'Then that's why they're your friends, isn't it? They say what you want to hear.'

'You were always so jealous of my friends. I could never understand why.'

'Bea, go home now.' Robert's face was tense. 'Please go home.'

'First I must use your bathroom. I need a wash.' Beatrice ran up the stairs, tripped against a loose fragment of carpet and screamed, 'Why don't you ever finish anything? That's bloody dangerous!'

Robert heard her going into the bathroom without closing the door, as though they still lived together. The lavatory flushed, the water cascaded from the taps, then she appeared once more in the kitchen. 'Has Alice got any make-up here? I must do something about my face.'

'No, she doesn't leave things lying around.'

'Like I used to. I'm still messy, it drives David crazy sometimes, especially when I use his shaving cream to do my legs.'

'I'm glad I don't have to put up with that any more.'

'David never shouts at me. He just says, "Beatrice, I'd be grateful if you could tidy a few things away." Very calmly. I've only seen him lose his temper once, when I put petrol instead of diesel in the car.'

'He's a good man.'

'I do try and be nice to him, really.'

'I wasn't accusing you, Bea. There's no need to be

154

defensive. Now, do you mind if I go and get some work done?'

She came closer, he thought she was going to kiss him goodbye, but instead she looked intensely into his face. 'Robert, darling, when you've had wonderful sex it never goes away, even if you're not living together any more,' she said. 'But you must never never tell Alice. I'd kill myself if she knew.'

'What a stupid thing to say.'

'It's not as though you've betrayed her with a stranger.'

'There's no need to be so dramatic about it. It was merely a quick, rather enjoyable fuck.'

'Very quick,' said Beatrice disdainfully. Then her eyes suddenly clouded. 'You don't regret it?'

'What?'

'Making love to me.'

'Fucking? No. Should I?'

'Of course, it's different for men. You'll have forgotten all about it in a few days. Or even tomorrow. But I won't. Which is your toothbrush?'

'The blue one.'

'Good, that's the one I used. Have I got any fatter?'

'You're just the same.'

'Do you still like my body?'

Robert smiled for the first time. 'You don't need me to tell you that. Your body is perfect.'

'Still?'

'Still.'

'David thinks I'm too thin.'

They both laughed.

Robert wasn't surprised when Beatrice rang later that night, whispering into her mobile standing pressed against the back wall of the corner shop they both used. The hum of the chiller cabinet obscured her words, but he caught the drift. In any case, he could have guessed. He mustn't feel bad, she had regretted nothing. It was their little secret, everyone had them. It was a natural occurrence, for old times' sake. She wouldn't dream of making a habit of it and anyhow she was so desperately busy. How on earth did people find the time to have lovers, she wondered? For a while, Robert put Beatrice out of his mind, although she was never far away.

Friday's lunch at the Café Royal with Gerald and Mary had started off haltingly, but by the end of the meal Robert was feeling more optimistic. Mary had acted as go-between, effecting the kind of compromises which, in the end, satisfied them both. After Gerald had left, he and Mary sat with coffee cups, chewing over what had been said. During their conversation Robert happened to mention that he really must find a secretary, the paperwork was piling up and he was so bad at getting down to it. Alice usually came to his rescue and sorted out that kind of thing, since she could type and he couldn't. He asked Mary if she knew someone efficient who could come for a few weeks, a retired secretary looking for a little extra money would be ideal.

'I've come to the end of the library phase with my research for Professor Norrington,' Mary remarked. 'It would be no trouble for me to get some of your paperwork out of the way. I was a secretary once, you know. Mother made me do one of those ghastly courses after leaving school, then I found work in an office. Only on a temporary basis, of course. I wanted to see what it was like to go to work from nine till five.' She laughed. 'Two of my bosses said I was the best secretary they'd ever had and asked me to stay.'

'Were you tempted?' Robert asked.

'Heavens no! Anyway, I'd be only too pleased to help if you need me. As a matter of fact, I find secretarial work rather satisfying. Why don't I just come along to see what needs doing?'

Robert took up Mary's offer. She came back briefly to

his house to make her assessment. Mary watched with amusement as he opened drawers stuffed with papers, unanswered letters, bills, enquiries he had failed to follow up and threw a series of bulging files onto the table. 'You could do with a little organising,' she said. 'I think you need some kind of system. Would you like me to set one up for you?'

Robert, secretly pleased, was showing reluctance. 'I suppose I could afford to pay someone now. In the past I've tried to economise on secretarial help. You get used to doing without. How much would you charge?'

'Well, I've a suggestion to make.' Mary paced round the room, settling with her back to the fireplace. 'It's only an idea, but you wouldn't want to have me bashing away in here and I wondered whether . . .' She seemed embarrassed.

Robert couldn't imagine why. 'Go on,' he urged.

'Just for a few weeks, well, there's all that space in the basement and it just so happens I'm absolutely desperate for somewhere to work. It's driving me up the wall trying to live and work in one room. Of course, I am looking for a flat, but in the meantime I thought you might consider an arrangement. While Alice is away, that is. I won't need longer than three or four weeks.'

'I'll have to think about it,' said Robert, taken aback. 'What kind of arrangement?'

'If I could work downstairs for a while, I wouldn't charge you anything for sorting out your papers, doing odd bits of correspondence, things like that. I'd take everything down there, so it would be clear in here for you . . .'

'It's a possibility.'

'As a temporary measure,' added Mary. 'I don't think Alice would mind, do you?'

'Why should she? She won't be moving her work-room until after we're married. That's the deal, we're both happy with that.'

'Oh, just one thing.' Mary twisted one of the rings round her finger. 'I don't always work conventional hours. Would that bother you?'

'I don't know what conventional hours are,' said Robert with a laugh.

'If it doesn't work out, just say. I won't be offended.'

'We'll give it a try. That's fine by me.'

When Alice made her weekly call from the clinic Robert did tell her that Mary was going to help him out with some secretarial work, as she had some time on her hands. He omitted to mention that she would be setting up in the basement, sensing that Alice might read something into it that wasn't there. Certainly Beatrice would. As far as he was concerned, it was a perfectly reasonable business arrangement and, most importantly, it would cost him nothing.

Nine

• • •

Having laid out the pre-cooked Turkish deep-fried meatballs and aubergines on a tray and covered them in Clingfilm (she always veered towards ethnic food, being unsure about sauces and distrusting ovens) Mary made her way to Holland Park. There was something about frying which permeated the skin, even when you were shrouded in a professional white overall. She had examined Robert's high-tech oven and decided that she could just about cope with roast rib of beef. The red wine sauce with shallots was ready prepared in a plastic container, the mange-tout topped and tailed, the jar of horseradish and carving implements neatly packed into her deep basket. Other people's kitchens, especially Robert's, made her feel ill at ease, as though she was about to leave a blackened residue on some priceless implement, which could never be removed.

Her delight in accomplishing a task perfectly was acknowledged by Robert as he watched Mary moving about the kitchen with deft fingers, seeking and picking out the right cooking tools from his aluminium cupboards without asking where they were to be found. (With Alice he tended to be slapdash about eating, he confessed.) 'Would you like me to help?' he asked, as she laid out the deep-fried morsels on an oval platter.

'No,' she said with a smile. 'This is my job. I enjoy it,

159

I really do. Go and have a glass of wine. I've opened a bottle, it's over there on the shelf.'

Mary had been working for hours, reducing his pile of intractable papers to slimness, organising a filing system, which was logical and easy to operate, finding receptacles for awkward objects scattered around his studio. As a final touch she had brought one of her own Parisian vases and made a splendid display of leaves and lilies bending over informally, but with a sense of predestined order. Robert found himself working well and productively, knowing that she was down in the basement ordering his life, yet never making him feel it was an effort. After a couple of days she began to arrive late in the morning and to stay until evening. Her rhythm of work coincided with his, which suited them both. When he suggested a take-away meal after they had both been working late, she told him it would only take a short time for her to prepare something simple. So much better than those dreadful pizzas and half-hearted, careless attempts at the great Chinese cuisine. Then, later, when she mentioned casually that it might be an idea to invite a few of his clients over to a meal, he could see no reason to object. There was so little time to think of entertaining and, to be honest, he had little inclination for organising evenings with duty guests. Mary reassured him she would look after everything. All he had to do was to make sure the wine was properly decanted.

The guests Mary had selected formed a harmonious combination and she took care to steer the conversation away from anything too learned which might make the less informed feel uncomfortable. Around the prettily laid-out table were Gerald Dinely with his wife Trish, a former Miss Blackpool; Max, a Knightsbridge estate agent and his wife June, plus a surprise couple, friends of Mary's, Norman and Teresa. Norman was an eminent gynaecologist at a London teaching hospital and his wife was Bolivian. Mary's mix ensured a perfect balance and Robert was surprised to find that he actually enjoyed the occasion.

It was around midnight and Robert was just about to help Mary clear away after the guests' departure when he was summoned to the front door. Thinking that one of the guests had left something behind, he opened it. Beatrice was standing on the doorstep, looking dishevelled and distraught. 'I've got to talk, Robert. I've had an appalling row with David and he's gone off to stay at his ghastly club. We never have rows and he's totally incapable of coping with passion. What on earth am I going to do? I almost smashed up everything in the kitchen. Thank goodness I didn't. I'm supposed to cater a wedding tomorrow.' She entered the hall and buried her head in Robert's neck. 'Oh, Robert, you're the only person who understands, who can calm me down. I feel absolutely dire.'

'Bea, everything's in chaos.' Robert slowly disengaged from Beatrice. 'We've had some people to dinner. I must clear up tonight.'

'We? I thought Alice was still away.'

Robert took a deep breath and guided her back towards the door. 'A business dinner.'

'Why didn't you ask me to cook?' She could hear sounds of clattering, plates being stacked. 'Who's in the kitchen, then? Simon, I suppose?'

'Bea, how about coming over for coffee tomorrow? Then you can give me a brief version of what happened.'

'I might be dead tomorrow.'

In spite of his resolve, Robert was unable to quell the turbulence raging inside him. It was as though Beatrice were still living with him, waking to each day with a store of weapons to goad his every nerve. Other occasions came flooding back, evenings ending

161

in the hurling of dishes, the crashing of saucepans, thundering feet, slammed doors, fury in the bathroom, either tears in the bedroom or savage bite-marks left on his arms to elicit abject apologies in the calmer morning. He wondered why the intervening years had done nothing to dampen down the emotion she aroused.

Mary emerged from the kitchen, swathed in her white overall. 'Hello Beatrice, we met at the Lansdale Club. Remember? Do forgive the mess. Can I make you some coffee while I'm clearing up?'

Rarely had Robert seen Beatrice silenced, but she recovered quickly. 'What are you doing here?'

'Just helping Robert.'

'What's that supposed to mean?'

Robert intervened. 'Look, Bea, you know the amount of work I've got at the moment. I needed someone to give a hand and Mary kindly offered.'

'I could have found you someone.'

'I really haven't time to talk now and I've some urgent work to finish. I'm sorry Bea. Let's discuss it tomorrow.'

He suddenly walked off and it took Beatrice a couple of seconds to realise that Robert had made his escape. 'Robert's gone out, hasn't he?' she said, staring straight at Mary.

'Not as far as I know.'

'Robert always avoids confrontation, he is so extremely sensitive. That's the trouble with architects, they think like artists and behave like plumbers. What are you really doing here, Mary?'

'All I've done is to organise dinner for a few clients,' replied Mary calmly. 'And I do the odd bit of secretarial work for Robert. He truly does need someone full time now.' Then she smiled at Beatrice. 'Do forgive me, but I must finish the washing up tonight. It's such a waste of time doing it in the morning.'

'Why don't you use the dishwasher?' said Beatrice,

watching as Mary laboriously filled a plastic bowl. 'Or isn't it working?'

'I brought along some of my French china, as it was a formal dinner. It's too good to put in a machine,' replied Mary, sorting the plates and cutlery into neat piles.

Suddenly Beatrice stood up. She had been invaded by one of her overwhelming intuitions, which had to be expressed. 'Do you think I'm totally blind? Do you think I haven't noticed that you're moving in to take Alice's place?'

Mary instantly realised that Beatrice was in a disturbed emotional state. Her mother, whom she rarely saw, behaved in the same way, making outlandish accusations because it was the first thing that came into her head. Mary moved quietly to sit at the kitchen table, opposite Beatrice. 'Listen, it's quite understandable for you to wonder what I'm doing here. But I'm really upset that you've jumped to such a ridiculous conclusion. I'm merely doing what I can to help out Robert while Alice is away. In any case, Alice knows I'm here. We're very close friends. Can I make a suggestion? While I'm getting all this out of the way, why don't you go into the living-room? There's some wine in the bottom cupboard on the left. Then I'll join you and we can talk. I'm sure Robert will come too.'

Unable to resist such a civilised invitation, Beatrice left the kitchen.

Ex-wives and ex-lovers usually created trouble, in Mary's experience. Some women were unable to let go and were by nature jealous and possessive, however innocent or harmless the circumstances might have been. She tried to avoid arousing such emotions, but sometimes it couldn't be helped, especially with volatile characters. Mary found it difficult to understand how an intelligent and sensitive man like Robert could tolerate Beatrice harassing him in the way she did. Still, some men liked (or thought they liked) women who weren't very bright and she was quite decorative in her way.

In theory, at least, Mary did understand. (During her research for Dr Bates's book on the crisis of male identity she had studied several texts on the dilemma of modern man, stripped of his manly role.) If she gained Robert's confidence, which she appeared to be doing, she could build up his belief in himself and enable him to free himself from the destructive influence of his former wife. This would have to be done subtly and unobtrusively, but she could end by being a force in his life, throwing light into dark shadows and helping him to achieve something really significant. They had a rapport which was unique, even though he was only just beginning to realise it. Although it seemed far-fetched at present, she would make an ideal business partner for him. For an architect to be truly successful he needed to gain the trust and confidence of influential and wealthy people. It had to be said that Robert was lacking in that respect, but she would make up for it. Yes, it would be an ideal arrangement.

Too often, apart from Roland, men had come and gone without trace. Whenever she believed she was in the midst of a grand affair of passion it suddenly petered out. It was difficult to determine why, because she cooked excellent meals, was a conscientious housekeeper and knew what to do in bed. If she chose the wrong men, it was because she was unable to resist talent, wherever she found it. She recognised her weakness, which stemmed from her lack of belief in her own ability. As a second best, she would be involved in others' talent. (There was substantial historical precedent for this female role, as she well knew.) No one apart from her could appreciate the latent genius that Robert as yet showed only sporadically. She would spur him on and give him a goal; she would be inspiration, critic and guru. He needed her, though he was still resisting the idea.

One day, Mary thought, she might create a little something of her own, but she doubted if anyone would think it significant. 'Now I've finished washing up, I'll make some more coffee and we'll talk,' she said to Beatrice, who was sitting on the floor in the living-room. She had found Robert's store of wine and was opening another bottle. The confrontation would follow its course, Mary surmised, then Beatrice would go home. Next morning there would be a phone call, a contrite message poured out into the answerphone tape. She was beginning to get the measure of this telephone-dependent neurosis.

'Are you living in this house all the time? I think I have a right to know.'

Mary smiled at the directness of Beatrice's question. There was just a trace of an Irish accent, which she found quite attractive. 'I stay over occasionally,' she replied. 'It was Robert's suggestion. Because there's so much to do, I sleep in the basement when it's too late to drive home.'

'Do you expect me to believe that it's just a convenient arrangement? Robert is an extremely attractive man . . .'

'I know women must find him so, but he doesn't appeal to me. Physically, that is. He's not my type at all. I am aware that people often misinterpret what I do, it's understandable. I happen to admire Robert but . . .' Mary paused, as though reluctant to talk further, but then she took a deep breath. 'When you've had the most amazing relationship with your husband, you never think for a moment of repeating it. My husband was perfect for me and I know I won't find another.'

'What happened to him, then?'

'He died, tragically young.'

Beatrice stared at the table for a minute. She felt ashamed that Mary was being so reasonable and she herself so hostile, making unfounded assumptions. It wasn't often that someone made her feel in the wrong but Mary had succeeded. 'I'm sorry, I'm really sorry,' she said quietly. 'But I am concerned for Robert and Alice. What are you going to do when Alice gets back?' She looked up expectantly at Mary.

'By the time she returns I'll have finished Robert's work. Then I'll be leaving the country to start doing my own research. I'm planning to write a book.'

Hearing voices in the living-room, Robert came out of his studio and decided to intervene. By now, he hoped Mary had calmed down Beatrice. She was more skilled than he was at saying the right thing. 'Bea, isn't it time you went home now?' he said as he entered. 'We're both exhausted.'

'Robert, I need to talk to you alone, just for a moment.'

'I'll say good-night, then. I'll do the rest of the clearing up tomorrow,' said Mary, leaving the room.

Beatrice shut the door firmly behind her and faced Robert. 'Are you and Mary having a scene? Be honest with me, Robert.'

'We're not, Bea. And we haven't.'

'How do I know?'

'Look around you. Has anything changed? Could you always tell when two people are having an affair? "They're doing it, I know they are," you used to say. Why should I need somebody else? I have Alice. She's everything I want.'

'Are you sure?'

'Absolutely. In any case, Mary hardly presents much of a temptation.'

'Really? She's got a good figure.'

'I suppose so. I hadn't really noticed,' said Robert with a yawn.

'I'm going to go now,' said Beatrice. 'But I don't suppose David will be back.'

'I'll walk you home.'

When Robert returned he was surprised to find that Mary was still cleaning up in the kitchen, washing down the floor on her hands and knees. 'There's no need to do that. You've done too much as it is,' he said. 'I'll finish it.' He pulled her to her feet and untied her apron.

'What a day!' she said, stroking his forehead. 'You must be exhausted. Isn't it time to go to bed, Robert?'

Simon had been depressed recently but he was reluctant to search too deeply for the cause. (The last time he had thought deeply, in the emotional sense, was after Alice confessed she had fallen in love with Robert. He never came to a definitive conclusion about where he had gone wrong.)

It always made him feel uncomfortable when he had to give instructions to someone about behaviour, since his own was frequently less than impeccable. However, he felt he had been right in telling Genevieve that they would see less of one another, that he wasn't ready for anything serious and maybe never would be. And she had made the mistake of assuming that marriage was round the corner, constantly inviting him to stay at her parents' pub. Although he refused every time, it made him feel anxious. It wasn't that he didn't appreciate her tidying up a bit, or sewing on the occasional button, or even staying the odd night, but what she failed to understand was that he positively enjoyed being a bachelor. He just didn't want her there all the time. Why couldn't she grasp that? Always trying to organise things, to make plans, to have people round. And he didn't really like her friends although he tried to be amiable. On the other hand, he did miss female company.

When he called Beatrice – really to ask if she had heard from Alice – she sounded pleased to hear from him. It was a shame they had stopped going to the club, but it wasn't the same without Robert and Alice. Then she asked about Genevieve and he told her what had happened in a sentence, which didn't satisfy her. Women often said in half an hour what he could say in a minute, which was puzzling.

'She wasn't right for you, Simon,' was the conclusion Beatrice reached after a thorough investigation lasting at least thirty-five minutes. Then she compared his troubles with her own – another feminine characteristic he'd observed. David was being unusually difficult, she said, but that was to be expected. At present, none of their star signs looked good. They were going through a turbulent period of planetary activity, which gave rise to unavoidable domestic conflict.

Simon was about to invent an excuse for putting down the phone when Beatrice suddenly changed the subject and asked if he might like to taste some olive oils she had to report on for a catering magazine. He found himself looking forward to it. He liked being asked his opinion and besides, away from Robert, Beatrice was good company even if she did talk non-stop. She accepted his invitation to come to his place for the tasting. He would slip in a few oil samples of his own which gave him an excuse to spend a couple of hours in his favourite food emporium in the King's Road.

'You haven't given a dinner party for weeks,' Beatrice complained as soon as she arrived, casting her eye round the fast-disappearing evidence of Robert's superb design. The carefully selected modern pieces had long gone. And the English traditional look that succeeded it had now moved east to somewhere like Afghanistan, with rough-hewn rustic objects and gaudy rugs more suited to a tribesman's tent than a made-over terrace house in Shepherd's Bush.

'Been busy.' Simon thrust a dish of olive oil under Beatrice's nose. 'What do you think?'

Dipping a morsel of dry bread into the oil, Beatrice sniffed it. 'Tuscan.'

'French.'

'Yes, on second thoughts, it would seem to be French. First pressing.'

'Naturally.'

Beatrice dipped into a few more of the tiny dishes before her. 'That one's definitely the best,' she said.

Simon decided to agree. 'Showing your customary discernment, Bea.' As he nibbled at a piece of ciabatta, he said, 'Have you spoken to Alice, by any chance? She wouldn't give me her number before she left. Where exactly has she gone? Some health club in the country, it sounded like. It's a mystery to me. Why go to a health club when she uses the Lansdale anyway?'

Knowing that Alice would be furious if anyone thought she had gone to lose weight, Beatrice had to think quickly. 'Premarital nerves, Simon. You know how it is? When you have everything you want, then start doubting that you know what you want?'

'Can't say I do,' said Simon.

'Women are much more subtle than men,' Beatrice offered in explanation. 'They live out their emotions.'

She looked carefully at Simon, as though weighing up several different conversations she could have had, important ones like diving into an investigation of female subtlety and male insensitivity, or less important ones, like comparing recipes featuring olive oil. Simon diverted her by pushing a few more bottles of the latter in her direction, so that she could continue her evaluation of the relative merits of Tuscan, Spanish, Greek and French. When they had reached agreement over the scoring and Simon had lent her a pile of cookery books, she settled herself on a traditional button-backed chesterfield, which Simon was attempting to disguise

169

by draping it with kelims. 'Simon, I just happened to drop in on Robert one evening. I hadn't seen him for a while. Well, we don't go to the club much any more and . . .'

'And what, Bea?' He smiled at her attempt to disguise the frequency of her visits.

Beatrice began cautiously, in case Simon dismissed what she was about to say. 'I can't be absolutely sure, but I suspect that Mary Bartlett has moved into Robert's house, supposedly acting as his secretary. Has he said anything to you?'

'Robert did mention it, told me she was catching up on the clerical backlog, coming round for the odd day. Good thing, if you ask me.'

'Mary has plans, I can sense it,' said Beatrice, forgetting her earlier resolution.

'What do you mean, plans?' Simon awaited yet another implausible interpretation of events.

'Plans for moving in. I can always tell, I can't help seeing beneath the surface. In a way it's a curse, not a gift, because once you know something it's so hard to stand back and do nothing about it. That's why mediums and astrologers have such a difficult life.'

'I'd never thought of that!' replied Simon, relieved that he had never been cursed in that respect.

'Can I tell you about it?' said Beatrice, restraining herself once more.

'Go ahead, Bea. I promise I won't interrupt you.'

The way Simon reacted, having heard Beatrice's account of the 'business' dinner and finding Mary clearly ensconced at a ridiculously late hour, was first to wonder why he hadn't been invited or even asked to cook. He wasn't exactly suspicious, but he did wonder. Was Robert trying to keep him at bay? Was it really the case that he was far too busy these days to meet at the club, or was he hiding something? Then he resisted the thought. There would be some perfectly rational explanation, though you could say his behaviour was a little tactless under the circumstances. 'When's Alice coming back?'

'Tomorrow if she's any sense. I'll call her when I get home.'

'There's no need to rush things. Don't make her panic, Bea.'

'I'll only talk to Alice about Mary if I think it's necessary. If I tell her that Robert is missing her desperately, can't work properly and so on, that'll probably be enough. Then I'll make sure Mary leaves.'

'Isn't this rather an extreme measure? After all, you've no proof of anything.'

'Who needs proof?'

'Well . . .' Simon stopped himself. This was not the moment to stress the importance of verification and he allowed Beatrice to continue.

'If I didn't realise what was going on, I'd feel quite sorry for Mary Bartlett. She's desperate. Behind that prim little face there's a determined woman who'll stop at nothing to get her way.'

'Sounds a touch over-dramatic to me. Which Hollywood movie was that? Well, do whatever you think's best.'

Simon piled up the olive oil marking sheets, and walked off to the kitchen to transfer the findings onto disk and print out a copy for Beatrice. The computer in his kitchen was surrounded by empty bags and food packets, but he cleared a space amid the crumbs and attacked the keyboard.

'Maybe I should send Mary along to you?' said Beatrice, smiling mischievously as she surveyed the disarray before her. 'She could sort out your kitchen.'

'No one touches my kitchen, not even my cleaning lady.'

Now that he had momentarily overcome his hurt, Simon allowed himself a few unfriendly thoughts.

171

Could it be that Robert was chafing against imminent coupledom? If Mary was digging in, perhaps he was using her as a way of avoiding . . . And then, perhaps in time Alice would realise that . . . It would be as it was . . . nothing need change . . . only slightly . . . Robert was happy on his own, it wasn't as though . . . lots of men preferred to have it that way . . . Alice would be heart-broken and he didn't want that. It didn't bear further contemplation. That way neurosis lay. Exit. Closedown Alicefile.

When Simon was faced with an unresolvable conflict he either cooked dinner, pitted his wits against the constructed master of computer chess, raked in obscure information from the Internet about gardening, third world economics, golf, genuine Afghani furniture sources or whatever interest he had on the go – or sent gobbets of information to his e-mail buddies. However, these diverting activities couldn't stop him from thinking about Alice. He often wondered about what would have happened if he had employed a woman architect instead of Robert to redesign his house.

Well past midnight, Simon was still seated in front of his computer, testing the alertness of his reactions by firing rocket launchers in a subterranean tunnel. Ruefully he admitted to himself that, once past the age of eighteen, one's speed of response and mental agility fell back in a disappointing curve. He wondered if there was a correlation between the falling off in the male sexual drive (hormonal) and the decrease in brainpower (neurological), since both of these functions appeared to have miniaturised into a sleeping icon for the time being.

Then he stopped wondering, abandoned the computer screen and settled in the kitchen. Failing to find his usual comfort in hot tea and a thick peanut butter sandwich, he started rearranging the saucepans, putting them in order of size along the hooks, for no particular reason. He repeatedly asked himself: should he or shouldn't he? A nagging desire to find out exactly what was happening between Robert and Mary kept him awake all night, even though he told himself over and over that it was none of his business. Not strictly. On the other hand, if he could find an excuse to drop in early in the morning, that meant he might be able to . . . Yes, he would. Simon went upstairs, jumped into bed, removed only his shoes and managed a few hours' sleep.

When Simon arrived at Robert's house, it was Mary who greeted him with a beaming smile. 'How lovely to see you, Simon. We see you so rarely nowadays.'

He winced at the 'we' and stood awkwardly by the door. 'I've brought something for Robert. Didn't know if he was up and about, he works late sometimes.'

'I know,' Mary said, smiling again.

Simon was staring without realising why, but then it registered. Mary was wearing the black satin embroidered kimono that he and Alice had chosen for Robert's birthday. He remembered Robert saying it made him feel like Ronald Colman, all it needed was the moustache. It was far too large for her, even though she had pulled the belt in tightly.

'We're just about to have breakfast, do come in.'

When he saw Robert in polka-dot black silk pyjamas sitting at the table in the living-room, the table covered in a white linen cloth (a white linen cloth? on that table?), slivers of toast in a silver toast rack (a toast rack?), curled butter in a tiny china dish, silver knives and forks, two floral china plates he didn't recognise and a copy of *Le Monde* lying open beside plate number two, Simon completely forgot the excuse for his presence and loitered by the window, deprived of speech.

'Fancy some breakfast? Mary's cooking bacon and

eggs.' This was Robert trying to pretend that everything was normal.

'No thanks, not at the moment,' Simon stuttered.

'Do you like my china?' said Mary in a morning-fresh, cheery voice, as she bore down with a pot of steaming coffee. 'I thought Robert might appreciate a little old-fashioned elegance once in a while. I was quite surprised when he didn't object.' Mary gave Robert an affectionate glance, which went through Simon like a cheese-cutting wire.

'So what brings you here? We haven't seen you for ages. Still, no doubt you're horrendously busy, as we all are.'

'Yes, rather busy.' Simon suddenly remembered his excuse, which was stuffed in his pocket. 'Robert, I thought you might like to see this. Rather a good article on the New Dynamism, found it in an American architecture magazine. You know me, I knew if I didn't drop it in to you, you wouldn't get it. I'd never use snailmail.'

'Thanks a lot, Simon.' Robert took it from him. 'Looks good, you're right.'

'How's the big project coming along, Robert?'

It was Mary who replied. 'Marvellously. Everyone's absolutely over the moon with Robert's designs. Are you sure you won't have bacon and scrambled eggs?'

'No thanks. I never eat breakfast nowadays,' he lied.

'I'll make some more coffee, anyway,' she said, well on her way to the kitchen.

Simon came over and sat down next to Robert. 'Hope you don't mind me asking, but is Mary living here now? I'm rather confused.'

'Her idea,' replied Robert with a smile. 'As I told you, she's been giving me some secretarial help. Then she asked if she could do some of her own work here, as she's terribly cramped in her flat. The obvious place for her to be was the basement, so she's down there at the moment. She felt very bad about not paying me rent, so she suggested working for me free of charge. It really is working out very well.'

'Is that wise?' said Simon. 'Have you told Alice?'

'Alice knows, of course. She thinks the arrangement is fine.'

'What about the bed bit?'

'What bed bit? What are you talking about?'

'Come on, Robert. A girl living here? Even if she is being your secretary. Am I meant to think nothing's happening?'

'Mary sleeps downstairs when she's working late, that's all. I put a bed in the basement, just a temporary arrangement till Alice gets back.'

'Are you saying it's all perfectly innocent, whatever that means?'

'Look, Simon. Mary's not unattractive, I admit. But that has nothing to do with it, I promise you. She's amazingly helpful. And fantastic with clients. She really understands people with money, knows exactly how they think. Unlike me. It's been marvellous to have her around, to have someone who appreciates what I'm doing. Try finding a secretary who could do that!'

'Who are you talking about? Your secretary or your mistress?'

'Simon, this isn't like you. I honestly don't know why you're getting so upset. Don't tell me Beatrice has been making trouble again? Has she contacted you, by any chance?'

Simon flushed slightly and hoped that Robert hadn't noticed. Probably not, since that was one advantage of having a ruddy complexion. 'Er, not recently.'

'Naturally Mary will leave immediately when Alice comes back. By that time she should have sorted herself out with somewhere.'

'And if she hasn't?'

'Oh, she'll find a place, she's had offers of rooms

from friends, but they're all rather far out from central London. Mary likes being at the hub of things, as I do.'

Buttoning up his jacket, Simon prepared to leave. 'I still think you're crazy. Do you expect Alice to come back as though nothing has happened?'

'Nothing has happened. Nothing at all,' Robert insisted.

'Somehow I can't believe that,' said Simon. 'Girls don't go around in dressing-gowns if nothing has happened.'

'I have to say, Simon, you can be naïve, sometimes. All right, I'll tell you. We have an affectionate relationship and we once spent a few hours in bed together when we'd been working all night. We both fell asleep instantly. That's all there is to it.' Robert broke into a smile. 'I'm working so hard I doubt I could manage it anyhow.'

'Same here,' said Simon, trying to sound light-hearted. 'Better get moving. Meeting at half-nine.'

After Robert had accompanied Simon to the front door he tapped him jocularly on the stomach. 'Why don't you come to the club next week? You haven't been for a while. Time for a tone?'

'I'll see.'

Simon went to his Covent Garden office, had four meetings, sent a few faxes, fiddled with a draft consultative document, decided he'd leave the rest of the tasks lined up on his DO TODAY file, left early and took a taxi home. He judged the confusion of his mind by the fact that Beatrice called to say she had no one to baby-sit and would be arriving at his house with Drusilla and Sasha, and would he mind cooking Munchy Monsters with oven chips because that's what they liked? While the children were ruining their taste-buds for life in the kitchen, they could sit upstairs and have a proper talk.

Simon's thought was: if Robert went in for being

unfaithful and had made a habit of it in the past, Beatrice was bound to tell him. Without him having to ask directly. Would she? Not that he really imagined Robert would be. Or could he? They'd never got round to talking about it. No need. Was he getting cold feet about marriage? Funny chap, complicated. Never could make him out. Not on that score. Could know someone for years and still not.

While his mind was racing, he typed a row of words across his screen.

AliceAliceAliceAliceAliceAliceAliceAliceAliceAlice AliceAlice . . .

Ten

• • •

Alice smoothed Aloe Vera bubbles over her body as she tried to dispel the grumpiness that threatened to escalate into a raging headache. It reminded her of school, having to clean off a grey band of dirt from around the bath rim before taking your clothes off. Kirsty said she still had to work on creating a positive karma and she was wondering whether it would manifest itself as ectoplasm so that she could see it in the mirror. The mirror was smudged and cracked, which made it unlikely. If only she could be lying in her bath at home.

Alice stretched out her legs to their full extent. Her thighs had definitely shrunk to a more reasonable proportion and when she had pinched the roll of fat round her waist there was less than she remembered. The steam had heated up the bathroom and she poured in some more of the large bottle of bath essence she had purchased in a rash moment from the Beauty Store. She ignored the rattling of the door handle and took a selfish delight in prolonging her bath. Finally, she stepped onto the disintegrating rubber bath mat and dried herself on a small towel embroidered with the words: I LOVE MYSELF. The pleasure of a long soak was dissipated as soon as Alice walked down the dingy, clammy corridor to the Cowslip Room.

On more than one occasion she had been on the point of packing her bag, but there were several things which held her back. First, Dr Grossman had recognised the difficulties she was having with the somewhat unconventional therapy methods practised in the clinic. Most women found them enormously helpful, not to say inspiring, but she could see that Alice was not the ideal candidate. Englishwomen, she observed, often resisted eclectic approaches to overcoming problems, preferring medical doctors to counsellors and therapists, scientific certainties to radical and uncertain philosophies. Sympathising with Alice's stance – and admitting that validation from the scientific community was her ultimate aim – Dr Grossman agreed to give her extra sessions without payment and a thirty per cent reduction on beauty treatment. However, she did suggest that she co-operated with the regime. She might even find that she derived some unexpected benefits from it.

It was only when she poured out a list of complaints to Mary that Alice realised she might have underestimated the benefits.

Right from the beginning, Mary listened patiently with an open mind. 'Yes, yes. It is sad that your particular group appears to be – let's be honest – rather tedious. You've just struck unlucky, Alice. One can never guarantee who's going to attend. But you haven't mentioned how much weight you've lost?'

'Oh, I'm losing weight all right. Up till now, about four and a half kilos.'

'That's brilliant, Alice. I'm so pleased. Aren't you thrilled?'

'I suppose so. But I'd lose weight in prison, too.'

Mary laughed. 'Prison food is very high-calorie stodge, the truth is exactly the reverse.'

'Not prison, then. But at least there I wouldn't have to go to rebirth classes. Today we had to pretend to be a butterfly coming out of a chrysalis. We were all given sacks and had to wiggle out of them. One of the girls got stuck. It was really funny, but I didn't dare laugh. And we do a lot of things like cleaning and washing up and getting in wood, which isn't so funny. Oh, yes, and we have to smile a lot. Apparently you need to do that in order to encourage the right karma. My mouth aches.'

After a pause, Mary said, 'It sounds quite fun to me. A new experience, anyway. Don't you like doing unpredictable things sometimes? Surprising people? I know I do.'

'I hadn't thought of it like that,' said Alice.

'Anyway, I do hope you're not disappointed in Dr Grossman. Are you still having individual sessions?'

'Oh, yes. We have great conversations, about all kinds of things. She said now I've proved I can lose weight, I shouldn't be frightened if my weight goes up and down. And she said I'm lucky because I respond to interpretation, which many women don't, apparently. I don't always agree, but she says that's all right, too.'

'So you've got a couple of weeks to go. I'm sure when you look back, you'll think it's all been worth it.'

'I don't know yet. I do worry about the money.'

'Why don't you bring that up with Dr Grossman? You know it's only a fear and you can always borrow from me.'

'That's really kind.'

After Mary's reassurance, Alice felt better enough to attend the Let It All Hang Out workshop that she had intended to miss. She listened to the frenzied outpourings, the hatred directed at the size eight ones, the slim-hipped ones, the ones who gorged on cream cakes and treacle pudding without so much as a tiny fat-wrinkle, the ones who wore bikinis without a qualm, the ones who drew admiring gazes from desirable men. When it came to her turn to voice her anger Alice was unable to muster the required degree of emotion.

Kirsty had to comment, 'Now, Alice. You're not coming to terms with your Angry Self. We want to hear how you honestly feel. We want you to lay your negativity on all of us. We can take it, can't we?'

'Yes!' came the chorus.

Seeing all those beaming faces turned towards her, Alice was overcome with irritation. 'Christ!' she yelled. 'Why the hell get angry about that? What good can that do? It isn't going to change anything. Why not just start eating less?'

Kirsty came across the room and gazed into Alice's eyes as she clasped each of her hands. 'Alice, that was truly wonderful,' she said. 'At last you have given voice to your Angry Self. This is the moment we'd all been waiting for. I'm so proud of you.'

The exercise classes were quite enjoyable, Alice found, since there was no need to talk and the twanging Indian music was not unpleasant. Sarita, the Indian exercise guru, intoned the instructions with an attractive lilt: *Stretch to the sky, stretch to the clouds, stretch to the sun, fall slowly to the earth; stretch to the sky, stretch to the clouds, stretch to the sun* ... Alice could feel each muscle doing its work, flexing with enjoyment. Standing up proud, shoulders relaxed, back straight, arms like folded wings, she even managed a suitably vacuous smile. Occasionally, catching sight of herself in the mirror, she was not displeased. I'm not bad, she thought. Not bad at all. Not a perfect figure, but nothing to complain about. Good complexion. Shiny hair.

The time began to pass more quickly. Alice would sometimes take herself down to the Beauty Store to experiment with pots and jars. Dr Grossman told everyone that frivolity was important and that they should all appreciate the role of adornment in women's lives. Anyone could take advantage of the extras offered by the clinic and pleasure therapy was freely available (price-list available on request) but not obligatory. Once Dr Grossman had told her that she was coming to terms with her anal impulses (fear of letting go, fear of losing money, fear of spending money), Alice rashly booked herself in for aromatherapy appointments, Tai Chi, massage, deep facial cleansing, hair revitalisation programme, decarcinogenised sunbed treatments and aquaerobics.

Mary was delighted that she was indulging herself and sounded envious. When she had the time, she said, she would book into the clinic herself. But at the moment she had her hands full, what with finishing off research for the book and trying to sort out Robert's books and files. To make things easier, she had brought some of her own files along and was working in the basement. She even slept over if she had been working late and she hoped Alice didn't mind. Of course she didn't mind! Her account of the dinner party made Alice admire her all the more. At last, someone who could stand up to Beatrice. Robert often let her get away with murder, especially when he was tired. Mary said Robert was fine, not too exhausted, just working very hard. She only saw him for the odd cup of coffee, and when she could be bothered she made a stew and left it in the oven for him. And very occasionally she ironed a shirt, because he hadn't time to do it himself. And he did need to look smart for meetings. You're doing enough already, Alice told her. You don't need to spoil him.

When Beatrice called her unexpectedly, Alice's Angry Self made another unscheduled appearance. She had rung while Alice was in deep relaxation following holistic aromatherapy and was lying on her bed in no mood to be interrupted.

'Bea, I can't talk for long. It's not a good moment,' Alice began.

But Beatrice was disinclined to stop her flow. 'I couldn't ring earlier. We're going out to dinner and I've got to talk to you.' As she listened to Beatrice, Alice was perplexed. Robert wasn't ill, merely missing her. And he was working far too hard. If he went on as he was doing he was sure to get ill. Beatrice thought it would be a good idea if she cut short her stay and came home early.

'Robert's never ill. And if he were missing me so much, he would have rung. I left him my number for an emergency. I don't believe you.'

'It happens to be true. But you know Robert, how proud he is, he'll never admit to his feelings, especially when they're dependent on somebody else. He'd hardly call you up and say. "Darling Alice, please please come home." But I know that's how he's feeling.'

'It's not the end of the world if he misses me. I'm not going to come running because he's a bit down, it won't be the first time,' said Alice tetchily.

'He's always vulnerable when he's working so hard,' added Beatrice. 'The slightest thing upsets him. And you've been away for days.'

'Don't be ridiculous,' said Alice.

'I thought you'd have been pleased to know what's going on.' There was a short silence before Beatrice continued, 'Are you having a good time at the clinic?'

'Quite.'

'You're disappointed, I can tell.'

'I'm losing weight, which I suppose was the reason I came.'

'Alice, do tell me. What's wrong?'

'Dr Grossman has been a great help. But the rest . . .

well, I'm making the best of it. It's like a cheap hotel for commercial travellers. Vegetarian ones. And there aren't any staff except secretaries.'

'It can't be that bad. Who looks after the place?'

'We do. We do everything except the shopping and the secretarial work, and they have a Portuguese lady to do that. It's meant to help the bonding process. I'm getting very good at making beds and peeling potatoes.'

Beatrice gave an incredulous laugh. 'I can't believe it. But surely, if it's as bad as you say you can tell them you've got to get back. Or invent some silly excuse?'

'It's not possible, Bea.'

'Why on earth not?' Alice was silent, too embarassed to tell her. 'For God's sake, how much did you pay for all this?'

'Quite a lot,' Alice said. Everyone around her was used to money flowing in a fairly continuous stream. A few thousand pounds could be spent on an unsuccessful holiday and neither Beatrice nor Simon would regard it as more than a bad choice. 'It's going to be at least four thousand pounds, I imagine.'

There was a horrified shriek from Beatrice. 'That's a huge amount. How can you afford that? You must leave immediately and ask for some money back. If I'd known you were so serious about going on a diet I'd have helped you. You know I would.'

'I can't, Bea. You have to stay the full time and once you've paid the deposit that's it. I know Mary meant well when she recommended this place, but she never thinks about cost. I should have known, having rich parents like she has. And a husband who must have left her masses.'

'But this sounds like an awful con to me. Mary must have realised what it's like. Who knows? She might be getting something out of it. Didn't you say she was a friend of that Doctor, whatever her name is?'

'I'm sure that isn't true,' Alice objected. 'She would have told me. Anyway, friends don't do that.'

Beatrice let her comment pass. There was little point in conveying her suspicion of Mary. 'Why doesn't anyone object? Here I was, thinking you were swimming in luxury.'

'Oh, I do loads of swimming,' said Alice in a vain attempt to make light of her situation. 'And I'm having lots of time to think about things. It's not all a waste of time. So I'll go along with it,' she added defiantly.

'Oh, Alice. You are being stubborn.' Beatrice sighed. 'I wish you'd let me help. I'm very good at sorting things out. I bet I could get your money back for you. Will you give me a chance? I could come up at the end of the week . . .'

'Thanks for the offer, but no.'

In the fourth week a special day was scheduled entitled: Seeking out Nature's Path. It would start as a hike (a card on the notice board advised lightweight mountain boots, which could be purchased in the boutique, and a thermal cagoule, also available) with a special midday Communing session. Kirsty refused to explain further, because she wanted them all to have a special revelation. On this day, they would be initiated into holy secrets.

There was a peculiar exhilaration about walking for miles and miles. After a while a slight breathlessness and gentle fatigue made Alice light-headed. She was acutely aware of the crackling sound of last year's acorns and fircones embedded in the woodland paths, the shrieks of magpies lurching from tree to tree, the breeze drying the skin, the scurry of rabbits hastening for cover, the tiny finches bouncing onto thread-thin twigs.

On arriving at a bird sanctuary in the middle of a wood, the group paused to put down their backpacks and bags. Although no one told them to sit on the ground in silence, they intuitively did so. Kirsty crossed her legs and looked up through the trees at the sullen sky where a small gap would get wider, to allow the fair-weather clouds to show their faces. 'Let us commune together and say our mantra,' she said eventually. They knew she would tell them when this special session was ended and they could open the pre-prepared lunches still untouched in their lightweight containers.

Beatrice refused to take no for an answer even though the receptionist's command of English demanded a little indulgence. 'I know she's here,' she exploded. 'Alice is a friend of mine and I have to see her most urgently. Do you think I'd have trekked all the way down here if it wasn't important?'

'Escuse me?'

'*Espagnol, Français* or *Italiano*?' Beatrice asked, exasperated beyond belief. It clearly wasn't *Deutsch*.

'*Portuges.*'

'Damn.'

Beatrice wrote Alice's name on a scrap of paper. 'Where is?' she said forcefully.

Whereupon the burgeoning jet-haired woman of uncertain age unfolded a map in front of Beatrice and pointed. '*Chia*. Dis place.' She then prodded Beatrice, pointed to a board marked DESTINATIONS and ran her finger down it until she reached '*Fuschia Group. Nature Communing Session. Leader Kirsty*'. '*Chia*. Dis one.'

Snatching the map from her, Beatrice rushed out of the clinic and jumped into her car. Luckily the large-scale map showed a wood, which was distinguished by a bird sanctuary. It couldn't be far. After asking a few locals and venturing into a pub, Beatrice parked her car by an English Heritage air-raid shelter from the second world war, pulled on an ancient pair of trainers and set off down a path marked: 'Caution: hatchery. Please progress in silence.'

Thinking about it afterwards, Alice never would have imagined that she could have spent an afternoon hugging the enormously girthed trunk of an ancient oak tree but as everyone else was nearby, doing the same to similarly broad trunks, it seemed churlish to refuse to join in. She wondered what her father and brothers would have thought had they seen her, but she would have replied that she was seeking inspiration from nature. Didn't Robert say that many of the best architects examined natural forms to create their buildings?

They were all leaning against Alice's oak, sucking through straws at cartons of Cloudesley Organics apple juice and salivating at the thought of sprouted grain sandwiches with tofu and marinated chick-pea salad, when the rapid crunching of undergrowth heralded a mammalian tread.

'Bea — what on earth?'

'Oh, Alice, thank God I've found you.'

Alice scrambled to her feet. 'Has something happened to Robert?'

'No and yes. Nothing terminal. Let's go and sit in the car. I'm parked at the edge of the wood.'

There were a few curious glances, but no one commented as she was about to leave with this strange creature from the outer world, except Kirsty. 'What a shame. Today of all days,' was all she said, looking sorrowfully at Alice.

Beatrice turned on the heater full blast in her BMW and scrutinised Alice. 'You've lost tons of weight. Well done.'

'Has anything happened to Robert?'

'Don't get alarmed. He's quite all right, getting on

fine. But I had to tell you that Mary has moved in and is intending to stay. That's why I thought you should come back immediately. I couldn't tell you when I phoned and I hoped she'd have gone by now. But she hasn't.'

'Why are you getting in such a state, Bea? I know Mary's been working in Robert's house, we've been in touch all the time. Robert needed someone to look after him, with all that pressure. It seemed a good arrangement for all of us.'

Beatrice clasped her forehead with both hands, summoning all the force at her command. 'Alice, you've got to see what she's doing. Mary is trying to take Robert away from you, it's obvious to everyone.'

'How can she possibly take Robert away? You're talking nonsense, you really are.'

'I wish I could make you believe me. But whenever I go round she's there. And she gives the impression that she intends to stay.'

'That's how you see it. But that's the last thing Mary would do. She never stays in England long in any case. She'll be off soon.'

'She won't, Alice. I know she won't. I can tell.'

'Why don't you be honest? You're loading the anger onto Mary that you feel against me. You've never been able to express what you felt about me marrying Robert. I'd rather you did. You feel he's yours, you still feel he's yours. And off he goes, marrying me. You've every right to be furious. And jealous. Why don't you yell at me and express your hostility? It's far better to do that than to create some ridiculous scenario involving someone Robert hasn't the faintest interest in. Mary cares about me and she cares about Robert. What's so strange about that? Why are you getting so worked up?'

It was impossible for Beatrice to take her eyes off

Alice. She seemed so calm, so self-assured, her face shining with a rosy glow. 'Do listen, Alice. Mary is sharing Robert's bed, I'm sure of it.'

'Sharing a bed doesn't mean you're having sex. There are other ways of relating, Bea.' Alice shifted away from Beatrice and drew a squiggle on the misted car window. 'There's no way on earth that Robert would sleep with Mary. Can I be honest with you?'

Beatrice sounded affronted. 'I'd expect you to be, Alice. We've always been open with one another. Or don't you consider us as friends any more?'

'I do and I know we are. But there have been all those times when you've been so wrong, not knowingly wrong. Just wrong. And you're wrong about Mary. She's always acted as though she had my interests at heart, she thinks about other people, Bea. She's really concerned, like a good mother.'

'Mary isn't the slightest bit motherly. What are you talking about?'

'We all have preconceptions of what mothers should be. That's why we make mistakes.'

'For Christ's sake, Alice! What has Dr Grossman been saying to you? You never used to talk like this. You're living in some weird corner of your imagination, as though you're a moon subject – and you're not. Please listen, Alice. How can I convince you? Come home now, see for yourself.'

'Robert isn't like that.'

'You know nothing about Robert,' Beatrice burst out. 'You're going to get hurt.'

'Your past with Robert has nothing to do with me. You knew a different Robert. You've invented someone I don't have a clue about.'

'More's the pity,' shouted Beatrice. 'Can't you see I'm trying to protect you? But you refuse to listen. You're falling straight into a ditch.'

'Listen, Bea. You have to confront your possessiveness,

your jealousy and your manipulation. If you still love Robert, for God's sake tell me. I won't hate you.'

With a sigh, Beatrice started up the engine. 'Will you come home tomorrow?' she asked as gently as she could.

'Why? It's not necessary. Anyway, I've got my session with Dorothea tomorrow,' said Alice. 'I'll walk over to the others. You go back to London. I'm staying. I told you I would, remember? I know you want to help, but everything's fine. Really it is.'

Beatrice revved the engine, swore and turned towards the south. When the planets were in such violent conjunction she knew better than to confront them with a paltry human will.

Dr Grossman happened to be in the General Office when a long fax came through, which jammed up the machine for far too long. At first she thought it was yet another of those clients who were so struck by her life-changing course that they sent off daily accounts of their everyday lives in order to keep spiritual continuity. Occasionally, she received a stream of abuse, but that was to be expected, as some clients were mildly psychotic. (She would shortly refer to them as 'patients', although her doctorate was in economics. Clients preferred to think of her as 'Doctor', as it lent a beneficial medical aura to the clinic.) The fax was addressed to Alice. She handed it back to Juanita.

Having digested the fax in her bedroom, reading it quickly once and slowly several more times, Alice immediately phoned reception and took herself off the list for the extra workshop: *Being Faithful to Myself – Jealousy and Competitiveness*. Before that, she had allowed herself to cry. The very banality of Simon's message, its slightly formal prose which ended in the symbol they used to have for hugs and kisses ***{}{}{}***caused a lump to rise in her throat.

190

(1)   He said sorry about grizzly handwriting but all three computers have gone down, unbelievable. Roll on the day they had enough brain to mend themselves. Pen feels like a prosthetic, forgotten how to use.

(2)   He said it was the last thing he ever expected to do, to write like this about the man she loved and was going to marry. But he felt it was right, in this case, that he should. She should realise he was merely expressing his own clumsy thoughts on the matter. Which were: a) he didn't believe it was very sensible to have Mary setting up her office in the basement of Robert's house, or b) living there full time in the way in which she was, not going back home at nights, which normal secretaries did.

(3)   He said obviously there was nothing between Robert and Mary but, old-fashioned and obtuse as he was, he did think it was extremely bad timing. He was sure Robert wasn't being unfaithful. He apologised, saying he was bad at writing letters, shame they didn't have e-mail. He hoped Alice would understand and come back quickly so they could get things back to normal.

PS Robert doesn't know I'm writing this neither does Beatrice. This is between us.

PPS When you come back, will you allow me to cook dinner for you? Promise I'll only use cream once. ***{}{}{}***

Following Simon's fax, Alice's reaction was passed on to Dr Grossman by Kirsty. She was worried about Alice, as she had appeared to be drawing back from the rest of the group. She was even talking of quitting the clinic, though she refused to say why. On hearing this, Dr Grossman thought it highly desirable, not to say essential, for Alice to have some individual therapy sessions. For Alice to leave at this juncture would totally negate the marvellous progress she had made.

Persuaded by the offer of a free session, Alice lay down on the couch in Dr Grossman's luxuriously furnished consulting room in the Annexe. Staring up at the slowly gyrating sun, moon and stars mobile hanging from the ceiling, Alice voiced her feelings by streaming out her consciousness and allowing each topic to link itself rather than being guided by the superego, as she had been taught. When she had finished, she was allowed to sit up on the couch facing Dr Grossman (she was just beginning to call her Dorothea) to receive her Summation.

'Alice, dear. You have an unresolved conflict about your role in the world and your role with your partner. You have projected Robert as that part of yourself which you admire, yet fear. Instead of standing alone, which you will be able to do after further sessions at the clinic, you have internalised the male side, namely Robert, as being an integral part of your animus. But in reality this has nothing to do with your acceptance of yourself as a woman. Whether Robert has sexual intercourse with another, with one woman or ten, is irrelevant. What is essential is that you feel whole, you feel right and you feel able to confront the day-to-day conflicts surging up from childhood. We are all traumatised and we try and lay on other people the reason for our trauma. That is only human. When you eventually leave I want you to be able to accept yourself as you are. Just as you are.'

Alice felt no desire to comment, even though Dorothea would expect it. 'I really can't say anything at the moment, but I've got to leave tomorrow. Something's happened at home and I need to sort it out.'

'Don't you think we should discuss it, Alice?'

'I'd rather not, Dorothea. Everyone's been so marvellous. I'm sure I can cope now.'

Dr Grossman was unable to disguise her trepidation. 'Alice, I'm deeply, deeply disappointed. This is the worst possible time for you to leave. The last thing we want is for you to return here in a more acute state than when you arrived. And I have to say that could happen.'

Alice looked down at her hands and decided to remain silent.

Dr Grossman continued. 'Alice, listen. We've all got to know you over the weeks, watched your amazing progress, your open-hearted participation. But you have reached a crucial stumbling block, which must be worked through. It could be dangerous if you neglect this final step. You might find yourself reaching once more for that diet sheet, wretchedly counting the calories, again a prisoner of the demon of obesity.'

Her words had barely sunk in. Alice calmly looked up at Dr Grossman, straightened her back and slipped off the couch, 'I'm willing to risk that. I have to get back to London.'

Dr Grossman appeared to recognise a moment of defeat – and graciously accepted it. She took Alice's hand in hers. 'You know we're always here for you.'

'Yes.'

She pressed the button of her internal phone and buzzed reception. 'Could you prepare Alice Miller's account? She wishes to leave tomorrow.' There was a pause as she looked up at Alice. 'Are you paying by gold card? We do accept dollars or deutschmarks if that's easier.'

'Cheque,' said Alice.

Dr Grossman produced an understanding smile, which gradually gave way to a frown. 'In that case, Alice, we will need to contact your bank manager. Just a formality.'

Alice wondered for a moment if she would be held prisoner if her bank manager were away on holiday, such was the severity of Dr Grossman's expression. But then she suddenly smiled again, went over to a shelf and took hold of a polythene packet from a pile of others. 'Here, Alice. I thought you'd like a little memento of the clinic.'

After she had packed her belongings, Alice found the polythene packet lying forgotten in a corner of the communal bathroom. She unwrapped it and found an Extra Large T-shirt in lollypop pink with gold letters on the front, which read: I Found Myself at the Cloudesley Clinic. Returning it in its folds to the packet, she placed the T-shirt in the one drawer of her rickety plywood chest that she managed to open. She missed the afternoon workshop on *The Creativity Surge – Holes, Trances and Frozen States*. Then she said goodbye to Juanita.

Eleven

• • •

Alice returned to London, having lost about seven kilos. She ran along the street, brimming with energy, enjoying the sensation of her bag bobbing against the bones of her thighs. When she saw the outside of her house she took a sudden dislike to the gaudy colours. She would repaint it white. (Robert would approve. He liked everything white. Or black.) In the hall there was the smell of neglect, like a turned-off fridge filled with mould, and the dust of Kensal Green had smeared all the windows and even entered her workroom. Tossing her tights, leggings and tops into the linen basket, she vowed to clean the whole place from top to bottom.

As she suspected, there were messages waiting on her answerphone, winking away conspiratorially in the corner. The hats in her workroom were just as she had left them, half finished, wrapped in polythene. This she removed, then she cast a critical eye over her past work. She had an impulse to pack away all her hats, clear out the room and start anew. She would do it differently now. Why had she chosen that bright yellow straw, why that particularly repellent violet hue for the trimming? She wondered if artists reacted this way — whether in one sudden transforming moment, without knowing the reason, they deserted figurative for abstract or selected one colour over all others, like Picasso. The difference was that she wasn't yet sure about the direction she would take.

Suppose she delayed her decision until she had moved into Robert's house? Would she ever? Had everything changed or was she merely projecting the change she had gone through at the clinic onto her future with Robert? She wanted to be with him, but feared it. She couldn't bring herself to ask him about what had happened. If she did, it would mean she had lost faith in him, as well as in Mary, the two people who had her interests most at heart, all the trust accumulated over weeks or months and years. And if he said nothing had changed, what then? Was she to destroy the future because of a mere suspicion that two people had conveniently come together who were not in love?

Alice paced up and down, wondering if she could ever settle back into tackling laborious tasks, all those mundane procedures she had put behind her at the clinic. She missed the odd characters in the group, the way they poured out their feelings even if it annoyed her. They talked of things that mattered to them, however ridiculous it sometimes seemed. Could she talk to Robert about things that mattered? Or was it better to keep them tactfully hidden, to remain on the even keel they had always maintained? Shouldn't she guard against Beatrice's mistakes, homing in on exposed nerves, destroying the calmness of comfortable, everyday being with someone? Did it matter, concealing things which were perhaps better kept concealed? She wanted to see Robert, right now, to hear his voice, to be in his arms, but she stopped herself. She wasn't ready quite yet.

The red notebook, where was it? And why couldn't she find a pen anywhere? She could no longer avoiding the winking light of the answerphone. Alice pressed the button. Apart from frustrated customers, enquiring more and more desperately about the progress of commissions (she would deal with that in the morning), there was a message from Mary, one from Beatrice and another from Simon. She was waiting for Robert's voice, which was absent from the tape. It looked as though it had run out. He would be working now. She would save up the moment to tell him that she was back home. He'd probably forgotten exactly when she was coming, with so much on his mind.

She spun through the tape once more, listening to the anxious voices of customers waiting for orders and some voices she didn't recognise. It didn't matter, Alice told herself. She could always suggest they went to another milliner. Why should she be bothered with dates and times and deliveries? The messages she wanted to hear were towards the end of the tape.

MARY: Hi, Alice. Got your message, couldn't ring you last night. It sounds as though you've had a tremendously valuable few weeks. How much weight did you lose in the end? Let me know. Very sorry, but I won't see you for a while. My sister's had a heart attack in Morocco, totally unexpected and I've got to fly out there at once. Her husband was involved in a car crash on the way to see her in hospital. So they're both there, in different wards. Shame it was Agadir but Lynn always goes for cheap deals. I'll write soon.

BEATRICE: Thank God you're back. Bet you're disgustingly healthy and slim. Guess what? Mary decamped yesterday without a word of warning, didn't even tidy her things away. I'm at Robert's, packing them up. Well, you didn't want to see her stuff all over the place, did you? Longing to see you. Club on Thursday? Lots of love.

SIMON: Now you're back, how about lunch on Monday? Remember what I said? Oh, yes, will I see you at the club on Thursday as usual?

WESTMINSTER BANK, KENSAL GREEN BRANCH: It has been drawn to our attention that your overdraft limit has been exceeded by a not inconsiderable amount. Please ring the Customer Services Manager.

WESTMINSTER BANK, KENSAL GREEN BRANCH: Please contact the Customer Services Manager urgently.

Alice prickled with annoyance, wanting to desert the house and leave everything behind her, like sloughing off an old skin. Then she caught sight of herself in the mirror, the one that always made her look fat because of the way the light fell. She stretched, pulled in her stomach and turned to view herself from the side. How gratifying. She couldn't be much over size twelve. Size twelve! Then the phone trilled. It was Robert, on site, using the mobile. She could hear the fatigue in his voice, Gerald wanted him to squeeze too much into the space. He was glad she was back.

Lying on the living-room floor in Robert's arms, clothes flung in heaps around them, Alice felt as though new life had been breathed into her. Even though he was tired and had apologised for his lack of vigour, it didn't matter. Really it didn't. But no, she didn't want to go up to the bedroom, not yet, she liked it so much down here. She was waiting for him to make a comment about the new slimmed-down Alice, but instead he laughed.

'I suppose you want a new bed? I know you don't find it comfortable. I promise I'll get one, once this business is out of the way.'

He went upstairs first, shouting down several times to ask when she was coming.

'Just making some tea. Won't be long,' she called back.

In the kitchen, Alice opened one cupboard after another. Inside, they were spotless, as usual. There was nothing she had not known from before, not one new jar of jam or a strange bottle of oil, or a packet of Earl Grey tea. Even her favourite biscuits, now stale, had not been touched. She put one into her mouth, but it didn't seem to taste quite the same. Was she imagining it, or had the china been rearranged in a slightly different order, small plates piled on top of big plates, matching dishes next to them when they were usually in a separate cupboard? How silly it was, expecting everything to have remained in exactly the same state, as though she had only gone away yesterday.

'Mary's gone, I expect she told you why,' said Robert, as Alice settled into bed beside him.

'Yes, she left me a message.'

'I was relieved that she had to go. But then I've always felt uneasy about having a secretary working here.'

'Wasn't she doing her own work as well?'

'I believe so. Using my phone, anyway. I know she's your friend, but I found her a bit much after a while.'

'Why?'

'It's difficult to say. She's the kind of person who has definite ideas about doing things.'

'That's her manner.'

'I suppose so. Still, she made herself useful.'

'Good.'

'And she managed to persuade Gerald to stick to our original plans. More or less, that is. But now she's left he's starting to see what he can get away with. It's so draining, having someone constantly nibbling away at what you want to do. Still, the contractors are on my side.'

Alice was waiting for Robert to tell her again that he was glad to have her back, that he had missed her – but she could see he was preoccupied. He would soon make a comment, she felt sure. 'It's good to be here with you,' she said, kissing him lightly on the neck and snuggling up to his back, his long back that she loved. He didn't move, so she drew him round to face her.

Then he placed his arm around her waist. 'The time's gone so quickly, I didn't think it would. You really are much slimmer, I should have told you earlier. The trouble is, when you spend all day looking out for an error of half a centimetre you want to come home and have everything a blur. Tell me about the health place. You haven't said much about the mysterious Dr Grossman. By the way, Simon's been putting on a bit since you've been away. Perhaps he should go there, too, maybe you could persuade him.'

'They don't take men,' said Alice.

'Isn't that rather sexist? Men need to lose weight, too. There are far too many fat men around.'

'And women?'

'They're better at hiding it,' Robert said with a laugh.

'Am I?'

'Don't be ridiculous, darling. You don't need to hide anything.' He stretched out his arm and dimmed the light. 'Do you mind if I sleep now? This job is so exhausting. I've got to be up at six tomorrow.'

Stung into wakefulness, Alice sat up and looked at Robert. After all this time she still gazed on him with wonder, his strong face abandoned on the pillow, with the serene expression of sleep, as though his lips would break out in a smile at any moment. Would he appear any different if he didn't love her? Would she cast such a lingering look over his face – ridiculous thought – if her love for him began to fade? Did he appear so composed sleeping next to Mary? If he had? Much slimmer, was all he said. He could have asked how she had lost all that weight or showed how pleased he was or even questioned her further about the clinic. She might almost have been away for a few days, instead of several weeks. Was he perhaps disappointed that after all this time she was not just a little thinner? Was he expecting her to come back a size ten? Was he dreaming of a slender woman whom he could toss in the air like an autumn leaf? Who would make no imprint at all on the hard bed?

The alarm clock beeped and Robert was immediately awake, resting for a few minutes in the warmth of the bed.

Alice rolled over and pressed herself against the length of his body. 'Robert.'

'Go back to sleep, darling. I'll be quiet.'

'I'm awake.' She was waiting for him to give her a morning kiss, until she remembered that when he was pressured he lay on his back, collecting his thoughts before springing out of bed. 'Can I ask you something?'

'Sure.'

'Did you have sex with Mary?'

'Why are you asking me now?' He didn't sound annoyed.

'I just want to know.'

Robert sat up, looking down at her. 'Of course I didn't. Whatever put that into your head? Why on earth should I sleep with Mary?'

'I'm glad you didn't. Would you have said anything if I hadn't asked, Robert?'

He looked suddenly serious. 'If there was anything to say, of course I would. But there wasn't. You know we've talked about this before. We were never going to embark on one of those restrictive, neurotic marriages, the kind where the man only has to mention some girl he fancies and the wife looks daggers at him. If you'd been attracted to someone at the clinic, do you think I would have hit the roof? Of course I wouldn't.'

'There weren't any men there,' said Alice crossly. 'I told you that.'

'If there had been, that is. The only thing that matters is what we feel for one another.'

'So you didn't fancy her?'

'Not for one second.' He then put his lips to hers. 'If I kiss you properly I'll never get to work. I'll try and leave early today. Shall we have dinner somewhere, later?'

Once Robert had left, Alice stayed for a while in his house. She kept thinking about Mary being there, occupying her basement, wandering upstairs into Robert's studio, into the kitchen. Up to the bedroom? The more she thought about it the more it began to haunt her. She would only succeed in putting Mary out of her mind if she concentrated on the bad effect it would have on Robert if she kept harping on about what had happened. There was no reason for him to lie to her and there was none for her to react in such a ridiculous manner. It was unlike her to be suspicious. She couldn't remember doubting or accusing anyone, it wasn't in her nature. Not like Beatrice.

It was Robert who brought up the subject. He wanted to tell her what it was like never to have a moment's peace. Only in the time he had known Alice had calm returned to his house. The rows with Beatrice usually centred round trivial matters. She was furiously jealous if he talked to any girl for longer than two minutes, imagining he was already making an assignation. Often, she used to go through his pockets, hoping to find a hotel bill. She never did, of course. It was so humiliating. Besides, if he put all that energy into making sexual conquests, how would he find time for his work? In the end, he had stopped the arguments, shutting his mouth hermetically tight. His silence, of course, she regarded as proof of guilt. The infernal debate used to go its inevitable round: innocent question, unacceptable reply, interrogation, loss of temper and screaming, throwing the first object which came to hand against the wall, down the stairs, towards the window. It was simpler to say nothing and leave the house. In the end, Robert developed a stubborn resistance to questions, any questions. But now he was making an effort to ignore the scars, to put all that behind him.

Alice resolved never to ask about past infidelities. It was better not to know whether Robert had ever been unfaithful, once or more than once, whether it was a figment of Beatrice's imagination or whether it had actually happened. All the same, if Mary had been fat it would have been easier to take. She was the shape he liked. And hadn't Mary always made it clear that sleeping with a married man was a mere question of opportunity? If you fancied one another and there was the opportunity, why not? Love was totally different. She had known both. Alice couldn't imagine how she could separate both experiences. How could you put sex into two different compartments?

Was it possible to go through life without asking questions?

Respecting Alice's wish to remain solo-cycling in concentrated silence, Beatrice refrained from chatting and just mentioned that she was making her a present of a holistic aromatherapy session. On first seeing Alice on her return from the clinic she had remarked only briefly on the weight she had lost. How many times, after all, had she scolded Alice for being unduly obsessed with her weight? However, she had emphasised how incredibly healthy she looked, with skin glowing like a moonstone.

They were both lying back on adjacent couches, their faces covered in hot aromatic towels infused with essence of jasmine imported from China. Alice felt able to talk, in the damp darkness. 'Do you think Robert would have gone to bed with Mary? I can't stop thinking about it.'

'What does your instinct tell you?'

'That he might have done.'

'I doubt it, Alice. He loves you, doesn't he? I should try and forget about it. Forget about Mary. She's gone now anyway, off to latch on to someone else. We can celebrate now that she's taken herself off to Morocco,' said Beatrice.

'That's a little unfair, Bea! She's been a good friend to Robert and me. She's done a lot for us.'

'Typical Gemini, ruled by Mercury,' Beatrice said scornfully.

'How do you know?' asked Alice.

'I can tell.' Beatrice pulled the towel slowly from her face and Alice did likewise. Then they turned to face one another.

'Did Robert have lots of other girls before you were married?'

'Oh, I imagine he must have done, all those temptations. When we were first going out, I'd see him watching some girl and I'd think why shouldn't he have her instead of me? What's stopping him? Then I'd get furious and accuse him of all kinds of dreadful behaviour. The rows! I can't tell you the number of things I broke. Once I tore up all his plans in blind rage, just blind rage. Mars must have been hovering over me at birth. Terrible, terrible.'

'Yes,' Alice persisted. 'But did he actually?'

'Does it matter? He never talked about other girls. It was a long time ago,' said Beatrice, covering her face again with a towel.

*   *   *

The bar was full, which was why Simon and Robert were without a seat, leaning with their backs to the counter. The concerted Internet campaign, suggested by Simon in conjunction with London's leading health clubs (http://www.feelgood.co.uk.) had resulted in a massive increase in membership. Alice was back at last. Simon felt on good form. 'When we've created the Brainlive Computer – I give it another hundred years – what question would you ask it first? I've been wondering about that all day.'

'Needs a few moments,' said Robert. 'It's like asking what you'd say for your last words on earth.'

'That's already decided. My last words will be: "Yes, I will have another one." The secret lies in the banality, like "Bugger Bognor". Come on, Robert. The question, what's it to be? I'm logging various responses, to determine the human as opposed to the techie factor.'

Resting his chin in his hand, Robert tried to conjure up an original, Simon-defying question, but it eluded him. 'Will the Brainlive computer produce pictures?'

'Naturally. Chimps can produce pictures, it's more advanced than that.'

'Right. My question would be more of a request.'

'Fine, fine.'

In the time it would take for Robert to figure out a question, Simon would be twenty thoughts ahead. He was now wondering when Alice would appear. It was like watching a film and suddenly being made to go back half an hour to the bit you'd already seen.

'I know what I'd do,' Robert proclaimed after a couple of minutes. 'I'd ask it to find a contemporary portrait of Helen of Troy. I've always wondered what she looked like.'

'Not bad, not bad. And suppose Brainlive is female?'

'That's a difficult one. There's no male equivalent. What would you ask?'

'Something more simple – like what is the meaning

of life?' What he really would have asked was what would it take for Alice to come back? If he entered some kind of chamber and emerged as Simon but with the body of Robert, would she . . . ? His speculation was halted by the appearance of Alice and Beatrice. 'Alice looks amazing,' he remarked, seeing her come in from a distance. 'I do hope she's had a good time at the fat farm. If so, I might give it a try.'

'Bad luck, Simon. They don't take men,' said Robert. 'And she had to eat a lot of brown rice and vegetables.'

'Yuck. No wonder they don't take men. We wouldn't stand for it.' As Alice came up to the bar, Simon gave a delighted smile. 'Welcome back. We've all missed you, of course.'

Alice turned round in front of him. 'Well? What do you think?'

'Come on, tell us. How much did you lose?'

She whispered in his ear. 'Nearly eight kilos.'

'I hear the food was dreadful,' Simon said, addressing the others.

'Very organic, naturally,' Beatrice replied.

'Sounds painful. Far too healthy for me. I don't think I'll go.'

'Dr Grossman wouldn't have you, Simon,' said Alice with a giggle, as she tried to imagine him lying on the therapy couch.

'Ah yes, the ubiquitous Dorothea Grossman, guru to the stars,' Simon said with a smirk. He had an annoyingly retentive memory for seemingly useless information. 'According to Hollywood gossip, Liz Taylor introduced her to Michael Jackson and she's never looked back. And apparently she's been shopping with Hillary Clinton. Very impressive. I wonder if Freud ever went shopping . . .'

Beatrice stopped him elaborating and looked hard at Simon. He was trying, as usual, to avoid the subject.

'Let's face it, since Alice has been away we've seriously let ourselves go. Simon, you really should stop drinking so much and put in some extra sessions. That's what I'm going to do, anyway. Even David, who never notices anything, said my face had got plumper.'

'Good. So you and David are talking again,' said Robert.

'I'm talking.' She put a hand on Robert's shoulder. 'A tomato juice, please.'

'Tonic water with lemon,' said Alice. 'And we must find somewhere to sit, I think I've strained something.'

By the end of the evening Beatrice had worked out the detail of a new diet regime which they would all follow. For a couple of weeks, anyhow. Beatrice had read somewhere that you are what you eat, and who wanted to be sausages and mash, and look at Alice, glowing with health after all that raw, natural stuff. Didn't they say it was energising? And why pay all that money to the club in order to keep fit and healthy, only to fill yourself up with fatty food immediately afterwards? Simon said he'd try it for a week because he wanted to see if diet affected the brain. Alice decided to go along with it, because you couldn't eat normally when everyone else was going low-calorie.

Instead of the usual breakfast of fried eggs and bacon, Alice was lying in bed eating a boiled egg, which Robert had cooked. Although it was only the third diet day, Alice was dreaming of a bagful of warm, soggy chips with lashings of vinegar and salt. The egg was slightly underdone and slimy, and she'd tipped too much salt into the shell, which made it inedible, but she was determined to eat it and said it was just how she liked it.

Robert went downstairs to replenish the supply of toast and coffee, and when he returned with the tray he

207

handed her several pages of a thick folded letter. 'Read this if you want to. It came yesterday from Mary. Boring stuff about some book she's researching and people I've never heard of,' he said.

The first paragraph described the scenery around Menton, a favourite spot of hers. She said how much Robert would like it. He should really be working in France, where they appreciated the aesthetics of design. If he (or Alice) wanted to take a weekend off she would find him a place to stay, she'd some very good friends in that area, well-known painters, musicians, actors, such fun . . . etc. etc.

'Why is she writing from France?' Alice asked, having given up on the tiny, laborious handwriting. 'I thought she was meant to be in Agadir. Does she say what happened to her sister, after that awful car accident?'

'Crippled apparently, though lucky to be alive. She's been flown to England.'

'And the husband? What about him?'

'She doesn't say. But she did say she'd gone to stay with friends in France, that she had some business out there.'

'Why did she write you such a long letter?' asked Alice.

'I imagine she had nothing better to do,' said Robert with a laugh. Then he took the last page of the letter and showed it to her. 'I don't know what this is about.'

PS Would you tell Alice that I have rather a signifi-cant cash flow problem? I'm sure she'll understand, it happens to all of us! I need to have back the deposit and the cash I lent her for the Cloudesley Clinic as soon as possible. She'll know the amount. I can't remember exactly, around two thousand pounds, I believe. Here are my French bank details so she can forward the money order. Naturally, I wouldn't ask this unless it was absolutely necessary.

Alice stared at the letter in disbelief, then quickly glanced above the postscript to see how she had ended the letter. 'Kindest regards to you and Alice.' She must have known that he would have shown it to her. 'I don't understand it, either.'

Unwilling to enquire further, Robert went back to reading his paper. It was understood between them that he would never probe into Alice's affairs. He respected her independence. Since she remained silent, he decided to comment. 'I'm sure she's not really that desperate.'

Alice tried to imagine the circumstances. Hadn't Mary told her that she would lend her the money gladly, that she mustn't give it a moment's thought, she wanted to do it, she could pay it back whenever it was convenient? Didn't Mary always say that money didn't matter, whether she had it or not? That the material things of life interested her little? But it was possible that she had had to pay for her sister's hospital expenses and didn't want to make an issue of it. Being discreet, she wouldn't have gone into detail. She was quite proud about managing her affairs, so she must have suddenly found herself in an embarrassing situation.

'I'm sure you don't have to pay it all at once,' said Robert. 'She wouldn't expect that.'

'I can't pay any of it at the moment,' said Alice, pushing the tray down the bed and reaching for her dressing-gown.

Robert stretched out to pull her back into the bed, but she was already on her feet. 'I'll help you out, darling. I've actually got some cash in the bank. But I'm sure Mary isn't exactly hard up,' he said.

'How do you know?'

'I don't, I'm only guessing. She bought a very expensive car recently.'

'Did she? She didn't tell me.' Alice read the postcript again and sighed. 'I will have to pay her, Robert.'

'Fine, but please let me help. You'd do the same for me, wouldn't you?'

'Of course. But I'd rather you didn't bail me out, not this time.'

'Stop being so stubborn, Alice.'

'Am I?'

'Sometimes.'

Alice Miller, bankrupt. No one in our family has ever been bankrupt, her father used to say with pride. Would she be the first one? Did the Loans Manager really mean it when he hinted that she should sell her house to maintain her 'liquidity'? There was only one alternative. She would have to sell her services to a manufacturer, churning out badly made crude shapes which would flatter no one, in cheap straws and tatty felts. Or perhaps she could sell something? She possessed nothing of value, nothing others would value. Take out a second mortgage on her house? Yet more debt? She couldn't dream of Robert coming to the rescue. How could she begin marriage owing vast sums to her husband?

When the friends next met at the club Alice was no closer to resolving her problem. There were some evenings when everyone was irritable and this promised to be one of them. Robert arrived late, just for a quick beer. Simon had overdone the weights and decided it was all a waste of time being fit as he much preferred the unfit state. Then Alice, in response to a question from Simon, made the mistake of saying she was wondering whether she wanted to go on making hats all her life.

Overhearing this, Beatrice hit the roof. 'What are you saying, Alice? When you've all that wonderful talent.'

'No one gets rich making hats. I'm sick of being poor.'

'Alice is worried about some money she owes Mary,' Robert explained. Then he turned to Alice. 'Why don't you just give her a small amount and stall her for a bit?'

'Why on earth did you borrow from her?' exclaimed Beatrice. 'I could have helped you out. And I'm sure Simon would have, too.'

'This is nothing to do with any of you. It's my problem.' Alice picked up her bag and started to put on her coat.

'Where are you going?' said Robert, puzzled at her behaviour.

'Home. My home.'

The others watched as Alice walked swiftly out of the bar.

'What's wrong?' asked Simon

'Mary lent Alice some money, quite a lot apparently, said to pay it back when she could and now she's suddenly asking for it.'

'Absolutely ridiculous,' said Beatrice.

'I offered to help, but she didn't want to know. What do you suggest, Simon?'

'Leave her alone for the moment. I'll think of a way out, make it sound like a business suggestion.'

'What Alice needs is another fat commission.'

'What Alice needs', said Simon tartly, sucking at his cigar, 'is to make her name and extend her clientele. We must devise a marketing strategy.'

When he returned home, Robert was uneasy. He had always thought of Alice as so independent, able to cope, and now he wondered if had misjudged her. Beatrice always said he liked to be in control and didn't allow her to go her own way enough. Was he going too far in the opposite direction? Should he have been firmer and immediately made arrangements for

211

Mary to be paid? When he phoned Alice she apologised for being in a bad mood. She sounded calmer, more positive, as though she had collected her thoughts. 'If I can't sort out the money myself, I'll ask you, I promise. But Simon's right, he's always telling me I must learn to manage better.'

'You're better at managing than I am,' Robert replied.

She sounded pleased. 'Do you really think so?'

'Yes, I do.' Robert paused a moment. 'Things are going to get better. Once we're married . . .'

'Then what?' said Alice.

'I'll get myself properly organised.'

'I thought Mary had done that already.'

Robert said nothing in reply. He could hear the trace of anxiety in her voice. Alice's remark must have slipped out without her meaning it. Not like Beatrice.

Twelve

* * *

Shortly after Mary had written to Robert she sent Alice
a letter. Her sister was progressing, having been moved
to a large hospital in Surrey. Her sister's husband was
still in Agadir, strapped up like a mummy, but he
was well looked after, however much he complained.
After a brief holiday in France Mary had decided that
she really must get down to writing a book herself,
instead of being the handmaiden for the works of
others. For her subject she had chosen to write a
biography, which would mean extensive travel and
Alice knew how costly that would be. There were
no package tours tailored for literary research. And
since it was notoriously difficult to find a publisher
she had decided to publish the book herself. She had
fixed her sights on the independent route, whatever
it cost. She was sure Alice, of all people, would
understand.

She thanked Alice for sending part of the sum she
owed and asked her, in the sweetest way, if she could
manage to pay back the rest in the next six months.
Otherwise the book would progress extremely slowly.
And she happened to have heard down the grapevine
that there was some academic who was pursuing the
same subject, so time was of the essence.

It took Alice a few days before she wrote back.

Dear Mary

I would hate us to fall out because of money, but it really is a dreadful time at the moment. I've just about persuaded the bank manager that my business is 'on the turn', Simon's expression, so he made me take out a loan and I pretended I had a monthly income to pay it off. I haven't. But I will find something. Could you possibly wait a little while? It would help so much if I knew you weren't absolutely desperate for cash. (I can't possibly borrow from Robert because how could I start marriage being in debt to my husband? Hope you understand.)

I'd hate it if you weren't able to do your book because of me. Please write back quickly.

There was going to be another paragraph, saying something like – I do need to talk to you. About you and Robert and Robert and me. Did anything happen? If it did, I try and tell myself it was just one of those things which happens when you're seeing someone all the time, as you were. I couldn't understand why you left so suddenly, without us talking. I suppose I want to know if we can still be friends. But she deleted it and wrote, 'Love, Alice.'

Ten days later Alice received a reply on a postcard from Mexico City.

Only just got your letter, forwarded from France. This is a magic place. Have been given five thousand pounds by a dear friend (surprisingly enough, he's a literary critic!) to complete my research. Isn't that incredibly generous? Hope everything is well with you. Plan to come to England soon. Love Mary.

Mary gave no address. It was difficult to read between

the lines, or for Alice to understand the content of her message. Did this absolve her, though only temporarily, from repaying the money she owed? When she asked Robert he was convinced that Mary would have asked if she needed it.

'What makes you so sure, Robert?'

'If she'd known you were so hard up I'm sure she wouldn't have insisted. Mary's not like that. In any case, she's plenty of rich friends she can borrow from.'

'How do you know? Why are you defending her all of a sudden?'

'I'm not, Alice.'

It irked her that there was a part of Robert she didn't know, which centred on those weeks when Mary had been in his house. She wanted to know not all of him, that was impossible, but to be familiar with all the characteristics that made Robert Robert and not, say, Simon. Her doubts were getting stronger. The more he refused to say, the more Alice suspected that Mary had been much more important than he would ever admit.

She decided to seek help from Dr Grossman. Who else could understand her dilemma?

Dr Grossman remembered all the details of her case and said she had expected her to call. It was always dangerous to leave the course too early, but she knew that Alice had a pressing reason. First, she enquired about Mary Bartlett, whom she greatly admired and who she understood was a good friend of Alice's. Then she asked if she was putting into practice what she had learned at the clinic. Her voice sounded intimate, close and concerned. Was Alice maintaining the positive thoughts? There had been lapses, doubtless. Everyone had lapses. If she had stayed longer these might have been less frequent. Was she still practising her smiling exercises? No? It really was crucial, like

215

pianists practising scales. 'Do you still find yourself thinking about your weight all the time, Alice? Can you answer me honestly? I do need to know whether you'll need further treatment.'

'I don't weigh myself morning and evening, like I used to. I don't think it worries me as much. I like being thinner, but I'm bound to put on some weight again eventually. I'm not obsessed by it any more. As long as I don't get huge and I don't think I will.'

Following ten more minutes of questions from Dr Grossman, Alice still hadn't said what was really on her mind. This was a delicate subject to raise, since it was through Mary's friendship with Dr Grossman that she had been given a place at the clinic. 'Do you mind if I ask you something which is, well, embarassing?'

'Sure, Alice. That's what I'm here for.'

Aware that she was entering the second ten minutes (another fifty pounds) Alice spoke as quickly as she could. 'When I came back from the clinic I thought that Robert . . .'

'Robert?'

'My fiancé.'

'Of course. Now I remember.'

'Might have gone to bed with a close friend of mine.'

'Ah,' said the disembodied telephone therapy voice. 'A man friend?'

'Goodness, no.'

'You sound shocked, Alice. It is very common for people, even heterosexual people, to discover that they wish to explore their own-sex tendencies. In these cases it's very rarely of long duration, but an essential process in the continuum of self-discovery.'

'The point is,' Alice insisted, 'I keep thinking he might have gone to bed with . . .'

'Are we talking intercourse, Alice?'

'Yes, yes. I mean, I don't know. It's likely, or perhaps it isn't really.'

'We have to be clear about these things.'

'I keep thinking Robert must have gone to bed with . . .'

'With whom, Alice?'

'Mary Bartlett.'

'I see.' Dr Grossman paused for a few seconds to collect her thoughts. 'Alice, dear. I do happen to know that Mary is your loyal friend – as she is mine. It could be that you have a problem relating to other women. So many of us do, since we are constantly surrounded by power-seeking men. It is in their interests to breed suspicion and distrust among us. Divide and rule. We need to explore this. Please say exactly what you're thinking at this moment.'

'Well, Mary is amazingly thin, she's size eight. Robert has always liked thin girls. However much weight I lose I'll never manage to be like her. My bones are just too big to make a difference. Every time I see her I feel threatened, I can't help it.' Alice could feel herself veering out of control, but Dr Grossman allowed space for her super-ego to take over. She counted several breaths, slowly in and out, then continued in a calmer voice. 'I've no reason to think that anything happened, but I can't get it out of my mind.'

'And does Robert comment on your body shape?'

'Oh, no. Never.'

'I see.'

There was a pause as Dr Grossman scrolled through Alice's case notes on the computer screen in front of her. 'When you are with Robert, you stop see-ing yourself as you are. You see yourself as you imagine he sees you. Big fat Alice. This is false, a false obsession. But he loves you for being you. Otherwise he would have said, "Dear Alice, I love you but how about losing some weight." Has he said that?'

'No.'

'Then what we have here is a conceptual problem . . .'

'But supposing he did?' cried Alice. 'Supposing he did end up in bed with Mary?'

'But you have no evidence that he did, Alice. Knowing Mary, I think it highly unlikely, although I'm not aware of all the circumstances. And I don't believe we can discuss this over the phone. We need to talk this through. This minor infidelity, if such it was, has traumatised you, but it clearly isn't mainstream to your relationship. We are not talking of a Don Juan complex here, persistent congress with another or others, from what you've told me. Are you sure you couldn't take a day off and come and see me for a session? Or, if you prefer, you could come to my Harley Street consulting room. Would you like an appointment?'

'I'd really like to,' Alice replied, looking at her watch and attempting to calculate the cost of the phone call. 'But I can't afford it just at the moment.'

'Perhaps I can help,' said Dr Grossman. 'With Mary and a few other friends I have a special agreement. When she introduces new patients to the clinic she receives a twenty per cent commission on the total fees. I find this quite satisfactory and fair. And Mary does know exactly the kind of women who would benefit from my treatment. Would you be interested in a similar arrangement?'

For a moment Alice was lost for words. The longer she stayed at the clinic, the more money Mary would have received. Putting aside such an ignoble thought, she told herself that she must have been really desperate. And too proud to tell her. 'I . . . I'm not sure if I know anyone. But I'll think about it,' Alice stammered.

She had an overwhelming urge to cycle off to Lidgate's and buy a huge chunk of that wonderful pork pie (four hundred and seventy-six calories) and pop a few doors down to Cullens where she knew exactly where to find those scrumptious crinkle-cut frozen chips (five hundred and eighty calories). She would fry up the chips, then put out the pie on a large plate, no need to cut it up in pieces, eat them both with eager fingers, sink her teeth into the dense flavourful pork and sweetly gelatinous binding, dollop on the mustard pickle (a hundred and seventy-eight calories) and consume it all in one go (total one thousand two hundred and thirty-four calories). That left one thousand three hundred and sixteen calories for the daily allowance, though really it should be less for her height. Cycling hard both ways would lose five hundred calories. Then she would go to the club.

From her cycle seat in a gallery above the display of human endeavour Alice looked down on the scene below. Every single machine was in motion. Weights were bobbing up and down like manic oil derricks in the Texas boom. An army of legs on the treadmills was going on a campaign trail to nowhere. She could see Simon and Robert vying with one another, piling on the weights, straining as the sweat poured off their faces. Alice came down to the floor as a rowing machine became vacant and vowed to punish her stomach muscles until they cried out for mercy.

By the time they had showered, Simon, Robert and Alice were in a state of blissful, catatonic collapse.

'I suppose nineteenth-century factory workers must have felt like this every day,' remarked Simon, stroking his aching leg muscles.

'Still, it would have kept the weight down. At least they weren't disgustingly gross like so many people today,' said Robert.

'Yes, but I bet they wanted to be fat.'

'What? How can you say that? Who on earth would actually want to be fat? Who would find folds of flesh attractive except sumo-wrestling addicts? Anyhow, fat people have always been figures of fun. Look at Billy

219

Bunter. Or Pavarotti. Without his voice, what could he be in life with a shape like that?'

Alice, whose gloom was deepening, longed for Simon to change the subject. At last Robert had come out into the open. She couldn't bear to hear any more.

But Simon continued, 'First point, Robert. In the last century factory workers didn't possess scales, so they wouldn't have known what they weighed. Second point, they probably dreamed of being fat like the factory owner. Being thin meant being poor for the most part.'

'Is that true, Simon or are you making it up?' asked Robert, with a laugh.

'Now, would a CD-ROM tell a lie? The whole of British history on a wafer-thin metal beer-mat. Isn't that amazing, Alice?'

'I suppose it is.'

'What's up? Is the health farm effect wearing off? Still, no wonder you sound tired. I was watching you in the gym. You must have rowed half way down the Thames.'

'I feel flat and fat, and I haven't an idea in my head. Don't take any notice.'

All Alice wanted was for Robert to take up her cue and say, 'Fat? Of course you're not.' But he didn't. Really she knew that he never would.

'Have you by any chance got hatter's block, Alice?' Simon asked. This evinced a half-smile. 'Apparently, the cure, for writers anyway, is to go for long walks somewhere like the outback of Australia or Dartmoor at a pinch. You get so sick of seeing nothingness that you're forced to invent.'

'Where would I go? The outback of Holland Park?' said Alice tartly. 'And anyway, I cycle.'

'I've been through it often, as Alice knows,' remarked Robert. 'It's as though your brain has slipped down a few notches. You try and think of something and whatever you do think of, you know it's second-rate or unoriginal.'

'Exactly.' Alice sighed, looking towards Robert with a softened expression.

Simon suddenly felt extraordinarily jealous. It was as though they were already married, exchanging those quick glances of understanding. 'How do you know if it is second-rate or unoriginal? It might be a really good idea and you just happen to have a headache at the time. Your perception might be askew and someone else might think it was marvellous.'

'You don't understand, Simon,' said Alice.

Rising from his chair abruptly, Simon went over to the bar to repeat his order. He was just contemplating whether to revive his thirst with a packet of Bombay Mix or some tempting salted Brazils, when he caught sight of Beatrice, laden with bags, smiling jubilantly as she entered the bar. 'And a double vodka for Beatrice,' Simon shouted to the barman.

It made it even more acute, when someone else was brimming with achievement. Alice looked glum and gave a faint smile when Beatrice flung herself into a chair with such energy.

'Bad day?' asked Beatrice with cheerful concern.

'Bad days, full stop. I can't get going again,' said Alice. Then she grinned. 'I know what you're going to say. My stars are bad.'

'I wouldn't say that, you must never say that. A flat period, perhaps. I suspect Vulcan overruling Mercury.'

'When are my stars going to change, Bea? What can I look forward to?'

Beatrice came nearer to study Alice more closely. She observed a slight greyness in Alice's complexion and faint circles round her eyes, signs of insufficient sleep. But she sensed something deeper. 'There's no need to be depressed. This is just a temporary period

221

of abeyance. Next month will be brilliant, really it will. A great flowering period with bursts of energy coming at you from all sides.'

'Well, I'll have to sit tight and wait for next month, won't I?'

Beatrice accepted Simon's large glass of vodka, checked there was enough ice and lime, not lemon. Then, suddenly it came to her, which happened occasionally when she was in a state of exhilaration and heightened awareness. 'Alice, I know what you must do,' she said, creasing her eyes in concentration. 'You must have a show, a proper show for your hats, models and lights and music and everything gorgeous and memorable.'

'Great idea,' Simon broke in. 'We should have thought of it before. When? Before or after the wedding?'

'Hold on!' cried Alice.

'After,' said Robert.

'Before,' answered Beatrice.

'Before. Definitely before,' added Simon.

'Stop. You're getting carried away,' said Alice in panic. 'I've nothing to work on. I can't possibly. And anyway, how could I afford it?'

Beatrice looked from Robert to Simon. 'We'll sort that out, won't we?'

'Certainly,' answered Simon, who was already producing mental rapidcalc figures in the region of a couple of grand. His wedding pres for RobAlice? 'That's my department.'

'Simon, why don't we all go back to your house and sort something out right now? Otherwise nothing will happen,' suggested Robert.

'Too right,' added Beatrice with a knowing glance at Robert.

'Group brainstorm,' added Simon. 'Excellent.'

Before Alice could object, she found herself propelled out of the bar together with Robert, Simon and Beatrice.

After they had drained several bottles of wine

and demolished a perfectly ripened unpasteurised Coloumiers as they sat round Simon's computer in the kitchen, a theme for the collection had emerged. Afterwards, they all claimed the idea for their own, but Alice thought it had been Robert's. Beatrice must have mentioned something about star signs and he must have said, 'Why not use that as an idea?' That's how she remembered it, anyway. And Simon said it was a very now concept and people would love it. Beatrice enthused about the lovely shapes of the star signs and the symbols, which she conjured up using Simon's computer Paintbrush. Alice sat at Simon's table, scribbling on sheets of paper, sketching vague shapes and making notes for colours.

By the end of the evening, Simon had minuted the decisions in Hatshow.doc:

HATSHOW

1 Beatrice and Simon to organise Event. Send invitations and get in press.
2 Models: Hattie, Pen, Genevieve and more of Alice's favourite clients.
3 Venue: chapel in Kensal Green, owned by a friend of Simon's and as yet unconverted (Action Simon).
4 Action Robert: map out simple structure for the stage and a rough design.
5 Action Beatrice: find suppliers for lights and materials at the lowest possible price. Plus cake, she insists.
6 Date: first week in September.

Alice read the printout and laughed. 'You haven't given me a job. What am I going to do?'

'Just make some hats,' said Robert with a grin.

A few days before the show there was the kind of

frenzied chaos from which – it seemed to Alice – order would never emerge. Simon busied himself by bombarding lady journalists with faxes and e-mails about the forthcoming supernova event of the year. Beatrice supervised the workers and made fleeting visits with sustenance. In vain did Alice protest that she wanted something small and intimate and unthreatening. No one listened. In her workroom, four girls sewed to her command. Alice panicked, calmed down and panicked again so that she felt like a yo-yo in the hands of a hyperactive child. The night before her show she complained that nothing was ready, that she couldn't go ahead, it should be cancelled. Then, when she saw the completed results, helped by a large quantity of champagne, she changed her mind. Some of the hats, she thought, were quite good.

To model the hats, it took little to persuade Pen and Hattie to take part. Three of Alice's favourite customers from student days agreed to make up the numbers. At the morning rehearsal they showed a surprising ability to hop gracefully onto the small stage, which had been constructed in the centre of the chapel by one of Robert's carpenters. After screams from Beatrice of 'No, not like that, like this!' they also managed to convey the necessary arrogance for a 'happening show'. Simon was updating action plans every hour, glued to his mini-computer. A composer friend of Robert's had provided the music, which took the form of an electronic fantasy on the theme of planets in motion. Robert wasn't madly keen on the finished work but said it was probably the kind of thing people expected. They all kept saying Alice shouldn't worry about a thing except her hats. So she worried incessantly about her hats.

On the night of the show, Beatrice predicted that it would be rainy and windy, and for once she was right. No one had considered the needs of taxis, cars and motor bikes that were jostling to find a parking place within high-heeled walking distance of the undistinguished red-brick chapel. Many had arrived late, since Kensal Green was not on the map of Central London. The Harrow Road, which was the nearest street anyone had heard of, was so long and featureless that some continued as far as Edgware. A few even ended up at the gates of the West London Cemetery, asking suspicious passers-by if there was a chapel anywhere near.

A small crowd did find their way to the venue, urged on by the promise of champagne. It was up to Simon to pacify the press and the impatient guests, including the whole of Alice's family. They were unable to understand why they couldn't take their seats immediately and had to stand outside in the pelting rain. Sam bellowed that they should organise it better and where the hell were they anyway? Alice swore it was a smart place, but he said if this was what they called smart he'd be buggered. Didn't they know who he was? Not Lord Miller yet, Alice remarked with a grin, at which he went purple in the face. Veronica tried clutching his arm but he took her hand firmly and said he was going in, damn it. At that point, Simon gave up. There was little likelihood of Robert coming to his assistance, as he was engrossed in conversation with someone from a Dutch cable company who was clutching a video camera and attempting in vain to distinguish the Somebodies from the Nobodies.

Alice, sitting at the side on the end of a bench, clenched her hands so tightly that her nails dug into her palms. She could hardly bear to watch. The models pranced up and down the ramp, only faces and hats lit by the laser beams, like disembodied cryonic heads floating in the ether. She pinched her eyes shut and just wanted it all to end. Then, furtively, she surveyed the audience, a mass of wriggling bodies trying to come to terms with the narrow benches. In the second row were

Veronica and Sam. Alice caught her mother's eye and gave an uncomfortable smile, so Veronica reciprocated by crossing her fingers and holding them up.

Then she heard the applause, clapping and cries of appreciation. She turned slightly to view the audience again, who sat thigh to thigh, crammed together on the hard brown benches, straining forward to remember the colours, the textures and shapes of the proudly carried hats. The cameras flashed as dark figures pushed their way to the front. The laser lighting changed hue, deepening or fading as they shifted from red to blue to green to yellow. The models all walked slowly forward and removed their hats in a simultaneous, sweeping theatrical gesture. Then the lights softened into a gentle flood and they filed down each end of the benches, carrying the hats aloft.

Beatrice came and stood beside Alice. 'They adored them, look at their faces,' she said in a whisper, bending down towards her.

The applause was still continuing when there was the sound of a scuffle, and the long-lensed cameras wielded by agile young photographers changed their aim from stage front to chapel back. Beatrice could just make out Simon beckoning wildly in her direction, so she ran from Alice's side and pushed her way down the packed passageway between the rows of benches. Suddenly she found herself plummeted against a security guard, over six feet tall with a baseball player physique. Simon was attempting to extract himself from an awkward encounter.

'You need to speak to Bea,' said Simon, trying to edge the giant away from the doorway. 'She's the organiser.'

'Dina Martin wants to see the show,' said the unmoving giant. 'She came late, rehearsing in town.'

'I'm awfully sorry, but it's just finished; but we can send a brochure,' replied Beatrice, flashing a tremendous smile while she tried to remember if Dina Martin was a movie star or a pop singer – must be one or the other. 'Or I can arrange an appointment.'

'Look, lady. Dina Martin wants to see the show.'

Beatrice stood stiffly, wondering what the correct procedure would be. Her girls were bringing in the trays of champagne. She was waiting for the moment to cue the Salsa music so that Paola (the latest au pair, waiting nervously backstage) could make her entrance bearing the Cake, with appropriate majesty. 'The show's over, I'm awfully sorry,' she said, trying to sound firm but pleasant.

'You know who Dina Martin is?' he said, looking at her straight between the eyes in grotesque surprise as though her nose was missing.

'Sort of.'

The giant laid a hand on Beatrice's shoulder and guided her to a position behind the stage. 'She's the most talked-about comedienne in New York. Why don't you get your girls to do a repeat performance? Dina would appreciate that.' He looked at her meaningfully.

'I'll see what I can do,' replied Beatrice, having made a swift decision.

It took a few entreaties plus a joke or two from Simon to persuade the audience to take up their seats again. Some left, but those who remained were roused into expectation, encouraged by more champagne and chunks of Beatrice's cake. There were whispered words to the lighting man, then a rustle and scuffle as someone entered the room. Preceded by a flamboyant entourage, Dina Martin swept in, wearing a satin Hollywood gown with a short, sugar-pink marabou jacket. On her head was a spangled marabou hat dipping over her eyes. Alice held her breath. She was enormous, stately and imposing, large enough to be a monument in a city centre.

'What can one say?' whispered Simon, coming to sit beside Alice and Robert.

'Grotesquely huge. But rather wonderful.'

'Honestly, Robert?' Alice's mouth dropped open.

'I mean, visually. With her onstage, you wouldn't need a set.'

Simon rushed down to Dina Martin and guided her to a space on the front bench. 'We're so glad you could come,' he said, as though expecting her.

She pulled out her skirts from under her and spread herself across a space in which three had been comfortably seated only half an hour previously. 'This bench is killing my butt. D'you have something I could sit on?'

'It might help to sit on this, Miss Martin,' Simon said, instantly pulling off his favourite ribbed silk jacket.

Accepting his offer, Dina raised herself carefully and arranged it on the bench beneath her. 'Call me Dina, honey,' she said, eyes twinkling beneath feathery false eyelashes. She leaned forward as the lights dimmed for the repeat performance, hand on chin, observing every movement of the girls on the stage in front of her. Then, as soon as the brief performance was over, without a word of warning or even a salutation, she rose and propelled herself in a straight line towards the exit like a submarine about to submerge.

Sipping champagne behind the stage, Alice, Hattie and Pen were having a post-mortem.

'I thought she might at least have been a Royal, with all those photographers snapping away,' Hattie said in a disappointed voice. 'But she wasn't. She was American.'

'Royals expect everything for free,' came Pen's rejoinder. 'Who needs them?'

'If she'd been well bred, she would have thanked everyone. Fancy rushing off like that. I mean!' exclaimed Hattie in a tone of pique. 'Still, anyone that huge is bound to have problems. I wonder if it's glandular, one could hardly ask her that.'

'She's probably got a rehearsal first thing, too tired to hang about. Stars don't have to follow the rules,' Alice explained.

Hattie sniffed. 'I don't see why not. Well, I hope she jolly well buys a few hats after all that.'

Alice thanked everyone for being so amazing and good-tempered, and giving up their time, and generally being marvellous friends. By now, she was barely able to take in what had happened. All she really noticed was that Pen was thinner than ever and Hattie had got a little fatter, hovering between sizes twelve and fourteen.

'See you later at Simon's. He's giving us a surprise buffet. Isn't that good of him?' said Alice, before going off to look for Robert.

She found him pressed against the wall of the narrow entrance to the chapel, surrounded by a small knot of people. All she wanted was for him to give her an all-embracing hug, to tell her that it had been marvellous even if it hadn't, that her hats looked spectacular.

'Shall we go now? I'm hungry,' was what he actually said.

'Was it all right?' she asked anxiously. 'I need a kiss.' Alice knew Robert didn't like showing affection in public.

'Brilliant,' he replied, kissing her briefly on the forehead.

'The *Standard* are interested in doing a profile,' Robert said, as they walked towards his car.

'I haven't done enough for that. What am I going to say? I can't bear being interviewed.'

Robert opened the car door for Alice and smiled at her. 'Don't worry. This time it's me they want to talk to – for the "Men in View" page.'

'Good. Very good, I'm really pleased,' replied Alice. Then, a second later, she found herself wishing that she had been asked instead of him. Although the press had taken plenty of pictures, no one had asked her for a personal interview. It would have been satisfying to say – perhaps, but I'm rather busy at the moment. 'Did you think the show looked professional? I wasn't sure about all the girls moving around so much.'

'I told you, it was brilliant,' Robert said a little distractedly. He was wondering what he would do when confronted by a journalist or how he would disguise his long out-of-work periods, the gaps in his career. Then it came to him. He would invent some design book he was working on, something which involved lots of research thought, and would take ten years to write. Mary would have come up with a suggestion immediately, the apposite subject, fashionable enough to be interesting, but not so fashionable as to be ephemeral.

It was around midnight, when his party was starting to be riotous and to elicit protests from the neighbours, that Simon received a call from Blakes Hotel enquiring if he was free to take a call from Miss Dina Martin. She regretted calling so late, but she had only just finished her last appointment. Simon listened gravely, nodding and scribbling notes on the back of a wine list lying next to the phone. When he put the phone down he scanned the room, looking for Alice, but she had gone home with Robert.

At that moment, Alice was leaning against Robert as he drove slowly past his house, seeking out a parking space. She suddenly sat bolt upright. 'Robert, would you mind staying with me, at my place?'

'No, no. If that's what you'd like.'

'I would.'

'Are you all right, Alice?'

'Just extremely tired. And I'll have to be up early to clear up the workroom tomorrow.'

He took one hand off the steering wheel, stroked back her hair and planted an affectionate kiss on her neck. Then they headed off towards Kensal Green.

The house was a mess, having been unkempt for the days and long nights when Alice was working. She wanted him to see what it was like, so that he could witness her chaos and mess, so unlike the careful order with which he surrounded himself.

'The hats were splendid, they really were. I heard people saying some very complimentary things,' Robert said, as he took off his shoes, preparing to undress, while Alice hastily pulled the bed together into a semblance of order and hid a half-empty packet of sweets behind her bedside table.

'It wasn't how I wanted it to be,' Alice said. 'I wasn't ready, the hats weren't finished properly.'

'Anyway, you can afford to give yourself more time for the next show. My shopping mall will keep us going for a couple of years at least.'

'Shopping mall?' Alice queried sleepily.

'Gerald's next project. A futuristic mall with tropical gardens. We were talking about it the other day. He wants me in on it.'

'I thought you didn't approve of them.'

'In theory I don't. But we have to live, don't we? I don't want Mrs Norham to have holes in her tights.'

Alice smiled back at him and watched him remove his clothes, fold his trousers tidily, arrange his shirt on the back of a decrepit chair and tuck his socks into his shoes. She waited on the edge of the bed until he had removed his underpants.

'Aren't you going to get undressed?' Robert said, getting under the duvet. She was just about to strip off when the telephone rang. 'Leave it, darling,' Robert murmured.

'It's Simon,' she whispered back to him.

She attempted to digest what Simon told her, as his

voice rose in excitement. Dina Martin wanted her to make a collection of hats for her British tour. She'd been seeing a load of young milliners, because she was wild about hats and featured them in all her sketches. When she saw Alice's she knew she'd hit the spot. That's what she said.

'I'm not ready. I can't possibly do it, Simon. I'll have to cancel all my orders.'

'And I doubled the price she suggested. Said that *Vogue* were devoting two pages to your work. Naturally, since you're the brightest talent around.'

'You lied. You shouldn't have. It'll come back on me, Simon. You're being daft and irresponsible, and getting me into trouble.'

'Good.' Simon gave an infuriating chuckle. 'And I've arranged for you two to have lunch at the Carillon. That took some doing, I can tell you.'

'You're fired,' Alice shouted. 'Anyway, what restaurant is that?'

Simon rattled off the credentials. 'The most fashionable place in London, opened last week, fabulous French cuisine, up for a Michelin star, design by Julian, backed by . . .'

'I don't care,' said Alice.

'Twelve thirty, Tuesday. Put that in your diary.'

'I need time to think.'

'No one thinks nowadays.'

'Simon, I promise I'll let you know tomorrow.'

Alice went upstairs, undressed and crept into bed, where she lay on her back, her head spinning. If she took on an enormous commission, how much would she see of Robert? What about the wedding? They'd have to postpone it.

When she mentioned her fears to Robert over breakfast, he appeared unconcerned. 'We're fine when we're both working hard, darling. That's how we're meant to be.'

Thirteen

• • •

Alice was just closing the front door that morning, intending to stock up on a few Danish pastries to keep her going, when she found Mary standing on the pavement, briefcase in hand. Her long white raincoat and white polo-neck shirt emphasised the colour of her face, a light biscuity tan. Long Mexican ear-rings hung from her ears, visible because of her short-cropped hair. Handing Alice a small bouquet of flowers, she kissed her on both cheeks. 'I've just got back from the States. I thought I'd drop by for a brief chat before we meet properly. Shall I come in?'

'Yes, yes, do,' Alice stammered.

'There's so much to tell you, I've had such an amazing time. Have you a moment for a quick coffee? Or are you going somewhere important?'

'Not really,' said Alice, immediately feeling guilty. She ought to have invited Mary to her show, even if she was out of the country.

Mary followed her into the kitchen. 'How is everything? How's Robert?'

'Fine, thanks.'

'It's the first thing I wanted to do, to see you. You're looking so well and much much slimmer. Congratulations, Alice! By the way, Jilly sends her love.'

'Jilly?'

'Of course! The last time I wrote I was in Mexico.

Well, I couldn't avoid going to the States after that. They have such professional libraries and treat one so well, it's a positive joy to work there. So I went to New York . . .'

'Has Jilly moved, then?' asked Alice.

'No, no. But the internal flights are so quick and easy, I flew down to see her. And when I asked if she could find me some cheap motel in the area she insisted that I came to her house. And refused to take a penny, or rather a dollar, though of course I bought her little treats for the children. She's so generous, wouldn't let me pay for a thing. I didn't realise Jilly had such respect for writers, it quite surprised me. I mean you'd hardly guess if you didn't know her. And Duane is unbelievably sweet, too. He's doing incredibly well, they've an enormous ranch. Anyway, we've so much to catch up on. Why don't we fix a time to have dinner? On me, you choose where to go.'

Alice took a sidelong glance at Mary, while she unbuttoned her raincoat. If only she hadn't looked so radiantly cheerful, as though she were in the middle of some passionate affair, which she probably was. She had put on a tiny amount of weight, Alice noticed, but it suited her. She looked almost sexy, with a gleam in her eye and colour in her cheeks. 'Robert's extremely busy at the moment. We both are, actually.'

'I haven't come to see Robert, I came to see you. I really am sorry to have stayed out of touch for so long.'

By now, Alice was about to apologise, then decided against it. 'I haven't forgotten about the money,' she said, trying to sound business-like. 'I'll be able to pay it all back now, don't worry. Things are looking up at last.'

'There's no hurry, Alice. Please don't worry about it. I'm so pleased you're becoming a success, but I knew you would.'

234

'Success? I wouldn't say that,' said Alice. 'It probably won't come to anything. But I think I've landed a big job. Fingers crossed.'

'Who is it?'

'Some American no one's heard of. She's called Dina Martin, a comedienne.'

Mary gave her a dazzling smile and Alice realised she was wearing dark-red lipstick, which completely changed her face. She looked compelling, having lost the slightly grey anonymity of before, and she had kept the hair colour she adopted for her cocktail hat, a deep, glowing chestnut. 'Oh, yes. Dina Martin. I do hope it works out,' said Mary in an offhand manner.

'What do you mean?'

'Never mind. Oh, well, I've seen her on American TV. She's immensely gross and I have to say I didn't find her particularly amusing. American humour is so different from ours. Rather crude, I think. Still, it's a great opportunity.' Mary glanced at her watch and gasped. 'Is it really so late? I'm so sorry Alice, I have to go.'

On her way out, Mary remarked, 'I hear you had a very successful show. I couldn't get a flight so unfortunately I missed it. Never mind, I'll look forward to the next one.'

Later that day, she left a phone message for Alice. Could she have rung from Robert's house? Or from a public telephone, as she sometimes did? Or she could have used her mobile phone. 'Alice, I've been thinking about what you told me. I do hope you don't mind me giving you some advice about Dina Martin. It's just that I don't want you to end up being exploited by someone who has the reputation of being terribly difficult. Incidentally, I knew someone who worked on her show and she drives everyone into the ground. Dina has the most appalling weight problem, which she tries desperately to turn into a showbiz asset.

Never mind, I'm sure I'm being silly and that you'll be able to handle her. By the way, I've moved from Earls Court, it was impossibly small and a good friend of mine, Lady Priscilla Sackville, has loaned me her flat in South Kensington. My new number is . . .'

Alice pressed the rewind button and deliberately lost the end of the message. Then she phoned Robert. 'Hi, I'm at home. Is Mary there?'

'No. Why? Have you seen her?'

'She's back in England.'

'Don't worry, if she calls I'll say I'm busy. She's the last person I want to see. Everything all right?'

'Everything fine.'

'Good luck with the lunch.'

Just when Alice had prepared herself for the Carillon, hair washed, shoes polished, make-up applied with care, Mary rang again. 'Alice, I'm really sorry to bother you, but I'm in a dreadful state. The most awful thing has happened. You know the flat I'm staying in? Lady Priscilla's? I've just heard she's been knocked down in the King's Road by a bus. And she's seriously injured, in intensive care. It's too, too awful . . .' There was a stifled sob. 'I only saw her yesterday. Such a marvellous girl. So pretty and bright. I did wonder if you could possibly come round. Just for half an hour. I'm not normally like this, but I feel so ghastly.'

'Honestly, Mary, I know how upset you must be – but it's really difficult to come today. I don't see how I can manage it . . .'

'Please. Otherwise I'm frightened I might do something stupid. However hard one tries, one can't be strong all the time. Just when I thought life was getting some kind of shape, a direction, this happens. It's as though there's some kind of curse over my life.'

'Mary, you mustn't think like that. You know so many people and accidents happen all the time. I could get knocked down on my bicycle tomorrow.'

236

'Don't say that,' Mary gasped. 'It's unlucky.'

It was unlike Mary to be superstitious and Alice was startled at her sudden outburst of emotion. She found it hard to believe that someone whose life was so calm and regulated, as Mary's seemed to be, could be prone to such violent tragedies. Still, Alice reflected, some unfortunate people went through unpredictable periods of disaster, just as others appeared to be accident-prone.

'You will come?' Mary repeated.

'Yes, of course. Give me your address. I'm going out to lunch but I'll come later.'

As she completed the final touches to her appearance, trying a succession of hats which might go with the full black suede jacket and straight skirt whose waist would be hidden under a pleated blouson, ancient Jean Muir, Alice pondered what would happen if there were such a thing as Fate and it had taken against her? Might she pass out in the Carillon and knock over her chair as she fell to the ground with an almighty thump? Develop a crippling syndrome in her hands so she couldn't sew? Go blind? Would the Customer Services Manager inform her that she must go bankrupt?

Then Alice realised that she was avoiding what she dreaded most. A brief exchange with Robert, which would probably take place over breakfast. *Darling. I've been thinking. I don't think it's a good idea for us to get married. It's not going to work.*

You mean because I'm too fat?

I can't help it. I've always liked thin girls.

She wondered if thinking about things made them happen, if Mary had secretly wanted Priscilla out of the way so she could take over her flat; if she had wanted her husband dead because memories were safer. Then she realised she was hearing Dr Grossman's voice, digging out the underbelly of events and giving them sinister shadows, like a child lying in the dark, convinced that the bedroom wardrobe was a giant about to devour the whole house.

With a shock, Alice caught herself reflected in the black glass of the approaching taxi. How grim I look, she thought. 'Cool green, cool green,' she muttered, and laughed. The driver must have had hundreds of mad people in his cab.

'The Carillon Restaurant,' she announced as she climbed into the back seat and pulled her skirt down carefully to avoid tell-tale creases.

The large circular table, intended to seat six, was swathed in pink linen, showing off a row of glasses and large bone-china platters. Several waiters had deserted their posts in the nether regions of the coolly lit restaurant and were concentrating their attention on table number seven, one of the star tables, their table. This was a celebrity restaurant where celebrities could bask in anonymity. Nervously having ordered the first dish that attracted her eye, Alice was already regretting her decision. She couldn't take her gaze from Dina's burgeoning breasts and plunging neckline, in the midst of which dangled a cluster of silver grapes suspended from her neck by a narrow collar.

'Now, Alice. Tell me about the British. How do they laugh?' asked Dina.

It was an impossible question, like describing the difference between the Nevada desert and the Cotswolds. Alice had no idea.

'But you're so British. You must know.' Dina's urgent tones had the effect of deadening Alice's responses. She felt she must make an impression, but failed to summon the brio that was expected. Dina sounded as though she had leaped out of bed, greeting the morning with a song from some Hollywood musical on her lips.

'I suppose we laugh at obvious things. Like people making idiots of themselves, things not working, bureaucracy, that sort of thing. And a bit of dirty stuff every now and again.'

'Is that so?' Her eyebrows shot upwards as though they would soar to heaven.

Alice searched for a suitable topic of conversation. 'When did you start wearing hats, Dina?' she asked, expecting a trawl through childhood.

'Okay. Let's talk hats,' said Dina with an evident intake of breath, changing her friendly tone into ferocious interview mode. She had become accustomed to the replays of standard questions. 'What do you want to know?'

'Things which interest you. I'd love to see you perform.'

'That's no problem. I'll get a tape sent round, give you an idea of Dina in action.' She suddenly stared down at Alice's plate, where a quail stuffed with pâté de foie gras in a treacly port wine sauce was congealing into inedibility. 'What's this? You're not eating? If it's no good I'll send it back.'

'No, don't do that, please.' Alice covered herself instantly. 'It's just, I'm not sure I really like quail.'

'How about the seafood platter? Would you go for that?'

'That would be lovely.'

'I'll get the waiter. Where's that god-damned waiter?' Since he was nearby, but behind her, he appeared in a second. 'My guest would like the seafood. Fresh, not frozen. Double portion so I can have a taste. And a big bowl of aïoli, tons of garlic, mind.' The waiter imperceptibly shuddered, but nodded and went away. Alice was now overcome with embarrassment. Aïoli – same as mayonnaise but more, a few dollops would be around seven hundred calories at least.

'Really I'd be quite happy just to have the salad,'

Alice said hesitantly, beginning to be overcome by waves of nausea, occasioned as much by nerves as by calorie guilt. If she had been alone it would have been different.

'No sweat. I'll take the rest.' She peered closely at Alice. 'You're not gonna tell me you're on a diet?'

'Well, I am meant to be. Robert and I are getting married and I desperately need to lose a few kilos before then.'

'You're kidding. You on a diet, Alice? For Chrissake, why? Not medical reasons, I hope. Never trust Herr Doctors, they don't have a clue. Myself, I've a Frau Doctor. She measures my heartbeat, takes my cholesterol level, tells me what to do and I pay her a thousand dollars. It's worth it, then I can eat and feel guilty. Guilty eating is like guilty sex, don't you think? Much more exciting. When's the wedding, Alice?'

'Just over three weeks. The twenty-seventh of September.'

'I adore weddings. Other people's. My own don't bear repetition. My last husband insisted we left the reception in a hearse, believing it was the ultimate in chic. Death-defying, he called it. Well, he was a stunt man. I was his challenge, like climbing Everest without oxygen.'

Chuckling while craning her neck and twisting round to observe the people around her, Dina bombarded Alice with further questions. She wanted to know who they were, what they were, where they lived, whether they had muesli or sausages for breakfast, where they bought their clothes, chainstore or designer, if they had jobs or private incomes, whether they paid cash or credit and if they were lovers or married.

'Okay!' Dina exclaimed, evidently satisfied with Alice's guesses. 'Now, d'you mind if I check out your views on millinery? What's your angle on outrageous hats? What do you see on my head?'

'Perhaps you should wear a Viking helmet,' said Alice, gazing in wonder at the exotic being in front of her. 'Or a Boadicea head-dress.'

'Who d'you say?!' Dina hooted.

Alice couldn't remember much about her or what century she lived in because history with Miss Holyoake was one vast, timeless blur spreading from cave men to the Industrial Revolution. But Pen said Boadicea was the first modern woman and Alice remembered that. 'An ancient warrior queen; she was English. Boadicea stood up to the Roman conquerors and killed thousands and thousands of them.'

'No kidding?'

The seafood platter and salad made their appearance, noiselessly set down with a large bowl of aïoli.

Dina absent-mindedly took a couple of langoustines from Alice's plate. Then she tore them apart with her fingers, which she wiped clean with her napkin and plunged into a bowl of rose water. 'I like hats which identify people. That's how I use them. I create these characters round the hats. Think about it. John Wayne without a Stetson, Audrey Hepburn without something gorgeous on her head, Harpo Marx without his floppy job. It was the hats that made them.'

Alice immediately retracted. 'I wasn't being serious about the Viking helmet.'

'I didn't take it personally, Alice. I've an acquaintance with British humour, though most Americans haven't.' She waved once again at the waiter, this time for more bread. By now everything on the plates and dishes had been demolished. Dina appeared more relaxed, leaning into the inadequate back of her spindly chair. 'Say, is it true women from the north are big, real big? 'Cos I'm starting my tour with Leeds, Sheffield, Manchester and Newcastle. Is it going to be the tour from hell? I need to know.' There was a look of repressed fear in the dense brown eyes, a terrible anxiety that touched Alice.

'They'll like you, I'm sure they will. You'll get a fantastic response.'

Dina leaned forward, her sleeve trailing across the empty plate. 'You know how I feel? Like shit.'

The waiter arrived, replenished the bread basket, then waited for a gap in the conversation to suggest a few puddings, elaborating with an over-enthusiastic, rehearsed description in a Maurice Chevalier accent.

'I would quite like a pudding, the chocolate one,' said Alice, overcome by creamy, treacly, chocolatey paeans of praise from the waiter. 'Would you mind?'

'I'd love it. And to follow? I know! Lemon cheese-cake! One pudding is a starter, two is starting to be satisfactory. But if you don't eat up I'll tell them to brown-bag the lot and insist you take it back home. Agreed?'

Alice nodded. She was going through a series of arguments, which ended in the most persuasive. How often would she be sitting in a restaurant like this where the cost of the meal alone would pay for one of her hats? And in such company? So what if the total was way over three thousand calories? She would eat nothing except raw carrots washed down by herbal tea for two days.

Dina's driver was parked outside the restaurant in a white Cadillac with ink-black windows. As Dina manoeuvred herself into the back seat she announced the itinerary and Alice realised she was expected to abandon the rest of the day to her wishes. She sank back onto a cushion, feeling huge and satisfied. The day was brought to a conclusion outside Claridge's, where Dina had an evening production meeting. By now, she had winkled out of Alice a whole gallery of characters, getting the driver to crawl around, circling the City, meandering through Kensington and Knightsbridge, so that she could observe the hat wearers of London. She even parked outside a church where a wedding was in progress to make notes on the type of headgear. Sadly, Ascot was long gone, but she would get some news footage sent over to her hotel.

'You know, Alice?' Dina said, giving her a hug as she hovered in the foyer of Claridge's. 'When I first met you, I thought will this girl have what it takes? Then I changed my mind. I think you'll come up with something fantastic. I'll call you tomorrow, I'll have an idea or two mapped out by then.'

'What changed your mind?' asked Alice.

Dina laughed. 'The way you ate that dessert. Like you loved every mouthful.' Then she laughed again and fished inside a huge leather satchel. 'My, I nearly forgot. This is for you. You can open it when you reach the bank.' She handed Alice a thick white envelope, on which was handwritten in a purple scrawl 'Alice Miller – Hat Lady'.

Alice couldn't wait to tell Robert. Her head was aching with it all as she squashed herself into the throng of people waiting in Bond Street tube station. The envelope, containing a hefty first payment for her services, was crushed in her jacket pocket, so she could reassure herself by feeling its presence through the soft suede. She felt as though she were being propelled along by a strong, warm gust of summer wind. It was with a jolt that she realised she had reached Holland Park. As she emerged onto the street and began walking towards Robert's house she undid the waist button securing her skirt and rolled over the top as she walked. Passing the patisserie window, where she automatically directed her gaze, now replete and lacking in desire, she smiled at the girls inside and shook her head as one of them pointed to a cream-filled gâteau. Not today.

Greeting Alice, Robert seemed preoccupied, but that

was nothing unusual. She was about to tell him how well the lunch had gone when he disappeared inside his studio. A moment later, the door opened again. It was Mary, dressed entirely in musty brown – a pencil-slim linen skirt topped by a tight-fitting ribbed-cotton sweater. She was so tastefully underdressed that Alice felt she had come out in the wrong clothes. Mary stood there without moving, still and unreal as a waxwork, looking at Alice with a slight smile, as though querying whether she was pleased to see her.

Alice flushed with embarrassment, only now remembering that she had promised to see Mary for tea. And it was getting on for eight in the evening. 'I'm so sorry, Mary, but I couldn't get away.' Alice approached her and kissed her on both cheeks (usually Mary initiated the greeting). 'Are you all right?'

'I had to get out of the flat. I rang Robert and he said you'd probably be coming at some point. He could hear I was upset, so he asked me over. So sweet of him.' Mary walked towards the living-room. 'We were just having a drink, Robert found me some sherry. He's finishing off a report, but he won't be long.' She settled herself on a cushion on the floor. Beside her was a pile of magazines and a half-empty sherry glass. 'Will you have something? There's some wine in the fridge, I know you're not keen on sherry.'

Taken aback by Mary's proprietorial tone, Alice stammered, 'That's all right, I'll help myself, thank you.'

Alice made herself a mug of coffee, then went into Robert's studio. He was leaning over his computer, typing rapidly with two fingers. Without looking up, he said, 'I hope you don't mind, but Mary rang, wondering what had happened to you. She was expecting you to come over and I didn't know where you were. Anyway, as she sounded a bit fraught, I asked her to come round.'

'You know where I was.'

At this, Robert suddenly turned round. 'Darling. I completely forgot. Your meeting with Dina Martin. How did it go?'

'It was great.'

Rising from his stool, Robert put his arms round Alice. 'I've had a hell of a day trying to get this damned thing finished. You know how I hate writing.'

'Yes, I do,' replied Alice, escaping his grip and leaving the study.

Reluctantly, she returned to the living-room, where Mary was seated cross-legged, tearing pages from a magazine, placed on a pile of others. She looked up at Alice, smiling. 'I expect Robert would like some more coffee. He can't work without it. I'll go and ask him,' said Mary.

Alice looked at her in surprise. 'You don't have to bother. He doesn't expect women to wait on him.'

'Of course he doesn't. But it's no trouble.' She tucked her legs under her, rose to her feet and disappeared into the kitchen. Her hips were impossibly slim, she moved with conscious grace, which Alice resented. Why couldn't she leave the room naturally? It was as though she were performing for some hidden video camera, assuming her movements would be recorded and examined. Alice leafed through the magazines, which she assumed were Robert's, all concerned with architecture and design, printed on heavy, glossy paper, in French, German and Italian.

'Aren't they beautifully produced? I bought those on my travels. You can't always get them in England,' said Mary, as she came back into the living-room. 'They were meant for Priscilla, well she's . . . I mean was . . . an interior designer. Such a talented girl and only twenty-six.'

'I'm really sorry,' Alice said.

'It's so awful thinking of someone younger than yourself suddenly disappearing from the face of the earth, like a round-the-world yachtsman who sinks a hundred yards from the port of departure.'

'It must be hard for you, Mary,' Alice added.

But Mary merely shrugged, lifting her bony shoulders in a gesture of resignation. 'I'm used to it, unfortunately. But I needed to see you.' She gave a shy smile, as though it was an effort to continue. 'I'm not very demonstrative, but I thought about you a lot while I was away. Whenever I saw something that took my breath away, a sculpture, a painting, a blossoming tree, I wished I could share it with you. I know you appreciate things in the same way that I do.'

Alice was uncomfortable. She felt she had let Mary down in some way, without quite knowing the reason why. 'How's your book coming along?' she asked.

'I'm really pleased with it. It's going better than I thought. Of course, it's a huge learning process when you haven't written biography before. But I think I stand up well compared with those whom the critics rave about.'

Mary rose and began to pace thoughtfully round the room. 'Alice, is everything going well for you? I do hope so. You know, if anything disastrous hit you I don't think I'd be able to take it. There have been so many friends recently . . .' Her face seemed to seize up, as though she were sucking back her emotions with an iron will.

'You mustn't think about it,' said Alice. 'Things do go well for people. I've just had lunch with Dina Martin; we got on fantastically well. And afterwards she gave me a cheque so I can pay you back nearly all the money I owe. I'll do it now.' Alice found her bag, extracted her cheque-book and carefully wrote out the amount.

Mary hesitantly took the cheque from her. 'I'm really grateful, Alice. I'm so hopeless at asking people for money, but I knew you'd remember. Would you like a receipt? For your records?'

'Heavens, no. I'm just glad I could pay it back.'

'You probably worry too much about money, Alice. It's easy to think that everything is solved by it. It really isn't that important.'

'Yes, it is,' said Alice. 'It is when you want to travel, and find fresh ideas and see new skies.'

'And now you've got someone to travel with . . . Mind you, I like travelling alone. When no one knows who you are they think you're terribly famous and important. I'm talking about places off the tourist track, of course, in underdeveloped countries. They still treat white women like queens. It's the only time I feel important.' She gave a self-deprecating laugh, as though expecting Alice to object. 'I've got some marvellous photographs of my trip and lots of Jilly and Duane and the children. Shall I show them to you?'

Before she could undo the clasp of her bag, Alice interrupted. 'I'd love to, Mary, but let's make it another time. I've a lot to do.'

'You've only two or three weeks before the wedding, haven't you? What are your plans for The Dress? Do you think you'll be able to fit into it now?'

'I haven't time to think about it, not with this huge commission.'

'Let me know if I can do anything. You know I'll always help.'

Alice left the room and stepped inside Robert's study. 'Mary seems to be perfectly all right. Couldn't you ask her to go? Can't we be alone for a while?'

'Tell her we're going out. That we're exhausted. Anything. She'll understand.'

'You tell her. You invited her to come over.'

Swinging round from his stool, Robert smiled at Alice. 'Only because she wanted to see you. Do go and see her. You're so much better at these things than I am, darling. And I must finish this.'

247

Alice went upstairs to change and on returning to the living-room found Mary tidying the magazines into a neat pile. She then carried them over to a table in the window. 'Do tell Robert he can keep the magazines. I've read them all.' Then she turned towards Alice. 'Oh, I meant to tell you. Jilly's coming over in a few months' time and I said I'd give her a party for the gang. The flat I'm in is so ideal for parties . . .'

'But surely you won't be staying there now?' said Alice quickly.

Mary gave a tremulous smile. 'Priscilla always said even if she got married and went away she would like me to stay in her flat. Isn't that extraordinary? She felt in some weird way that it was part of me. Anyway, I've decided Jilly's party will be an all-day event, then she can ask lots of people to drop in. I've never known anyone with such a range of relatives and friends, all over Britain and America.'

'I know,' said Alice. 'I've known Jilly since I was six.'

Mary smiled broadly. 'Anyway, I want to be sure you can make the date, so that you're not off with Robert somewhere. I'll let you know when it is.'

'If she'd like a party, then she can have it here,' said Alice firmly.

'But Robert doesn't like parties, does he? I'd be very happy to do it for her. We really did get on enormously well. I never expected to. Do you know, she's started to read books? She never did at school.'

As she put on her coat, Mary said, 'I shouldn't have said what I did about Dina Martin. I'd be the last person to make an issue of it if someone happens to be vastly overweight. In the end it doesn't matter, does it? It's only Western society that is obsessed by fat women. Don't you agree?'

'I suppose so,' replied Alice.

'How can the anorexic possibly be an object of

desire? I'm coming to the conclusion that women are to blame, though I hardly dare say it. Eventually, men will come to their senses, I'm sure of that. If all the advertising agencies began promoting plump women that would be a start.'

'Would you try and put on weight, then?' Alice asked, with a hint of malice, as Mary pulled in the belt of her coat to fit round her tiny waist.

'Me? I've quite a small appetite, I couldn't alter that. Goodbye, Alice. Say goodbye to Robert for me. I don't want to disturb him.'

It was hard for Alice to comprehend why she still listened to Mary. She asked herself time and time again why she hadn't made herself unavailable, hadn't dismissed her in the nicest possible way, but couldn't find an answer. Mary had a disturbing way of making her distrust her own instinct, as though she had a mind which could leapfrog to infallible conclusions, could see round corners and through doors. Mary made her uneasy, yet she found it impossible to close her ears.

'I'd rather not see Mary, at least not for a while,' Alice said to Robert when they were alone together at last.

'Poor Mary. Nothing seems to go right for her. But I've given her a bit of work to do, to take her mind off things. She tries not to show it, but she finds life hard. I feel sorry for her.'

'Do you?'

'Yes, because she's intelligent, sensitive – and not bad-looking. With those qualities she should have got somewhere by now, don't you think?'

Alice drew in her breath. 'Do you find her attractive, Robert?'

'Not particularly,' he answered.

Next morning, when Alice put her head out of the window she could smell a slight tang in the air, the nostalgic tinge of early autumn when you can still remember summer. She decided to walk home, striding along the endless length of Ladbroke Grove, and she could tell where she was by the cars parked on either side. The great divide, Holland Park at one end and Harrow Road at the other, metamorphosed gradually from freshly painted pastel colours and glossy parked cars into grey unkempt walls and ageing bangers with handwritten 'for sale' signs in the back window.

She wondered how it would be, day in, day out during the stretching years, to be with the same man, the same friends. It was an awesome thought. Dinner parties, friends, club, work, holidays, occasional Sunday visits to his family, her family. She didn't know if there would be children, but assumed that one day she would find herself pregnant and Robert would be first resigned, then delighted. Mary's life seemed so much more inspiring, in spite of the disasters. She roamed the world, risked, loved, lost, made her home in different cities and seemed to have the kind of freedom that Alice envied but could never attain.

It would be so much easier if all life's unsatisfactory creases could be ironed out by becoming a size ten. Alice began to have doubts. If she could fit into her wedding-day dress, what then?

Not long afterwards she took The Dress and put it into a Sainsbury's carrier bag. Then, along with some hats she despised, she deposited it at the local charity shop. When she walked out it was as though she had lost at least ten kilos.

Fourteen

• • •

Mary was relieved to be back among the faded colours of London's early autumn. Her plans were progressing well. Now she was thinking about Robert. She had to move gently because he was difficult to know, but she had suspected right from the beginning that they had a common understanding, that their minds were in tune. She wondered if Robert realised how incredibly rare it was to come across someone who understood the intricacies of his thought processes and had his interests at heart. However, he seemed to appreciate her more and more, recognising that he needed her guidance and support. He even confided that he had never known anyone like her, a loyal friend who combined insight with a sense of purpose. They did not share the irresistible physical attraction which had bound her to Roland, but that could be overcome. Once their business partnership had been finalised the rest would follow.

She had taken to arriving at Robert's house in time for tea, since he appeared to appreciate her little ritual. Today she had come earlier than usual, but she remembered to bring a few things along, including a packet of Earl Grey and some gaufrette biscuits, knowing full well that Robert would have had little inclination to be concerned about the empty state of his store cupboards. 'I've brought you something to fall back on,' she said, giving Robert a gracious smile. 'I'm sure you don't have time to go shopping. And neither does Alice, of course.'

Robert accepted the Selfridges Food Hall bag and allowed Mary to unpack its contents, putting each in the appropriate place. Today, he noticed, she was wearing a pair of finely cut, cream linen trousers, having abandoned the full cotton skirts she had favoured earlier in the summer. Her hair was freshly cut into a perfect shape, too often she looked as though she had done it herself in a quick chop. 'You look elegant,' he said.

'I thought it was time for a change. When you've grown up with a mother who's obsessive about clothes you tend to go in the other direction. But I'm off to see a publisher today, so I've made an effort. I've decided not to publish the book myself. I believe it deserves a wider audience. Does that sound boastful?'

'Not at all. How is the book?'

'Coming along very well.' Mary gave a wry smile. 'But it's so hard choosing the right publisher. I refuse to compromise and of course they all want something commercial, even in the academic field. In any case, I try not to dwell on it. There are more important things, after all.' Opening a document-sized Mulberry bag, Mary withdrew a large brown envelope and spread its contents on the table. 'I saw my lawyer yesterday. He really has been very efficient. The partnership agreement is ready for you to look at. It's what we discussed, very straightforward.'

Robert took the sheets of paper and read quickly through them. 'I'm hopeless at this kind of thing. It looks all right to me. But are you still convinced you want to go ahead? I mean, it's quite an investment for you. I might not get any more work, who knows?'

With a laugh, Mary said, 'Have you forgotten about the Chicago project? It's looking extremely promising.

There's a good chance we might get a substantial financial commitment for initial plans. Dear Robert, do you think I'd be doing this if I didn't believe in you?'

'I suppose not. Really, I'm very touched. What do I do now?'

'Just sign at the bottom. Then I'll get it witnessed.' She offered Robert her pen and he scrawled his signature. 'I haven't said anything to Alice yet, but I will when the moment is right.'

'I'd be quite happy to tell her. It's not as though Simon and I haven't talked about it before, finding a business partner.'

'It's probably best if I explain our arrangement to Alice. Recently, though, I've hardly seen her. That American woman seems to be taking up all her time. She'll need to pursue the orders which followed her show. I hope she's not going to drop everything, that would be such a waste. Then she's got the wedding to think about . . . Are you still planning to get married at the end of September? That's barely two weeks away. Isn't it going to be rather a rush for you?'

'The register office is booked for 27 September. Both our parents will be there. And Simon and Beatrice. Then we'll go out for lunch.'

'And afterwards, I hope you're off to somewhere hot and exotic.'

'Oh no. We'll have our honeymoon early next year. Alice wants to go to Barcelona.'

As she filled up the kettle, Mary seemed pensive. Her back was turned to Robert. 'Unfortunately I'll be out of the country by the twenty-seventh,' she remarked. Before Robert had time to explain that he would have invited her except for the presence of Beatrice, she turned round and smiled at him. 'You should go away afterwards, even if it's only a long weekend. I think you both need it.'

'We probably do. I'm sure you're right.'

'Sometimes it helps to have a friend put things into perspective,' Mary said, as she took the cups from the cupboard, instantly opening the right door. 'It's so hard to see what's right under your nose, don't you find?'

'What, exactly? What have I missed?' asked Robert with a smile.

'Friends can say things other can't. I'm a bit concerned about Alice,' she announced, once she had selected her favourite china teapot and completed the ritual of tea making. 'I expect you've noticed that she's putting back quite a lot of weight, in spite of her efforts at the clinic. Such a waste! I have to say I was a little shocked. Not that I said anything to her, of course.'

Robert looked at Mary with amazement; it hadn't entered his mind. The observation he brought to bear on structures and buildings did not extend to Alice. Why should it? Alice was there; he was familiar with every contour of her body, each comforting fold. Measurement didn't enter into it, not when someone was part of your existence. He sensed her rather than looked at her. 'I can't say I've noticed. Alice's weight has always gone up and down, it's how she is. It's hardly surprising she's put on a bit recently. Dina Martin spends her time devouring the contents of London's best restaurants and she insists on taking Alice along.'

'I even wondered if Alice might be pregnant,' Mary said. 'But I haven't had the opportunity to ask her. You can't ask that kind of thing over the phone. I mean, it would be wonderful if she were . . .'

'She isn't,' Robert said quickly. Then he poured some milk into his cup.

'Milk? In Earl Grey? You never have milk.'

'I forgot,' Robert said with a grin.

'If she isn't pregnant, then Alice has a serious weight problem. I'm not saying this for aesthetic reasons, one has no right to criticise anyone's shape after all.'

'Alice has always put on weight easily. She'll take it off when this job is finished. She's just unfortunate that way. I don't see that it's important.'

'That depends.' Mary broke open a packet of wafer biscuits, inserted one gingerly into her mouth and passed the packet to Robert. 'These go well with Earl Grey,' she remarked, but Robert refused her offering. Mary took a deep breath and loosened the silk scarf round her neck. 'I keep having this recurring dream. You and Alice are flying off to your honeymoon and Alice is suddenly taken ill on the plane. You ask for a doctor, but there is none on board. By the time you land, she's – awful of me to say this – she's had a massive heart attack. I had the same dream about Roland shortly before he died. Every time I get really close to someone something awful happens. And then Priscilla . . .'

'Come on, Mary, you're sounding like Beatrice. You must get on with your book and try and forget things for a while. You've nothing to fear. Alice is happy and working well, and so am I.'

Extracting another biscuit, Mary ate it distractedly and drew out another. Then, realising what she was doing, she closed the packet. 'You must stop me eating these. I've a weakness for gaufrettes. Roland was always hiding the biscuit tin.' Then she delicately cleared her throat. 'I know you think I'm worrying unnecessarily, but I do think Alice should see a doctor. Carrying that amount of weight for her height means she's a prime candidate for high blood pressure and escalating cholesterol levels. And that is extremely dangerous. It should be taken seriously.'

'What on earth am I meant to do?' said Robert indignantly. 'Drag her off to the doctor when she's perfectly healthy? Persuade her to go on yet another diet? There's absolutely no need for it, she's slightly plump, that's all. Don't be ridiculous.'

'And if she does get pregnant, that is if you decide you do want children . . .'

'We're not thinking about it at the moment. That's not the reason we're getting married.'

'. . . it would be even more dangerous. I don't want to be alarmist, but even with modern medicine women still die in childbirth.'

Was Mary trying to say that Alice's life was in his hands? Robert shuddered at the thought. He couldn't bear to think of her ill. How would he know what to do? In the past, he had never concerned himself with health matters. Beatrice was the one who interfered, who made doctor's and dentist's appointments, decided on vitamin supplements and mineral supplements and told him when he was unfit. How was he to know whether a condition was serious or not? 'What do you suggest? How on earth am I going to put it to her? There's no way I can tell her she's too fat and should see a doctor.'

'I wasn't suggesting that, Robert.'

Robert watched Mary collect the cups and dust away the crumbs. He started to be invaded by guilt, by irrational fears. He was so used to Alice being healthy and strong. 'What do you think I should do?' he asked, following Mary to the kitchen.

'Well, there is one solution,' she said, as she filled the washing-up bowl. 'You could say that you're taking out a life policy now you're getting married and that you'll both have to go to the doctor to have a health check. That would be the sensible way of doing it.'

'Do you really think it's necessary? How do you know about these things?'

'I happen to have a fair amount of medical knowledge. You pick up all kinds of things in libraries.' Mary slowly began the delicate process of drying the cups.

When he had asked her on another occasion why she insisted on drying she had said it helped her to think when she carried out simple manual tasks. 'You don't have to take my advice – I won't be offended if you ignore it – but as a friend, I had to say something.'

Driving out to Gerald's site, Robert kept hearing Mary's words in his head. He felt guilty about Alice. Beatrice had taunted him many times, saying he was so locked up inside himself that even if she were dying of AIDS he wouldn't have noticed. The rows they'd had, the bitter disputes. Beatrice screaming, 'You selfish bastard!' him screaming, 'You're the one who's selfish. When do you ever think of me?'

Was Mary exaggerating or was Alice really swelling to an unacceptable size? If she was right, had he truly failed to notice? He wanted to look after her, to protect her. Soon she would be his wife. Robert began to rehearse how he would broach the subject. He could be accused, quite rightly, of neglecting Alice recently. But he was confident that she would never condemn him for submerging himself in work. By now, she must have become used to his failure to notice everyday things. Hadn't he confessed, after they'd gone to bed together, that he was difficult and moody, and sometimes retreated into himself? Or was that the picture reflected back from Beatrice?

For the next few days, Alice and Dina had several meals together, which broke every rule Alice was determined to observe. Lunch had become a daily ritual, sometimes accompanied by showbusiness contacts whose brains Dina would pick as though sucking out a lobster claw. She wanted to know why, where, when, how long, how much, who . . . Alice reeled at her energetic questioning and began to see why Americans made it big and the Brits made little miniatures of success, then retreated to a country house in Sussex.

Alice had stopped counting her intake and in any case had managed to lose her calorie counter. Together they consumed pies and sausages and chips and offal, deep-fried everything and loads of sauce and wedges of bread. Sitting in a Real Ale pub where Dina was waxing lyrical over Shepherd's Pie, Alice said she couldn't go on like this. After a couple of weeks she was escalating to over size sixteen. Many shops didn't go beyond size sixteen.

'So? You get a good dressmaker.'

'That's not the point. I was only a little over size twelve not long ago.'

'I'm just the same. My weight goes up and down like crazy. You know what to do? Get two sets of clothes – one for thinner times, one for fatter. That's what I do. Come on, you're not getting all screwed up about the kilos, surely?'

'*I* don't mind. Not any longer, anyhow.'

'So who does mind? Go on, tell,' said Dina, looking quizzically at Alice.

'I'm going to marry someone who only really likes thin women. So I thought I'd lose some weight before the wedding. And now it's all going on again, that's all.'

'That's all? Who is this jerk? Has he said awful things to you?'

'Goodness no. Robert has never said anything, but then he wouldn't. He wouldn't want to hurt me.'

'So, he's a paragon? First one I've ever met. Not that I've met him. But I hope I will. Look, Alice. If the guy says nothing, why the hell worry?'

Alice made a wry face, then decided she might as well confess. 'Oh, you know. I think one day he's going to clear off and he'll meet someone else and he'll say, "It's so difficult to say, Alice. But I couldn't bear you being fat."'

'Are you really saying he's a jerk?'

'No, not at all, Dina. He's great, absolutely fantastic. And I love him.'

'Jesus, you're a muddled kid. Gonna take me time to make you out.'

'You don't have to. Just stop taking me to so many fat-food places!'

Alice told Dina about the size ten Dress, about her stay at Dr Grossman's clinic, about all her diet programmes, her attempts and struggles to reduce her weight. She supposed that Robert had become used to her by now, but she still had to persuade herself every time the subject arose that he did really love her as she was.

Dina listened attentively, restraining her desire to interrupt. Then she burst out, 'Haven't we all tried that, Alice, dear? You know how many diets I've gone through? Thirty-four. You name it, I've done it. Ten years I spent counting calories, weighing myself three times a day. For what? I'd never be Audrey Hepburn. My, she was thin. Know something? I was wild about a guy and lost twelve kilos in eight weeks for him. Then you know what? He ran off with someone fatter than me. Jesus, was I mad! You think Orson worried about being the size of a cruise liner? For sure, he didn't. And neither do I.'

The arrival of her driver cut short the imminent lecture. As she gathered up her bags, Dina turned to Alice with a grin. 'Mind if I use the dress story? It's such a fabulous idea, it really grabs me. I can do something with that.'

'Can't imagine what,' said Alice. 'No, I don't mind as long as you don't have a girl called Alice.'

'How about Mary? I used to think all English girls were called Mary. John and Mary. I'd love you to meet John and Mary, such awfully good people . . .'

Alice worked all through Saturday night catching up on the 'Dina collection' and on Sunday she cycled over, against a stiff breeze, to Holland Park. Soon after she arrived at Robert's house she disappeared to study herself in his bathroom mirror (the only one in the house, he disliked mirrors). Then she recoiled when she saw the darkening circles under her eyes and the chin that seemed to have acquired an additional fleshy fold. On closer examination she realised it was only due to a trick of the light and the way she was standing. Even if she was a little fatter than when she had returned from the clinic, she told herself, once Dina had gone she would cut down and return to her former size. Or thereabouts.

Alice was looking forward to Sunday breakfast. (Beatrice's diet had been abandoned.) Robert would rush down to Cullens to bring back fresh croissants, crusty bread, new-laid eggs and bacon and a pile of oranges for squeezing. This Sunday he appeared to have forgotten or to have decided against it. He asked if she would mind making some toast and tea. He was dressing hurriedly, as though it were a weekday.

'Simon's asked us over for supper tonight,' Robert remarked, as he climbed into his clothes. 'He's finally released himself from the clutches of Genevieve, which is a relief. And he's promised to create a special menu. He's into Japanese food at the moment, so it won't be heavy and fattening.'

Alice looked at Robert with alarm. 'Why did you say that? Do you think I'm fat?'

'No, of course I don't.'

'If you don't mean it, I'd rather you told me now.'

'Told you what, Alice? Don't be silly. You're not fat.'

'I know I've put on weight again. It's all those meals with Dina. I suppose I am a bit plump.'

'All right, if you will, a tiny bit plump. I like you that way.'

He talked with such affection that Alice was ashamed. If only he hadn't been what she'd always wanted, dreamed about, found and now wished to turn her back on. What kind of perversity was this? Alice was irritated that she was irritated, which didn't make it any better. Why was it, when you had everything you could possibly desire, that the desire itself could suddenly subside into a grey heap and leave an aching need to be somewhere else?

'Robert, I can't come to Simon's. I'm really sorry, but Dina has booked tickets for a comedy show. She wants to see some man she might use in her act. It was the only night she could manage. Fantastically important, she wants me to go with her. And she promised to introduce me to her American agent who's coming as well.'

'Darling, I do think you should keep some life of your own. You've been devoting yourself to Dina Martin for days. It is Sunday, after all. Shouldn't you have an evening off?'

'Not tonight. Actually, I'm quite looking forward to it. Simon will understand.'

Robert had cast aside the shirt he had chosen and was stretching up to find another in the shelf of his wardrobe, so that Alice could see the taut muscles of his waist. His arms were thin, his skin was so white, vulnerable as only white skin could be. She wished they were fuller, more rounded with muscle and realised she had never studied them before. 'You're not cross, Robert?'

'Why on earth should I be cross? You're right to go along with Dina, she could be your entrée into the American market. I'd do the same if I had the chance. Gerald mentioned a development in Chicago, by the way. Imagine if we were both working out there!'

Alice glanced at Robert. Her stomach felt queasy all of a sudden. She was about to explain that she didn't see America as a Mecca, that she loved working in England, that Dina had become a good friend, nothing to do with feathering her business nest, then she thought better of it. Robert had lived so long on the margins of success, he deserved a big break. If he had a major assignment over there, she wondered if she would abandon her workshop and follow him to America. Suppose he liked it and she didn't? Suppose nobody wanted her hats? What if he were to be chased by a tall, willowy, bubble-blonde, blue-eyed, red-lipped American heiress? Hadn't Beatrice said that American women were voracious when they set their sights on a man? How would she stand a chance with this super-race of supercharged egos?

'I'm not sure about America,' Alice said. (I might lose you, she thought.)

'We should go just for a short while, I'm sure it would do us both good. I think the time has come for us to open our eyes to something different. We need to spread our wings, see new things, get shaken up and spend some time away from this tiny island. I feel enormously excited at the idea, don't you?'

Alice was puzzled. In the past, Robert had been critical of American culture, only grudgingly admitting that it had energy rather than style. He preferred the quiet, considered statement. Or she thought he did. 'It's not a good place to bring up children,' she said, thinking of her mother's diatribes against that dreadful American education where all they did was answer yes or no in little boxes, absolutely frightful that they couldn't even spell or punctuate.

'I'm not talking of living there permanently,' Robert replied. Then he suddenly looked her up and down. 'Alice, you're not pregnant, by any chance? You are still on the pill?'

There was a trace of tenseness in his voice and Alice flinched. It was as though he was accusing her of deceiving him into having a child without his consent. 'Why did you say it like that?'

'Like what, darling?'

'Never mind. No, I'm not pregnant. Are you trying to say I'm fat enough to be a mum?'

'I've told you, you're not fat.'

Still dissatisfied, Alice continued, 'But you'd hate me to be pregnant. If that's how you feel, tell me Robert.'

'Of course I want us to have children, but I want it to be when we both want them.'

'Don't you think I do?'

'Alice, darling. I know it's Sunday, but I have to see Gerald today. Can we talk later this evening?'

Alice was out of bed, struggling with a tunic she had fitted into a few weeks ago, tugging at it crossly. She managed to pull it up, frowned at the wrinkles spreading from her hips over her tummy, considered a moment, then said 'What the hell' as she buttoned up the two buttons which still met across her breasts. 'Anything the matter?' she said, as she caught him staring at her.

'Nothing at all,' he replied. 'I just like looking at you.'

'What you really mean is why are you putting that on? It's far too tight.'

Robert laughed. 'I like tight clothes, you know that.'

How could he ever tell her? He found it difficult to avoid considering her shape, or to stop imagining her heaving heart struggling to push the blood through the arteries. He thought he had heard her puffing as she came up the stairs. The idea of Alice being ill was something he had never considered, surely it only happened to those over the hump of middle age? Suppose it meant Alice should never have children? Choosing between the wife and the baby, the ultimate horror? He wished the conversation with Mary had never taken place.

*   *   *

263

It was a disappointing meal, as Simon had overreached himself with a host of dishes, each of which was slightly underdone or slightly overdone. And he was offended when Robert gently pointed out to him that it was not possible to eat practically raw tuna, not unless you were a cat. His supper had been continuing for three hours, which was a record even for Simon.

By the time Robert arrived home, he was in the listless state that follows a dismal meal. It was late when Alice returned. The evening with Dina had been sparkling, even though only a few Americans in the audience had grasped the New York humour punched out by the comedian.

'And he was almost as big as Dina,' concluded Alice. 'So I suppose that's why she's thinking of him for her show. Fatties unite!'

'Simon was saying that the Americans have produced a new pill. Apparently you can lose weight without any side effects. Ask Dina if she's heard about it. It's got to be cheaper than going to a health farm.'

'Are you saying I should try it?'

'Just a thought.'

Alice fell silent. Robert realised he had offended her. If only she had hit back, or reacted so that he could have apologised. He had been wrong in attempting to bring up the subject. Taking hold of the remote control, Robert switched on the television set and proceeded to rove through a few channels, finally alighting on a sequence which caught his attention. 'I fancy seeing a movie on TV. Are you up for it?'

Alice looked from Robert to the screen several times. He always watched television like an addict, as though he was about to succumb to a state of heightened consciousness. It was some thriller set in Chicago. She knew that he switched on the set to distract himself from something he wished to avoid, something with emotional consequences, a relic from Beatrice days when she had tried to argue him into a corner, growing ever more furious when he refused to engage.

Without realising it, Alice began to breathe faster, as though she were preparing to jump a hurdle or run a relay. She could feel words congregating in her head, about to burst from her mouth and sensible Alice was repeating – no don't, no don't, no don't. Think about Beatrice. Don't, don't. Think of his fear. I'm in the same trap, all women are the same. Don't bring it up, don't stir the settled waters. 'Robert, I'm not going to take any pill.'

He half turned from the screen. 'It wasn't a serious suggestion.'

'Yes, it was,' said Alice. 'You don't want to hurt me but I'd rather you said it.'

'Said what?' answered Robert evasively. 'What are we talking about?'

'You think I'm too big. And you're trying in the nicest way to get me to diet again. Wouldn't it be better if you just came out with it? That in spite of everything, you can't help having a feeling of revulsion?'

'What on earth makes you think that? Would I be here, would you be here, would we be going to bed together if I found you repulsive? All it was, I was thinking about Dina. You have been putting a lot back, eating with her at all those restaurants. I'm not criticising, not at all, but it can't be very good for you to go on constant binges like that. It doesn't seem healthy to me.'

'I feel absolutely fine.' He turned away and continued watching the screen. 'Robert, we can't go on not talking about it. Would you mind turning off the set?'

'Sure.'

Once the screen was blank, Robert stood up and leaned against the marble fireplace, staring towards the window. 'All I'm saying, darling, is that when you

265

get over a certain size it's dangerous for the heart. Every doctor agrees about that. I don't want you to get to that stage. That's all there is to it. I don't want you keeling over with a heart attack, do I?'

'Has Beatrice been saying something by any chance?'

Robert turned on her in surprise. 'Why should she? Alice, what on earth is going on?'

'You wish I were slim. You wish I could be more her shape. Or Mary's. You try and avoid looking at me too much. Like now. You're staring at your hands. It's no good pretending you're worried I might get a heart attack. You've never worried about it before. I know you're revolted, but there's nothing I can do about it. I'm not interested any more in getting thinner. I feel good as I am.'

'Alice, is that really what you imagine? It's an un-believably stupid thing to say. How can you possibly revolt me?'

'Beatrice once told me you'd never fancied fat women. The skinnier the better, the nearest you could get to a stick insect, that's how you wanted them to be. Then she said how pleased and surprised she was that you'd found someone of a normal size.'

Robert looked across at her, an angry frown distorting his brow. 'I thought you knew by now that Beatrice is constantly inventing the past. She creates a fiction around me, around David. She's incapable of seeing things as they are.'

Alice shifted nervously on her chair. 'So you're saying that she never said anything of the kind? That she made it up? Why would she want to make up something like that?'

'If I knew that I'd have the secret of the universe. Maybe she wanted to upset you, maybe she's envious.'

'How can you say such a thing? She's always gone out of her way to be encouraging, she's a generous person in spite of her faults.'

Robert laughed dismissively. 'Oh, she can put on a good show, I'll admit that. She'll never admit to being jealous, but you do have everything which she lacks.'

'I can't see what, apart from being kilos heavier, and having you . . .'

'Beatrice doesn't want me, she never has. All she wants is to be a genius, a comet in the sky that the whole world stares at in amazement and awe. She's always dreamed of being an absolutely extraordinary woman and she is merely an ordinary woman who puts on an act of being extraordinary. Unlike you, she has never done anything which people have admired. That's all she really wants.'

Alice was still dissatisfied. Unless she knew what he really thought their marriage would be a charade. They would rub along like so many others and Alice didn't want that. She came and stood in front of him. 'Robert, you would tell me if you're unhappy about . . . I mean, you haven't mentioned it for so long. You do want us to get married?'

'Of course I want us to get married, you know I do. Why on earth do you imagine I'd want to change my mind?' Robert replied calmly. 'But it's not as though our life is going to change direction, not as though we'll stop doing what we do now. You'll be working here, that's the only difference.'

'And eating and sleeping here all the time,' Alice added quickly.

'I did assume that,' Robert said teasingly. 'Though you might get fed up with me sometimes and want to spend the odd night in Kensal Green. I won't mind.'

Alice looked up, startled. 'But I was going to sell that house. Did you think I'd keep it?'

'I thought you might want to keep some independence. We don't need the money at the moment. And when we do, you could let out a room or two. It's an investment.'

'An investment?' said Alice. 'Are you being serious? You sound like my father.'

'As I'm not giving you diamonds or a portfolio of shares, why not? Everyone needs something to stop them touching rock bottom.'

'You've never worried about that before,' said Alice.

'One gets older,' replied Robert, as though it had happened overnight.

Finding herself wandering over to the fridge, Alice opened it and peered inside. There were an ageing bag of mixed salad leaves and some shrink-wrapped, brown-tinged carrots, hallmarks of the local late-night shop. There was just enough stale bread in the stainless steel bin to make herself a Marmite sandwich. Which she did.

'Surely you're not still hungry at this hour?' remarked Robert.

'We only had a tiny sandwich before the show,' she replied, biting into the wodge of bread. 'In any case, even if you want me to, I'm not going to be able to lose weight before the wedding,' she added.

'Please, Alice. I'm not asking you to go on a diet. Besides, how much weight can you lose in five days?'

'Everyone will gawp at the photos and say, "Is that big girl really Robert's wife?" I know you mind, you don't have to deny it.'

'Do you want me to mind, Alice? Do you want me to say, for God's sake make an effort and lose a few kilos?'

'So you do want me to lose weight?'

'All right, if you insist. You could do with losing just a bit.'

'How much is a bit?'

Without answering, he stalked towards the kitchen and Alice was unsure whether he was angry or was about to make coffee. Robert came back with two mugs. 'If I said ten kilos, you'd say twenty kilos. There's no point in having this conversation, Alice. You could cut back a little, that's all.'

'How much is a little? I need to know.'

'Stop asking me to define boundaries. Just enough so you feel comfortable.'

'I do feel comfortable.'

'Then that's fine.'

'No, it isn't. You don't like me fat.'

'Do we have to argue about it? It isn't an issue, Alice.'

'It is to me.'

'Then for Christ's sake go on another diet if it makes you feel better. But do we have to talk about it? It makes no difference to me one way or the other.'

Alice shook her head angrily. 'Then why did you say I should lose a bit?'

Suddenly, Robert put his head in his hands. It was the last thing he wanted, to be boiling up for a row. There was nothing he could do to reassure her, any more than he could convince Beatrice that she was the most beautiful, perfectly proportioned woman he had ever been to bed with. What was it about the female psyche that resisted praise and preferred to lie low, cowering in inferiority? Why was it that he had always known he possessed a distinctive talent . . . whereas they . . . It was tempting to generalise – they, them, they all – but now that he knew two women so well, wasn't he justified in leaping to certain conclusions? 'Don't let's have a row, Alice.'

'I can't work at the pace I am and go on a diet. It's just not possible. And I'm not going to take any pill.'

Robert left a message for Mary the following morning. It had been a failure, Alice had responded badly.

Fifteen

• • •

Next day, Robert met Gerald and Mary for lunch, but he had thought better of mentioning it to Alice. He had booked a table in an out-of-the-way little place in Islington, a side-street brasserie where Dina Martin was unlikely to make an appearance with Alice. Soon, Dina would be returning to New York before starting her British tour. He agreed with Mary that the strain of dealing with this difficult woman had made Alice uncharacteristically moody and he would be relieved when she had gone.

As arranged, Mary arrived early. She had already received copies of his sketches for the shopping mall, which she had considered. She passed Robert a file containing typewritten sheets with her comments, cross-referenced with the sketches. 'As you'll see, I did think it needed toning down just a fraction.'

'What do you mean?' said Robert apprehensively.

'The drawings are good, they really are. But I'm not sure this will go down well in Cheltenham. Perhaps you might modify the main area, make it less complex.'

'It really isn't my kind of thing. In fact, I loathe shopping malls. I don't know why I took it on.'

Mary rested her hand in his. 'You know why you did.'

'All right, Mary. Yes, I do,' replied Robert with a laugh. 'To give you a return on your investment.'

'That would just be a bonus! What we're doing is building up for the future, laying a solid base and so forth. Aren't we?' She cast him a glance, then began to study the short menu with devoted attention.

Robert ordered her sherry, his beer and suggested that the set menu would suit all three of them. He didn't want to waste time pondering indifferent dishes.

'Absolutely right,' Mary said, as Robert gave the order. 'We've far more important things to consider and Gerald never looks at what's on his plate.'

'What matters to me, above all . . .' Robert began hesitantly, 'is that we get on so well together. I feel so positive with you – which I don't with anyone else. One day I'd love to design your home. It would sprawl right across the top of a tall building, like a giant eagle's nest.'

Mary laughed as she slipped off her linen jacket to reveal a subtly patterned silk blouse, unbuttoned past the undetectable divide of her breasts. She caught him looking at it with an approving smile. 'Do you like it?' she said, glancing down, then raising her head to his level. 'I felt like being extravagant. Vastly overpriced but perfectly made.'

Robert continued to take her in. He hadn't realised before what a graceful, long neck she had, perhaps because she had cut her hair shorter since they last met. Nor had he noticed her long, white fingers, glistening with Victorian silver rings. 'Splendid rings,' he commented. 'Bea used to love them, too. Alice won't wear them because they get in the way of sewing. It's a shame. I used to like choosing them.' There was one in particular that caught his attention, with a large green stone. The setting seemed too elaborate to be holding a chunk of green glass. 'That's not an emerald, is it?'

'Actually, yes.' Mary looked slightly embarrassed. 'I know one should keep family heirlooms in the bank, but I'd rather take a risk and wear them.'

Robert smiled appreciatively and went on to ask his usual question, as he did every time he saw her. 'How's the book progressing?'

'One can't rush these things. I'll need to go back to Mexico soon to continue my research.'

The thought of Mary being in another continent gave him a moment of panic, for now he couldn't imagine undertaking anything substantial without her. 'Will I be able to contact you? What if I have a serious problem with the shopping mall?'

'Oh, there's no need to worry. I'll make sure we're in e-mail contact.'

The waitress placed a basket of dry, stale-looking rolls on the table. Mary selected one, delicately tore off a morsel, then left it on her plate. 'I know it's difficult, but I do think we should talk frankly about Alice before I go away,' she said. 'I got your message. At least you managed to bring up the subject.'

'I tried. But it was very hard for Alice to understand that I was merely concerned about her health. She couldn't get it out of her head that I was being critical about her weight, that I'm put off by her being . . . well . . .'

Mary interjected softly, 'Fat. We hate using the word, but one can't avoid it beyond a certain point. And I loathe the word obese. I don't know why the medical profession insists on using it.'

Having demolished the stale roll, Mary grimaced. 'Can't resist bread, even a stale roll. Roland loved to dip it in olive oil. I wonder if they have any?'

'I doubt it,' replied Robert, making no move to summon a waitress. He suddenly noticed that she had pushed her chair closer to his.

'Robert, could I ask you something personal? Don't answer if you don't want to, but it would help me to clarify certain things about Alice's health. I need to form a complete picture, so we can decide what to do. Is everything satisfactory with you and Alice in the bed department?'

The question was so direct that Robert was unable to hide his astonishment. Mary had a way of bringing up the trivial alongside important matters, as though her mind were constantly running on double tracks. It might have brought him up short, but he was compelled to answer. If Beatrice had asked him such a question he would have ignored it. 'Yes, most times.'

'So you aren't put off? Physically, I mean.'

'I don't know. I hadn't thought about it. Maybe, a little.'

Mary sighed. 'Such a shame. These things shouldn't matter, but often they do. Especially when one has an intense aesthetic awareness – which we both share.'

An image slipped into his mind: slim legs, delicate knees, small feet and breasts like those on the court ladies painted by the Flemish school.

Robert opened his file and began skimming Mary's pages. 'This is amazingly thorough,' he remarked, wondering how she would appear naked. She would have trim pubic hair and slim thighs, he thought. He would run his hands down the bony line of her hips. He had a suspicion that she might be sensual in bed. Some women hid it well.

'Remember that night when we both collapsed in bed together without undressing?' Mary giggled. Then, as though divining his thoughts, she added, 'I sometimes think we should have had proper sex. Maybe we should try it some day.'

At that moment Gerald came through the glass doors and gave a cheerful wave. 'How's tricks?' he said, as he approached their table and deposited an overpolished briefcase at Mary's feet. 'Excuse me, must make a call.' He wandered off to a corner of the brasserie and took out his mobile.

'I always think he looks like a flasher on Hampstead

273

Heath,' Mary said in a whisper, shielding her mouth with an upheld hand. 'There's something irresistibly vulgar about Gerald. How's tricks indeed! But one can't help liking him. And I know he likes you.'

Under the table, Robert was aware of light fingers stroking his thigh. He wondered if he had imagined it, for Mary was looking towards Gerald as though nothing had happened. It made him feel uneasy that Mary was able to revive the brief sensations of desire he had felt when she was staying in the house, which had nothing to do with how he intended to live now.

'I think about you a great deal, Mary. You're very important to me, but . . .'

'Yes?' she replied, urging him with her eyes to finish his sentence.

He wanted to say that a time might come when . . . then he stopped himself. It was too soon to admit his feelings for Mary, which he was making every effort to deny. 'I don't think it would be a good idea to go further. Neither of us wants to hurt Alice.' Then, fearing he had been too abrupt, he added, 'Not for the moment, anyway.'

Mary smiled broadly and touched his hand. 'I've never understood women who are possessive – I suppose because I'm not. Roland used to say I was like a man in that respect. Maybe I am.'

'And did Roland sleep with other women?'

'Strangely enough, he didn't. I always said I wouldn't mind if he did, but he seemed completely satisfied with me. Heaven knows why, I'm no sex goddess. I suppose I just did what he liked, there's no mystery to it.'

While she was speaking, the waitress arrived with their order and proceeded to set down three soup bowls, but Mary appeared to be unaware of her presence.

How did she manage to fascinate and disturb him? If any other woman had said such things it would

274

have seemed like an act. He would have made some flippant comment and laughed it off. Could she be right? Were they wrong to deny themselves the natural consequence of their closeness? She would have made it easy for him. There would have been no reproaches, no rows, no demands, merely a satisfying release in the afternoon, and back to work. Then he thought of Alice's loving embrace, the gentle morning kiss and the angelic look of her face in the first light. There had to be limits. He and Mary would have a satisfying working partnership. For Alice's sake he would make sure that it didn't go further than that.

With a clatter, Gerald arrived at the table, pulling out a wooden chair while stuffing his mobile phone back in his pocket. After apologising – important callbacks, always get guys at lunch, best time – he launched into an overview of his latest projects, including the purchase of a peach of a site against tough opposition. Mary allowed his ego an appropriate amount of time to float on the clouds of achievement, then she pulled out Robert's file. She would have made an excellent senior civil servant, Robert thought, nudging ministers round to her agenda. There was a brief staccato discussion. Gerald would leave the boring detail to Mary. Following yet another summons from his mobile, he left the brasserie with his first course barely touched.

Mary was satisfied with the meeting and said she could handle Gerald's objections. These things took time and needed patience. 'I enjoy working with you,' she began. 'You're the kind of man it would be very easy to fall in love with. And I was very happy being in your house.'

'You're always welcome to stay, Mary.'

'I wouldn't dream of moving in on you,' she replied with a slight laugh. 'Anyway, you'll be married to Alice very soon.'

'That won't make any difference. You know how fond she is of you.'

Mary glanced away, as though it didn't need saying. Then she clasped her hands together and a wistful expression came over her face. She glanced to either side of her and leaned towards him. 'Robert, I know it's silly of me, but I'd rather you didn't tell anyone when I go to Mexico. One has to be so careful nowadays. Before you know it you find someone else writing about your subject – it happens all the time. And then, of course, you can't get published. You're the only person who knows what I'm doing. I haven't even told Professor Norrington.'

It had crossed Robert's mind that he had no idea of what she was researching, nor the subject of her book. But the occasion to ask had never seemed to arise. Now he said, 'You've never told me what your book's about, Mary.'

'Then you should have asked,' she replied, glancing at him coyly. 'There's a lot we don't know about one another. Isn't it better that way?'

Robert smiled and suddenly put his arm round her shoulder. 'Tell me. I won't steal the idea,' he said, aware that she hadn't flinched away as she might have done.

'A world-famous, wildly beautiful Latin-American ballet-dancer who became involved in the Mexican revolution. That's all I can say.'

'Fascinating. It sounds like a marvellous idea for a film.'

Mary put two fingers to her lips to demand silence, then rested them on Robert's hand. 'I'm really upset that I can't come to your wedding.' She looked straight at him like a portraitist memorising her sitter. 'Why don't we have a bottle of champagne together before I leave the country? And I promise not to talk about work.'

Suddenly they both looked down at the rapidly cooling plates of pasta in front of them.

'Shall we leave it? Would you mind? I'm not hungry,' Robert said.

'Neither am I,' replied Mary with a smile.

He escorted her out of the brasserie and into Islington High Street, where groups of passers-by were devouring the shop windows of boutiques and bars and restaurants. They were lingering by a shop that stocked one of Mary's favourite designers, when she suddenly took Robert's arm. 'Isn't that superb?' she whispered, gazing at a deep-purple velvet cocktail dress with a sculpted fitting front and tiny *diamanté* straps.

'You'd look fabulous in it,' Robert said.

'It's not really my colour, but why not? Shall I be really extravagant and buy it?'

Robert began to open the glass door of the boutique. 'No,' he said firmly. 'I'm going to buy it for you.'

For a few days, exactly how many Alice was unable to tell, she had forgotten to weigh herself. The scales, which had seemed like a constantly admonishing friend, were buried somewhere in a heap of dirty linen, which she hadn't had time to wash. Dina had returned briefly to the States before embarking on her tour and Alice had little more than a week to complete the hat collection before she became Mrs Norham. There was no time to cycle down to the patisserie, none for lingering moments at all. She had taken to collapsing onto an old mattress, which she had put down in her workroom, and would start up again as soon as she was sufficiently revived. Beatrice pleaded with her several times to take an evening off and come to the club, but Alice refused. After a few phone calls Beatrice took matters into her own hand.

Alice was thankful that she had come by without Drusilla and Sasha. For once, Beatrice was wearing minimal make-up, with her hair tied back severely and secured by a strip of cotton. Her trousers were baggy and she was wearing a T-shirt, very un-Beatrice. She sat on the client armchair in the workroom, while Alice manipulated the materials for Dina's parade of hats.

'Those hats, Alice! They're absolutely remarkable. You always dream up things which are really special, that no one else could make.'

Alice smiled as she glanced at Beatrice and continued the painstaking stitching. When she looked up again she noticed Beatrice scanning the workroom with a critical eye. 'I know it's in a terrible state, Bea. But I'll clear up when all this is out of the way.'

'You need a cleaning lady, Alice. Still, you'll have one once you're married. Robert has a thing about dust.'

Before Alice could reply, Beatrice walked purposefully out of the workroom. After a few minutes she heard the rumble of the Hoover sucking out weeks of dust, travelling round the house like a manic robot. When Beatrice reappeared she demanded a tea-break and produced a cake.

Alice continued sewing and allowed a small portion to be inserted into her mouth. 'Light and subtle,' she said, knowing Beatrice would expect a comment. 'And it would be very good with cream in the middle.'

'That's what I would do,' said Beatrice with a laugh. 'Cream's out, so they tell me. But I'll put some on your wedding cake. You won't be keeping it afterwards in some ghastly tin, will you? Because I . . .'

Alice interrupted her. 'Bea, we've decided to have a party early next year for our friends. Why don't you save it up for then?'

'That's a much better idea.'

Beatrice appeared to be satisfied, which puzzled Alice, and she gave an impression of tranquillity, which also puzzled her. Then, all of a sudden, she came and sat on the edge of the table where Alice was working. 'I'd better tell you, I'm pregnant again. And before you say anything, I'm over the moon. I hope it's going to be a boy and with any luck, a Gemini. That's a good sign for a male.'

'Oh, that's wonderful, Bea.' Alice got up and embraced her. She could feel the slight swell of her normally pancake-flat stomach. 'Perhaps he'll keep your girls in order for you.'

They both laughed, then there was an awkward silence from Beatrice.

'It's not what David wanted,' she said after a while. 'In fact, we really don't want the same things at all. Isn't it strange? It's taken me all this time to realise we're totally unsuited. Really he would have liked one of those placid English roses who never drops things and has a nice low voice and . . .' She bit her lip. 'I got him drunk at the right time of the month. Otherwise it would never have happened.'

'What?' queried Alice, finding it hard to concentrate on the implication of her news while attempting to finish a hat.

'I wanted it to be his. I couldn't have him disowning my child.'

Alice put down her needle. 'That's ridiculous. David's not like that. Why on earth would he do that?'

'We haven't been doing it for months. If a man goes without, anything can happen. He doesn't have to spell it out, Alice. I know his work means much more to him than life with me.'

'I'm sure that can't be true. He'd be lost without you.'

'Maybe for a week or two. He doesn't love me, not in the way I want anyway.'

'And what's that?' said Alice with a smile.

'Lust and passion and poetry. Isn't that what we all want?'

'I think I'd settle for not having too many arguments and being nice to one another. And having fun sometimes.'

'Dear Alice, if only life were as simple as that,' said Beatrice. Then she stood up, hands on her hips, and scrutinised Alice. You haven't really put on that much weight since you came back from the clinic. Considering all those meals you've been having with Dina.'

'Do you know, Bea, I can't remember when I last weighed myself. I've no idea what I am now. I suppose I ought to find out.'

'Does it worry you, not knowing?'

While she was threading her needle, Alice paused to think. 'I'm not sure. To be honest, I don't believe it does.'

'Oh, God, Alice. I'm so happy. Whenever you got depressed about your weight I used to feel awful. Nothing I said would have made any difference.'

'There's one thing which still bothers me, Bea. Do you remember when you told me that Robert only really liked thin women? Had he met me when he told you that?'

'What are you saying, Alice? I never said anything of the kind.'

'You did, Bea. How could I forget something like that?' Alice replied.

Beatrice looked so hurt that Alice almost regretted bringing up the subject. 'I think I know what you're thinking of, Alice. Do you remember when I told you about that ghastly holiday Robert and I had in Spain? He kept going off all day to look at examples of Spanish architecture. I didn't go to Spain to stare at buildings, so I used to lie on the beach the whole time. And when I wasn't doing that, I'd be downing Spanish brandy and stuffing myself with fried tapas. When we got home I really was disgustingly fat.'

'You fat?' said Alice, laughing at the thought.

'I was, you know. Well, fat for me. Then Robert said something about not liking me fat, that it didn't suit me – and I stormed off in a temper. For heaven's sake, Alice! It was nothing to do with you. Did you think it was?'

Alice nodded.

Beatrice came up and hugged her. 'How awful. I'm so sorry. I do say brainless things sometimes. Alice, I'd never ever want to do anything to upset you. Please believe me.'

Beatrice rushed out to the kitchen to make a pot of tea and vowed to take Confession with Father Thomas the following day. It was hard for her to accept that one chance remark could alter someone's life for months and months. How Alice must have brooded, how insecure she must have felt. Why hadn't she said anything before? When she returned, she masked her guilt and regret with exuberance. 'Where's that lovely dress, Alice? If it needs a slight alteration I could do it for you.'

'I don't have it any more, Bea. I gave it to the Oxfam shop.'

'You did what? That fabulous material? Have you gone mad?'

Beatrice's face was such a picture of horror, as though Alice had just given away all her possessions, that she burst out laughing. 'Not really. I never felt like finishing it off, anyway.'

This time next week, Alice reflected, she would just have become Mrs Norham. After the brief words in the register office they would all have lunch, her family, Robert's family, Simon and Beatrice, then everyone would go back to work. When the cold evenings drew in, she and Robert would plan a glorious Christmas, alone on some sun-filled island. Afterwards, they would have their New Year's party. That was Robert's idea. Why had Beatrice imagined that he hated parties?

*   *   *

Robert parked his car in the brightly lit mews in South Kensington and looked up at the row of cottagy film-set houses newly painted in pink, green and yellow. As indicated in Mary's directions, Priscilla's house was illuminated by a reproduction Victorian street light outside.

She greeted him wearing the velvet dress he had bought her, with a black lacy shawl slung over her shoulders. 'Make yourself comfortable,' she said, pointing to a sofa in the cluttered sitting-room. 'I won't be long.'

Robert could smell her perfume lingering in the room. He felt uneasy. How could he have any control over what would inevitably happen? It was fortunate that Mary was about to go away. He would find the right time to tell Alice about their partnership – once she felt secure in their marriage – and he hoped that one day she'd understand how much he owed to Mary. As a working partner. He wanted to tell Alice that Mary made him feel as though he could achieve everything he set out to do.

Mary entered the room, bearing a tray with the champagne in an ice bucket and two tall fluted glasses, which she set down on a walnut table. Then she sat opposite him, leaning forward in a chintzy armchair, so that he could see the slight swell of her breasts. He had an intense desire to slip down the *diamanté* straps and carry her off to bed.

'Robert, I know I said we wouldn't talk about work, but as I'm going away for some time . . .'

'How long?'

'A couple of months, maybe more. I had another talk with Gerald and I'm afraid he's being rather stubborn. He wants you to change the concept of the shopping mall.'

'What do you mean, change? I thought we'd agreed on the basic idea. I've spent a lot of time . . .'

'I know,' replied Mary calmly. 'But he wants something on a slightly smaller scale and a little more, well, traditional. Just for this development. I suspect he has problems with the council. Someone is creating local opposition and they're worried.'

'What's that to do with me? Gerald has to sort out that one. If he's going to settle for some crass Disneyworld shopping centre with plastic trees and mini-fountains, then he can find someone else. I'm not interested.'

'You'll have more scope with Chicago. They're much more adventurous over there. But for the time being, I think you ought to go along with what Gerald wants. If he hires another architect because he thinks you're going against his wishes he might not be too keen to come back to you.'

'That's a risk I'll have to take, Mary.'

'No, Robert. That's a risk *we* won't be taking. At this stage we're not in a strong enough position to be dogmatic.'

'We? This is my decision.'

'Our decision. I'm your partner, remember? I invested in you because I want you to reach your full potential, to be famous enough to choose your own projects. And to have a comfortable life, that goes without saying. But if you start being difficult now it doesn't bode well for the future. Of course, if you want to go your own way, you can always buy me out.'

'What are you talking about? You know I couldn't possibly do that.'

Robert drained his glass of champagne, but Mary immediately filled it again. 'Is it so hard, to make slight concessions?' she asked.

'For me, yes. It's how I am.'

'Heavens! I forgot the pistachio nuts. I bought them specially for you.'

Mary quietly rose to her feet and disappeared to

the kitchen. Robert could hear the tearing of foil. He suddenly realised that he had made an appalling mistake. Mary had assumed that she would have total control of his life, of the way he worked, of the projects he undertook. He would be a puppet in her hands. How could he have failed to see what she was doing? How could he have allowed himself to accept her as a partner? Without consulting Alice? Or even Simon? It was strange how little it took to see someone you knew well in a totally different light. How would he be able to escape from her now? I must keep control, he told himself, as she came into the room again carrying a dish of nuts.

'Robert, before I go away, do you mind if I say something? It's so awful to see someone you care for making the wrong decision. More than anything, I want things to work out well for you.'

'Let me think about it. I'll have another talk with Gerald,' said Robert, trying to relax back into a corner of the sofa. Mary came to sit next to him, but he avoided looking at her.

'I wasn't meaning Gerald. I was referring to your marrying Alice. I think she has a bad influence on you. She's holding you back, Robert. Basically, all she wants is a cosy little life in Holland Park making a few hats and having babies. And I know you don't want that. In a few years' time you'll be deeply frustrated, miserably unhappy and longing to escape. One should do everything to make second marriages an improvement on first ones. But that's only my opinion. Some people can't resist repeating their mistakes and there's nothing one can do.'

Suddenly Robert got up to face Mary. She was reclining on the sofa with an unlit cigarette in her hand. She handed him a lighter and as he lit the cigarette his hand was shaking. Taking a deep breath, Robert tried to quell the waves of anger sweeping over him. 'What do you want, Mary? What are you really after?'

'You don't need to ask me that,' she replied, smiling. Then she took his hand and pulled him towards her.

He could feel her hands stroking down his back. As in a bad dream, he was rooted to the spot, even though he had an overwhelming desire to run out of the flat. He never wanted to see Mary again. Perhaps something might happen to her in Mexico. No, nothing ever happened to Mary, only to others. Everything was swimming before his eyes. Now he could never tell Alice. 'I have to get back, Mary,' he said with a forced smile.

As she let him out, Mary kissed him goodbye like a lover. 'I'll keep in touch,' she whispered.

Two days before the wedding Robert was overcome by fatigue, not the tiredness of every day but as though each bone in his body had turned to lead. Was it flu? Or some all-invading virus, unclassified by doctors? He threw himself onto the bed, thinking he would take a quick nap, but he did not awake until eighteen hours later. Mary's face seemed to be just in front of his, looking slightly down with a satisfied smile. Her words raced through his head like a stream of projectiles. Would he ever be rid of her? Was she another Beatrice, destined to haunt him for ever? He could only imagine one solution. If he worked hard enough, for long enough, he would buy her out. It would mean abandoning his principles, fulfilling what was expected of him without complaint. It would mean long weeks in Chicago, away from Alice. For the moment he couldn't think how he would put it to her, but he knew he could never admit how foolish he had been. His head was throbbing and crawling out of bed took an enormous effort. He just managed to ring Alice.

When she came round, Alice was horrified. She had never seen Robert in a state of weakness, eyes closed, lying on his side with his arms spread out limply over the pillow. He wanted only to sleep, but Alice promptly called the doctor, even though Robert said it was nothing, just tiredness. When he eventually came, he backed up Robert's diagnosis. Exhaustion and stress had taken their toll, but nothing was wrong physically. All he needed was to remain in bed until he felt stronger. Alice wanted to care for him, to be there for his needs, but he murmured that he was perfectly all right, she must get back to finish her work. Although he was against it, Alice made the necessary calls and Robert finally agreed that they should postpone the wedding. 'Did anything happen?' asked Alice, seeking desperately to find a cause. 'Or maybe it was something you ate.'

'No, Alice. It couldn't have been. All I did was to have lunch with Gerald on Monday, some boring brasserie in Islington.'

'What did you have?'

'I honestly can't remember. Pasta probably.'

Alice phoned Beatrice to tell her they had decided to delay getting married until Robert had recovered.

'That's a relief,' Beatrice said. 'I did an in-depth reading of your sign and Robert's, and things appear to have changed. They do occasionally, you know. The date you've chosen wasn't propitious. The heavens are telling us something and we have to listen. You needn't tell Robert any of this, he doesn't have to know. I'll find you another date.'

Alice acknowledged that the delay of a few months was practical and sensible. She would have more time to finish her hats. Robert would get better and back to his usual self, then they would be married.

Robert gradually grew stronger and insisted on keeping

his projects on the move, working from his bedroom that now doubled as an office. Alice could do nothing to slow him down, but he agreed that they would get married the following April, before he went to Chicago.

Beatrice did not offer her opinion about Robert's illness, even though she had one. Whatever she said might be taken the wrong way. She suspected that Robert was terrified that once they were married Alice might get pregnant. His illness was a symptom of his unresolved fear, she was convinced. There was no point in reminding Alice that Robert could never face being a father. But perhaps he was different with Alice. Robert might slowly be getting used to the idea. Why else would he have recovered? To recover, you needed to trust the future. You should always give people the chance to change. She began to believe that Robert had changed.

Alice decided not to sell her house in Kensal Green. Now that she was becoming known, with orders flowing in from the States following Dina's triumphal return, she needed to hire a couple of assistants. There wasn't space in Robert's basement and in any case, as Simon pointed out, she could easily have another workroom by building an extension at the back of her house. This would also mean that Robert could use his basement as a permanent home for his architectural models and plans of past projects, so that potential clients could see at a glance where his genius lay. In any case, that part of the house belonged to neither of them. It would always remind her of Mary.

Alice often wondered why Mary had disappeared so abruptly. She had never paid back all the money she owed – but Mary had never asked for it. Robert said she'd had to rush off to Mexico to interview important people for a book before someone else got there first. Alice was waiting for a postcard, but it never came. Robert assured her that he hadn't heard from Mary either. Eventually, he did tell her that he was slightly attracted to her at first, but that it never came near to an affair. Alice believed him. She didn't wish Mary ill. Why on earth should she? It was only Beatrice who had some weird notion that Mary carried evil. Still, she was a Catholic and they believed that kind of thing. If it hadn't been for Mary, Alice would never have visited the clinic, never have met Dr Grossman and would still be trying new diets. She now hovered between sizes twelve and fourteen. Sometimes more. It didn't bother her unduly. There was no reason to talk about Mary any more.

They all began to meet regularly again at the Lansdale Club. Beatrice's baby was expected in June. She was disappointed to learn that it would be a girl, even though she'd performed all the right rituals to produce a boy. Simon? He was making more money than ever, continuing to date unsuitable girls and was about to change the interior of his house for the umpteenth time.

One late night, cruising through his favourite sites on the Net, Simon happened to alight on one he hadn't noticed before: www.desperately.seeking.co.uk. His eye was caught by the names, which apparently belonged to one person: Dr Mary Norrington aka Duchesse de Guerlidan aka Myra Jackson aka Joan Kentucky. Real name Mary Bartlett. The story, although written in some Gallic version of English, could just be deciphered. He produced a more correct version, printed it out and presented it to Alice.

My name is Roland Lamotte. If you have come across the above person, who uses different names, who is by profession a literary researcher and could be somewhere in America or Europe, please contact me urgently.

I was married to Mary for six years, without realising who she was. I believe Bartlett is her family name. It is possible to be married and not to know your wife, isn't it? She was good to me at first. I am unfortunate as I suffer from schizophrenia, but I controlled it through taking drugs. My family, who is well-known in France, disowned me when I was diagnosed as schizophrenic. Mary persuaded me that my drugs would eventually kill me so I came off them. My condition deteriorated. She had me committed to a private mental hospital outside Paris. It was easy for her to secure the power of attorney from a corrupt solicitor who had influence with the court. In this manner she was able to take anything from my estate she wished – furniture, money and family jewellery – saying she needed the money for my medical expenses. While I was in the hospital, I started getting better. The doctors were fantastic. When I came out, after about a year, I found there was nothing in my flat, all my possessions had gone and my savings had disappeared along with Mary.

Mary is clever. She liked inventing stories to gain people's sympathy and they always believed her. Because they felt sorry for her they would give her money or help her in some way. She told the French lawyer that I had made several suicide attempts, that she could no longer cope and that I should be kept in hospital for my own safety. She told the hospital that she loved me and was totally distraught at having to send me away. All completely untrue. I hate having to write this. We were not unhappy together. I came to love her, but I was never sure if she loved me or not. I know she believed I was a genius. (I painted a little.) She used to say genius is akin to madness. I am neither mad nor a genius. And I have to find her.

Sixteen

• • •

Alice wondered if it was true, what the old wives told. Inside her stomach, a tiny creature was giving an almighty kick just as the Corsham Jubilation Anthem drew to a close with a corresponding thump of chords. He, the unborn boy, was going to be a musical genius. Would she give birth to the next Mozart if she went to enough concerts?

Five years had passed since she had last attended a reunion, enough time to inspire gossip throughout tea. The recently appointed headmistress, in her inaugural speech, announced clean sweeps and a programme of regeneration. The new had to replace the old, even though the essential traditions would remain. There was little sign of essential traditions, Alice thought, for she no longer recognised any of the teachers, who were all young and clad in a uniform reminiscent of hostesses working for a thrusting cut-price airline.

In the assembly area next to the hall there were several new display cases with objects professionally laid out by the Marketing and Media A level students. To her amazement, Alice found one of her hats tilted jauntily in a corner of a cabinet, with a handwritten label beside it: *Alice Miller, one of our distinguished old girls, is now a top milliner. This hat was donated by the owner, Mary Bartlett, also an old girl and now a famous author (see Case Three).* Alice drew in her breath. She could instantly conjure up the scene. The cocktail hat. Mary staring into her mirror, turning her head with a half-smile of pleasure and approval, standing ramrod straight in the workroom of the little house she had once owned in Kensal Green. Quickly passing to Case Three, Alice found herself standing next to Pen. Pen had changed little, except her hair was now orange with black flecks, rather like a tropical parrot.

'Typical, isn't it?' said Pen, as they both stared at a small privately published volume with a hand-stencilled cover which said, *The Travails of Dolores Del Monte: Mexican Dancer and Revolutionary* by Dr Mary Bartlett.

'Trust her to write about a person no one's heard of.'

'We never did Mexico in history. But whoever she is, she's probably quite famous over there. Like Emily Pankhurst here.'

'Who?' asked Pen.

Hattie inserted herself between Alice and Pen. 'Gracious, look at that! Dr Bartlett? I didn't know Mary studied medicine. I do hope she hasn't decided to come along today. Do you think she might have been sitting at the back somewhere?'

'She won't be here, I'm sure she won't,' remarked Alice with authority. 'I've loads to tell you about Mary Bartlett.'

'Tea at the Corsham Grange, then?' said Hattie.

A matronly Jilly put her hands round Pen's and Alice's shoulders when she caught up with them walking down the drive. 'I saw you guys in Hall, but I got stuck out front. It's so exciting, being here on my own. Duane booked me a ticket to England for my birthday. Isn't that darling of him? I'm dying to catch up. Isn't it just awful about the Grange becoming a Sunset Home?'

291

'I don't believe it!' exclaimed Hattie. 'How on earth could they do that? Still, I'm sure I'll end up somewhere like that – making cuddly toys with a big needle in an old people's home.'

'Hattie, don't be daft. Of course you won't,' said Alice. 'Anyway, we'll all be living for ever by the time we're old.'

'You really believe we will?' said Jilly.

Pen licked her finger and slicked back an orange wisp from her forehead.

'Lovely ear-rings,' commented Hattie, wishing she had the nerve to exchange her tiny studs for Pen's swinging candelabra.

Since the Corsham Grange Hotel was now out of bounds, forbiddingly encircled by high walls and security gates, the group made their way to a new French wine bar advertising afternoon tea, which Jilly had noticed as she drove through Corsham village. Being greeted by a cheery waiter in a black polo-neck T-shirt ('What can I do for you, my name's Eddie?') was not what they expected, but the chocolate croissants were exotic enough to hold their attention.

Only Hattie had remained in touch with Alice.

Jilly was full of apologies. 'I'm so bad at writing. Remember how you used to write my essays for me? And quite honestly, I thought you'd be too famous to keep up with boring old friends. But I did hear some of your news when Mary came out to see me.'

Pen looked outraged. 'Mary Bartlett? Did she stay with you? What a cheek!'

'We're always getting people passing through. You can't say no, not when they've come all that way. Well, the house is big enough. Mind, she did stay quite a few days.'

Hattie tried not to stare at Jilly, who had gained at least twenty kilos by her reckoning since they'd last met. She didn't do herself a favour by wearing that gathered skirt and embroidered peasant blouse. Still, being married to an American, living in the country miles away from decent dress shops, she probably lived in jeans most of the time. It wouldn't matter over there, since they didn't have a clue about fashion. Pen was still the same size, even after another child.

'Guess where Mary's landed up?' said Alice.

'Bet she's married again, to some fuddy-duddy old professor.'

'Oh, no, not Mary. My bet is she's landed a rich, ugly guy in real estate.'

'You're both wrong,' said Alice. 'She's in a French prison.'

Hattie was lost for words. Pen gave a hoot.

Jilly's eyes opened wide in astonishment. 'My! You mean she murdered someone?'

'Goodness, no.'

They all laughed with relief. It was too shocking to contemplate. Then they looked expectantly towards Alice.

'Mary never told us when we last met, but she was married to a very rich Frenchman called Roland. He was a schizophrenic. Apparently he never wanted to marry her, but she persuaded him she could cure him – so he changed his mind. They had a huge wedding and it was in *Hello!* magazine. Lots of famous people came along.'

'How fabulous!' Hattie sighed. 'I wonder how I could have missed it? My favourite reading, isn't that dreadful?'

'Do go on, Alice,' said Pen.

'After the honeymoon she took away his drugs. She said they were killing him. So then he got uncontrollable and she had him locked up in a mental hospital outside Paris.'

'That's almost the same as murder,' added Pen.

'But it wasn't murder. So why did she go to prison?' asked Jilly.

'While Roland was in the hospital, Mary took everything from his Paris apartment and removed it to England. She kept the family jewellery, sold most of the furniture at Sotheby's and Christie's, but kept the best pieces for herself. Then she sold his country house, which was worth a fortune.'

'My!' exclaimed Jilly. 'That's just incredible. I can't wait to tell Duane.'

'Anyhow, Roland stayed in hospital a while and got better. He went home again and found – no Mary, nothing. She'd stripped his place bare and he didn't know where she was. Roland advertised on the Net and told the whole story – which Simon happened to see. Simon had met Mary once, so he told us all about her. Poor Robert, it was so awful for him. He didn't say anything for ages – he was so embarrassed – but Mary had put some of the stolen money into his company and he had agreed to it.'

'Why did he do that?' asked Hattie. 'I thought Robert was doing all right.'

'He was,' Alice replied. 'But Mary persuaded him that he couldn't be really successful without her. She was planning to dominate Robert as she had dominated Roland. Mary wanted power over people, but she wasn't satisfied with that. It was even better if she could get loads of money out of them. Then she'd take off for exotic holidays, saying she was researching a book.'

'Wasn't she interested in Robert for other reasons? She probably fancied him,' suggested Pen.

'That's what Beatrice thought,' said Alice. 'But I believe the money was more important. Every time Robert got a big project, most of his earnings would go to her. I couldn't understand why he always seemed so broke. Then it all came out about their partnership.

294

Robert said he hardly ever saw her in England – she was always travelling around the world. He never knew quite where she was, but e-mails kept coming from her. She wanted to know every tiny detail of his work. And he even had to send her financial statements.'

'That's dreadful. How on earth could he have allowed that?' said Hattie.

'He had no choice. She threatened to bankrupt him if he didn't toe the line. He wouldn't have been able to practise as an architect. Anyway, it was Simon who winkled Mary out. He contacted the French police and suggested they could find her by monitoring the sources of her e-mail. Eventually they tracked her down to a hotel in Ecuador and found out she was about to fly to Paris. Then, when she landed in France, they arrested her.'

This news warranted a change from pots of tea to a bottle of wine while the implications were discussed. They decided not to inform the present headmistress of Corsham Towers, even though it was tempting. Although they searched their memories, they had never heard of an old girl who had 'done time', as Pen put it. She remembered a girl caught dealing in drugs but that didn't really count.

'I still don't understand how the police found out,' said Hattie, who was constantly amazed at how everyone knew so much more than she did.

'Oh, you can find out anything nowadays,' said Pen.

When Jilly was passing round her latest batch of photographs she suddenly had a chilling thought. 'Alice, don't mind me asking, but you're not divorced from Robert, are you? Or is Simon one of your brothers? Awful how you forget names.'

'I never married Robert. Simon's my husband,' said Alice with a proud smile.

* * *

There came a point at which you went through so many changes that it was difficult to summarise them over tea. Even Hattie had only a vague idea why it had happened. She assumed that Alice was no longer in love with Robert, since that was the easiest explanation to give. How could Alice expect anyone to see it differently? Shortly after Beatrice became pregnant again and Robert had that strange illness, Alice started to wonder if she really wanted to live with him, in the house that would always be his. If Robert had asked her a few months after they had met, she might have moved in instantly, without thinking of the future. Or would she? By now, Alice had forgotten the real reason for her decision.

She remembered voicing her doubts to Beatrice, sitting by the pool of the Lansdale Club. Their conversation took place during that cold February, two months before she and Robert had fixed their new wedding date. She wasn't sure she really wanted to marry Robert, after all. Beatrice was aghast. Then Alice told her how Robert had insisted that she saw a doctor about her weight and cholesterol levels. He said it was needed for some insurance policy. How could she possibly believe that? It was his way of saying that she was too fat. What else could it be? And she began to wonder if he really loved her.

A few weeks later, after Robert had revealed his partnership with Mary and Alice pulled back from the wedding, Beatrice told her that she had made the right decision. (Also, it was in her stars to cancel a long-standing arrangement.) How could he have been taken in by Mary Bartlett? Beatrice thought he might have changed, but he hadn't. Why had he listened to Mary when he never listened to anyone else? Hadn't she warned him? He was impossible and always had been.

Looking back, it amused Alice that in spite of Beatrice's

tirades, it only took her three more years to leave David and live with Robert again. Sasha, Drusilla and baby Leonora spent alternate days in his house and David's home. She had kept her amazing figure, hovering, as ever, between sizes eight and ten. Some women never got fat, even after having children. They were still having arguments, she and Robert, though Beatrice had given up smashing plates and no longer locked him out of the house. The Lansdale Club had built a special pool for children. They all met up there, once in a while.

It was unsettling, talking about Mary again. Alice could never quite accept that she was either evil (according to Beatrice) or manipulative (according to Simon). Didn't Mary have good sides and bad sides, like most people? Although Beatrice was convinced that Mary had sent her to the clinic so that she could move in on Robert, Alice was sceptical. In spite of Beatrice's denials, Alice still believed that Robert would never have been trapped if Mary hadn't been size eight. Size eight was Robert's weakness.

At first, Alice found it impossible to remove Robert from her life and her heart still missed a beat when she saw him walking into the club. There were moments of regret and pain, but as the months passed, they began to fade. She was enjoying her success, laughing at her mistakes and muddling through in her own way. Gradually, she stopped wondering what Robert would have thought. And she began seeing more of Simon. She shared his mad crazes, didn't worry about leaving her things around his house or tidying up, and they cooked together and laughed a lot. She didn't remember laughing much with Robert.

Although Simon had stopped seeing other girls, Alice doubted if he could ever forgive her for running off with Robert. That would be too much to ask.

*   *   *

Simon couldn't see that Alice had changed, although she insisted she had. She was the same Alice he knew and loved, and always would be. He suspected that even though Robert had let her down, her heart was still with him. It was best not to discuss it. However, he would have to put the question once more. Then he would know. Had to know. Odd, that. He knew Alice better than anyone and hadn't a clue what her answer would be.

After he had asked several times if she would like to go abroad with him, she eventually agreed to a short weekend in Paris, to see a millinery exhibition at the Pompidou Centre. He planned to take her out for a magnificent lunch, master his pride and propose marriage for the second time. His short speech on hearing her inevitable but kind rejection of his offer had already been prepared. Disappointment and desolation would be warded off in the short term by pre-booking seats for *The Marriage of Figaro* at the Paris Opéra, for old times' sake. Sensibly, Simon had booked two rooms at the Ritz, but as it happened he only had need of one. She said yes with tears in her eyes, which was unlike Alice.